AF422115

THE
LONG TRAIL
WEST

Historical Fiction By Steve Stephens

The Restless Journeys Series

A World Away From Home
Further From Home
The White Medicine Woman
A Search For Gold

Translation By Steve Stephens

The Poems Of Undina

THE LONG TRAIL WEST

A TRUE NOVEL

STEVE STEPHENS

Cover and book design by
Amy Livingstone, Sacred Art Studio
sacredartstudio.net

Cover Photo: Cowboy/ChatGpt & Handwriting: Shutterstock/Marie C Fields
Vintage paper and pen: Shutterstock/Chepko Danil Vitalevich
Horseshoe: Shutterstock/NamlessK

ISBN: 979-8-9951291-0-3

WINTER CREEK
— PUBLISHING —

DEDICATION

To Allen John Herbert Stephens—
A cowboy with a story for every situation.

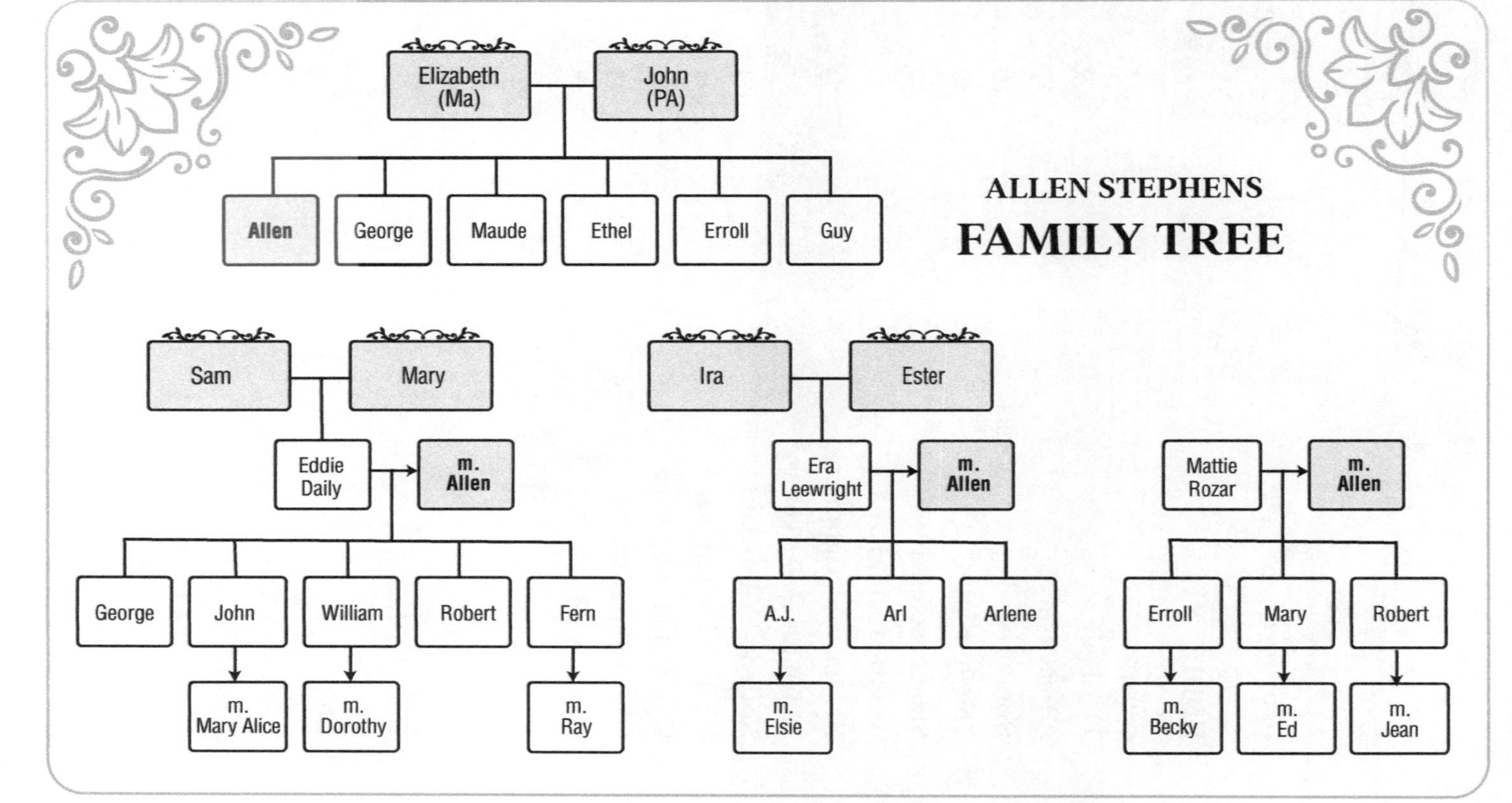

ALLEN STEPHENS
FAMILY TREE
Elizabeth (Ma)
John (PA)
Allen
George
Maude
Ethel
Erroll
Guy
Sam
Mary
Eddie Daily
m. Allen
George
John
William
Robert
Fern
m. Mary Alice
m. Dorothy
m. Ray
Ira
Ester
Era Leewright
m. Allen
A.J.
Arl
Arlene
m. Elsie
Mattie Rozar
m. Allen
Erroll
Mary
Robert
m. Becky
m. Ed
m. Jean

TABLE OF CONTENTS

SUNSET

(1925-1958)

MATTIE

SUNRISE

(1893-1911)

EDDIE

Escape

The Trail

A Real Cowboy

Horse Thieving Scoundrels

The Prettiest Girl

Stagecoach Drivers

A Little Red House

Dreams and Nightmares

When the River Thaws

Nothing Left to Say

Waiting for Summer

One Sunday at a Time

Oklahoma Drought

Bittersweet

ESCAPE

If I stayed, I knew I'd die.

I lingered outside the barn, cool wind on my face, full moon spilling silver across the fields. I glanced back at the house. Ma's oil lamp flickered in the window. The dog barked once, then fell silent. I turned away, my throat tight, and walked into the dark.

My parents were good people—but content to live simple and small. My pa was a farmer who worked the wheat fields sunrise to sunset. My ma was a God-fearing woman, worn to the bone trying her best to care for five kids. I was the oldest. You might say I was restless. Some would call me a rebel. I'd say I just needed to see more, feel more, experience more. I was bored.

So one morning I stole a horse from Pa's barn and galloped west across the wide, flat prairie under the glowing light of a flower moon. I didn't know where I was going. I didn't care. I just knew that I was free—and it felt so good I wanted to shout at the top of my lungs, "World, watch out! Allen John Herbert Stephens is about to wrangle you to the ground! So you'd better get out of my way!"

When you're fifteen and riding high on your pa's whiskey, you think the world belongs to you. I once asked Pa how he could afford a bottle when he could barely feed his kids. He beat me with a leather strap until I couldn't sit for a week. I deserved it. I wasn't good at showing proper respect. After all, if you piss into the wind, you're bound to get your face wet. Later, Pa told me he never bought his whiskey—he traded eggs from our hen house with old man Miller, who had a still hidden behind bales of hay in his barn.

Settling in the saddle, I took one final look at the farm. I imagined Pa waking up to the empty stall, the hoofprints heading west. He'd shake his head, curse under his breath, and then go on to his daily work. That's how he handled everything—just kept moving forward, like feelings were weeds you could pull up and burn.

I'd miss Pa—but I'd miss Ma more. She had a stubborn strength. No matter how poor, or broken things got, she didn't give up. She'd say to me, "Where there's a will, there's a way." And my way was to leave before the quiet desperation destroyed me. I had to escape. Not in anger or hurt, but simply to find a way to breathe.

Ma said I always had to learn things the hard way. People could tell me something a thousand times, but I had to find out myself. Don't touch the hot stove or you'll get burned. Are you sure? Don't stand behind a wild horse. Why not? Don't walk through tall grass barefoot. What's wrong with that? I never liked being told what to do—not even at four. If I wanted to play in the tall grass without boots, that's what I damn well was going to do.

It was a blistering summer day. I must've been four. I remember the way the grass tickled my ankles as I ran barefoot through the field behind our sod house, chasing a butterfly like it held the secrets of the world. I wasn't more than ten paces in when I heard it—that low, dry rattle. It sounded like dry beans in a tin cup—slow, steady, deadly. I froze.

The grass around me swayed just slightly, and then I saw it. Coiled, thick, and mean-looking, its body blending with the straw-colored stalks. That rattlesnake stared at me with eyes that didn't blink. The tip of its tail shook like a corn husk in a windstorm.

And then it struck.

I didn't even have time to scream before its fangs sank into my right leg—once, then again. A white-hot pain shot up my side and dropped me flat. I screamed—loud and raw—and it brought Ma running like death itself was on our heels. She reached me in seconds, rifle in hand. My leg was already turning red and purple. I could barely see her through the blur of pain and tears. She looked at the snake, then at me, and without hesitating, she raised Pa's Winchester and fired.

Once. Twice. Three times. Four. Five.

The snake jerked, twisted, then went still—torn apart in the dirt.

I remember Ma scooping me into her arms like I weighed nothing. Her voice was steady, but her hands shook as she wrapped a strip of her apron around my leg. "Stay with me, Allen," she whispered. "You stay with me, you hear?"

I nodded, but the world was spinning. I felt like I was sinking into the earth.

The fever came fast. I burned up for days, sweating and thrashing, while Ma sat at my bedside, changing the rags on my leg and whispering prayers between songs I barely recognized. Pa paced the floor like a boxed in bull, muttering about how he should've cleared that field weeks ago. But I survived and learned my lesson. After that, I never left the house without boots. I carried the scars of that rattler the rest of my days. That's what the Sioux called a big dose of coyote medicine.

Ma taught me to read when I was five. She should've been a schoolmarm. I wasn't good at numbers or memorizing facts, but I loved to read. Anything I could get my hands on, I devoured. Pa thought it was a waste of time and kept me from my chores. My favorite book was *Tom Sawyer*. I don't think Ma realized that books could be dangerous. After all, that's where I got my ideas about whiskey, smoking, and running away. If Tom could do it, why couldn't I?

My folks homesteaded ten years earlier in a sod house on the northern edge of Nebraska. You stepped off their property and you were in the Dakotas. You were also on the Rosebud Reservation. The Indians didn't like white folks stepping on their land. It was sacred soil—where the Great Spirit left footprints and the Ponderosa Pine pointed to the shining circles in the sky. The Sioux weren't happy about the shooting of Chief Sitting Bull. Rumors spread like wildfire—Ghost Dances, black and red war paint, broken peace pipes, and retaliation for Wounded Knee, where 3,000 Sioux were killed. A lot of our neighbors moved south to avoid being scalped or shot through the heart with an arrow. But Pa said, "Nobody is going to force me off my land."

It was late fall toward the end of the day. Pa had worked all day mending fences and now he sat on the porch, whittling on a stubborn piece of red oak. "The world don't owe you nothing," he said. "But it'll take everything you let it." He sighed and motioned me to sit next to him.

Pa was as quiet as winter and when he spoke, I listened. "Fifteen is almost a man," he said without looking at me. Then he reached under his chair and set a bundle wrapped in oilcloth on my lap. My hands knew what it was before I unwrapped it. The revolver. His Colt—blued steel, pearl grip, worn smooth by years of use and care. I picked it up. It was heavier than it looked. The cylinder clicked as I spun it once, then stopped it with my thumb.

Pa smiled. "Don't use it unless you have to. But if you have to, don't hesitate."

I nodded. But he didn't seem to notice. He was already back to whittling something that refused to take shape. I looked at him— really looked. The lines on his weather-worn skin were deeper than I remembered. The calluses on his hands were cracked and stained. But what caught me were his eyes. They were the color of storm-washed stone—gray, steady, but sad in a way that crept into your bones. We sat in silence until the stars came out. Then he stood up and walked inside. And I sat there, revolver in my lap, knowing that he'd told me everything he ever would.

That was six months ago, now it was mid-May 1894. It was at least three hours until dawn when I rode away. All I had was a bedroll, three pieces of Ma's cornbread wrapped in a red bandanna, the revolver Pa had given me, an old army canteen, a tin of chewing tobacco, the clothes on my back, and a hat on my head. But that was enough.

As my chestnut mare sauntered west beneath a steel and starry sky the saddle creaked under me and dust puffed up with every stride. The prairie smelled of sage and old earth, and a coyote howled somewhere to the north. My thighs ached already, but I didn't care. The sky was so wide it made me feel like anything was possible.

For the first time, I knew no one was coming to check on me. No Pa, no trail boss, no boss man, no hand to steady me, no dog to watch my back. Just a dream of going west and a hunger I couldn't keep quiet.

My head swirled. If I could do anything, what would it be? After careful thought, I narrowed it to three pursuits even Tom Sawyer might savor—a soldier, a cabin boy on a whaling ship, or a cowboy. None of those sounded boring. But the army had just massacred the Sioux in South Dakota and they were on the warpath, so I wasn't too keen on that. Nebraska was 1,500 miles from the nearest whaling port—and I didn't think my horse was up for that sort of journey. That killed that dream. The only option left was cowboy, and that's what I set my sights on.

Now, I knew a little something about life on the trail—and it wasn't as romantic as the dime novels made it seem. But I didn't care about romance. I wanted adventure. Even if that adventure quickly turned out to be more hard work than excitement.

As dawn broke, the sky turned the color of fresh peaches and blood. I crested a hill and saw nothing but prairie stretching to the horizon. No fences. No voices calling me back. Just possibilities. A rooster crowed to the west as I turned my horse south toward the biggest cattle operation in these parts: the JR Bar Ranch. It was a half-day's ride from where I was, tucked into a pretty valley where White Snake Creek emptied into the Niobrara—a place the Sioux called "the land of the wide waters." The ranch was owned by Mr. Jack Rhodes, known throughout Cherry County as an honest and fair man. If he gave me a shot, I'd be the luckiest kid west of the Mississippi.

I stopped at noon in the shade of a pine to eat my cornbread. Wolfed down two pieces in half a minute and saved the rest for later. About now, my folks were probably wondering where I'd gone. Pa would be mad that I took one of the workhorses. Ma would be worried. She'd be praying I was safe and that I'd come to my senses and hightail it home before something bad happened. But once you leave, it's hard to go back—at least not until you've proven yourself. And I needed to prove I was a man who could take care of himself. I felt bad about upsetting them, but I figured fate was calling me forward. So I put on my hat, climbed back into the saddle, and tried to outrun the sun.

About five o'clock, I rode up to the ranch house. The cowhands paused to watch me as I rode up, their expression unreadable beneath wide brims. One spat into the dirt. Another just nodded slightly. The house loomed above me—two stories of weathered pride. Word in town was that Mr. Rhodes ran his place like a general, fair but fierce. I straightened my shoulders and dismounted, trying to look older than I felt. I walked with my head high to the massive front door and knocked hard. An Indian woman in a long black dress asked me what I wanted. I said I wished to speak to Mr. Rhodes and she led me to his office. It was the nicest room I'd ever seen—spacious, high-ceilinged, with a large western window flooding the space with light. Before me stood a mahogany desk, leather chairs, crystal lamps, and a wall of books. A sizable man in a white suit sat behind the desk, silently signing papers.

"Excuse me, Mr. Rhodes," I said, stepping forward and removing my hat. "My name is Allen Stephens, and I've journeyed all day to ask you a question."

The man with golden hair and a bushy mustache set down his pen. "Then I suppose you'd better ask it." His deep, booming voice reverberated through the room, pushing me back a step.

I swallowed hard. "Would you consider hiring me as a cowboy?"

Mr. Rhodes smiled. "Well, you're not shy about asking for what you want."

"No, sir." I straightened my legs to hide their shaking. "My pa said if you want something, you've got to ask for it."

"But that doesn't mean you're going to get it."

"I understand. But asking's a step closer to getting."

"Kid, how old are you?"

I looked him in the eye. "Sir, I'm much more mature and responsible than my appearance might indicate."

He studied me, clearly surprised by my confidence. So was I.

"Can you throw a rope?"

"Yes, sir."

"Ever herded cattle?" He lit a cigar and exhaled a cloud of rich, earthy smoke.

"Yes, sir," I said. Pa told me never to lie to a boss. "I worked springs and summers at Mr. Palmer's farm near where I grew up. Five dollars a month to feed the herds and bring them into the barn at night."

"How many head?"

"Seven head and two milk cows."

"Can you handle life on the trail?"

"I've lived on the range since I was one."

He gave me another once-over, then shrugged. "Suppose a boy has to start somewhere."

"I'll do whatever you ask and won't cause trouble."

After a few more questions, he agreed to hire me for one cattle run to the reservation. If it went well, he'd extend the contract. If not, we'd part ways like gentlemen. I thanked him and shook his hand with all the strength I could muster. My hand felt small in his, but I didn't let it show.

He said, "You'll ride with Joe and Tom. You do whatever they say like it came from me. If they say jump in the river, you dive like your pants are on fire. If they say sleep in a tree, you hum yourself a lullaby until you're snoring."

"Pa taught me to work hard and show respect."

"The run takes seven days if all goes smoothly. Four more to return. Understand?"

"Yes, sir."

"I expect to see you back here a week from Friday to find out if you're man enough to lead a herd. My men will be watching."

"I'd expect nothing less." The excitement was almost too much to contain, but I kept nodding calmly.

Mr. Rhodes tapped his cigar. "Looks like we have a deal. Go to the bunkhouse and get your gear. Juan has beef stew on the fire if you're hungry."

I nodded, trying to keep my stomach from growling. I was hungry—but that was nothing new. When you live on the edge, you eat when you can.

"The drive starts at dawn. Hit your bunk early."

"Thank you, Mr. Rhodes. You won't regret this. I promise."

"I'd better not, Kid. Now get out of here before I change my mind."

I stepped outside, threw my hat into the blazing blue, and hollered, "Yippee! Yee-haw! Hallelujah!"

I was grinning like a fool, but something heavy tugged at my chest. I wasn't sure if it was guilt or fear—maybe both. You don't just ride away from your whole life and expect to feel light.

Even as I whooped into the sky, I knew the trail wouldn't be easy. Freedom was earned mile by mile, through country where the wild made its own rules.

But I was ready. No map. Just a vague dream of work out west and a hunger I couldn't quiet. Nothing was going to stop me. Not storms. Not hunger. Not fear.

The sky was wide, the trail was open—and for the first time in my life, I was free.

THE TRAIL

Joe didn't like me very much. He hadn't liked me since we first met years ago—and he sure didn't like me now. I didn't blame him. I hoped he wouldn't recognize me when I walked into the bunkhouse, but he did. He knew exactly who I was—and he would've done anything to get rid of me. He shot me a look and spit in the dirt.

When I was ten, I worked at Palmer's Farm doing odd jobs—cleaning stalls, milking cows, feeding chickens—just about anything nobody else wanted to do. I was full of piss and vinegar. I worked hard but didn't have a lick of horse sense.

Mr. Palmer had a daughter about my age, and I would do most anything to get her attention. Joe was the foreman at that farm. He took his job seriously. He was tall and lean, about ten years older than me. Problem was, he didn't have much of a sense of humor.

One summer day, Joe set his new Stetson on a fence post while he washed his face in the horse trough. I was always pulling pranks, but this time I went too far. I scooped fresh manure and set it in his hat. When he put it on, the mess ran down his face.

Joe was as mad as a hornet in a tin can. The Palmer girl and I laughed so hard our sides ached, which only made him madder. He glared at me like he meant to kill me. He threw the hat at me and came after me like a man possessed.

I ran as fast as I could. He'd have killed me if Mr. Palmer hadn't intervened. The boss made me clean Joe's Stetson and shine his boots every day for a month. But that wasn't enough for Joe. He never forgave me.

"What are you doing here?" Joe was sitting at a long table with ten cowboys. His words cracked like a whip and left me frozen in place. My heart pounded so hard it hurt. My legs went weak. The room went silent. Everyone stared at me.

I took off my hat and spoke as respectfully as Pa had taught me. "Mr. Rhodes just hired me as a cowhand. I'm to report to you and Tom to get my gear for tomorrow's run to the reservation."

"Get outta here before I beat the daylights outta you!" Joe stood and pointed to the door.

"Yes, sir." I put on my hat and left the building. I sat down in the shade with my back against the bunkhouse and breathed deep to calm my heart. I took a swig from my canteen. The water was warm, but it filled my belly enough to stop it from aching. I wished it was stronger than water.

A small, mangy dog came up to me, licking my face like we were old friends. Black with a white chest and so thin I could feel his ribs. I unfolded my bandanna and broke my last piece of cornbread into two even pieces. I set one in front of the dog and gobbled up the other. He ate his piece in one bite. His tail wagged so hard I laughed.

Juan came out of the bunkhouse. "You hungry?"

I nodded, and he handed me a ceramic bowl of stew—beef, onions, potatoes, carrots. It was delicious. I emptied the bowl and thanked him. When I set it on the ground beside me, the dog licked it clean.

"What's his name?" I asked.

"The men call him Pup, since he isn't full grown yet."

"He seems like a good dog." I scratched his head, and he nuzzled me for more.

"He's a stray who steals scraps," said Juan. "Showed up a few months back. The men aren't too fond of him. They kick him and throw things at him, but he won't stay away."

"Maybe he's just lonely. Pup isn't a proper name. I think I'll call him Jasper."

"Well, you and Jasper best sleep outside tonight," said Juan. "Joe isn't too happy that Mr. Rhodes hired you."

"But I'm supposed to ride with him to the reservation tomorrow."

"Kid, you'd better pray he calms down by morning. Otherwise, you're in for a rough time on the trail."

"Knowing Joe's history, I don't think he'll calm by morning."

"Then you'd better be prepared for the worst."

I told him I was tougher than I looked and that I'd take whatever Joe dished out. For the next ten days, I never complained. Joe was determined to get even and show me who was in charge. I was determined to take it like a man. He put oats in my bedroll, filled my boots with molasses, assigned me night watch every night, and made me chase down every steer that wandered from the herd. It was a grueling trip.

We started at dawn the next morning. Jasper wanted to join me on my first run, but Joe chased him off with a rock. He shouted that no scavenging son of a bitch was welcome on his drive across the open range. Jasper ran off with his tail between his legs, but when I turned back from the trail, I caught sight of him watching from the brush. He didn't bark—just sat there, quiet and still as a stone.

Our outfit had a crew of six to move three wagons of supplies and sixteen head of cattle. Joe and Tom were in charge. Juan was our cook. The three of them drove the wagons—loaded with everything from flour to fabric to fishhooks, along with grammar books and U.S. history texts. Two ranch hands were armed with Winchesters across their saddles and Colt six-shooters on their hips. This was rustler country, and Mr. Rhodes wasn't taking chances.

Since I was the greenhorn, I was the drag rider—pushing the stragglers forward through dust so thick it blinded my vision and choked my lungs. After a long day, I did whatever else nobody wanted to do. But I never fussed or grumbled, though I had good reason.

It was my third night on watch, and I hadn't had more than six hours of sleep in three days. The prairie was black as pitch except for a thin sliver of moon hanging like a curved knife in the sky. The fire had burned down to embers, and I sat with my blanket wrapped tight, revolver on my lap, eyes fighting to stay open.

Somewhere out beyond the herd, a coyote let out a lonesome cry. The cattle shifted, hooves crunching dry grass, then settled again. I leaned back, trying to stretch the ache from my spine, when I caught the faint shimmer of eyes in the dark.

I reached for my revolver, heart jumping.

Then a shape moved through the grass—low, steady, familiar.

"Jasper?" I whispered.

The dog crept forward, tail wagging low, and slinked up beside me like it was the most natural thing in the world. He laid his head on my boot like he belonged there.

"I'll be damned," I said, stunned. "You followed me?"

He licked my face and let out a sigh like he'd been through hell to get here. I scratched behind his ears, still trying to believe it. "You don't listen too good, do you?" He thumped his tail and didn't move.

For a while, we sat there—just me, the mutt, and the stars. The wind stirred the grass, and the fire hissed softly behind me. I wondered if Ma and Pa knew I wasn't coming back anytime soon— or if they were still holding out hope.

"Guess we're both out here chasing something," I whispered.

I loved the blue-green buffalo grass prairie that spread in every direction. It was as flat and free as when Tom Sawyer floated his raft down the mighty Mississippi. Sure, it was hard work, but I was a cowhand riding my chestnut mare beneath the big sky, doing what I'd always dreamed. I smiled as a west wind blew the dust out of my face for a brief moment. After a few days, my back stung with strain and soreness—but that just meant I was pushing my limits. I grit my teeth and rode a little harder.

The night was cold, and every bone in my body reminded me that the trail won't tolerate the weak. My hands were blistered, my legs ached, and the smoke from the fire burned my eyes. Tom sat on a stump nearby, nursing a tin cup of coffee and whittling a stick down to nothing. I dropped onto a flat rock close to the fire, my plate empty but still warm in my lap.

We didn't say anything for a while. The fire cracked. Somewhere out on the prairie, an owl called.

"You're tougher than you look," Tom said after a while. His eyes fixed on the flames.

I looked up. "Thanks," I muttered.

He took a slow sip. "First time I rode out, I was sixteen. My horse threw me into a prickly pear patch two days in. I still got the scars."

I blinked. "Bet that hurt."

He gave a short nod. "Out here, pain's part of the job. Dust, bruises, sunburn, saddle sores. But that ain't what breaks a man."

He tossed the stick into the fire and watched the sparks leap. I watched them too.

"You'll learn, son. It ain't the miles or the dust that wear you down. It's what you carry."

"What do you mean?"

Tom didn't look at me, just stared into the coals like they held answers.

"Regret. Guilt. Loneliness. Whatever's in your gut when the trail gets quiet. That's the heavy stuff."

I didn't say anything. I didn't have to. I knew what he meant.

On the fifth day, we crossed out of Nebraska onto the reservation. It was a brisk and beautiful morning, but I was so tired I could barely stay in the saddle. We were headed for the agency headquarters to drop off supplies and a small herd of cattle. As usual, I was at the rear, wrangling a stubborn steer that lagged behind.

Three Indians on horseback came galloping from the east. They didn't look friendly. I kept my hand close to my revolver. I'd seen these men years ago on Pa's farm. I called the leader Chief White Hat because of the white cowboy hat he wore, with an eagle feather tucked into the brim. The other two were younger.

It seemed like a lifetime ago that I was doing chores in the barn when they'd come demanding to see Pa. I told them he was out in the fields but I could go get him.

"We will wait," said the chief. They sat down in front of the barn. That made me so nervous my hands began to shake. I stuck them deep in the back pockets of my well worn pants. As far as I know, they didn't notice my fear. Pa once told me that if you show fear, Indians will scalp you. So I kept quiet and prayed like Ma had taught me.

One of the braves pulled out a long knife and wiped it on his buckskin legging. So I called him Long Knife. I went back into the barn to finish my chores. He pointed at me and said, "I have my eyes on you." His crooked smile gave me the chills. I wouldn't have been surprised if he scalped me on the spot.

I called the third one Sitting Fox because he sat so quiet and still. I was afraid they'd hurt Pa, but there was no way to warn him. Ma kept the kids inside the soddy until things seemed safe.

When Pa came home, he walked right up to Chief White Hat. He wasn't afraid, and the Indians respected that.

"One of our cows wandered this way," the chief said. "Did you see it?"

Pa said he saw a cow near Little Beaver Creek. The chief frowned and stared Pa down. "If you're not speaking the truth, we'll come back and burn your barn. Maybe with your boy inside." That threat gave me nightmares for months. But they rode south, and I hadn't seen them since—not until now.

As they got closer, that old fear came roaring back. I pushed the steer toward the herd as fast as I could. The last thing I wanted was a face-off with three braves who were each twice my size. I rode fast, but they rode faster.

One of them threw a lasso around me and yanked me from my horse. I hit the ground hard. They took my gun and tied my hands behind my back. The steer bolted north into the dust.

"What do you want?" I asked.

"That steer," said the chief.

"I can't give it to you," I replied, trying to stay calm.

Long Knife hit me across the face with a willow switch. It stung bad.

"It's not mine," I said, sucking blood from my lip. "This herd belongs to Mr. Rhodes. In two days, it'll belong to the reservation."

"But our people are hungry." Long Knife struck me again.

"I'm sorry." I looked him square in the eye. "Follow us to the agency headquarters. Ask them for supplies."

"Two suns is a long time when your children beg you for food," said the chief.

I nodded. "Come with me to our camp. Maybe our cook can give you some beans and bacon."

"Why should we trust you?"

"Because my pa was an honest man."

"Do we know your pa?"

"My pa farms just south of your reservation. A few summers back you were out looking for a lost cow."

"I remember." The chief nodded. "The soddie with the big barn."

"Pa could've butchered your cow. He didn't. He told you the truth. I'll do the same."

They spoke in their own language and pointed at me as they argued. I sat there, bound and terrified—but I wasn't about to show it.

"How do we know this isn't a trick?" said Long Knife.

"If you don't believe me," I said, "just scalp me and let the vultures pick my bones clean."

Eventually, they agreed to follow me to camp. I explained the situation to Joe and Tom. Tom listened with a furrowed brow. Joe just stared at me, like he was chewing rocks. For a second, I thought he'd let the braves take my scalp. But then he gave the slightest nod. "Feed 'em. Then get that steer back." It wasn't much. In Joe's world that was as close to praise as I was likely to get.

Afterward, I talked to Juan, who gave me extra supplies for the braves to carry home. Nobody wanted women and children to starve.

They were grateful—and I was grateful to still have my scalp.

When we returned to the ranch, Juan told Mr. Rhodes I was a hard worker. I said I just wanted to prove myself. Mr. Rhodes said he appreciated how I'd saved his steer and offered me a job. Twenty dollars a month.

No fifteen-year-old kid I knew had ever been that rich. When I left the ranch house, I whooped and hollered so loud the whole crew probably thought I'd gone crazy. Truth was, I was the happiest kid in the state of Nebraska.

I missed Ma and Pa—and hoped Pa would forgive me for stealing his horse. I hoped someday I'd ride home and make him proud.

But first, I had a trail to ride and a life to build.

A REAL COWBOY

"You make it through the summer as a cowhand, and I'll make you a cowboy."

That was a promise Mr. Rhodes made to me, and I wasn't about to let him down. Who wouldn't want to be a cowboy? I worked hard to make everyone happy. It was a hot summer, with a few days climbing to 110 degrees, but I did my best to keep moving and stay out of trouble.

But not everyone was so lucky.

Joe's bad luck came early. Tom's trouble was waiting just around the bend. Joe got bit on the thumb by a rock rattler out on the trail. He pulled out his revolver and shot his thumb clean off. His scream echoed across the prairie, sharp enough to startle the herd. We found him hunched over, his hand clutched tight around his thumb, blood trickling between his fingers. The skin was already turning purple, swelling fast. His revolver lay in the dirt beside him, still warm. The smell of gunpowder and blood hung in the air.

"I had no choice," he muttered through clenched teeth. "It was already goin' numb."

Tom wrapped a bandana around Joe's wrist to stop the bleeding while I fumbled in the medicine chest for whiskey and clean cloth. Joe's face went gray, but he didn't make a sound as we poured the whiskey over the wound.

Later, he leaned back against the wagon wheel, sweat dripping down his temples. "Don't tell my wife how loud I screamed," he said.

I nodded. "You've got my word."

Tom's situation was much worse. When we were out on the trail, it wasn't unusual for Tom to disappear. Nobody knew where and nobody asked—some things are better not talked about. Besides, out on the prairie, a man respects a man's privacy. At least until he can't any longer.

Tom was a rambler. Sooner or later that catches up to a man and the devil gets his due. I woke once and saw his silhouette slipping out of camp. Horse saddled. Rifle across his back. No one else stirred. All I heard was the sound of hoofbeats in the dark—barely a whisper against the ground. By morning, he was always back like nothing happened, sipping coffee, and cracking jokes.

I asked him about it once.

"Just needed some air," he said, flashing that crooked smile. "A man gets restless out here."

But restlessness don't usually leave you with smudged paint on your hands and feathers in your saddlebag. I didn't press. Even cowboys need their fun.

But there was a particular morning in mid-August that was different. I felt a foreboding in my bones. It was sunrise on the prairie and Tom was still gone. We were eating breakfast and talking about organizing a search party when two Indians rode up to our camp. It was Long Knife and Sitting Fox with red paint streaked across their faces. They were mad.

"How can we help you?" Joe asked, forcing a friendly smile.

"Chief White Hat has been humiliated by one of your men."

"How can that be?" I said.

"Follow us." Long Knife motioned toward us. It was more an order than a request. I had a sneakin' suspicion that if we didn't cooperate, there'd be trouble. So Joe and I mounted our horses and rode toward the sunrise. Twenty minutes later, we entered a circle of about a dozen colorful teepees. In the middle of the village was Tom, standing buck naked and tied to a wooden post. The place was dead quiet except for the crows squawking overhead. Tom's face was streaked with dust and sweat, his arms rubbed raw from the ropes. He looked more pitiful than scared.

"You gonna let 'em do this to me?" he barked.

Joe didn't answer. He just stared, jaw tight. "What's going on here?" he asked.

"Your man slept with Chief White Hat's daughter," said Long Knife.

"I'm sorry," said Joe. The truth was, there wasn't much to defend. Sleeping with the chief's daughter was a grave insult. In their eyes, it was war-worthy.

"Red Thunder is promised to White Eagle's son during the next Raccoon Moon. Your man took what was not his."

"We are honorable men. We will do what we can to atone for this grievance."

"Honorable men?" Sitting Fox spit on the ground. "There is nothing honorable in what that man has done to our tribe."

Someone threw a stone at Tom. He groaned when it hit his chest.

"Your man must pay or he will die," said Long Knife.

"What must be paid for you to free him?"

"Five horses."

"We only have two extra horses," said Joe.

"What about two horses and his horse?" Long Knife pointed at Tom.

"But a cowboy needs his horse."

"That man doesn't deserve a horse."

Joe looked at Tom. A group of women stood around him, pointing and shaking their heads. A young boy threw rotten tomatoes and watched the red juice drip down Tom's face. The boy's friends laughed and threw more.

"You're probably right." Joe shrugged. "Keep his horse. We'll go back and get two more."

"When you return, we will release him," said Sitting Fox. "But if this ever happens again by any white man, we will not be so tolerant. Do you understand?"

When we rode out, I looked back and saw Red Thunder standing near her father's tent—head bent, face looking down, clothes torn. I couldn't tell whether she was sad or ashamed.

When Mr. Rhodes heard about this incident, he was as mad as a mule with a mouthful of bumblebees. Horses were very important to him and I'm not sure whether he ever fully forgave Tom for this indiscretion. Yet the bossman had a soft spot for me since I was the youngest hired hand on his ranch. When I wasn't out on the trail, he'd invite me to the ranch house to eat supper with his family. I washed up real good, combed my hair, and wore my least worn-out clothes. I even used the best manners Ma had taught me. Unfortunately, I'd forgotten a lot, but his family was still polite to me. These were the best meals I'd ever eaten—thick beef steak, canned oysters, celery, asparagus, banana pudding.

Mrs. Rhodes always set the table like it was Sunday supper. Real linens. Polished silver. Candles flickering in glass holders. I sat at the end, careful not to spill anything. The youngest daughter giggled at my nervousness. Nancy passed the potatoes and smiled at me when I said "thank you" with my mouth full.

Mr. Rhodes asked me about the trail, and I tried to tell it straight. But I didn't say it all.

He nodded and said, "A good cowboy knows when to speak, and when to keep his mouth shut." I took that as a compliment.

After dinner, he let me pick a book from his shelf. I chose *The Prairie* by James Fenimore Cooper. I didn't understand half the words, but it felt good just touching it's leather binding.

Nancy always insisted I take some table scraps for Jasper, who wolfed it down like he'd never eat again. This is where I had my first drink of fizzy water. It took me a while to take a hankering to it since it made my mouth feel all bubbly and bitter. Yet I must admit that as a kid I liked it a lot more than Pa's whiskey, though it didn't have nearly the kick. But what does any fifteen-year-old kid know about anything?

Yes, I was the youngest worker on the ranch so everybody just called me "Kid." "Kid, get the water." "Kid, get some wood." "Kid, lay out my bedroll." That's all I seemed to hear day and night. Mr. Rhodes told them that if they kept ordering me around, he'd put me in charge of the next cattle drive, and I would get the chance to order them around. After that, the guys were a lot nicer—at least when Mr. Rhodes was around.

At the end of the summer, Mr. Rhodes called me into his office. Jasper followed me for moral support. I knew this was going to be my judgment day. I was either going to be a real cowboy, stay a cowhand, or be booted from the ranch. I knocked on his door. He yelled to come in. I patted Jasper's head and he laid down in the shade of the porch to wait for my return. I was as jumpy as a jackrabbit being hunted by a hungry coyote. I took off my hat, stood straight, looked Mr. Rhodes in the face, and waited. He looked at me and smiled.

"Allen, you've made me proud. Today you're a cowboy and I'm raising your pay to $30 a month."

"Thank you, sir."

"But there is one problem."

"Yes, sir?"

"It's time for you to get a different horse."

The horse I stole from Pa was a gentle mare, but she was an old workhorse. Pa called her Mrs. Steady since she was strong and slow. The guys made fun of me because I had a troublesome time keeping up with them. I tried the best I could, but Mrs. Steady was never going to be a champion no matter how hard I pressed her. I knew that Mr. Rhodes was right.

So the next day I went out and got myself a little sorrel filly, which I called Nancy. She was named after Mr. Rhodes' daughter, who was my age—bright as a button and as sweet as honeysuckle in June. My new filly might have been small, but she was as fast as a thunderstorm on the wide open prairie. I bought a used saddle and bridle from Joe at a good price. Mr. Rhodes gave me a pair of silver-plated spurs and that was when I felt like a real cowboy. I buckled them onto my boots and danced about like a bantam hen. Those spurs were the prettiest looking things I'd ever owned. Then he put his arm around my shoulders and said, "Son, I want you to remember three things. Speak slow, ride fast, and don't trip over your spurs."

I smiled. "Yes, sir."

Nancy wasn't a big horse, but she had fire in her legs. The first time I took her out, she tossed her head like she had something to prove. I leaned forward and whispered, "Let's see what you got." She took off like lightning. Wind in my face. Hills rolling beneath us.

I whooped and leaned low, letting her stretch her legs. For the first time since I'd left home, I felt like I belonged in the saddle—not just sitting in it, but moving with it, part of something faster, stronger, freer. Nancy ran like she had wings instead of hooves. Each stride was a promise. Each breath between us was trust.

We crested a ridge and the world opened up. The prairie rolled out ahead like a painted canvas, and I felt like the luckiest boy alive. I let the reins go slack and she kept her pace, steady and fearless. "You and me, girl," I whispered. "We're gonna go places."

Fall in Nebraska was my favorite time of year. The brilliant colors were enough to make you smile. And the temperature was just right, not too hot and not too cold. By October, there was a bitter bite in the morning, but by noon it's comfortable enough for one to lounge in the sun—that is, if a cowboy ever had time to lounge. By November the north wind blew and the prairie has a thin layer of snow. With a few days off, I rode into Valentine—Jasper on my heels—to buy winter gear. I picked up knee-high boots, an army coat, and a wool cape, all for five dollars flat. Now I was ready for anything the prairie might throw at me.

We were out on the trail when the first snow hit. We had a thousand head of cattle and it was a hard drive. With such a big herd Mr. Rhodes hired on a few extra cowhands. Two of these were brothers who were drifters from Oklahoma. We called them Big Smith and Little Smith. The wind from the north was about ten degrees below zero.

We battled snow and bitter cold all day and barely made five miles. We camped in the protection of a high bluff. Fuel was scarce with only willow branches and cow dung to keep us warm. All night long the coyotes howled and Joe figured they were out scavenging for food. We were lucky just to be alive by sunrise—cold, stiff, exhausted. Juan made us coffee and beans for breakfast.

The wind didn't let up. Nobody wanted to leave the fire, but the herd still needed moving. Joe, Tom, and I pushed harder than ever, but the Smith Brothers were a lazy lot. They let the cattle wander all over the prairie. Joe said he'd talk to them, but I said I could handle it. Big Smith loomed over me like a thundercloud. "You think you're man enough to boss me around?"

I didn't flinch. "I don't think. I know."

He didn't expect the rope. It snapped across his cheek and left a welt. I hit him again before he could draw.

"You're fast, Kid," he said, rubbing his face.

"Now can you follow orders?" I asked.

He reached for his gun, but I pulled mine first. His brother made his way toward us. Joe stepped in and said that if there was any more trouble, he'd beat the hell out of both of them.

I looked them in the face and said, "It seems to me you got two options. You can agree to take orders from me or you can quit."

They looked at each other and then back at me. They agreed to take my orders since they were both broke, having spent all their money at the saloon in Valentine the day before we left. From that moment on the Smith Brothers kept their mouths shut and did whatever I asked.

Two weeks later was my sixteenth birthday and Mr. Rhodes gave me a few days off. It had been six months since I'd seen Ma and Pa and I really missed them. Ma had written me a letter almost every week since June. I'd sent one or two, letting them know I was okay, but I never was much of a writer. I was glad Pa wasn't mad at me for stealing his horse, and I promised I'd return Mrs. Steady first chance I got.

They asked if I could meet them in town to celebrate my birthday and catch up on old news. Valentine was a rough-and-tumble town of about 800 folks, barely ten years old but bustling. It had everything you needed—school, jail, post office, bank, train station. But the real traffic was at the saloons, where cowboys spent their pay faster than they earned it.

Ma looked robust and healthy, her cheeks as cheerful as ever. She wrapped her arms around me and I wondered if she'd ever let go. Pa looked withered and worn out, as skinny as a rail.

We sat on the bench outside the general store, eating peppermint sticks and watching the train roll past. Ma asked about Jasper, and I told her how he chased coyotes like they owed him money. She laughed, a sound I hadn't heard in six months.

Pa gave me a package wrapped in newspaper. Inside was my old pocket knife—cleaned, sharpened, and oiled. Pa had given it to me when I was eight.

"I figured you'd want this back," he said. "There are some things you don't want to leave behind."

I gripped it tight. "Thanks, Pa."

He nodded. "You're doing fine, son. Don't forget where you came from—but don't be afraid to keep riding."

"Riding the range makes you grow up fast," I said. "How's the family?"

"God has blessed us," said Ma. "Your brothers and sisters are faring well. And Erroll just had his fourth birthday."

"But the harvest was not plentiful this year," said Pa.

"Mr. Rhodes says that two years of drought have forced a lot of people out of the county."

"We had to butcher half our herd since they didn't have enough feed to survive."

"Pa, you should have told me. Mr. Rhodes would have helped you."

"Don't insult me," Pa said. "I don't need anyone's charity. If I can't make it by the sweat of my brow, it's time to move on."

"Are you moving on?"

"Got a job as ranch foreman. We're moving to Norfolk, over in Madison County, at the end of the month."

"But that's 200 miles east of here," I said, shaking my head.

"A man's not a man if he can't feed his family."

"Pa you've always fed your family. Even if you had to go hungry to do it."

"You're damned right about that! No real man shirks his responsibility. It might be hard, but I'd rather be face down in my grave than let my family down."

I nodded slowly, watching the train disappear into the horizon, and realized—for the first time—home wasn't a place you stayed. It was something you carried, no matter how far you rode.

HORSE THIEVING SCOUNDRELS

It was a cold March evening, and Mr. Rhodes had invited me to his office after enjoying a meal of fried chicken and mashed potatoes. He sat behind his big mahogany desk and looked at me so seriously that I started to squirm.

"Are you ready for an adventure?" he said.

"I'm ready for anything you ask me to do."

"Tomorrow morning you and I are heading to Wyoming."

"What about Joe and Tom?"

"Joe will join us," said Mr. Rhodes. "And Tom will make the Rosebud Run."

"Do you trust him?"

"I think Tom has learned his lesson."

"I hope so." I shrugged. "So what are we doing in Wyoming?"

"I need another 6,000 head of cattle." Mr. Rhodes slapped my back. "And you and I are getting them."

That night, I packed light and tried to steady my nerves. I wasn't sure what to expect, and I certainly didn't want to disappoint Mr. Rhodes.

The next morning I saddled Nancy in silence, while Jasper circled the hitching post—whining, ears flat. He knew something was happening.

"You're not coming this time," I told him.

He sat down hard and let out a huff, tail twitching like he wanted to argue.

I scratched his head. "Don't worry. We'll be back soon."

As we rode out, I looked back once. Jasper was sitting there alone, watching the dust we kicked up, head high like he still thought he might catch up if he just ran fast enough.

Mr. Rhodes led Joe and me west toward some big ranches near Lightning Creek, Bear Creek, and Chugwater. After gathering more cattle for his herd, he hired a few more cowboys from Cheyenne, and we started the 300 mile trek back to the JR Bar Ranch.

So far, it had been a good journey. When traveling the prairie in March, there were only four things to worry about—snow, wind, Indians, and rustlers. We could deal with the first three. It was the rustlers that made me nervous. Horse thieves have a short life in the West. So do cattle thieves, but that doesn't stop unscrupulous men from taking whatever they think they can.

It was past midnight, and the cowboys were snoring in their tents. Three shadows crept into the camp from the north. Eight horses slept in a wooden corral, with a young cowhand keeping watch—at least when he wasn't nodding off. One of the shadows cut the ropes while another led three horses toward freedom. The cowhand spotted the movement and yelled for help.

Bang! Bang!

One of the shadows shot the boy in the leg. His cry pierced the night.

Now everyone was awake—shouting, swearing, scurrying about half dressed and looking for someone to shoot.

"Joe and Allen, come with me!" ordered Mr. Rhodes as he mounted his horse. "The rest of you help the boy and watch the cattle."

"Nobody steals our horses," said Joe.

"Especially not Nancy," I mumbled.

It was a bright, moonlit night, and we followed the criminals west. But the prairie was rough, and the thieves were fast. They knew every shortcut and creek crossing. We chased them all night and into the next day. At times we gained ground on them, only for them to disappear again. I was hungry, tired, and could barely sit in my saddle. But Mr. Rhodes never slacked—not even for a moment.

"There's no way we're going to let these good-for-nothing rascals get away."

We searched high and low, but they were gone. It was six o'clock. The sun was setting, and a mist shrouded the canyon we rode through. Suddenly, Mr. Rhodes raised his hand and motioned for us to keep quiet. He was like a hound dog that caught a scent. He quietly dismounted and crept toward a large boulder. We followed.

"Look." He pointed to a cave beside a creek, where three men were crouched around a small campfire, cooking coffee and beans. Our horses were tied up in a ravine not far off.

Mr. Rhodes crept closer and aimed his gun as steady as any man could. Then he shot the main man in the back of his head. The poor bastard never saw it coming.

The second man grabbed his six-shooters, and the third—who'd been riding Nancy—kicked dirt on the fire.

"Shoot!" shouted Mr. Rhodes.

Joe and I fired. Both men dropped to the ground at the same time.

All three were dead, laying in the dirt.

The silence afterward was heavier than any gunshot I'd ever heard.

This was my first kill, and I didn't like it—not one bit. My hands were still shaking when I lowered the smoking pistol. My heart was pounding like a drum in my ears, drowning out everything but the crackle of the dying fire and the soft wind running through the canyon. For a second, I couldn't breathe. The heat of the moment vanished, and cold realization rushed in behind it.

I just killed a man.

I replayed the moment over and over. The way he'd spun when the bullet hit him. The sound—dull and final. The look in his eyes. I hadn't meant to kill him, only to stop him. But out here, lines blur fast. You aim to protect, and end up burying a man.

I tried to convince myself he had it coming. That stealing horses and pulling a gun sealed his fate. But that didn't stop the bile that crept up my throat, or the shaking in my hands long after the gunshot echoed out. I wasn't sure if I'd ever feel clean again.

"You did what you had to," I whispered, but even I didn't believe it. I set my gun at my feet and closed my eyes.

Above me, the stars blinked like distant, indifferent eyes. I thought of Pa and what he'd say. Be careful who you shoot, son. Bullets don't stop once they leave the barrel. Not out here. Not in here. I pressed a hand to my chest.

"Good job," said Mr. Rhodes, patting us both on the back. "We taught those horse-thieving scoundrels a lesson. Now let's take it easy."

Mr. Rhodes picked up my gun and pressed it back in my hands. Then we went to their campfire and ate their beans.

He was mighty proud of us. I wasn't about to argue with him, but those beans were hard to swallow.

"Should we call a sheriff to take care of the bodies?" I asked.

"There's no lawman within a hundred miles of here," said Mr. Rhodes. "Besides, the coyotes will take care of the bodies."

I went over to Nancy, petting her and making sure she wasn't hurt. The man who'd taken her had laid a colorful Navajo saddle blanket on her back. He'd replaced my worn-out saddle with a new hand-tooled one—one of the prettiest I'd ever seen. I showed it to Mr. Rhodes.

"You can have it," he said. "After everything you've done today, I suppose you've earned it."

I was so tired I could hardly think, but sleep wouldn't come. So I just sat there, staring into the fire as it burned down to nothing. When the sun finally broke over the hills, I saddled up and rode back—quiet, worn, and sick with shame.

None of this felt right. Mr. Rhodes said they deserved it. That messing with another man's property was asking for a bullet. But the man I shot was just a young guy—maybe five years older than me—with his whole life ahead of him.

I wished I hadn't had to kill him. Ma would've been disappointed. She always said the Good Book tells us, "Thou shalt not kill." And I agree with that. But sometimes, you gotta do stuff that's not decent. When Mr. Rhodes started shooting, I did the same. He said if we wanted our horses back, it was going to be them or us—and I wasn't about to die. There's too much life I want to live: fall in love, own a ranch, read every Mark Twain book, go to Colorado and Montana.

Killing a man should never be taken lightly—especially not when you're only sixteen. I felt sick to my stomach, had nightmares for the next year. That's why Mr. Rhodes said never look at the face of the man you kill. But I couldn't help myself.

He was lying on his side, face in the dirt. I turned him over and looked him straight in the eye. I figured I needed to own what I did. There are some things you can't run away from, even if you want to. And I wanted to.

Especially when I realized I knew this person.

My eyes started to water, but I wiped them dry before Mr. Rhodes could see. To him, a cowboy did what he had to do. He was tough as nails, sharp as barbed wire, and as cold blooded as a rattlesnake in winter. That was just life in the Wild West.

I looked at Frank Douglas' smooth face and blue eyes. He was a handsome boy, but none too smart. His ma and pa had a small farm five miles south of where I grew up. They were good, hardworking folks. What was he doing out here rustling horses? How did he get mixed up with those thieves? Why did I have to be the one to shoot him?

"Son, are you okay?"

"I don't know," I said.

"You look like you just saw a ghost."

"I did." I shrugged. "I knew the boy."

"If you hadn't shot him, he would've shot you."

That's when I saw something peeking out of his shirt pocket—a folded square of paper. I slid it free, expecting some map or note. But it was a photograph—sepia-toned and creased at the corners. A young woman with soft curls and bright, intelligent eyes that seemed so full of dreams. And then there was a mysterious smile that felt both proud and shy.

Her name, Emma, was scrawled in pencil on the back.

I stared at the picture a long time, longer than I meant to. She looked like someone who still believed the world was good. That stung worse than the bullet. The wind stirred the dry grass, and the paper fluttered in my hand. I folded it gently and slipped it into my saddlebag.

I didn't feel like a hero. I felt like I'd done something awful—like I'd stolen someone's future. Folks said Frank had a girl in Valentine. They were planning a May wedding. She might've been a banker's daughter or a schoolteacher's—stories varied. But now she'd be a widow before she ever got to wear her white dress. The thought made my stomach twist.

I started to hate myself.

I sat back and stared at the dirt, wondering if Frank's family would ever know what happened. Would they hear the truth? Or just that he vanished, shot by an unknown hand somewhere out past Lost Creek? I'd taken a life, and with it, shattered a wedding, a future. I thought about writing a letter. Not to confess exactly—just to say he died fast, that he didn't suffer. Maybe send it unsigned, let Emma know he was brave. But what good would it do? Would it ease her grief—or make it worse? I couldn't be sure. And if I told the truth, I'd have to face what that truth might cost me.

Joe got the fire going again, its orange glow flickering off the cave walls. I sat a little ways off, nursing the bottle Mr. Rhodes handed me. The whiskey burned my throat, but it numbed the edge just enough to keep me from unraveling.

The others were quiet, too tired or too used to death to speak.

But I sat there watching the flames dance, wondering what Ma would say if she could see me now. Probably nothing. Maybe just lay a hand on my shoulder, let her silence speak what words couldn't. I remembered her humming a lullaby when I was small, when I'd wake crying from nightmares. Funny how something that simple could steady you more than whiskey.

The days that followed blurred together. I kept my head down and worked hard, but the memory stayed with me. Some nights I'd wake gasping, the gun shots still echoing in my dreams. I never spoke of Frank—not to Joe, not to Mr. Rhodes.

Six months later, on a hot August day, Joe and I packed our saddlebags for a trip to Pelican Lake—about twenty miles from the ranch—to drive some stray cattle home. I didn't call for Jasper. Didn't have to.

He showed up with his tail wagging, nose in my bedroll like he was making sure I had everything.

"Looks like you don't want to be left out on this ride."

He barked once and trotted off toward the gate.

I slung the saddle up on Nancy and smiled. "Guess that's a yes."

By the time I finished strapping down the bedroll, Jasper was waiting at the edge of the road, tongue out, ready as ever.

A few days later, with the stray cattle rounded up, we were riding along the bend of Snake Creek when Jasper froze. He stood stiff, tail up, ears sharp forward. Then he let out a sharp bark and darted ahead.

"Jasper, wait!"

But he was already halfway down the creek bed, cutting through the brush like a jackrabbit.

I kicked Nancy into a trot, following him, and that's when I saw it—a broken-down wagon, wheels stuck in a rut, a woman trying to calm a crying baby, and a boy struggling to lift a feed sack that was twice his size.

Jasper reached them first. He trotted right up to the boy and licked his hand, tail wagging so hard it stirred up dust.

The boy was rail-thin, cheeks hollow, dirt caked under his nails. When he looked up at me, his eyes held the same wide, scared look I'd seen on my brother George the night a twister tore through Cherry County. The baby in her arms had a sunken face and a deep cough, wrapped in a feed sack like it was the only blanket they had. The woman rocked him gently, her knuckles raw and red from days of work and worry.

They weren't just stranded—they were near giving up. They were out of food and looked mighty poor. A weight settled in my chest. I'd seen hard times, but not like this. I offered them my canteen. The woman handed it to her son, and then took two gulps herself.

"So grateful you wandered this way." She sat on the tailgate of the wagon. "Someone stole our horses, and my husband is out searching for them—and whatever else he can find."

"What's your name?" I asked.

"Shirley."

"Well, Shirley, how long has he been gone?"

"Since yesterday morning." She held her baby close.

"The scoundrels who stole your stuff are probably long gone."

"They took all our food," she said. "If my man can't find them, we're going to starve."

"We won't let that happen," I said. Something about the woman reminded me of Ma—maybe the way she squared her shoulders despite how tired her eyes looked. Her daughter, no older than two, clung to her dress just like my sister used to cling to Ma when thunder rolled across the plains.

I remembered nights back home, when we had nothing but dried cornmeal and a prayer to keep us going. Ma would light a candle, smile through the hunger, and say, "This too shall pass." I didn't know if that was true for this family. But I knew what it meant to need help and have none come.

"Here's something to tide you over." I reached into my saddlebag and handed her some beef jerky, hardtack, and dried fruit.

Joe did the same. "When we get back to the ranch, I'll ask the boss for some grub."

"We'd be mighty grateful." She smiled.

When I told Mr. Rhodes, he said, "You two need to take supplies to that family at first light."

"Boss, you're being very generous," said Joe.

"I just don't want women and children dying on the prairie."

By ten in the morning, we were back at the broken-down wagon with a quarter beef, a sack of flour, a box of vegetables, and two workhorses.

"I never thought you'd return," said Shirley, smiling, like a barn cat with a mouse in its mouth.

"Well, we did—and all of this is yours."

Her husband, Jake, sat on the wagon tongue, sunburned and sweating. "Thank you so much," he said, "I couldn't find the horses anywhere."

"If you had, there might've been a shootout," I said. "These wranglers can be dangerous people."

"That's true. How can I repay you?"

"My boss doesn't expect repayment. He just wants you to get where you're going and settle down."

"Where are you headed?"

"To Cheyenne," said Jake. "I'm setting up a blacksmith shop."

"You can make it there in two weeks," said Joe.

"You saved us," said Shirley. "We'll never forget it."

"My ma says helping strangers in need is what good people do."

"Thank you for listening to your ma." Jake shook our hands, and we rode back to the ranch.

A week before my seventeenth birthday, Joe and I took a trainload of cattle to the stockyards in Omaha. It was an easy trip—better than twelve hours in the saddle and sleeping on cold ground. I was especially looking forward to it, since Ma and Pa's place was on the way and I hadn't seen them in a year.

They were so surprised to see me they both cried.

"I thought you were going to work as a ranch foreman?"

"So did I," said Pa, as we sat in a small living room several miles outside of Norfolk. "But then I found out that growing beets for the sugar factory was more lucrative. We've made more money in the past year than the previous three on the farm in Cherry County."

"That's mighty impressive!"

"Why don't you move here and farm with me?" Pa asked.

"That's an excellent idea," said Ma.

"Let me think about it," I said. "Mr. Rhodes is a good man and a fair boss. It would be hard for me to leave his employment."

"I understand." Ma patted my hand.

I didn't say yes, but the thought stuck with me longer than I'd admit.

"Where are all my brothers and sisters?" I asked.

"George spends most of his time working the fields," said Ma.

"I'm sorry I left him to do the heavy chores."

"He's a hard worker and never complains," she said.

"What about the girls?"

"In school," said Ma, "The schoolmarm says they are smart as whips."

"That's one of my greatest regrets."

"What?" said Pa.

"Not finishing school," I said. "Ma, you taught me how to read as good as anybody. But I never learned grammar, mathematics, history, or geography."

"Some folks learn in a classroom. Others learn on the open prairie," said Ma.

"But I still love to read," I said. "I always have a book in my saddlebag."

"Good," said Ma. "And since tomorrow's your birthday, we have a gift for you."

"I hope it's a book."

"Of course it is." She handed me *Tom Sawyer Abroad*. "It's Mark Twain's latest."

"How special!" I held the book to my chest and hugged both my parents. "I can't wait to read it. Anything with Tom Sawyer in it will keep my attention."

"You've always been drawn to anything with adventure."

"That's certainly true." I smiled. "So is anything exciting happening 'round here?"

"Not really," said Pa.

"There is the mystery of the Douglas boy," said Ma.

I froze. My face flushed hot, and my gut twisted into a knot.

"Which one?" I asked, already knowing the answer.

"Frank, the oldest," said Ma. "They found his body out on the prairie near Lost Creek. Shot right through the heart."

I felt the blood drain from my face. My hands went cold. I forced a nod, careful not to let my voice crack. "That's awful."

"They say he was a good boy," said Pa. "Engaged to be married, too."

I swallowed the lump rising in my throat. My palms were sweaty, and I wiped them on my pant legs beneath the table, hoping Ma didn't notice. I stared down at the floor, trying not to picture his face. But it was there, plain as day. Dead in the dirt, the photo of Emma still warm in my hand.

"His parents are devastated," said Ma. "He was a nice kid. And it was just two months before his wedding."

"Do they know who did it?"

"Not yet," said Pa. "But his bride-to-be is the daughter of the sheriff of Cherry County. He promised the Douglases he'd leave no stone unturned until he found the killer."

My mouth went dry. I gripped the edge of the table, hoping they didn't see my knuckles go white. Part of me wanted to run—to mount Nancy and disappear into the hills. Another part wanted to tell them everything. That I hadn't meant to do it. That it had all happened so fast. That I had just been trying to stop him. But the words stuck like burrs in my throat. Instead, I just nodded and kept my eyes on the floor, letting the silence do what my voice couldn't.

And somewhere deep down, I knew that silence wouldn't last forever.

THE PRETTIEST GIRL

Sometimes I get impatient and restless. I can't breathe. I can't think. Darkness pins my shoulders to the ground and knocks the wind clean out of me. And if I can't escape, something terrible is going to happen. I'm Jonah in the whale or Daniel in the lion's den. Life is getting skinny and time is running out. I need to ride my horse as fast as she'll go, directly into the eye of the storm with a devil-may-care that would drive Ma to her knees and Pa to his whiskey. Only then will I survive to see another sunrise.

So that's what I did.

It was past midnight and a cold November wind whistled through the cracks of the old bunkhouse as I climbed out of bed. I'd been at the JR Bar Ranch for two and a half years and had learned a lot. Mr. Rhodes had been both kind and fair, but I'd had too many days in the saddle and nights sleeping on the hard ground. I put on my warmest dirty clothes and wrote him a note.

Mr. Rhodes,

Thank you for believing in a greenhorn like me. I'm headed out, but I won't forget what I learned here.

Allen John Herbert Stephens

I stared at the note a long time before setting it down. I remembered my first morning at the JR Bar Ranch—green as spring grass, my boots too big, my rope too loose. Joe had begrudgingly helped me tighten my saddle. Tom had tossed me a biscuit and called me "runt." Mr. Rhodes hadn't smiled that day, but he did look me in the eye and shake my hand. I was just a kid, but they gave me a chance. That counted for something. And now I was leaving them behind.

I folded the note in half and set it on the front porch of the ranch house. Jasper followed me. He knew something was up and stayed close beside me. I scratched him behind the ears, and he licked my hand.

Jasper whimpered and pushed his cold nose into my chest. He circled twice, let out a low whine, and sat at my feet, refusing to budge.

"I'm sorry, but I can't take you."

I knelt beside him, running my hand down his back. "You wouldn't like it where I'm going. It's not the open prairie—it's rows of sugar beets and long days with no room to roam."

He tilted his head, unconvinced.

"Besides," I added quietly, "Ma's not too keen on dogs in the house. And I've already got too many questions in my head to be worrying about keeping you fed."

I scratched behind his ears again, my voice catching a little. "It wouldn't be fair to you."

He sat down and stared at me like I'd just betrayed him. I tried walking past him, but he blocked the gate, tail stiff, head held stubborn and high.

"So you're going to make this difficult?"

He barked and licked my hand.

"Fine," I muttered. "But no chasing chickens or getting me kicked out of Ma and Pa's place."

His ears perked up, tail wagging so fast it thumped against the fence post.

"You're lucky I'm a soft touch."

He barked once and took off toward the road like he'd gotten his way and knew it.

Truth was, I was glad for the company. Even if I didn't know yet where the road was taking me—or who I might meet when I got there.

I packed all I owned in my saddlebags and climbed onto Nancy. The north wind cut through my army coat and wool cape. I lowered the brim of my Stetson, covered my face with my bandana, and rode east. Jasper ran alongside Nancy, his tongue out and tail high like he knew something exciting was about to happen. I'd been a cowboy, but now I was ready to settle down. Pa had invited me to join him and work the farm. So, in the darkness, I followed a crystal moon toward Norfolk to be a sugar beet farmer.

Frost shimmered on the prairie grass like spilled starlight. Nancy's breath steamed in the cold, rising like smoke from a winter fire. The wind carried the smell of pine and snow, and I could hear coyotes howling somewhere far off. I pulled my coat tighter and tried not to think about what I was leaving behind—just focused on the trail ahead, each hoofbeat carrying me toward something new. Or maybe away from something old.

I should have felt sad for leaving, but things were changing at the JR Bar Ranch. Joe had taken a job as a deputy in Valentine, earning twice what he'd made at the ranch. And Mr. Rhodes had finally had his fill of Tom. It all came to a head when Tom started a fight out at the Rain Man Ranch—though I can't say it was all his fault. He was dancing with one of the Indian girls, and her father didn't like how he was treating her. The father grabbed him from behind, but Tom was faster and stronger. He picked the man up and threw him across the dance floor. Then the whole place broke into a fight. The next day, Mr. Rhodes fired Tom. Without Joe and Tom, things just weren't the same.

I rode into Valentine that morning, just long enough to get warm and fill my belly with a double portion of biscuits and gravy. A few days later, on a rainy Saturday afternoon, I rode into Duff. It was a two-horse town in Rock County with not enough history to have a reputation. It was raining hard, and I was tired of the saddle. The place had a fine-looking livery barn. The owner was named Sam. He was a friendly man in his thirties with a bum leg and a thick beard.

"How much would it cost to leave Nancy here for the night?"

He looked me over. "Twenty-five cents for a clean stall and a bucket of oats."

I took off my hat and asked real polite, "How much for me and my dog to sleep on the hay in the back?"

"Another twenty-five cents."

I gave him two shiny coins. He smiled and put them in his pants pocket.

"Where are you headed?"

"Norfolk," I said, taking off my cape and shaking off the water. "To see my folks."

"Sounds like you're a good son."

"I try my best."

"Just spending the night?"

I nodded.

"There's a dance down at the schoolhouse tonight," said Sam. "My wife and I are going, and you're welcome to come as our guest."

"That's very hospitable of you, but I don't dance."

"Then it's about time you learned." Sam smiled. "Dancing is a fine way to meet a wife."

"I'm not looking for a wife. At least not yet."

"Looking or not, there'll be plenty of pretty girls at the dance."

"Then I'll certainly accept your invitation."

"May I make a suggestion?"

"Most certainly." I was curious.

"If you want to make a good impression tonight," said Sam, "take a bath and scrub your clothes."

I paid two nickels for a cold water bath and twenty-five cents for a haircut. Sam loaned me a clean shirt and I shined my boots until they almost looked new. I looked so fine and dandy that I hardly recognized myself. Jasper watched me like he couldn't believe I was cleaning up. I rubbed his ears, and he licked my boots.

"What do you think, Jasper?"

He wagged his tail once.

"You think I can find a girl to dance with me?"

He let out a low whine and laid his chin on my foot.

"Yeah, me neither. But a cowboy's gotta try."

That evening, Sam and his pretty wife, Mary, walked me down the dirt street toward the dance. The rain was still pouring, but that didn't dampen the cheerful spirit of a Friday night. The schoolhouse was packed with people, and the music of the band could be heard nearly all the way to the livery barn. Jasper found a dry place beneath the eaves and rested in the shadows.

The moment I stepped onto the dance floor, the schoolhouse erupted around me. Boots stomped on the hardwood in time with the fiddle, shaking dust from the rafters. Skirts swirled like prairie fire, flashes of red and blue and white cutting through the crowd. Someone whooped, and another voice laughed, high and wild and full of whiskey. The air was hot and heavy, thick with the scent of sweat and sawdust, perfume and pipe smoke.

I was jostled from behind by a farmer in suspenders spinning his wife like a windmill. A drunk cowboy stumbled through a reel, nearly knocking over a table of pies. I side-stepped just in time to avoid him and caught myself on the back of a chair. My heart was thumping like I'd just been thrown from a bronc.

It was chaos. Beautiful, joyful chaos—but chaos all the same. And then I saw her.

"What do I do?" I asked Sam.

"Just go up to her and ask her to dance."

I could wrangle cattle with all the confidence in the world, but asking a girl to dance made my legs shake like a willow in a windstorm. I looked across the brightly lit room and saw a girl in a red dress with high leather boots. She shimmered in the lantern glow, light catching in her hair like silver thread, and I couldn't take my eyes off her. At that moment, the room closed in on me and all I could see was her. I'd swear she was the prettiest girl I'd ever seen. She had long black hair with a touch of red flowing over her shoulders and eyes as dark as the obsidian shards of the Sand Hills. She looked back at me and I gritted my teeth. She pointed at me. My heart was beating fast and I wiped the sweat from my face with my bandanna.

"Do you see her?" Sam said.

I nodded.

"Her name is Eddie," he said. "Go dance with her."

"Are you sure?"

"She's asking you to dance," said Sam. "She'll give you one chance. If you don't take it, she'll never give you another."

"Then I'd better take my chance."

I walked across the room and led the glowing girl to the dance floor. I stumbled on the first step, clumsy as a newborn calf, and muttered an apology. She smiled and took the lead for a few counts until I got my feet under me. "You don't do this often," she said, teasing.

"Never," I admitted.

"Well, you're doing fine."

We swirled past couples in boots and bonnets, laughter floating in the air like fiddle notes. Between songs, I asked where she was from. She said, "Nowhere yet," and smiled like she had a secret. We didn't say much, but sometimes silence speaks loudest.

She followed me with more confidence than a storm stirring on the horizon. But I held my own, and we danced until the last song. It was a slow two-step, and she leaned close, resting her head on my chest. I held her tight, and she held me tighter. I'd never felt so alive in my whole life as we swayed to the smooth fiddle music. Her eyes were closed, so I closed mine, and the magic of the moment transported me beyond the prairies of Nebraska.

"Thank you for coming to the festivities," said the leader of the band, "and I hope you all had fun."

The crowd cheered.

"Have a safe trip home," he continued, "and I hope to see you all at next week's dance."

Eddie reached up and kissed me on the lips. Then she was gone.

I stepped out into the night air, trying to steady myself. The schoolhouse door creaked behind me and then clicked shut. Rain still fell in a fine mist, glittering in the lamplight. I walked toward the edge of the porch, wiping the sweat from my brow.

"You looked like a man in need of fresh air," came a voice behind me.

It was Eddie. She leaned against the railing, arms crossed, her red dress darkened at the hem where it brushed the wet floorboards.

"You dance like you've been on horseback your whole life," she teased.

"Not far from the truth," I said, chuckling.

She stepped closer. "You've got kind eyes," she said softly. "I noticed that before you ever asked me to dance."

"I noticed everything about you," I admitted.

"I know I come off strong," she said, almost whispering. "Tough girl from New York, chasing cowgirl dreams, drinking whiskey. But sometimes I get nervous."

She looked away and exhaled slowly, the rain misting her lashes.

"I act brave because it's easier than admitting I don't always know what I'm doing. Back home, they said I took up too much space—too loud, too wild, too much of everything. I came West 'cause I had to. That old life was closin' in—getting so small even the cat was feeling cornered."

She gave a crooked smile, the kind that tried to laugh off what hurt.

"But the truth is, every time something good shows up, I half-expect it to vanish. So I keep my boots by the door and never unpack all the way."

She tucked a strand of wet hair behind her ear and met my eyes.

I looked at her carefully. "What are you so nervous of?"

"Of getting stuck. Of getting close. Of someone leaving before I'm ready." Her voice had a tremble in it. Not much—but enough.

"I guess I've just always felt like I needed to keep moving," I said. "Like there's something out there I haven't found yet. And if I stay in one place too long, I might miss it."

She tilted her head, studying me. "You think you'll know it when you find it?"

"I think... maybe I just did."

She smiled then—just a flicker, but it lit up the shadows around us.

Eddie leaned over and kissed me. It was slow, deliberate—like she wasn't in a hurry to prove anything. I kissed her back, a little unsure, but wanting nothing more than to stay in that moment. I hadn't known a kiss could feel like that. And as much as I tried not to need anything too much, I found myself wishing it wouldn't end.

Then she pulled away, just like before, and disappeared into the dark.

My head swirled. I turned toward the spot where she'd been, but her red dress had vanished into the crowd. I stepped into the open, hoping to catch a glimpse of her retreating form. But the night was dark, and the pounding rain swallowed up what little light the moon and stars had left behind.

My heart broke.

"Where'd she go?" I asked Sam.

"Home."

"But she didn't even say goodbye."

"Eddie doesn't linger." Sam laughed.

"Where does she live?"

"With me and Mary. We live right next to the livery barn."

"So you know her well?"

"As well as anyone in these parts," said Sam as we walked back. "She's Mary's little sister."

"Our folks live in northern New York, near the Canadian border," said Mary. "Eddie's a restless girl. She wanted to come west and be a cowgirl."

"That's mighty ambitious," I said.

"Once the girl gets a notion in her mind, there's no stopping her." Mary shook her head. "When she heard that Annie Oakley and Calamity Jane were cowgirls with Buffalo Bill's Wild West Show, she figured she'd come to Nebraska and do it herself."

"So the girl's got spunk?" I asked.

"More than anyone I've met," said Sam. "She's only seventeen, but she can shoot a bottle from a fencepost at a hundred feet, rope cattle like an old-timer, and sit in the saddle from sunrise to sunset."

"She can also handle her whiskey better than most cowboys." Mary laughed.

"She sounds like a girl I'd like to get to know."

"Too bad you're headed out in the morning," said Mary.

"And it's too bad Norfolk is a hundred miles from here," Sam shrugged.

"Well, thanks for inviting me to the dance. It certainly is a night I won't forget."

I went into the barn and gave Nancy a good brushing. She whinnied and I gave her a handful of oats. I laid back in the hay, boots off, hat over my eyes, with Jasper breathing slow and even beside me. We slept like two strays who'd finally found somewhere worth staying.

I woke up with the roosters crowing. The rain had stopped, and the sun was breaking through the clouds. I sat up and stretched, but I had a strange feeling someone was watching me. I rubbed my eyes and stared into the hazy yellows of early morning.

"I was milking the cows and thought you might want a drink." Eddie was sitting on a hay bale ten feet in front of me. She looked like an angel—bright smile, cowboy hat cocked to the side. She handed me a glass of milk.

I drank it and started coughing.

"This has quite a kick."

She gave me a sly look. "I mixed it with whiskey. It goes down smoother that way."

"It certainly wakes you up," I said. "Thank you for the drink. And thank you for last night." She nodded and sat down next to me.

"Are you really leaving today?"

"That was my plan."

"Plans sometimes change."

"That's true." I nodded.

"I was hoping today might be one of those times."

I looked at her. She had straw in her hair and milk on her boots, and she was the most beautiful thing I'd ever seen. "Why'd you come west?" I asked.

She smiled. "Because I was tired of waiting for life to come to me."

"And has it?"

"Sometimes." She paused, then leaned her head against my shoulder. "Last night was one of those times."

She kissed me again, slower this time. It wasn't a spark or a dare—it was a promise. And I never wanted it to end.

"Don't forget me," she whispered as she walked away.

I stood up and said, "Please don't go."

She turned around, and her obsidian eyes glistened with dewdrops. "I'm not the one who's going."

I stood frozen, her words echoing in my head as I watched her walk out the door like a damned fool. Not knowing what to say.

My boots felt heavy—not from mud, but from something deeper. I walked to Nancy and ran my hand down her flank, gripping the saddle horn like it could anchor me to a decision.

One part of me wanted to climb up right then—ride out before the sun had even cleared the ridge. Keep moving, like I always had. Norfolk was waiting. Ma's stew. Pa's quiet nod.

I didn't know what I was doing—but I knew I wasn't ready to leave. At least not yet. The barn still held her warmth, her voice, her scent. I stood there for a long while, thinking about Norfolk, thinking about her.

That was the moment I first fell in love—and I fell hard. Eddie was like no other girl I'd ever known. And from that point forward, my life would never be the same. But what about Norfolk with its freshly painted houses and rows of sugar beets growing in straight lines? Solid. Predictable. Safe.

But Eddie wasn't safe. She was the storm I'd always felt brewing just beyond the horizon. The rain picked up again, tapping harder on the roof. I stepped outside and let it hit my face. The clouds rolled low and heavy, wind tugging at my coat like it was trying to pull me somewhere I hadn't planned to go.

And maybe that was the point.

Every so often, life hands you a moment where the choice you make'll shape everything that comes after. I knew this was one of those moments.

I looked down the road toward Norfolk—toward the harvest, the folks waitin' on me, the life I was familiar with. Then I looked back at the little house where Eddie lived, sunlight catchin' the edge of her porch rail.

One road led to what was expected of me. The other led to her.

STAGECOACH DRIVERS

I tried to leave. That morning was bright and brisk. The mud was dry and the road east was clear. I knew Ma and Pa would be so happy to see me. If I left now, I'd be home by Monday night and beat any winter storm that might push across the prairie. So I packed my saddlebags, put on my hat, and rode Nancy out of the barn. But that's as far as I got. I just couldn't leave. Jasper trotted up behind me as I sat there staring at the horizon, unsure of what to do. He sat at my side, ears twitching, waiting for me to make a move.

"You think I'm a fool, don't you?" I said.

He tilted his head, then whined.

"Yeah, me too." I patted his head. "But I can't ride away just yet."

When I turned Nancy toward Eddie's house, Jasper followed without hesitation, like he already knew which choice I was going to make.

That one night at the dance had stirred up feelings I didn't know how to shake. Eddie was in my heart and I could think of nothing else. It seemed a bit ridiculous since I'd only met her the night before. But feelings can be as unpredictable as prairie weather—and just as sharp. Leaving her seemed impossible. If it didn't kill me, it'd leave me riding through a storm without a way back, wondering if the rain would ever stop.

I rode to the house next to the livery barn, took off my hat, and pounded on the door. Eddie opened it and stepped onto the porch.

"Well, young cowboy," she said, "I thought the trail was calling you."

"I thought so too."

"But here you are with your hat in your hand." Her smile made me want to kiss her, but that didn't seem like a very gentlemanly thing to do.

"Did you mean it when you said don't go?"

"I don't say things I don't mean."

"So you'd like me to stay?"

"Only if you really want to." She sat on the porch rail, swinging her boots. "You're not the only one trying to figure out where they belong," she said. "My folks wanted me to marry a banker back in New York. They told me ranch life was no place for a lady. But I didn't want pearls and piano lessons. I wanted wide open spaces and horses and a rifle by my side."

"I'm glad you didn't stay in New York."

"So am I." She smiled. "Out here, I get to be who I really am."

"Isn't there another dance next Saturday?" I could feel my confidence growing.

She nodded. "I believe so."

"I'm thinking that I'd like to attend that dance."

She leaned forward. "Are you in need of a dance partner?" Her scent was as sweet as prairie flowers on a spring morning.

"I am particular. I only dance with cowgirls who know how to rope and ride."

"Anyone can rope and ride," Eddie smiled. "The real test of a cowgirl is how well she can handle a gun."

The next thing I knew she had a Colt single-action Army revolver pressed against my chest. I almost pissed myself. I pushed the barrel away. "Didn't your pa teach you to never draw a gun on someone unless you plan to pull the trigger?"

"What makes you so sure I wasn't planning to?"

"I would hope not." I sighed.

"I'm sorry for that," she said, placing the gun on a table beside the door. "But if you're still interested, I'd enjoy dancing with you."

"I'd like that. Except there's one thing I need to know."

"And what's that?"

"Are you really as good with that gun as your sister's husband says?"

"What did he say?"

"That you can shoot a bottle off a fence post from a hundred feet."

"That was my record last month," she said. "I can shoot further this month."

"I won't believe it until I see it."

"Willing to bet on whether I can do it or not?"

"What do you want to bet?"

"A bottle of whiskey," she said.

"It's a bet!"

She won that bet, and I stayed for the dance. Afterwards, we stayed up talking past midnight, and by sunrise, I knew I didn't want to leave. We fell madly in love.

A month later we stood just outside the livery barn, where the snow had quieted the world. Eddie was bundled in a wool coat, arms crossed, eyes fixed on the horizon instead of me.

"It's time for me to head home," I said as I threw my saddle on Nancy.

"Reckon I'll miss you," she said, almost like a challenge.

"I know I'll miss you," I replied. "More than a cowboy ought to admit."

She stepped forward, reached into her coat pocket, and pressed something into my hand. "Don't open it until you're home."

I gave her a puzzled look.

"Just promise me," she said.

"I promise."

Then she went and surprised me—kissed me real soft. But it hit like a punch to the gut. Next thing I knew I was in a dither—heart thumpin', head spinnin' with a mess of thoughts I couldn't put into words even if I tried.

"Go on now," she whispered. "Before I make you stay."

"I'm already having second thoughts."

"Your folks need to see you," she said. "And if you go now you'll make it to Norfolk just in time for Christmas."

I rode away with the cold in my bones and her gift tucked deep in my saddlebag. When I opened it days later, it was the red ribbon she'd worn during our first meeting and a note: Come back to me.

Jasper loped behind Nancy, never straying far, as if he felt the weight in my heart and meant to shoulder some of it.

There was a light snow falling as I rode up to the small two-story farmhouse. The folks must have seen me coming, for Ma and Pa stood on the porch. Ma held an infant in her arms and smiled as broad as usual. Pa looked tired, but he always seemed tired.

Jasper bounded up the porch steps ahead of me, tail wagging like he remembered the place. One of my younger brothers squealed and clapped when he saw him.

"Jasper!"

"You brought a dog?" Pa asked.

"He's smarter than most folks I've met on the trail," I said. "Figured he'd fit right in."

Ma smiled, "Well, if he doesn't chew my slippers or chase the chickens, he can stay."

My four siblings stared at me, probably wondering if I was really their long-lost brother.

"The prodigal son has finally returned," said Ma. She handed the infant to my sister and wrapped her arms around me. "Like the Good Book says, we must kill the fatted calf, prepare a feast, and celebrate."

"Son, it's good to see you," said Pa. "We might not have a fatted calf, but we've got plenty of chickens—Rhode Island Reds—we can butcher."

"I'm not a prodigal son."

"I know," Ma laughed. "But you've been far away in a distant land."

"And I have some great stories to tell," I said.

"Cowboy stories?" Six-year-old Erroll tugged on my pants.

I bent down to my haunches and looked my brother in the eye. "I've got stories about life on the trail that will make your toes curl. Stories about Indians, cattle rustlers, and the biggest, wildest, man-eating coyotes you could ever imagine."

"Now, don't scare the boy," said Ma. "He'll have nightmares for a month of Sundays."

"I want to hear Allen's stories," said Erroll.

"So do we," said Maud and Ethel as they moved closer. Maud was eleven and Ethel nine. They'd both grown so much that I barely recognized them.

"I'm full of tall tales." I smiled and tipped my hat to them.

The girls giggled bashfully.

"Tell us one," said Erroll.

And so I did as the three sat wide-eyed while I told cowboy stories that had a grain of truth in them.

Jasper settled near the fireplace like he'd been there a hundred times before, soaking up the warmth and attention like a favored child.

After an hour, Ma said, "Storytime is over. You kids go and do your chores."

Then Ma took my hand and led me into the parlor. "How long do we get to enjoy your company?"

"As long as you'd like," I smiled. "I quit my job at the JR Bar Ranch, and I'm a free man."

"But you've always been a restless pilgrim," said Pa. "You've never been one to let grass grow beneath your boots."

"That's true, but I'm hoping to stay through planting season. That is, if you've got a place I can rest my head."

"Our house might be small, especially for seven of us," said Ma. "But there's always room for one more."

"What about two more?"

"Two?" said Pa.

"I met a girl about a hundred miles west of here." I paused. "She's quite a girl, and one of these days I'd like to fetch her so you could meet her."

"Son, you are full of surprises," said Pa.

"She's welcome anytime you want," said Ma, barely holding back her excitement. "What's her name and what's she like and where is her family from?"

"Now Ma, slow down," said Pa. "Let the boy settle in. There'll be plenty of time for questions and conversation between now and planting time."

Late that night, after a bountiful feast of fried chicken, creamed corn, and salad greens, I sat by the fire and took out my journal.

"What are you writing?" asked Ma.

"My plans."

"What sort of plans?"

"My plans for 1897." I smiled.

"That's mighty ambitious," said Ma. "Does this girl know about your plans?"

"Not yet."

"Son, I'd suggest you talk them over with her. Especially since she might think differently about these things than you."

"I've never been much of a talker."

"But if you want to settle down," said Ma, "talking makes life go smoother."

I nodded.

"Do you mind me asking about your plans?"

"Not at all. In March I'd like to bring Eddie out to the farm to meet the family."

"I'm looking forward to meeting this girl who's stolen my son's heart," said Ma.

"In April I'll plant sugar beets with Pa."

Pa, who was reading the newspaper, said, "I'd like to plant a hundred acres. George and I would sure appreciate your help."

"Then from May through August I'll drive stagecoach."

"Stagecoach?" said Pa. "Where will you drive stagecoach?"

"There's a run in Western Colorado where the railroad hasn't laid tracks yet. It's a patch of treacherous terrain, but they pay well."

"That should be quite an adventure," said Pa.

"In September I'll be back here to help with the harvest."

Pa nodded. "That will be greatly appreciated."

"Then in November I'll get married."

"Lord willing," said Ma.

"Lord willing, and if Eddie will have me."

"Are you sure you're ready?" said Ma.

"How do you know if you're ready?"

Ma shrugged. "You just know."

Throughout the winter I made three or four trips to Duff. Each one was better than the last. I never knew life could be so good. A pretty girl can put you in a flutter faster than anything I'd ever experienced. In mid-March I brought Eddie to my folks' farm for a week. Everybody loved her. She taught Erroll how to shoot and rocked baby Guy to sleep each night.

One morning, I came into the kitchen and found Ma and Eddie kneading bread at the long wooden table, flour dusting both their aprons and streaking their cheeks. The scent of yeast and warm milk filled the air. Sunlight poured through the lace curtain, catching the fine flour in the air like snowflakes dancing in a golden breeze. They were laughing—genuine, full laughs that curled at the edges like old friends swapping secrets. Ma wiped her brow with the back of her wrist and said, "You've got good hands, girl. You ever consider being a midwife?"

"I've never been good with babies."

"Give them time and they tend to grow on you."

"Maybe," Eddie grinned, rolling the dough with a firm press. "But only after I've raised a little hell."

Ma let out a free-spirited laugh and shook her head. "That's fair. Children can tie you down, but they can also warm your heart."

They bent over the dough again, pressing and folding in rhythm. Jasper nosed around the edge of the table, tail wagging as if he hoped someone might drop a crust or offer him a bit of dough. I stood in the doorway, unnoticed for a moment, just watching. I hadn't seen Ma smile like that in months—not since Christmas, maybe not since before I left the first time. There was something easy between them, like two parts of my life finally meeting and getting along just fine.

Eddie looked over her shoulder and caught me watching. "You just gonna stand there and let us do all the work?"

"I thought I might," I said, grinning.

Ma tossed a lump of dough at me—it hit my shirt and stuck like a cow pie. "No loafers in this house," she said, and Eddie laughed so hard she nearly dropped the dough.

For the next hour, we worked together, shoulder to shoulder, shaping loaves and brushing egg wash, Ma telling stories I'd never heard before—like how Pa once built her a rocking chair out of scrap fence posts—and Eddie soaking it all in. It was a picture I wanted to hold onto: my Ma, my girl, both with their sleeves rolled up, baking bread like they'd done it together all their lives.

That evening, after supper and dishes were done, I stepped out to check the barn roof for leaks. When I came back, I found Eddie on the porch steps, wrapped in Pa's old blanket. The stars were out, and the night was still.

"Ma says you're good for me," I said, sitting beside her.

"She said that?" Eddie asked, smiling faintly.

I nodded. "Said I looked settled."

"She's kind. I like her."

"She likes you too."

We sat quiet a moment. Then Eddie asked, "You want me to keep showing up?"

"Yeah," I said. "I do."

She didn't answer with words—just reached for my hand under the blanket. We sat like that with our fingers laced, enjoying the quiet and closeness, hoping it would never end.

The next afternoon Eddie and I sat on the front porch watching a storm gather on the horizon.

"I've been thinking about the future," I said.

"What about the future?"

"What do you think of me driving stagecoach this summer?"

"A man must do what he needs to do," said Eddie. "But I'd miss you."

"It'll only be four months."

"Four months is a long time."

"So let me ask you a question."

"Fire away."

"Are you as good with a rifle as you are with a pistol?"

"I'm even better." Eddie smiled. "I can shoot the hat off a man at two thousand feet."

"That's impressive."

"I'm no ordinary cowgirl."

"That's for sure." I paused. "Why don't you join me on the stagecoach run in Colorado? I can be the driver and you can ride shotgun."

"What if I want to be the driver?"

"You are a better shot than I am. If anyone wants to cause trouble, I'd rather the rifle be in your hands than mine."

"I can't disagree with that." She smiled.

A month later Eddie and I rode west to Colorado. We were hired for the two-day stagecoach run of seventy-four miles from Wolcott to Steamboat Springs, then back to Wolcott. After that we'd do it again, all summer long for some fifty trips. Drivers got fifty dollars a month and shotguns got twenty-five. But we pooled our money, and by the end of August we'd saved two hundred and fifty dollars. It was a fancy and rugged coach pulled by four horses that carried mail and up to nine passengers. Eddie and I sat on top where we could see for miles. The fresh air and majestic view of the Rocky Mountains made me fall even more in love with her.

Jasper took to the stagecoach like he'd been born for it. He'd ride up top with us, paws planted firmly and ears flapping in the wind like a flag. When we hit a steep grade, he'd bark encouragement at the horses as if his voice alone could push them uphill.

Passengers loved him. One little girl gave him a peppermint, which he accepted with solemn dignity—only to sneeze five times in a row and fall off his seat. Eddie laughed so hard she nearly dropped her rifle.

"He's better company than half the men in these hills," she said.

And she wasn't wrong.

The trips weren't easy. The grades were steep and the road was narrow. But we kept up the pace since there were schedules to meet. The weather was hot and dry with the sun beating down on the two of us. We never complained. I kept reminding myself of something Mr. Rhodes once told me: "The trail may be tough, but a cowboy is tougher." Eddie and I were determined to prove my old boss right. Luckily, we carried a lot of water and whiskey. When we got hot, we drank water. When we got nervous, we drank whiskey.

There were two passes we climbed on our route with a deep valley in between—Red Dirt Pass and Yellow Jacket Pass. Both were higher in the mountains than either of us had ever been. I gripped the reins and Eddie gripped her Winchester. We tipped over several times. Eddie and I were able to jump free with only a few bumps and bruises. The passengers were rattled, but there were no serious injuries. With the help of the men on board we were able to get the coach back on its wheels before too much time had passed.

The only other major trouble was on an August morning as we were climbing toward Yellow Jacket Pass. A large rock was in the middle of the road, and when I climbed from my seat to move it, two shots rang out from a cliff to our right. I took cover and Eddie fired in the direction of the shots. Two men stepped into the road with rifles and demanded that everyone get out of the stage. Eddie shot one in the leg. He fell, and the other bandit let out a blaze of bullets toward Eddie. I fired my rifle several times at him. He picked up his companion and they made their escape. I climbed up on the stage to check on Eddie. She was lying on her back clutching her right shoulder.

"I've been hit," she said, as if she couldn't believe that such a thing was possible.

Her shirt was bloodied. I looked at the wound. "I think the bullet might still be in there. We gotta get you to a doctor. Just lay down and press this on the wound to stop the bleeding." I handed her my bandanna.

I jumped down and checked on the passengers. They were okay. Then I moved the rock, climbed into my seat, and sped the stagecoach toward Steamboat Springs as fast as the horses could take us.

The town came into view just as the sun climbed over the peaks. Wood smoke hung in the air like a curtain, and the narrow main street was thick with morning bustle—wagons groaning under sacks of flour, dogs chasing chickens, and a pair of boys sweeping out the front of the saloon. A preacher tipped his hat as we passed, and a woman at the general store covered her mouth when she saw the blood on Eddie's shirt.

We rolled to a stop in front of the doctor's office, dust swirling around us. My hands were shaking as I climbed down from the coach.

"You're a lucky young lady," said the doctor as he bandaged her shoulder. "The bullet didn't hit any bones or arteries. So take it easy, and you'll be fine in a few weeks."

"Did you hear that?" I said as we walked out of the office.

"I can't take it easy," said Eddie. "You know that I'm not a quitter. We've got a job to do and our contract goes to the end of the month. And I plan to work come hell or high water, in spite of a bullet to the shoulder."

I crossed my arms. "Eddie, you just got shot."

She narrowed her eyes. "And I'm still breathing, ain't I?"

"That's not the point. You don't have to prove anything to anyone."

She stood, slow but steady, pain flashing across her face. "I'm not doing it to prove something, Allen. I'm doing it because I made a promise. And because I love this job. I love the road. I love that it's hard."

I didn't say anything right away. I just looked at her—this stubborn, fearless, incredible woman I couldn't imagine losing.

"Is there any use arguing with you?"

"No. My mind is made up."

I gave her a kiss on the lips.

She smiled and said, "Give me some whiskey to try to kill this pain."

That night, as Eddie lay curled on her side in the inn, I sat by the window with my rifle across my lap. Jasper lay curled at her feet, his ears twitching every time she stirred, guarding her like he understood just how close she'd come to crossing that last divide. I couldn't stop seeing her face when she was hit—the shock in her eyes, the way her body buckled. She'd been brave and steady. But in that moment, she looked small. Fragile. And it scared the hell out of me. I'd nearly lost her, and the thought of it hollowed me out like nothing ever had.

We worked out every day of our contract and her shoulder fully healed, except for a jagged scar. She was proud of that scar and said it proved she was a real cowgirl. Whenever possible she'd show it off. "See this mark," she'd say. "Doesn't it look like lightning? That's 'cause I'm so fast that not even a bullet can do me harm."

Whenever I heard this, I'd smile and thank the Good Lord for His protection.

On the first of September we took a slow ride back to Ma and Pa's farm to help with the sugar beet harvest. I hadn't worked up the nerve to ask her to marry me yet. But I was still hoping for a November wedding.

I didn't have a ring. I didn't have a speech. But watching her there—sunlight on her face, wind in her hair—I knew I didn't want a life without her. And sometimes, knowing that is enough to begin.

A LITTLE RED HOUSE

"Let's run away and never go home." Eddie leaned on my shoulder.

"Where would we go?"

"It doesn't matter as long as we're together." She kissed my cheek.

We sat side by side next to a campfire, watching the embers collapse on themselves in iridescent reds and yellows and blues. The prairie was peaceful at night and it felt perfect.

"But we're just a day from Norfolk," I said without looking at her.

"Your folks are the salt of the earth, but I need something more than the prairie." She threw a piece of wood onto the fire and smiled as it burst into flames. "I need to move beyond Nebraska."

"What if we could bring life to this place?"

"Is that even possible?" She shrugged. "Look at Sam and my sister. They started out so enthusiastic, and now it's like they've been drained dry."

"That would never happen to us."

"That's probably what they said."

"But I promised I'd help Pa and George with the harvest."

"A man is only as good as his word." She slipped her hand into mine. "But what about after that?"

"After that I was hopin' we'd get married."

For a moment, the words just hung in the air between us. I hadn't planned to say them—not like that, not here—but the firelight on her face and the way she held my hand made it impossible to keep quiet. My heart beat like a war drum. What if she laughed? What if she said no?

She looked at me with those steady eyes, like she could see the whole world in front of her and wasn't afraid of any of it.

"Allen John Herbert Stephens," she said, "did you just ask me to settle down with you?"

"I sure did." I squeezed her hand tight.

"But shouldn't you get down on a knee and take your hat off?"

I took off my hat and leaned on my right knee. "Eddie Dailey, would you consider being my wife?"

"Yes, yes," she said. "But I need you to promise me one thing."

"And what is that?"

"Please don't ever try to wrangle the cowgirl out of me."

"Why would I do that?" I sat down beside her. "It's the cowgirl in you that I fell in love with."

"Then let's get married." She jumped into my lap with such vigor that I almost fell over. "The sooner the better."

"What about November in Norfolk?"

"It's a deal." And she smothered my face with kisses.

The day we got married was the most wonderful, amazing day of my life. That morning I went outside to greet the frosty dawn with just my long johns and Stetson on. I whooped and hollered until Ma and Pa came out on the porch to quiet me down.

"What are you doing out here without your boots on?" said Pa.

"I'm celebrating!" I shouted, throwing my hat into the air.

"Get yourself in here before you catch your death of cold," said Ma.

I came in and my brothers looked at me like I was crazy loco. Maybe they were right. Love does peculiar things to your head. But if I was crazy I didn't care, 'cause I felt as happy as a buck in an open field. Ma gave me a cup of coffee and I drank it in one swallow. Life could not have been any better.

Pa bought me fancy clothes from some haberdashery in Chicago—a dark gray double-breasted jacket with matching trousers, a stiff white shirt, and a red necktie. It must have cost him a fortune. But he said that a man has to look as refined as possible at his wedding and his funeral. I'm not sure whether I looked refined or like a peacock on parade. Ma said I was as fine a looking fella as she'd ever seen. But a mother always thinks the best of her son, even if it's not true.

Even my brothers and sisters were dressed fancier than I'd ever seen. The girls were especially excited because they'd never been to a wedding before. Ma braided their hair and they wore colorful wreaths of dried flowers around their heads. The boys had shined their boots and scrubbed their faces until they almost looked like city folk. Ma rocked the baby and prayed he wouldn't cry through the ceremony.

A half hour before the wedding, I found Pa in the barn brushing down Nancy. He wasn't dressed yet, just in his shirtsleeves, suspenders stretched over his shoulders.

"Nervous?" he asked without looking up.

"A little."

He nodded. "That's natural. Getting married's like roping a wild horse. You don't know if it'll buck you off or carry you home."

"Thanks, Pa. That's... encouraging."

He cracked a rare smile. "Just don't forget—love ain't just about feelings. It's about sticking through the hard winters and the dry spells. If you can do that, you'll be alright."

It was a small wedding with just family. Sam and Mary came from Duff, but the rest of her family lived too far away to make the trip. We got married in a nearby Baptist church at one in the afternoon on a cold November day, just about a year after I first laid eyes on the prettiest girl I'd ever seen. But when I saw her walking down the church aisle all spiffed up, she was even prettier. I just stood there with my mouth wide open, wondering how I could be hitching up to such a sweetheart.

My throat was dry as dust. I kept thinking I'd mess up the vows or stumble over my own name. When the preacher asked if I took Eddie to be my wife, my "I do" came out rougher than I expected, but sure as sunrise. Her hands were warm in mine. I couldn't stop looking at her fingers—calloused from riding, nails chipped from gardening. They were real hands, strong hands, and I had the crazy thought that maybe we could hold up the whole world together with just those two hands and a promise.

That winter was the coldest, windiest time I'd ever known. Eddie and I thought we'd freeze to death, but I suppose it wasn't our time to meet our maker. As soon as the land thawed, I took the money we'd earned driving stagecoach and built us a little house just up the road from Ma and Pa. I painted it red because it reminded Eddie of strawberries, and she loved strawberries. It was a simple one-room structure with a fireplace, two windows, a double bed, and a bookshelf that held my meager library. Ma had recently given me *Moby Dick* and I was obsessed with the wide open sea. Books reminded me that there was a giant world out there that went far beyond the flat prairie. Next to our new home was an outhouse, a woodshed, a well, a brick oven, a chicken coop with three Rhode Island Reds, a two-stall barn for Nancy and Eddie's horse, Thunder, and a root cellar for vegetables and meat. Jasper paced from the woodpile to the well to the barn like he was in charge of everything. Whenever I stepped out of the house, he'd drop a stick at my feet and wag his tail expectantly. Eddie and I were as happy as two clams in high water.

That first night in our little red house, we lay down on the bed, the fire crackling soft and warm at our feet, and the smell of pine smoke hung sweet in the rafters. Eddie curled up against me—pressing her cold feet to my calves until they were warm—and we listened to the wind brushing the windows like it had missed us. The rooster crowed in the middle of the night, tricked by the heat of the hearth, and we laughed until we cried. We didn't have much, but it was ours—and that made it everything. Jasper curled himself into a tight ball near the fire, one ear flicking every time the wind rattled the windows. He was home too, and he knew it.

When spring came I got a job breaking horses and Eddie planted a garden with enough vegetables to feed an army. But she did a lot more than that. While I was off with the horses, she roamed the prairie looking for game. Some days she'd come home with prairie dogs or a white-tail deer. Other days she'd catch bass or catfish from the Elkhorn River. We ended up with so much more than we could eat that we often helped Ma and Pa put food on their table. With seven hungry mouths to feed, they never had quite enough. Ma must have thanked us a thousand times for our generosity—or should I say Eddie's generosity. Mr. Rhodes used to say that a full belly makes for good times.

August in Nebraska can get so hot and humid that your skin sticks to your clothes. One Saturday afternoon, we rode out to the river to eat a picnic lunch and cool our feet in the water. As we were eating, something rustled in the bushes behind us. I froze. Jasper bristled and let out a low growl, circling between us with the sound like he was ready to take on whatever threat was waiting there. Before I could move, Eddie jumped to her feet, drew her Colt, and fired. Then she strode to the bushes and lifted a two foot rock rattler by the tail—she'd shot its head clean off.

"I've never seen a snake that long," I said.

"Or a gun that fast." She smiled.

"Or that accurate."

"Well, next time you're going to have to shoot a snake." She paused. "I'll be busy with more important things."

"More important things?" I stared at her, trying to understand what she was referring to.

Eddie dropped the snake and sat down beside me. "I'm pretty sure I'm expecting."

Maybe I'm thick in the head, but I still couldn't figure out what she was trying to tell me.

"I'm in the family way," she said as plainly as I just wrote those words.

I stared at her, speechless.

"Yessiree! By the next spring moon, we'll have a child."

"So I'll be a father?" I looked at her in disbelief. "What should we do?"

"We don't need to do anything." She put my hand on her belly. "The little one will just grow and grow until he's ready to come out."

"Don't you need to lay down and rest?"

"I'm tough as the Rocky Mountains," she said. "After all, I just blew the head off a rattler at twenty feet. I'm a cowgirl and nothing is gonna slow me down."

"I'm not about to argue."

"Good," she said, raising her pistol and letting two more shots crack the sky.

"Ma will be so excited when she hears the good news."

"Then let's go tell her."

Seven months later, shortly after midnight, the two windows of the little red house were full of light. Ma and Eddie were inside. Pa and I were sitting in the barn with the horses, waiting for news about the baby. I was so wound up I couldn't sit still. Pa told me it would be alright and that every father is as nervous as a turkey on Thanksgiving Day. "But after that first birth, the rest are as easy as breaking wind."

Even Jasper seemed nervous, pacing circles in the barn and nosing Pa's boots until he finally settled at my feet with a heavy sigh.

Ma had been the midwife to many mothers in northern Nebraska and no one questioned her care. An hour passed, and then two.

Ma gave us updates that the baby was coming, but he didn't seem to be in any hurry. She said Eddie was tired and determined, but was as hardy as a quarter horse. At about three in the morning, Ma announced that we had a healthy little boy and that we could come check him out. He was beautiful and we named him George Allen Stephens. I don't think I'd ever been this happy. I kissed Eddie and the baby. Then I kissed Ma and Pa. If Mr. Rhodes was there, I might have even kissed him too.

Jasper took to baby George like a second shadow. Whenever Eddie rocked him to sleep, Jasper curled at her feet, tail thumping in rhythm with the creak of the rocker.

When George cried in the night, Jasper was often first to the cradle, nose nudging the wooden rails until I stirred.

"He's got the heart of a nursemaid," Ma said one evening, watching Jasper trail George and Eddie around the yard. "And smarter than most people I know."

Eddie was a loving mother, but she wasn't going to let a baby slow her down. As summer hit the prairie, she rode her horse faster, shot her gun further, roped cattle better, and drank whiskey more often. She even learned to play poker and could beat any man within fifty miles of Norfolk. Motherhood tames some women. It only made Eddie wilder. One day Pa and I were walking his sugar beet fields and he looked me square in the eye. "Son, you know we think the world of Eddie, but…" He paused and rubbed his face. "…but be careful. That cowgirl is as wild as a tumbleweed."

I laughed and said, "I know. That's why I married her."

Pa didn't laugh. He stopped walking, rubbed his chin like he was working through something harder than he wanted to admit. "Firecrackers light up the sky—but mishandle one, and it'll blow your hand clean off."

I blinked, caught off guard.

"She's got a good heart, but her fuse is short, and her feet ain't planted. Son, just be careful."

He placed his hand on my shoulder, gave it a firm squeeze. Then he walked away, leaving me in the quiet field with the wind rustling through the beet tops.

I watched him go, wondering what he saw that I hadn't. Eddie was wild, yes—but wasn't that what made her beautiful and exciting? Still, a part of me couldn't shake the chill his words left behind.

I thought about the time Eddie climbed the roof of the livery just to hang a wind-vane, or when she rode bareback into a thunderstorm just to see what it felt like. I loved that part of her—but maybe Pa was right. Maybe the wind that stirred her spirit couldn't be fenced in, even by love.

Time passed in a blur of seasons and baby steps. Two years after George entered this world, John Lewis Stephens was born. It was a tough birth.

After that Eddie stopped singing. That was the first sign that something was wrong. Eddie always sang—while cooking, cleaning, even hunting. But for weeks now, the house had been too quiet. Some days she'd wander the edge of the prairie for hours with John in a sling around her waist and her rifle over her shoulder, not saying a word when she came home.

At night, she'd lie awake staring at the ceiling. She stopped pressing her cold feet to my legs. I'd reach for her hand, and she'd squeeze it, but her mind was already somewhere else.

Then one night Eddie snapped.

John had started crying again. George was asleep in the loft. The fire had burned low, and I was fixing the door latch. Eddie's footsteps crossed the floor—quick, tense. She set John down and spun to face me, fists clenched.

I stood there with a screwdriver in hand, no idea what I'd done— just knowing I was about to find out.

But nothing happened. She just stood there with blood in her eyes, snorting and shaking like a bull in a pen.

After that, the days grew quieter. The house, once full of humming and laughter, felt still. Eddie stopped singing—her melodies silenced like a wind chime with no breeze. She swept the floors in silence. Rocked John with a faraway look. Some days, she'd disappear for hours, wandering the edge of the prairie, rifle slung across her back, eyes scanning the distance like she was expecting something to break through the horizon. Even Jasper grew restless, whining at the door when Eddie wandered the prairie, then laying his head on the windowsill to watch for her return.

I tried asking, but she'd just nod and say she was fine. I didn't believe her.

"Please tell me what's wrong."

She stared at me, long and hard, determining whether to respond. Then she said in a voice slow but fierce, "I'm leaving the prairie."

I straightened, tools in hand. "What?"

"I can't stay here. This place is killing me. Flat, quiet, small."

"But we've made a home here."

"I didn't come here to die." Her eyes were blazing now. "I want to chase buffalo, ride trails through pine forests, wade across raging rivers, sleep beneath mountains. I need to feel alive again, like a primeval land that hasn't been tamed."

"There's snow on the ground."

"Then I'll wait for the thaw," she said. "But I'm not waiting for permission."

She turned toward the fire and pressed her hands to her head as if to keep it from exploding. "Allen, I'm not just restless. I'm drowning."

"But we've started something good here," I said as calmly as I could.

"I'm leaving here with or without you." She sighed. "But I'm not staying a minute longer than I have to."

"Where do you want to go?"

"West," she said. "Maybe Oregon or Idaho or Montana, anywhere that a cowgirl can feel free."

"So there's no way you can feel free in Nebraska."

"No way in hell." She stared at me like I'd lost my mind. "I need to feel the wind in my face, the ground shifting under my boots. I need to be moving, reaching for something bigger. That's how I know I'm alive."

"If you want to leave, then let's do it together."

"Together or alone, I'm moving on." She slammed her fist against the wall. "I'm almost twenty-two years old and I've got to rope life before it gets away from me. I'm not spending another summer wasting away on this godforsaken prairie."

A month later we heard the snow had melted in Montana so we bundled up our two boys. Eddie stood in front of the little red house, holding John on her hip with George clutching her hand. I walked the perimeter one last time—ran my fingers over the doorframe we carved, touched the tree stump we used as a chopping block. The barn creaked, and the prairie wind carried that smell of dry grass and smoke. Eddie didn't cry. She just stared west. I realized then— she wasn't leaving something behind. She was chasing something ahead.

Two hours later we boarded the Union Pacific for a thousand-mile ride through the Rocky Mountains. We secured Nancy and Thunder in the stock car, making sure they had plenty of hay and water for the long ride. There was no way we were going to Montana without our horses. By now they'd become just as much a part of our family as George and John. Mr. Rhodes used to say that a cowboy without a horse was like a sailor without a ship.

The train rattled and groaned, cutting its way west through plains, hills, and into the jagged shadows of the Rockies. George pressed his face to the glass, wide-eyed at the forests and snowy peaks. Eddie kept one arm around him and the other on John, who squealed with delight every time the whistle blew.

I held her hand across our laps. Her eyes were locked on the horizon like it held a secret. I didn't know what Montana would bring—but I knew this: wherever she was going, I was going too.

Two days later we arrived at Kalispell. It was an isolated community, at the foot of massive granite mountains and some fifty miles from the Canadian border. Eddie said it looked like a tough cowboy town. After lunch at Heller's Saloon and a few stiff shots of whiskey, Eddie and I rode our horses up Stillwater River to look at one of the cattle ranches. It was a wild country with a majestic natural beauty that was truly a sight to behold.

The cowgirl couldn't have been happier.

DREAMS AND NIGHTMARES

The summer of 1901 was better than either of us could have imagined. Flathead Valley was paradise. The cowboys called it God's country. We soaked in the beauty, embraced the wildness, and lived our dreams to their fullest.

In the morning we rode in silence, just the rhythm of hooves brushing against dry grass and the soft creak of worn leather. The air was warm already, thick with the scent of dust and wildflowers. In the east, the sky unfurled in a quiet bloom of rose-gold, spilling over the prairie like paint across canvas. Streaks of peach and powder blue chased each other into the sky, lighting up the world without a sound.

Eddie rode ahead a few paces, her silhouette bold against the rising light. The sun caught in her hair, turning it copper-bright, and for a moment, she looked so wild and free. She twisted in the saddle, gave me that sideways grin. "Ain't no prettier time to ride," she said.

The mountains in the distance wore a soft haze of violet, their peaks rimmed in gold. Birds darted low over the fields, and the tall grass glistened with dew, catching the sunlight like threads of silver. Somewhere nearby, a meadowlark sang. I didn't say a word—just kept riding and watching Eddie, thinking: this is what forever ought to feel like.

The following summer we built a house on the Stillwater River, five miles north of town. I broke horses for the local ranchers, while

Eddie hunted in the hills and fished in the streams. In October, during the first snowfall, William Henry was born. The world hushed that morning, snow falling soft as whispers. Eddie wrapped William in a quilt her mother had sewn, handed her to me, and put on her riding clothes.

"What are you doing?" I asked.

"I need fresh air," she said, pulling on her boots. "Thunder and I are hitting the trails on the other side of the lake."

"But your baby needs you."

"Don't try to control me."

I didn't say a word—just kissed Eddie goodbye and watched her walk away. You can't rope the wind or talk sense to a storm— it's gonna blow through no matter what you do. All a man can do is brace himself and wait it out. William cried the whole day and no matter how I tried to comfort him, he wouldn't quit.

I know Eddie loved her boys—no question about that. But that third one added more weight than she'd counted on. She held it together most days, but now and then, I saw a tight, glassy look in her eyes—the kind you get when you're hangin' on by a line with time runnin' out."

That winter life got bleak—work was hard to find, money running low, there was not enough food to fill our bellies. Some of the cowboys told me they'd found work in Butte, Montana.

"What kind of work?" I asked.

"In the copper mines."

"But that's five hundred miles from here," I said. "And I hear it's mighty dangerous."

"That's true," they said, "but the pay is good."

So after Christmas I boarded the train for Butte. Once there, I found a job working in the smelter of the Anaconda Copper Company, pouring molten metal into molds. It was a miserable job— sweltering heat, toxic fumes, poor ventilation, steam explosions, long back-breaking labor. Not to mention that every week, workmen were burned or severely injured. Sometimes even killed.

Eddie wasn't in favor of this, but I felt we had no choice.

"I thought you were a cowboy," she said on the day I left.

"Desperate times require desperate measures."

"So you are abandoning your family when we need you the most."

"No, I'm doing everything I can to take care of you."

"You know family life is hard for me."

"I wish I wasn't leaving," I said.

"But you're going anyway."

She swore at me, slammed the door in my face, and refused to go to the train station to see me off. I stood there a long moment, bags at my feet, hoping she'd reconsider. But the door stayed shut. I touched the handle, thought about staying. Then Jasper came trotting around the side of the house, his tail wagging low and uncertain. He nudged my leg with his nose, then sat down at my feet, watching me with those steady brown eyes.

"You don't want me to go either, do you, boy?" I said, scratching his ears.

He gave a low whine, leaned into my side, and licked my hand.

"I have to," I whispered. "But I'll come back. I promise."

Jasper whined again, like he didn't quite believe me.

I slung my bag over my shoulder and forced myself down the steps. Jasper didn't follow. He stayed planted there, tail drooping, watching me walk away like he was trying to memorize every step.

When the cupboards are bare and the cold creeps in, you don't wait for something better. You grit your teeth and do what needs doing, even when your cowgirl—and your dog—don't understand. It took her a week to forgive me, and it felt more than twice that long.

The work was hard, but the loneliness was harder. I counted the days by letters, not shifts, and the distance between us stretched wider with every passing hour. I wrote to her three times a week from Butte. At first, Eddie responded to every letter with long, detailed descriptions—what George had said at breakfast, what John had caught near the creek, how William was growing, what she'd cooked, who she'd beaten at poker. She described the wildflowers blooming near the barn, the sound of rain on the roof, the smell of fresh coffee in the morning. I'd read her words slowly, imagining her voice, feeling close to home even though I was over two hundred miles away.

But over time, her letters grew shorter. One page instead of three. A quick note instead of a story. Then she wrote only once a week. Eventually, it became every two. Meanwhile, I kept writing three times a week like a fool in love. The less she wrote, the more I missed her. I counted the days between letters like a prisoner scratching marks into a wall.

Eddie felt hollow without me. I could read it between the lines of her letters. She'd never say it outright. She felt overwhelmed by three children. She was thankful for them, but they ate away at her freedom. She was trying to hold the homestead together with bare hands and no rest.

So I hired Kathryn, an older Irish woman with silver streaks in her red hair and a no-nonsense way about her. She helped around the house—watching the boys, cooking meals, patching clothes. She was kind and gentle with the children, and Eddie trusted her more than most.

Life settled into a hard, steady rhythm. Days blurred into weeks, and weeks into seasons. Eddie worked the ranch and rode the hills; I poured my sweat into the smelter miles away. Letters flew back and forth like migrating birds, carrying little pieces of our lives to each other.

Then one cold morning in January, Robert was born. He was smaller than the other three had been, but he had the biggest smile. Kathryn helped with the birth and assured Eddie that four boys were no more work than three. I didn't believe her, and neither did Eddie.

As life closed in on her, Eddie escaped more and more. At first, it was to the mountains to hunt or fish or just ride Thunder as fast and hard as she could. But then she discovered the saloons. Kalispell had more saloons than all the other businesses combined. There, she could drink and gamble and forget her troubles.

It started with a dare. One of the ranch hands in town had teased her about being too pretty and too wild to stay home forever. She laughed him off, but that night, with Thunder already saddled and her boots itching for movement, she rode into town.

The Silver Dollar Saloon glowed like a furnace in the dark. Music spilled out through the swinging doors, and voices lifted in laughter and cursing. Eddie paused just outside, brushing dust off her shirt, adjusting her hat, as if stepping into battle.

Inside, the warmth hit her first—whiskey, sweat, cigar smoke. The piano pounded something ragged and cheerful. A few men turned to stare, but no one dared say a word. She walked to the table like she'd been born there. The dealer looked her up and down and asked, "You in?"

She was.

That night she won twenty dollars and a bottle of rye. More than money, it gave her something she hadn't felt in months: control. Word spread fast. By the next morning, ranch hands were whispering about the "cowgirl with fire in her veins." Some said she cleaned out half the table with nothing but a pair of twos and a smile. Others said she didn't smile once. That she sat stiff as a gun barrel, eyes fixed, voice low.

After that, Eddie was hooked, and every Saturday night she'd ride Thunder into town like the mountains themselves couldn't hold her back. She headed straight for the Silver Dollar Saloon, where the smoke hung low and the men cleared a seat at the table without question. The deck was always stacked in her favor. I've never seen so many royal flushes and aces. She called her winnings her "whiskey money," and no one dared argue.

Eddie started with shots at ten cents apiece. But as her winnings grew, she graduated to the bottle. After all, the harder stuff carried a stronger kick and only cost a dollar fifty. She often polished off the better half of a bottle during the game and took home a few more to help her get through the week.

The train from Butte to Kalispell took nearly ten hours, but it was worth it. So every month I took the rails home, spent a few days with the family, and then hauled myself back across the mountains for work. That rhythm was the only thing that kept me going—until the rhythm was broken.

I came in late from a twelve-hour shift, exhausted and half-covered in coal dust. There was a letter waiting. The envelope was thin and folded crookedly, stained with soot and something else—maybe tears. My name was written in Eddie's rushed hand, beneath it the word URGENT. I stared at it for a long while, afraid to touch it.

It wasn't the kind of letter you just tear open. I slid my thumb beneath the flap like I was opening a wound. Inside was a single sheet, folded once. My fingers trembled as I read it.

Allen,

Robert is gone. Gone forever. I don't know how to live with it yet.
Please come home.

Your cowgirl,
Eddie

For a moment, everything in the room went still. I stood in the bunkhouse with the letter in my hand and the wind knocked out of me. Robert was just an infant. I'd held him a month before and watched him fall asleep—so small, so innocent. How could he be gone?

I thought of his tiny hands, the smell of his hair, the weight of him resting in my arms while I read from *Moby Dick* by firelight. He was such a beautiful baby. He had Eddie's obsidian eyes. I remembered the last time I kissed him goodbye—his cheek warm and soft, his fist gripping my shirt. I said I loved him and I'd be home soon. I could never have imagined that would be the last time I'd ever see him.

I sat on my bunk, clutching the letter to my chest. I shook like a man with a fever. After a while, I stumbled outside and threw up behind the bunkhouse. When I wiped my mouth and looked up, the yard spun sideways. The walls of the bunkhouse felt too small, the roof too low. I needed air, but no air could fix what was broken.

I sank down on the stoop, head in my hands. A stray dog wandered up—thin and scrappy, not half the dog Jasper was. He sniffed at my boots, looking for a friend. I turned my face away.

Nothing would ever be the same again. I wiped my eyes, packed my bag in silence, and went to find my boss. I told him I had to go—that something terrible had happened. He nodded and clapped me on the shoulder, the way men do when words are useless.

I caught the next train back to Kalispell, and the ride felt like it lasted a hundred years. I couldn't sit still. Couldn't sleep. I paced the aisles between cars when no one was looking. Every snow-covered tree outside the window blurred into the next. In the dining car, I sat with a cold cup of coffee and a thousand thoughts I couldn't settle. A woman across the aisle kept knitting, her needles clicking like a clock counting down something I didn't want to face.

At one point, a porter asked if I needed anything. I shook my head. He looked at me twice, like maybe he recognized grief when he saw it. I don't know. All I wanted was to get off that train, but I dreaded what waited on the other side.

I imagined the house now—cold, quiet, empty. Heavy with something that wouldn't lift. I stared out the window at the endless snow-laced trees, thinking of all the things I'd never experience—his first words, his first steps, his grown-up smile. A life stolen before it even started.

Every sound, every jolt of the tracks, echoed the pounding of my heart. When we pulled into Kalispell Station, I almost didn't get off. Part of me wanted to stay on that train, ride straight into Canada, and never look back.

But I didn't.

As I trudged up the path toward home, the cold gnawed through my coat and into my bones. The house stood dark against the pale snow, smaller somehow than I remembered.

Then a familiar bark shattered the stillness. Jasper tore around the side of the house, skidding in the snow, his whole body wagging with joy. He barked once, sharp and sure, and leapt toward me. I dropped my bag and knelt, burying my face in his fur. His tail whipped back and forth like a broom, sweeping away the cold, the sorrow, the miles between us.

I didn't realize I was crying until Jasper licked the tears off my face.

"Good boy," I whispered, holding onto him like he was the last true thing I had left. "Good boy. I'm home. I'm home."

Jasper stuck close as I pushed the door open and stepped inside. He padded at my heels, tail lowered now, as if he could sense the weight that hung in the air.

Eddie was there—pale and thin with dark circles under her eyes. She stood by the stove like a shadow that had forgotten how to move. She wouldn't talk about it. Said it was too painful. When I tried to hold her, she sighed and pulled away. She ignored me and the boys, spent more time with the bottle. The smell of whiskey clung to her like a second skin

I tried to be understanding. I tried to give her space. But I needed answers.

So I asked Kathryn.

"I don't want to speak out of turn," Kathryn said. "But you deserve to know."

She looked down at her hands. "She wasn't herself that night, Allen. I've seen her ride through hail without flinching—but that night, she could barely stand. Her eyes were glassy. Her breath smelled like whiskey and smoke."

"She came in late. After midnight. Face white as frost, eyes rimmed in red. Brushed Thunder, slow and quiet. Walked inside like her boots were made of lead. I asked if she was all right. She nodded, muttered something about a headache. Her hands were shaking."

"I offered to help with Robert, but she just said, 'I'm his mother,' like that made her bulletproof."

Kathryn's voice wavered.

"I should've taken Robert myself."

I stared into my coffee, hands clenched around the mug. Jasper shifted at my feet, ears twitching. The silence pressed in, heavy as snowfall.

"She laid down beside him like it was any other night. Kissed his head. Whispered something I couldn't hear. In the morning, she screamed loud enough to wake the chickens. And I came running. The baby was cold. Lifeless."

She paused. "We tried everything, Allen. Warm cloths. Water on his face. I even did compressions. But it was too late."

She took a shaky breath. "I buried children back in Ireland during the famine. I never thought I'd see another one this close. Not like that."

The words hit like cold water to the chest. I wanted to stand up, pace the floor, rage at the ceiling. But instead, I just sat there, staring at the knot in the wood grain on the table. I could see Robert's face in it—his wide eyes, the roundness of his cheeks. And I hated the silence that followed. Hated that I'd never hear him cry again.

Her voice fell to a whisper. "I didn't want to say this. But there's something else I can't forget." She looked down. "When I came into the room that morning, the whiskey bottle was tipped on its side on the nightstand, half-empty. The glass was broken on the floor. Like maybe she reached for it in the night. Maybe she dropped it. I don't know."

"So what do you think happened?"

"Seems she'd been drinking too much and rolled over on him in her sleep. It was an accident—God-awful and tragic—but he suffocated."

Then Kathryn leaned in close. "I know you love her, but love doesn't always protect us. And sometimes the wild ones... they burn everything in their path."

I didn't speak. I couldn't. Kathryn took a deep breath and looked me in the eyes. "I'm worried for the boys. Eddie's not the same. She rides the mountains for hours, doesn't always come back by sundown. Leaves the kids with me. Some nights she doesn't come back at all. Says she's staying with friends in town, but I don't know who."

I sat on the porch after Kathryn had left, holding my face in my hands, listening to the chickens cluck and the wind rattle the window panes. I couldn't move. Couldn't speak. Couldn't cry. I felt like the world had tilted and nothing would ever feel steady again.

The house felt hollow, like the air itself had given up speaking. The fire had burned down low. The boys slept fitfully in the next room, George complaining of a stomach ache and John having a nightmare. I was at the table, staring at the pages of a book. Eddie stood in the corner, arms crossed, eyes glassy with drink.

"You want me to pretend like everything's fine?" she snapped.

"No," I said gently. "I just want to understand."

"Understand what? That I'm tired of chickens and laundry and waiting on a man who's never here?" She slammed a mug onto the floor. It shattered against the hearth.

"Eddie..."

"I used to be something, Allen." Her voice cracked. "I used to be wild and alive. Now I'm just a woman cooking and grieving in a house that forgot how to live." She fell to her knees and stared into the fire. "I killed Robert," she whispered. "I drank too much and I killed him."

Her whole body trembled. She picked up a piece of the shattered mug from the floor and turned it over in her fingers, like she could glue it back together and fix something larger than ceramic.

"I remember lying down with him," she said. "He was warm. I kissed his head. I told him I loved him. But I was so tired, Allen. I didn't mean to fall asleep like that."

Her breath caught in her throat. "I thought I'd hear him cry. I always did. But that night... I didn't."

I knelt beside her, but she flinched.

"I don't want to be forgiven," she whispered. "I want to suffer. Because he did."

I reached for her again, but she leaned away. Not in anger—just distance. Like we were standing on opposite cliffs of the same canyon, both looking down, unable to cross. I wanted to tell her it wasn't her fault, that we'd find a way back to each other. But the words got stuck in my throat, too heavy with sorrow.

I loved her. I wanted to comfort her. But Kathryn's last words haunted me. "Be careful," she had said. The exact words Pa had once told me. "Be careful. That cowgirl is as wild as a tumbleweed."

Back then, I had laughed it off. Now, I wasn't so sure. Could I ever trust Eddie again?

What I was sure of was that I couldn't go back to Butte. I sat at the table for hours with the telegram to my boss half-written. My hand hovered above the paper. What do you say? That your boy died and your wife is breaking and you can't work another day knowing what you left behind?

That job had meant something. It meant I was a man providing for his family. A man with backbone. But now, the house needed me more than the smelter ever had. I walked into the boys' room and watched them sleep. William was as still as a statue. John's legs twitched like he was dreaming of chasing rabbits. George's lips moved, mumbling to someone in his sleep. Maybe Robert. Maybe me.

I knelt down and kissed their foreheads. That was all it took. I knew then—I wasn't going back.

Some choices don't come with thunder or tears. Sometimes they arrive quietly, like a bell ringing in the frost—sharp, certain, impossible to ignore. I went back to the table, picked up the pen, and finished the telegram.

I cleared my throat and set the mug down gently, as if any sudden movement might break something between us. "I'm not going back to Butte," I said, my voice barely above the creak of the fire.

She didn't move, didn't speak—but I saw it. The way her shoulders eased, just a little, like a rope gone slack.

"I don't know what comes next," I added. "But I'm here. For the boys. For you."

She stayed quiet, then gave the smallest of nods. No words. No smile. Just a slow, tired gesture—like the faintest crack in a long winter's ice.

WHEN THE RIVER THAWS

The thaw came late that year. Snow clung to the edges of the riverbanks like regret that refused to melt. But when it finally broke, something in Eddie shifted too.

She started riding again—first just down to the creek, then into the foothills with Thunder kicking up mud behind her. It was like she found pieces of herself with the wind in her hair and color in her cheeks.

One evening, after a long ride, she came in quiet. Not tired, just thoughtful. I was shelling beans by the window when she sat down across from me, pulled off her gloves, and said, "I've been thinking about how I want to live."

I looked up.

She picked at a spot on the table. "All that whiskey, all that poker—it made me feel like I had control. Like I was still the one holding the reins."

She paused, then looked me in the eye. "But I wasn't, was I?"

"No," I said gently. "You weren't."

She nodded. "I don't want to be that woman anymore. I'm not sayin' I'll never touch a deck again, or that I'll turn down a drink at Christmas. But I'm done chasing the bottom of the bottle. And I sure as hell ain't gonna gamble with what matters."

Her voice cracked a little on that last line.

I reached across the table and took her hand. "That's what I've been praying for."

She squeezed my fingers. "I want to be here. Really be here. With you. With the boys. With whatever comes next."

One morning I heard it. A soft humming from the kitchen. She was elbow-deep in dishwater, swaying her hips in time with the tune. It wasn't loud, just a whisper of melody—but it stopped me in my tracks. I hadn't heard her sing in almost a year.

I leaned against the doorframe and smiled. She looked over, caught me watching.

"Don't just stand there gawkin'," she said. "You want breakfast or not?"

"I'd rather listen to you sing," I said.

She rolled her eyes, but her grin betrayed her.

As the days lengthened and the earth softened, so did we. Spring brought more than warmth—it brought a quiet kind of healing.

That night we sat on the porch wrapped in a quilt, watching the moon rise above the barn roof. The stars blinked soft as candlelight. Eddie leaned against me. "You really done with Butte?"

"I'm done," I said. "I'll never leave again. Not unless you're riding beside me."

She didn't answer right away. Her hand found mine under the quilt.

"I still wake up looking for Robert," she whispered. "Some nights I swear I hear him breathing."

"I know," I said. "But I'm here now. I'm not going anywhere."

"You promise?"

"I promise."

She nodded, quiet and still. Then, so soft I almost missed it, she said, "Thank you."

Summer brought more than sun. It brought new life, again. We were planting potatoes in the back garden when she stood up and wiped her forehead with her sleeve. "Hope you're ready to do more than just dig holes for the garden," she said with a grin.

I looked up from my row. "What's that supposed to mean?"

She tossed me a grin. "We've got another little one on the way."

I dropped the spade. "You serious?"

"Serious as a snakebite," she said. "Due sometime just after the new year."

She dusted off her hands and gave me a look I'd never seen before—not just happy, but downright joyful.

"Maybe it'll be a girl this time," she said, almost to herself. "Someone to braid hair and ride bareback and raise a little hell with me."

She stared out across the fields for a second, her hand drifting down to rest flat against her belly, like she was already cradling a dream.

For a second, the joy twisted sharp in my chest. I thought of Robert—of the things he'd never see, the laughter he'd never join.

But I pulled Eddie close and held onto the hope instead. This time, we'd be ready for whatever came. I stayed kneeling there, hands still in the dirt, heart full to bursting.

Then I crossed the patch in two strides and scooped her into my arms.

"You hear that?" I shouted to the prairie. "We're havin' another baby!"

Jasper barked from the porch like he knew what we were celebrating.

As summer gave way to gold and the cottonwoods rustled dry and bright, we made plans for a journey. I hadn't seen Ma and Pa in over four years, and I missed them more than any cowboy ought to admit. They'd moved from Nebraska to Oklahoma not long after we left for Kalispell. Pa said the land was cheaper and the opportunities better down south—but truth be told, I think he was just as restless as me, chasing some dream he never could explain. Ma just shook her head and said only the good Lord knew what went on inside that man's mind.

Eddie was itching for a change, I was longing for home, and the kids could use time with their grandparents. So we figured we'd spend the fall and winter in Oklahoma. Ma could lend a hand when the baby came, and I could help Pa with whatever needed doing around the homestead. Come spring, we'd ride the train back north—and at least we'd miss the Kalispell winters that could freeze the clothes on your back before you made it halfway to the barn.

The train ride to Oklahoma was too long for a dog, especially one who hated loud noises and tight spaces. Jasper had never taken to travel—not by wagon, not by train, not even in the back of the buckboard. Whenever we packed our bags, he'd pace the porch with a worried look, like he knew something was up but didn't quite understand what.

"He can stay with me and the girls," Kathryn said, kneeling to rub behind his ears. "He'll guard my house and sleep at the foot of my bed. Might even fatten him up a little."

As we got ready to leave I bent down beside him. "We'll be back before you know it."

Jasper nuzzled my hand, tail giving a single half-hearted wag. I rested my hand on his back, feeling the steady rise and fall of his breath, and for the first time in a long while, I let myself believe we were going to be alright.

We left him there with a fresh ham bone and a promise to bring back a treat. As we walked toward the station, he trailed behind us to the gate, not quite ready to say goodbye. Eddie turned back and waved. "Be good, old boy."

He didn't wag his tail. Just watched, quiet and patient, like always.

I almost turned back right after seeing him like that.

As we headed down the road, I heard George call out behind us, his voice small but sure. "Bye, Jasper!" he said, waving so hard his hat nearly flew off.

Eddie slipped her arm through mine but didn't say a word. The whistle of the train howled through the hills ahead.

We rolled into Fairfax with the prairie wide open and the

creekside trees burning gold and rust. The train ride had been loud and rattly, but the boys handled it like seasoned travelers, their noses pressed to the windows, eyes wide with wonder.

Pa and Erroll met us at the station with a buggy. "Well, look who the prairie blew in!" Pa said with a big grin.

When we arrived at the homestead Maud and Ethel greeted us with warm lemonade and bright smiles. Guy, who was now five, hid bashfully behind his sister's long dresses.

I bent down and said to Guy, "Do you know who I am, little fella?"

"You're the famous cowboy Ma and Pa talk about all the time."

I chuckled. "I don't know about famous. But I'm your oldest brother." I turned and motioned for my boys to come over. "And these here are your nephews."

Guy squinted up at me. "What's a nephew?"

Suddenly Ma came running up, apron still on, tears in her eyes. "My babies," she said, gathering all three grandsons into her arms.

Ma and Pa's new homestead sat on a gentle hill with cottonwoods whispering around it. Down the road was a ramshackle gray house with a red roof that looked like a good gust could blow it away. But the barn was big and Ma had planted a line of sunflowers in front to add some color. It wasn't Norfolk, not by a long shot—but it had the same warmth.

That night, we sat around a firepit with coffee and peach pie, the boys chasing lightning bugs while Pa rocked in his chair and said, "A man's rich if his grandchildren are loud."

Eddie laughed, a soft, unguarded sound I hadn't heard in too long. She leaned in and whispered, "Guess we're millionaires, then."

Eddie leaned closer to the fire, the glow catching the red in her hair, and absently rubbed her stomach. "If this little one's a girl," she said, "she's gonna give those boys a run for their money." She smiled, not her usual teasing grin, but something softer—something almost tender with hope.

I kissed her temple and thought there wasn't a king alive who had more. Eddie rested her head on my shoulder, one hand on her belly, eyes on the stars. The wind howled across the Oklahoma plains that night, rattling the windows and piling snow against the door.

Eddie's labor started just after midnight on the sixth of January in '06. Ma boiled water. I chopped firewood until I couldn't feel my fingers.

Fern Elizabeth Stephens came into the world screaming and perfect—dark hair, tiny fists, lungs like a cattle bell.

The boys all fawned over their little sister.

"She's so tiny," said George.

"And loud," said John.

William wouldn't take his eyes off her.

"She's ours," I said.

Eddie smiled through tears, cradling Fern against her chest. "She's gonna be spoiled rotten," she said.

"Already is," I replied.

Eddie rocked her gently, almost without thinking, her voice cracking with wonder. "A girl," she kept whispering. "My precious little girl." She pressed a kiss to Fern's tiny forehead.

"Lord help her," I said, proudly. "She looks just like you."

"And I bet she's gonna ride faster and cuss louder than all her brothers put together."

We both laughed.

The days passed slow and sweet after Fern's birth. One evening, I heard the old porch rocker creaking and stepped outside. Ma sat there cradling Fern, her face lit by the last light of day. For a moment, it hit me just how far we'd all come—and how much we owed to the quiet strength of women like her.

I sat down beside her, the boards groaning under my weight. The air was warm, smelling of sweetgrass and dust. "I still can't believe you're all the way out here," I said, watching the sunset melt across the open prairie.

She smiled, her face weathered but kind. "Your Pa was tired of fighting the same patch of ground year after year. The droughts, the grasshoppers... it just wore him down. When the land agents came around talking about cheap acres in Oklahoma, he figured we'd better take our chances."

I glanced out toward the road, where the town sat low against the horizon. Fairfax wasn't much more than a scatter of wooden storefronts, a livery barn, a couple of churches, and a grain mill that puffed out dust all day long. The streets were rutted and rude, and the prairie pressed in on every side, wild and stubborn.

"It's a rough land still," Ma went on, brushing Fern's tiny hand with her thumb. "But your Pa's got a few cows out on pasture now. Planted sorghum and corn too. Sorghum's tougher than wheat out here—it don't mind the heat so bad. We ain't rich, but we're getting by."

I nodded, swallowing a lump in my throat. They hadn't just moved to Oklahoma—they'd built a whole new life out of nothing but grit and stubborn hope.

Time moved quicker than we figured, and we ended up staying longer than planned. Pa needed help with the planting, and Ma was glad to watch the kids so Eddie could have a little freedom—to ride the open prairie, fish Salt Creek, and hunt pronghorn in the Osage Hills. I got to spend time with my brothers too—herding cattle, shooting groundhogs, and spinning tall tales about Eddie and me driving stagecoach and climbing the massive mountains of Montana. Erroll and Guy had only ever lived in Nebraska and Oklahoma, so they didn't have the faintest idea what a real mountain looked like.

By June it was time to go home, we packed up our things, said our goodbyes, and boarded the train back to Montana, just as the cottonwood trees were shedding their fuzz like snow across the pasture.

Pa gripped my hand at the station, rough palms squeezing tighter than his words ever could.

"You take care of 'em," he said, nodding at Eddie and the kids.

"I will," I said.

Ma hugged me hard, her apron dusted with flour and wildflowers, and whispered, "Don't forget where you came from, son."

"Never," I promised.

The sky was wide and blue, and the air carried the scent of sage and dry soil. But it was too flat and colorless for me to ever call home. I looked back one last time as the train pulled away, watching the land roll past in waves of gold and dust. Fairfax wasn't much yet—just rough ground and stubborn dreams—but it was where Fern had taken her first breath. Where Ma and Pa had staked their hearts one more time against the wind. Where my brothers and sisters were growing up and finding their footing.

I tipped my hat toward the fading horizon and whispered a silent promise: I'll make you proud.

Jasper was the first to spot us coming up the lane. He launched off the porch like a shot, tail whipping back and forth in a wild blur. The boys whooped when they saw him, dropping their satchels and racing ahead to tackle him in the dust. He barked and barked, licking their faces, whining with excitement.

Then he saw me—and something in his expression changed. He froze mid-wag and padded over, slower now, eyes locked on the bundle in my arms. He sniffed the air, then stepped closer, cautious but curious. I knelt and lowered the blanket so he could see Fern's round, sleeping face.

"This is Fern," I said. "Your new job's watchin' out for her."

He sniffed her once, then again, ears perked. After a long pause, he gave her a single lick on the top of her head, then sat down beside me like he'd already claimed her as his.

Eddie smiled, brushing the dust off her skirt. "Looks like she's got herself a guardian."

"Best one in the territory," I said.

"This girl's gonna be tough," she said, her voice rough with pride.

"Tough enough to ride the wind if she's got a mind to."

She laughed, but for a moment her gaze drifted past us, far-off and longing, like part of her was already chasing the horizon again. I tucked Fern into her cradle and told myself it didn't matter. We were home. We were together.

As the sun sank low, the house felt full again. Jasper curled up beside Fern without needing to be told, his nose tucked under his paw, as if he'd been waiting for her all along. Eddie hummed by the hearth, and the boys snored soft from their bunks. Outside, the prairie sighed under the stars—and for once, my heart was still.

But even as the stars twinkled overhead, I knew nothing stayed still forever—not children, not cowgirls, not even love.

NOTHING LEFT TO SAY

After we came back from Oklahoma, life settled faster than Eddie could stand.

It started small, the way most things do. At first, it was just a look. Eddie would sit on the porch after supper, staring out at the empty road like she was waiting for something. It was as if it didn't stretch near as wide as the dreams she used to chase.

Some nights she sang while she churned butter or shelled peas, the way she always used to. But other nights, she was too quiet, moving through the house like a ghost no one dared disturb.

But there was work that needed to be done. The garden needed weeding, the boys needed tending, Thunder and Nancy needed new shoes—good, honest work.

Eddie rode Thunder more than she stayed home, kicking up dust on the road before breakfast some mornings and not coming back until the sun slipped behind the hills. When she returned, her cheeks were flushed and her hair tangled with wind, but the wild look in her eyes never softened. If anything, it sharpened.

I tried not to notice the way her eyes stayed fixed on the open road, or the way her voice got sharper when the boys got too loud, or the way she said "out" when I asked where she'd been—like it was a warning more than an answer.

We were happy for a while. Or at least we told ourselves we were. But trouble was already riding the fence line, waiting for the right moment to break through.

One night, we sat by the firepit, Jasper stretched out at our feet, the stars spilling overhead. Eddie stirred the embers with a stick, her motions sharp, restless. "Do you ever think about going farther west?" she asked. "Maybe Wyoming. Or Idaho. Someplace wild again."

I didn't answer right away. The fire cracked between us.

"We just got settled here," I said finally.

"But maybe that's the problem." She poked at the coals again. "I don't want to be settled anywhere."

"Our children need a home," I said.

"A home is anywhere they're loved," she said, her voice low.

"And for now, that home is in Kalispell."

She tossed another stick into the flames, sending up a burst of sparks. "Yeah," she muttered. "And already it feels like the walls are closing in."

The days got shorter, and so did Eddie's temper.

I found her one afternoon slamming the barn door so hard it rattled the hinges. "You don't get it, Allen," she said, voice rough with something deeper than anger. "I spent my whole damn childhood being told where to stand, when to speak, how to breathe." She turned, hands shaking as she brushed the dust from her jeans. "I ain't going back to that. Not for you. Not for anybody."

"I'm not telling you to do anything," I said gently as I could.

She didn't say a word. Just gave me a look, swung up onto Thunder, and rode off into the dusk—leaving behind nothing but fading hoofbeats and the hollow where her warmth used to be.

Being a cowgirl wasn't just about horses and hats. It was rebellion—pure and simple—against everything a "lady" was supposed to be.

Every time she rode fast against the wind, played a hand of poker, or out-shot a man, it was her way of spitting in the eye of every cage they'd ever tried to build around her.

Another evening, we rode side by side at sunset, somewhere beyond the homestead. The sun was sinking behind the hills, stretching the shadows long across the prairie. We rode without talking for a long while, the horses' hooves thudding soft against the dry ground.

Eddie shifted in her saddle, adjusting her hat against the glare. "You ever wonder why I can't sit still?" she asked.

I glanced over. "Sometimes."

She smiled, but it was a tight, far-off kind of smile. "Home was a place where you kept your mouth shut, kept your head down, and waited for the hammer to fall. That's the first thing I learned."

I didn't say a word—just rode alongside her, knowing sometimes that's the smartest thing a man can do.

She leaned forward, brushing Thunder's mane with her fingers. "My brothers got to run wild. I got told to sew and smile. 'A good girl don't argue.' 'A good girl don't drink.' 'A good girl don't dream too big.'"

My heart broke with each word she said.

Then she snorted. "Hell with that."

The horses kept plodding forward, the leather creaking softly.

"The first time I rode out past the riverbank on my own, I swear the sky cracked open. I wasn't scared. I wasn't trapped. I was just finally free. That's when I decided to head for Nebraska where Mary and Sam had a patch of ground. I knew Mary understood. She would let me be me."

Eddie fell quiet, twisting a leather strap between her fingers like she was trying to keep her hands busy so her heart wouldn't show.

"Sometimes," she said, voice lower now, "it feels like if I stop moving, they'll catch up to me. All those folks who said I'd never be anything but somebody's wife, somebody's problem."

I opened my mouth to speak, but she shook her head.

"I ain't askin' for pity, Allen. I just... I want you to know. It ain't about not loving you or the boys or the baby. It's just... some nights, the wind gets in my blood, and I remember how it felt to be free."

She looked at me then, real and raw.

"I don't ever want to forget that girl who crossed the river."

The last of the light caught in her hair, turning it to copper fire. I wanted to reach for her, pull her close. But I didn't. I just nodded once, quiet, and we rode on together into the falling dark.

I remembered the way Eddie once described her father—hard as dry oak and twice as brittle.

"My father wasn't a cruel man," she said once, voice low. "Not exactly. Not in the way folks think. He was just... hard. Hard enough to break you without ever raising a hand.

"He believed in work, in discipline, in earning your place every single day. And if you slipped up, even once, he made damn sure you knew it. A wrong word, a broken dish, a stitch outta line—those things weren't just mistakes. They were failures. Personal insults. He had a voice like a leather strap, snapping out blame sharper than any belt ever could.

"You ain't worth the boots on your feet," he'd growl if she lagged behind in chores. "Ain't no room in this world for girls who can't pull their weight."

And when the bottle was in his hand, it got worse.

Then everything became a test. A test I was afraid she wouldn't pass.

Eddie learned real young: stay quick, stay tough, never let 'em see you bleed. and don't let anyone hold you down or hold you back. You live life on your own terms—nobody else's.

The first fight snuck up on us, the way spring storms sometimes do—calm skies one minute, black clouds the next. I was splitting kindling behind the barn when I found three empty whiskey bottles, hid behind a bale of hay beyond the reach of sunlight or shadow. The sight hit me like a punch to the gut. I stormed into the house, bottle in hand.

Eddie was standing at the stove, stirring a pot of beans, humming low under her breath. I dropped a bottle onto the table hard enough to make her jump.

"You want to tell me about this?" I said, my voice already tighter than I meant it to be.

She didn't flinch. Just kept stirring. "It's none of your business," she said calmly, too calmly.

"None of my business?" I barked. "You got four kids asleep in the other room—the youngest still in diapers—and you're sneakin' around drinkin' yourself stupid, and it's none of my business?"

She set the spoon down with a clatter. "I'm not drinkin' myself stupid. And I don't need you sniffin' around my life like I'm some damn outlaw."

"You went out Saturday night too," I said. "Gambled half the night away."

She shrugged. "So what?"

I slammed my hand down on the table. "So what? I married a woman, not a ghost I have to chase down in every saloon between here and Kalispell."

She turned, arms crossed over her chest, mouth tight. "You married me, Allen Stephens. Not some porcelain doll to set on some fancy shelf. I don't answer to you."

"I know, but a man has his limits," I said.

"And so does a woman. I'm wild, and no man's gonna rope me down—not now, not ever."

The fight burned hot for a few minutes longer, both of us too angry and proud to back down.

Later that week, when our anger had cooled, I found her sitting by the fire, head bowed.

She apologized first, voice small. "I'm sorry," she said. "Sometimes I just get rattled. And say things meaner than I should."

I crouched down in front of her, took her hands in mine.

"We all get rattled, Eddie," I said quietly. "Ain't a soul alive who don't. And sometimes... sometimes I don't know how to help you without making it worse. I don't always get it right. I just don't want to lose you."

Her fingers tightened around mine.

"I get rattled too," I said, my voice rough. "Only difference is, I hide it better."

She let out a broken little laugh and wiped at her eyes.

For a long time, the fire popping and crackling between us, neither of us ready to let go.

For a while, things held steady. We patched over the cracks and told ourselves they weren't growing wider. We smiled, we worked, we slept side by side.

But spring turned into summer, and the strain stretched thin again.

Our next fight wasn't loud—not at first. It started low, in the pit of my stomach, and crawled up into my chest—a slow, twisting kind of fear that left me raw. She said she was going for an afternoon ride. Kissed me quick on the cheek, swung up onto Thunder, and was gone, kicking up dust down the road out of the valley.

By nightfall, she still hadn't come back. I fed the kids supper and tucked them into bed. Then I sat out on the porch, staring up at the stars, telling myself she'd just made camp by the creek.

When the sun rose and she hadn't come back, I stopped lying to myself. I spent the next two days scouring every trail I knew, hollering her name until my throat went hoarse. The boys asked where she was. I told them she was just out riding. Even Jasper kept pacing the fence line, nose to the wind, whining low in his throat like he knew something wasn't right.

By the third evening, I was half-crazy with worry, when she finally rode in like nothing had happened. Dust on her boots. Wind in her hair. A half-wild look in her eyes that made my heart crack wide open.

I met her halfway to the house, still in the saddle. "Where the hell have you been?" I said, voice breaking sharper than I meant it to.

She swung off Thunder like she hadn't care in the world. "Out," she said. "Just taking in some fresh mountain air."

"Three damn days, Eddie! No word, no note, no nothing—you could've been dead out there!"

She tossed the reins toward the hitching post, not even looking at me. "I'm a grown woman, Allen. I don't need permission to breathe."

My fists clenched at my sides. "It ain't about permission," I said, trying hard to keep my voice steady. "It's about not scaring the folk who love you."

She barked a laugh, dry and bitter. "Love? Do you call this love?"

I took a step toward her. "I was worried to death about you, Eddie."

Something flickered in her face then—pain, regret—but she stuffed it down fast.

"I don't belong to anyone," she said, turning away.

I stood there, fists useless at my sides, watching her walk into the house like she'd just torn my heart out. "Yeah, I know," I muttered to myself.

We barely spoke for a week after that. The house felt wrong—too small, too quiet, too full of things we weren't saying.

Then one night, when the boys were asleep and the fire burned low, she came and sat beside me without a word. She didn't apologize right away. Just picked at the seam of her dress like she was unraveling herself one thread at a time. Finally she whispered, "I'm sorry."

I didn't look at her. Just stared into the fire.

"I just needed to feel… free," she said. "Just for a little while. Like I could still choose who I was, not just wake up and be what everyone needed."

My throat tightened. I was somewhere between hurt and angry. But I reached out anyway and set my hand on hers. "You don't have to run away to be free," I said, so low I wasn't sure she heard me. "You just have to let me walk beside you."

She squeezed my hand once, light as a bird's wing.

We sat there in the half-light, not sure what to say or do. But there was a kind of peace in it—small and fragile, but real. For a moment, we both let our guards down. And I let myself hope, just a little, that maybe we could make it last.

Summer burned hotter than any I could remember. The days dried up and blew away like brittle leaves, and whatever was holding us together wore thin and frayed.

The third fight didn't sneak up like the others. It came roaring in—like a brush fire riding a high wind, burning through dry grass without mercy.

She didn't come home Saturday night. I sat up with the lamp burning low, counting every endless hour, every creak of the house, every sigh of the wind. When dawn broke gray and empty and she still wasn't there, something inside me snapped.

She stumbled in around eight in the morning, reeking of smoke and whiskey, hair wild, eyes glassy. Thunder's reins were dragging in the dirt behind her, forgotten.

I met her at the porch steps, heart pounding. "You've been out all night," I said, voice shaking.

She looked right through me. "That's the truth."

"A neighbor dropped by earlier today."

"That's what neighbors do." She rubbed her eyes.

"He said you were in Kalispell," I said.

"It's none of his business where I was."

"He saw you in the saloon sittin' on some rancher's lap."

"Like I said, it's none of his business."

"Maybe it's none of his business, but you're my wife. I love you." I looked away for a moment. "He said you were kissin' the rancher like you meant it."

She laughed—a sharp, bitter sound that didn't belong to the woman I married.

"You can't believe everything you hear?" she said, pushing past me toward the door.

"But I believe what I see," I snapped. "I see a woman throwin' away everything she's got for a bottle and a cheap hand of cards."

She whirled on me, eyes blazing. "I didn't do anything wrong!"

"You didn't come home!" I shouted. "You left your children sleeping in the house wonderin' if their ma was dead in a ditch somewhere!"

Her face twisted, rage and guilt battling behind her eyes. "You're makin' something out of nothin'," she said. "He's just a friend."

"Does your friend know you have a husband and four kids?" I said.

Her jaw clenched.

"You think you own me, Allen?" she spat. "You think you get to tell me who I am, what I do, where I go?"

"I think you drink too much," I said, voice low and lethal. "And you're acting like a saloon girl, while your kids sit at home wondering if their moma gives a lick about them."

Once the words were out, I knew I'd gone too far.

For a second, she just stared at me—like she didn't even recognize the man standing in front of her. Then something inside her broke.

"I will not live with a man who talks to me like my father did," she said, voice shaking with fury. "I'd rather rot in hell."

She stormed into the house, yanked a satchel from the closet, started shoving clothes inside with rough, jerky movements.

"You leave, Eddie, but you ain't takin' the kids," I said, following her.

She turned, eyes wild. "They're mine."

"They're mine too."

"You try to stop me," she said, reaching for the gun belt hanging by the door, "and we'll find out who's the better shot."

Jasper barked once, sharp and startled, from where he lay by the hearth.

I raised my hands slow, heart hammering.

"Go on then," I said, my voice hollow. "Take 'em. Take everything."

She scooped Fern up from her cradle, roused the boys with soft murmurs and promises of an adventure, stuffed what she could into a threadbare carpetbag. Then they were in the wagon, fading in the distance.

I stood there like a fool while she walked out that door with my whole life in her arms. The screen door slammed behind her, banging in the wind like a loose shutter before a storm. I didn't move. A part of me wanted to climb on Nancy, chase them down, beg her to come back. But I knew I'd just be trying to lasso a dream that had already slipped outta reach.

Outside, the wind picked up, kicking dust across the yard. Jasper whined low in his throat and pressed against my leg, trying to steady me, like he knew how close I was to breaking.

But it was too late. The house was empty. The only thing left inside was the echo of words I could never take back. I kept replaying the fight in my head—all the things I should've said, all the things I never should've. But words, once spoken, don't take themselves back.

She was gone. All I had left was four walls, a roof over my head, and a dog at my side. That was the truth of it—plain and hard. And the sooner I learned to live with it, the better off I'd be.

WAITING FOR SUMMER

The nights were the worst. That's when my mind started talking louder than anything else.

The days dragged by, slow and mean, and when the work was done and the sun slipped low, all I had left was the weight of everything I couldn't undo.

I never thought I'd find myself here—sitting alone on a porch that used to feel so full of life, just listening to the wind and the sound of my own breathing.

The fields were burned up from the August sun, nothing but dry stalks and stubble. Even the river looked tired, just a thin strip of muddy water winding through the cracked banks.

The house sat heavy and hollow behind me, like it was grieving too. You don't know what you've got 'til the house is empty and the wind's the only thing answerin' you. I kept thinking maybe I'd wake up and hear Eddie in the kitchen, humming low while she stirred a pot of coffee, the kids' footsteps thudding across the floor. But it stayed quiet. Always quiet.

I knew why she was gone. It wasn't just the fighting. It was the way I let my anger flare—sharp and ugly—the way it must've reminded her of things she spent her whole life trying to outrun. I saw it in her face that last morning—that look like she wasn't staring at me anymore, but at someone else entirely. Someone she was scared of.

And God help me, I didn't know how to pull it back once it was out. Didn't know how to fix what I'd broken. I wished I hadn't said what I said. I wished I had gotten down on my knees and begged her not to go. I wished I had done a hundred things differently. I loved her. I still do. I thought love was enough. Maybe I was a fool for believing that.

But even knowing all that, it still burned—the way she packed up and left without a word, like I wasn't even worth a goodbye. After everything we'd built. After everything we'd survived. I hurt her, sure. But she didn't just hurt me—she cut me clean out of her life, like I was something to be thrown away. And that... that's the part I don't know how to live with.

I sat there in my rocking chair, Jasper at my feet, waiting and watching. Hoping they'd come back so I could hug them, kiss them, tell them I was sorry—promise them this would never happen again. I was their father. I'd always be there for them, no matter what.

The house was too damn quiet without them.

I could still hear their voices if I closed my eyes—George shouting after a runaway colt, John laughing low at some joke only he understood, William banging his boots against the doorframe because he was too impatient to untie them. And little Fern, as fragile and beautiful as a rose, cradled in my arms, cooing and smiling while I rocked her to sleep. She was mine to protect. That's all there was to it.

I loved each one of them in their own way.

George was my wild one, always pushing the limits, always testing his weight against the world. Eight years old but already carrying himself like he had something to prove, like he knew the horizon wasn't gonna wait for him. He loved horses the same way his mother did—with awe and a little recklessness. Always trying to be brave for the others, even when he was scared. And sometimes he got that look—Eddie's look—like the world better get out of his way.

John was the opposite of his brother. He saw the world quieter, deeper. Six years old and already had hands steady enough to shoot a tin can clean off a fencepost with his first rifle. Eddie taught him herself, and he took to it like he'd been born for it. Deadeye shot, sure as any man I ever knew, but never showy about it. He was a fixer too—always turning over broken things in his hands, figuring how to make 'em whole again. I guess maybe I should've listened closer when he spoke, those rare times he did.

And William—five years old and stubborn enough to wear down a mule. Always trying to catch up to George and John, fists balled tight, daring anyone to tell him he was too little. He had a fire in his belly—God help the man who tried to put it out. He was rough sometimes, sure. But he had a heart the size of Texas. He'd give you the shirt off his back without blinking. Some days, I wished I had half that in me.

Then there was Fern. My little girl. Barely more than a baby, but somehow wise already in a way none of the boys ever were. She was sweet—so sweet it hurt sometimes just to look at her. She'd sit for hours in my lap, her tiny hand clutching the front of my shirt like she thought if she let go, she might drift away. She didn't cry much—no fussing, no tantrums—just leaned her head against my shoulder and trusted me to hold her up. She had this way of smiling, slow and soft, like sunshine easing through a window after a storm. She was every soft thing I never thought I deserved.

And now they were gone. All of 'em. Out there somewhere with Eddie, somewhere beyond my reach.

All I had left was the echo of them—the weight of loving 'em heavy in my chest, heavier than any work I ever did. I reckoned I could live a hundred more years and never fill the empty space they left behind.

She had made this place a home. Without her, I wasn't sure what to do. I knew she'd never return. But still, every night, I listened for her anyway.

The sun slipped behind the hills, dragging the last light with it. The wind stirred the dry grass, making it whisper against the porch steps. Jasper lifted his head, ears twitching, like he thought he heard something I didn't. But there was nothing. Just the emptiness, and the sound of my own heart waiting.

I waited through the fall and halfway through the winter. The cottonwoods along the river turned yellow, the mornings froze solid, and the mountains wore a crown of snow by November. The cold settled in early that year—the kind that stiffened your hands and made the days feel twice as long.

Kalispell wasn't the same without her.

Didn't matter where I went—the mercantile, the livery, the back trails—it all felt hollow without Eddie beside me. Every time I rode Nancy toward the mountains, I half-expected to hear her laughing behind me, daring me to catch her. Every time I passed the Silver Dollar Saloon, my gut twisted tight—thinking about all the nights she spent there, and all the nights I spent waiting.

By Christmas, the snow lay deep and mean, the river frozen over like an old scar across the valley.

I told myself to wait—wait through the holidays, wait through the worst of the cold. But waiting didn't fix a damn thing. It just hollowed me out a little more each day.

Two days after Christmas, a letter came from Eddie.

She said she'd taken the kids—all four of them—and gone to Duff. She was living with Sam and Mary now. She said she was sorry for the way it happened, but she hadn't seen another choice. She asked me to be patient. Said she'd never come back and that maybe by summer she'd be ready to let me see them again.

I sat out on the porch with that letter crumpled in my hand, the cold chewing its way up through my boots, trying to make sense of a life that didn't make much sense anymore.

Tucked near the bottom was a small request. Eddie asked if I'd send Thunder to her by cattle car. I didn't even think twice. I made the arrangements the next morning, clinging to the thought that maybe this was a step—however small—back toward something good.

I would've done anything she asked. Anything at all.

It wasn't much to hang my hopes on. But it was something. And I needed something.

A week later, I packed what little I had left, saddled Nancy, and rode out of Flathead Valley for good. For the first time in months, the air didn't feel so heavy in my chest. Jasper trailed close behind, kicking up little clouds of snow, never once letting me out of his sight.

We wandered aimlessly through the frozen hills and battered trails of Montana, camping wherever we ended up after a long day's ride. The snow was thick on the ground, and the nights cut through every layer of clothing I owned.

Some days, I thought about turning south, about disappearing altogether. But mostly, I just kept moving—one slow mile at a time.

A few weeks later, we reached Butte. I wasn't chasing a future. I was just buying time.

A man needs to work if he wants to eat and feed his horse, and I needed to earn every dollar I could before summer came.

Nancy was tired too—her coat dulled from the cold, her legs stiff—and she needed a barn to keep her out of the wind.

I rode straight back to the smelter. The boss took one look at me and hired me back without asking any questions. It was a filthy, brutal job—hotter than hell and cruel on a man's lungs—and I hated it even more than I had before. But I figured maybe that was the point. It was my penitence. My punishment. And I took it without complaint.

All I had left was work, waiting, and the hope that it wouldn't be for nothing.

At the end of May, I quit my job at the smelter and hit the trail for Duff, Jasper trotting close at my side.

I rolled into Duff on a Wednesday afternoon.

The town hadn't changed much in ten years—same dusty streets, same leaning buildings, same air that smelled of horses and old wood. The sun was sharp overhead, the streets half-empty, the whole place holding its breath between the bustle of morning and the lull of evening. But riding into Duff this time felt different. The last time I came through, I was chasing a dream. Now, I was chasing something I'd already lost.

I tied Nancy outside the livery, pushed through the doors, and looked around for Sam.

Sam and Mary had met years ago in New York—two hardworking souls who built a life on faith, grit, and love. They'd been married sixteen years, and though God hadn't blessed them with children of their own, they poured their hearts into being the best uncle and aunt they could be. Fiercely protective of family, especially of Mary's little sister. Good people, through and through.

Sam was mucking out a stall but froze when he saw me.

"Still charge twenty-five cents for a clean stall and a bucket of oats?" I asked.

He narrowed his eyes. "The price has gone up a dime," he said. Then, after a long pause: "You here to start trouble?"

I took off my hat and met his gaze head-on. "No trouble. Eddie told me I could see the kids this summer. That's all I'm here for. Just wanna spend some time with 'em. Let 'em know I still love 'em."

Sam didn't answer right away. Just kept looking at me, weighing my words like a man sizing up a snake—trying to judge if it was worth trusting by the warmth of its skin. "A man's promises don't mean much around here unless he keeps 'em," he said finally.

"I know," I said, voice low. "That's why I'm keeping my distance. Took a job at the Triple R Ranch in Long Pine—twenty miles north. Breaking horses. Herding cattle. Mending fences. I'll work during the week and ride down here on Sundays to see my kids."

"How long you planning on hanging around?"

"Just through the summer," I said. "Then I'm heading south to see my folks in Oklahoma."

Sam looked me over for a long moment, weighing more than just my words. Then he gave a slow nod—like he didn't much like it, but figured it was fair enough. "Well, keep your nose clean, and you won't have any problems with me."

"I appreciate it," I said, meaning it.

We were still standing outside the livery barn when Sheriff O'Brien came walking by, his boots heavy in the dust, his eyes sweeping the street like a man who didn't miss much.

"Everything all right here, boys?" he asked, his voice low and steady, like a man used to being obeyed.

"Just fine," Sam said easily, though he stood a little straighter.

"Good." O'Brien hooked his thumbs into his belt. "I aim to keep this town quiet. You understand?"

We both nodded.

The sheriff then tipped the brim of his wide cowboy hat and moved on, his boots leaving small puffs of dust behind him.

Sheriff O'Brien was a big man, early fifties, broad through the chest, with a thick handlebar mustache that made him look like he belonged on a recruitment poster—or maybe the front line of a cavalry charge.

I settled Nancy into a stall, brushed her down, and forked some hay into the trough. Jasper curled up in the straw nearby, keeping one eye open like he was still half on guard.

"Where does she live?" I asked.

"Nearby," Sam said cautiously.

"Can I speak to her?"

"I'll let her know you're in town," he said. "Give her a little time." He wiped his hands on his leather apron and jerked his chin toward Main Street. "Go on over to the Broken Spur. Have yourself a drink. I'll check in with you after I've talked to her."

I nodded, though my boots felt heavy under me.

I didn't like the waiting. Didn't like standing still when my whole heart was ready to run ahead and find her. But I knew better than to push it. If she wasn't ready, no amount of chasing would change that. So I walked over to the Broken Spur and ordered the stiffest drink they had.

Two drinks later, the door creaked open and Eddie walked in. She didn't hesitate. Just came straight to the bar and sat down on the stool next to me. She didn't say anything at first. Just sat close enough that I could feel the heat off her skin. Her hair was longer than I remembered, pulled back in a loose braid. She looked stronger somehow—leaner, harder around the edges—but good. Real good.

"Hey, Allen," she said, voice soft but steady.

"Hey, Eddie."

I swallowed down the lump in my throat and lifted my glass halfway to her before setting it back down.

"You look well."

She gave a little smile, polite but tired.

"You, uh... you look about the same."

Her eyes flicked over me—the worn shirt, the rough hands, the weathered face—and for a second, something almost like a laugh tugged at her mouth.

"Guess that's either a compliment or a complaint," I said, trying to keep it light.

"Maybe a little of both," she said, and this time she really did smile, just for a second.

I turned my drink in my hands, not sure what to say next. The saloon was half-empty, just a couple of ranch hands hunched over a poker game and the barkeep polishing glasses that didn't look like they'd ever been clean.

"How're the kids?" I asked finally.

"They're good. Growing like weeds." She hesitated, then added, "They miss you."

I nodded, feeling the loss of not seeing them for nearly a year.

"I miss them too. Every damn day."

She traced the rim of her glass with her fingertip, staring down like she was weighing something heavy in her mind. "I'm glad you came," she said after a moment. "I wasn't sure you would."

"Wasn't sure you'd want me to."

"I wasn't sure either," she admitted. "But I guess… I figured we owe it to the kids. And maybe to ourselves too."

I nodded again, not trusting my voice just yet.

Outside, a gust of wind rattled the windows, and the smell of old whiskey and woodsmoke hung thick in the air.

"I don't want to crowd you," I said quietly. "I'll stay in Long Pine, keep my distance. Just want to see 'em when you say it's alright."

She looked at me then—really looked—and some of the wariness in her face eased, just a little. "That sounds fair," she said.

We sat there in silence for a while, wondering how we'd moved from carefree partners out to conquer this wild and exciting world to sad eyed strangers in a saloon aching from the same wound. Finally, she stood up, smoothing down her skirt. "I'll talk to the kids. What about a visit on Sunday?"

"I'd like that," I said.

"What time on Sunday?"

Eddie glanced away for a second, then said, "High noon. After church."

I raised an eyebrow. "You going to church now?"

"That's what respectable people do in Duff."

I nodded once. "Then I'll see you next Sunday at noon."

She gave a quick nod and started to turn away.

I cleared my throat, stopping her for half a second.

"How are you getting along?" My voice came out rougher than I meant. "I've been saving up some money. For you and the kids. I know renting a place in town can cost a lot."

She shook her head gently.

"We're alright," she said. "Sam and Mary fixed up a couple rooms for us over the livery barn. It's not much, but it's enough."

I nodded, not trusting myself to say more.

She smiled—small, tired—and then turned and walked out into the day.

I stayed where I was, staring after her longer than I should have. Then I finished my drink and sat there thinking about her words.

Upstairs over the livery barn, Sam and Mary had fixed up a couple of rooms for Eddie and the kids. It wasn't much—just a narrow staircase leading to a low-ceilinged loft that smelled faintly of hay and old leather no matter how much she scrubbed. Most folks might've found it rough living, but Eddie didn't mind.

She said she liked the way the warm, earthy scent drifted up from the stalls below—said it made her feel more alive than any four walls ever could. The floorboards creaked underfoot, and the windows rattled when the wind came up out of the south. But she made it home the best she could—a battered stove in the corner, a few quilts stitched together to keep the drafts out, four straw mattresses lined up along the back wall like soldiers.

It was tight living, but it was hers. Hard living, sure. But sometimes hard was the only way you stayed free.

Sunday couldn't come fast enough. I couldn't sleep. I lost my appetite. All I could think of was my four kids and the pain I'd put them through.

I just wanted a chance to make things right. And for the kids to still want me when it was over.

ONE SUNDAY AT A TIME

The morning was bright and clean, the kind of day the prairie seemed made for. The grass moved in long, slow waves under a wide blue sky, and the air smelled like wild clover and warm earth. If there was ever a day made for starting over, this was it. It had been months since I last saw them—long enough for their faces to blur in my memory, but not long enough for the ache to fade.

I waited by the livery, boots planted firm, but my hands kept fiddling with the brim of my hat. Nerves I hadn't felt in a long time gnawed at my chest. Then I heard them—three sets of boots pounding down the alley, a burst of laughter chasing after them like a windstorm.

George was out front, all arms and legs, running hard like he was racing the whole world. William came next, fists pumping, face fierce with determination to keep up. John trailed a little behind, his pace steady, his smile easy. They pulled up short a few feet away, breathing hard, looking me over like a stranger they half-recognized.

"Hey, boys," I said, clearing my throat.

"Hey, Pa," George said, voice cracking like a colt's first whinny.

William just nodded, eyes darting to Jasper and back to me.

John tilted his head and said, dead serious, "Jasper's gotten fatter."

That broke the tension like a boot through thin ice.

Jasper barked once and bounded straight into them, tail wagging like mad, knocking William backward into George. The boys laughed, shoving and jostling the way brothers do, and for a second, it felt almost easy again.

"Thought we might ride out to Skull Creek," I said, jerking my thumb toward the horses tied nearby. "Maybe get our boots wet. Maybe a whole lot wetter."

George grinned wide. William whooped. John just nodded, but the way he swung up into the saddle told me all I needed to know.

We rode out slow, Jasper cutting back and forth through the tall grass, stirring up grasshoppers and the sweet smell of crushed clover. The sun was warm on my shoulders, the wind gentle, and for the first time in months, the world didn't feel so heavy. When we reached Skull Creek, the boys didn't wait for an invitation. They peeled off their boots and shirts and charged into the water, splashing and hollering loud enough to scare the fish into the next county.

I waded in up to my knees, letting the cold shock of it bite into me, clean and sharp. It felt like washing six months of sorrow clean off my skin.

George dared William to jump from a low-hanging branch. William dared him right back. John floated on his back, arms spread wide, his face turned up to the sun. Jasper crashed through the shallows, barking and spraying water everywhere, getting more laughs than the boys knew what to do with.

The awkwardness faded, little by little, like a splinter working its way out of skin. There was no talk about the past. No heavy words. Just water and sun and the pure noise of boys being boys.

Later we stretched out on the warm bank, drying off in the sun, the grass whispering all around us. George carved his initials into a driftwood branch. William tried to catch a grasshopper with his bare hands. John lay with his arms folded behind his head, squinting up at the clouds, the quiet king of his own little kingdom.

I leaned back on my elbows and watched them, letting the peace of the day seep into places I hadn't even realized were hurting. For the first time in months, it almost felt easy. Too easy, maybe. Like something you find washed up on a riverbank—whole and shining—only to realize the current's still tugging at it, ready to pull it under again.

As we saddled up to head back, I caught their eyes and said, "See you next Sunday."

George whooped and threw his hat in the air. William grinned so big it nearly split his face. John just nodded—steady, sure, the way he always was.

And for that precious moment, I believed it.

We rode back into town with the sun low behind us, and the boys ran off toward the livery, laughing and shoving like pups let off the leash. I watched them go, a smile tugging at my mouth for the first time in what felt like forever.

The next Sunday, I arrived an hour early. I couldn't help it. I was so excited I felt half-crazy, like a boy waiting for Christmas morning. Eddie was already there, waiting by the livery barn, Fern bundled up in her arms.

For a long minute, all I could do was stand there and drink her in. Fern was even sweeter, even more beautiful than I remembered—little fists clenching and unclenching, her eyes wide and curious, a soft coo slipping from her lips.

Eddie hesitated, then stepped closer and let me hold her. I cradled Fern in my arms like something holy, breathing in the warm, milky scent of her. Her little hand curled around my finger like it was the only thing keeping her tethered to the earth. I bent low and whispered to her that I'd never let her down again.

For ten whole minutes, I just held her, swaying gently on my feet, whispering promises I hoped she could feel even if she couldn't understand the words. After that, the boys dragged me off for target practice.

Sam had set up some empty tin cans along a fence post, and I took turns showing them how to steady their hands, how to breathe, how to squeeze the trigger like you were shaking hands with it.

John hit the can every single time from fifty feet—calm, quiet, deadly steady.

George, on the other hand, missed twice, then nailed one can so hard it flew off the post. I ruffled George's hair as he stomped past, muttering under his breath. The scowl he gave John could've stripped paint. It stung him bad to be outshot by his little brother.

William was more interested in catching grasshoppers, than shooting cans. So we just let him be.

After practice, we lazed in the sun awhile, no one in much of a hurry to head back. George found a jagged little rock near the creek, white as bone, and held it out like he'd discovered buried treasure.

"Lucky rock," he said, grinning wide. "Gonna keep it in my boot for good luck."

I told him he'd get blisters, but he just laughed and shoved it deep in his pocket.

William spent half an hour trying to teach Jasper to fetch a stick — and Jasper spent half an hour pretending he didn't understand a word of it. Every time William tossed the stick, Jasper would look at him, bark once, and trot the other way, tail high in the air like he had better things to do. William hollered after him, red-faced and laughing.

John wandered off and flopped down in the grass next to me, arms under his head, staring up at the wide, blue sky. Before long, he was asleep against my side, his soft breath rising and falling in rhythm with the breeze. Across the clearing, I caught Sam leaning against the fence, watching us. Arms folded, face unreadable. Maybe he was hoping I'd pull it off this time. Maybe he thought I wouldn't.

I sat there for a long time, not moving, not even daring to breathe too deep, afraid I'd wake him. The sun dipped lower, the crickets started up, and for the first time in a long while, the world felt just about right. But deep down, I could see it—the same restless fire in him that I used to carry.

The Sundays rolled by like warm river water—easy at first. But cracks were starting to show.

Several Sundays later, we were out by the creekbed, letting the boys chase minnows and throw rocks, when it happened. George, determined to show off, climbed a low tree near the water. I warned him twice to be careful, but George had his mind set on impressing his brothers—and me. He lost his grip halfway up, hit the ground hard, and didn't get up.

I was at his side before I even thought about it. One look at the angle of his arm and my stomach twisted. I sank to my knees beside him. His face was pale and tight, his breath coming in short, shallow pulls. I scooped him up carefully. He leaned into me, so small and light—the way he used to feel when I carried him piggyback after long days in the field.

"I'm fine, Pa," he muttered through gritted teeth, though his whole body shook against mine.

I tightened my arms around him anyway, wishing I could somehow soak the pain right out of him. Wishing I'd made him stay on the ground. Wishing a hundred things too late. I wrapped his arm as best I could, hands clumsy with guilt, then swung into the saddle with him cradled close against me. All the way back to town, every jolt, every stumble, felt like another failure. George bit his lip until it bled, fighting back tears he didn't want me to see.

And I kept whispering that it was gonna be all right—even though I wasn't sure either one of us believed it. Eddie was waiting at the livery when I rode in.

The second she saw George's arm, she went still—the kind of stillness that comes right before a storm. Her face drained white, then flushed deep red. Her hands shook as she snatched George from my arms, holding him so tight he let out a soft grunt of pain.

"What the hell were you thinking?" she shouted, her voice breaking around the edges. "You were supposed to be watching them, Allen! Not letting them climb trees like a pack of wild wolves!"

George whimpered and buried his head into her shoulder, and she ran a trembling hand through his hair like she could fix everything if she just held on tight enough.

I tried to explain—tried to tell her he'd been stubborn, that I hadn't looked away for more than a second—but the words dried up in my throat. She wasn't just mad. She was terrified. And to her, I'd already failed.

July brought hotter days and heavier silences. One Sunday in July, I showed up at noon sharp, only to find Sam waiting at the barn door, arms folded tight across his chest. He looked uncomfortable, almost guilty.

"Eddie's... not feeling well," he said.

When I pressed, he jerked his thumb toward the Broken Spur.

"She was out late. Drinking. Cards."

It hit me like a hammer to the chest. I clenched my fists, trying to keep my temper in check. How could she be doing this again?

The boys came out a few minutes later, wide-eyed and smiling, still glad to see me. I ruffled William's hair a little rougher than usual, trying to mask the tightness in my chest.

Later, when we were down by the creek tossing stones, I said something I shouldn't have. Something about their mother spending more time in a saloon than with them.

I muttered it low, but it was loud enough.

George squared his shoulders. "Don't talk about Ma like that," he said, voice firm.

John looked away, stiff and quiet.

Even little William crossed his arms and glared at me. Their loyalty was fierce. Unwavering. And it made me feel about as tall as a prairie dog—proud they stood up for her, and petty enough to feel downright embarrassed.

The next Sunday, Eddie was waiting for me. Arms crossed. Eyes hard. The second I swung down from Nancy, she lit into me. "I heard what you said to the boys," she snapped.

"I didn't mean it," I said.

"Then why did you say it?"

I opened my mouth to explain, but she cut me off.

"This is exactly why our relationship will never work!" she said, her voice shaking with anger. "You don't trust me. You don't respect me. You sure as hell don't know when to keep your damn mouth shut."

Sam and Mary appeared behind her, silent but solid. They were there to support their blood, regardless of her actions.

Sam shifted his weight and crossed his arms. "If you ever badmouth her around the kids again," he said quietly, "you won't have to wonder whether you're welcome in Duff. You'll be riding out faster than you can blink."

Mary didn't say anything, but the cold look she gave me said enough.

I apologized. And I truly meant it. But apologies were only words—and I could see plain as day they weren't buying them anymore.

By the end of August, the heat was thick enough to bend the horizon, and my Sundays had turned into silent battlegrounds.

Midway down Main Street one Sunday, I saw her. She was standing outside the Broken Spur, laughing. She leaned in close to a tall, handsome cowboy—clean shirt, clean shave, standing like he owned the ground under his boots. He said something low, and she laughed again—not the careful, guarded laugh she used to give me, but a bright, reckless laugh that carried across the dust and heat.

She touched his arm—a soft touch, lingering just a beat too long. He didn't move. He just smiled down at her, slow and sure, like he already knew she was his for the asking.

I froze in the saddle, every muscle wound tight as barbed wire.

The reins bit into my palms, the leather cutting deep, but I barely felt it. My jaw clenched so hard it sent a pounding ache up into my temples, but I held my feeling back—held everything back—like a dam fixing to burst. As each second passed I felt the pain and the pressure build.

Under my breath, I said to myself. "Be smart and just turn away. Don't look. Don't let her break your heart."

But I couldn't help myself. The harder I tried to look away, the harder I stared. She was laughing like she didn't have a care in the world. Like what she'd done last year in Kalispell didn't matter. Like I didn't matter. A low, dark heat started boiling up in my chest, burning through the hurt.

She was still my wife. Even if she didn't live under my roof or share my bed. Even if she'd quit wearing my ring months ago.

A piano tumbled out a tune from inside the saloon—light, careless, like nothing in the world was wrong. Jasper whined once behind me.

I felt it then—not just the anger, but something colder underneath. Fear. I was losing her for good, and part of me could already feel it slipping. But I couldn't stop myself. Before I knew it, I was stepping off Nancy, boots hitting hard enough to raise dust. My hand shook as I stormed across the street, the world narrowing down to her and the bastard smiling at her like he belonged there.

"What the hell is this, Eddie?" I barked, my voice sharp and hard, cutting through the afternoon like a blade. "You're still my wife."

She spun around, furious.

"We're not anything anymore!" she shouted, her face blazing. "I don't ever want to see you again!"

I raised my voice. Said things I don't even remember, stupid things.

"You can't talk to a woman like that." The cowboy she'd been laughing with stepped forward.

"You got something to say to me?" I growled, taking a step toward him.

"She said she don't want to see you anymore," he muttered like he was her rescuer.

"You little..." I tightened my fists and moved closer to him.

He shifted his weight, ready to stand his ground.

Before either of us could move, Sam barreled between us and shoved the cowboy back with a firm hand to the chest. "This isn't your fight," he said, low and dangerous. "Get out of here. Now."

The cowboy hesitated, looked like he might argue—but one glance at Sam changed his mind. He backed off and slipped into the saloon. Eddie turned and walked away with her chin high and shoulders square, each step measured like she was done taking orders from anyone. She didn't run. She didn't look back. She followed the cowboy inside.

I stood there breathing hard, fists still clenched. The street had gone quiet, like the moment after a storm when all that's left is broken fences and bent down crops.

If Sam hadn't stepped in, I don't know what might've happened. I'd already killed one man. I might've killed another. I wasn't thinking straight—just burning with rage, too far gone to care.

Sam turned to me. "That's enough, Allen."

I knew he was right, but I met his eyes and muttered, "I ain't leaving."

He squared up, jaw tight. "You are," he said flatly. "And you're gonna do it now."

I didn't move.

Sam called out, "Sheriff!"

Sheriff O'Brien strolled up, his hand resting casual on his belt.

"You can ride out peacefully," he said, "or spend a few nights in our fine little jail. Your call."

I glared at them—Sam, the sheriff, the whole damn town—until my vision blurred at the edges. Then I yanked Nancy's reins loose and swung into the saddle, kicking her into a gallop like I could outrun everything.

Jasper tore after us, paws chewing up the August dust.

At the edge of Duff, I jerked Nancy south and leaned low over the saddle. Then I took one look back.

Sam stood silent beside the sheriff, watching me. He didn't shout. Didn't shake his fist. But the way he looked at me—like a man who'd just watched someone burn down his own house—cut deeper than any word he could've said. I turned away, pushed my hat low on my sunburned head, and rode south. Just me and the dog and the road ahead.

I was heading for Oklahoma—but it didn't feel like going home. It felt like I was running—from my kids, from the only woman I ever truly loved, from the dream we tried to build. Every step away from Duff felt like another piece of me breaking loose and scattering in the dust. I gritted my teeth and pushed Nancy harder, trying to outrun the gnawing in my gut.

The wind in my ears, the saddle creaking beneath me, Jasper's paws steady behind. Every mile felt like losing them all over again— Skull Creek, their laughter, the way John leaned into me as he slept. But I didn't stop. I didn't even slow down. I just kept going, like a mad man running in the opposite direction of dreams and a broken man aching at the pain of losing everything that ever mattered.

Eddie wasn't just gone. She was ripped clean out of me—and no amount of miles or time was gonna fill the hole she left behind.

OKLAHOMA DROUGHT

It was the first week of September when I made it back to the folk's homestead. The air still held the weight of summer, but the light had changed—longer shadows, slower evenings. The cottonwoods along the edge of the property had just started to yellow, like the season was trying to turn the page but hadn't quite worked up the nerve.

Ma and Pa had done what they could with the land. It wasn't rich ground—not like they'd hoped—but it held if you treated it right. Pa stuck to sorghum and kept the cattle lean. Ma grew what she could in the garden behind the house, though even hardy beans and tomatoes didn't always make it through the heat. They stretched every inch of what they had. Ma canned and patched and made do, and Pa ran his fingers over the dry soil like a man reading old scripture. They hadn't come to Oklahoma looking for comfort. They'd come chasing survival. And most years, they found just enough.

Nancy nickered as we crested the last rise, and just beyond the trees, I saw the house. The red roof had dulled some, and the porch sagged a little on the right side, but it still stood—weathered, waiting. A thin ribbon of smoke curled from the chimney. Supper hour.

We rode in slow. Jasper trotted ahead, tail up, nose twitching. He gave a single bark and took off toward the house like he'd never left. I let the reins go slack. I wasn't ready yet.

We dismounted behind the house. Erroll heard me coming, and walked out of the barn.

"I can't believe my eyes," he said, taking off his work gloves. "I wondered if I'd ever see you again."

Last time I'd seen my brother he was a kid now he was a full grown man—tall and broad-shouldered, with thick brown hair and piercing blue eyes. He looked like every girl's dream—and knew it. He moved with the easy confidence of someone who'd never been told no. Handsome, athletic, and full of bravado. Every girl in the county probably dreamed of a date with him.

"Good to see you, brother," I said, slapping him hard on the back.

"It's been three years or more," he said. "We wondered where in the world you were?"

"Montana, Nebraska, mostly drifting."

"Well Ma and Pa will be mighty happy to see you."

"Where are your brothers and sisters?" I asked.

"George, Maud, and Ethel are all married and have moved on. It's just Guy and me still on the Homestead."

"It'll be good to see Guy again."

"Hey Guy," yelled Erroll. "Come on out here and see who's dropped by."

Guy stepped out of the barn a moment later, blinking into the sunlight. He was lanky and quiet, barefoot in the dust, sleeves hanging past his wrists. Twelve now, but still had that same gentle, curious way about him. "Hi there," he said, not quite looking me in the eye.

Then Jasper came bounding from behind the house. Guy froze— eyes wide, a grin blooming across his face. The dog ran straight to him like they'd never been apart.

"Hey there, boy," Guy said, crouching low.

Jasper gave one sniff, then flopped over, belly up and tail thumping hard.

Guy laughed softly and rubbed his ribs. "You're not shy, huh?" He slipped a half biscuit from his pocket.

Jasper snatched it, tail wagging faster than a prairie wind.

I stood a few steps back, arms crossed, watching them. Jasper had always followed me without question. Now he hardly looked my way. Maybe the way to a dog's heart really was through his belly.

Then the screen door creaked, and Ma stepped out onto the porch, drying her hands on her apron. Her hair was almost entirely white now, twisted into a loose bun. She raised a hand to shade her eyes, and for a moment, she just stared.

"Oh, my Lord!"

Then she came down the steps fast for a woman her age, calling my name in a voice thick with disbelief and excitement. "Allen?"

I wrapped her in a tight, teary hug. She pressed her face against my chest and stayed there, not speaking, not letting go. She smelled like flour and soap and home.

"You didn't write," she murmured. "We didn't know where you were."

"I'm here now," I said, voice rough. " I know I should've written, but... but I didn't."

"What's the racket out here?" Pa appeared in the doorway, leaning on the frame like he wasn't sure whether to step out or stay back. His face was harder than I remembered. Grayer, too. But his eyes—his eyes locked onto mine like they hadn't aged a day.

"Evening, Pa," I said.

He gave a slow nod. "Well, I'll be hogtied!"

Pa looked dumbfounded, with tears forming in his eyes as he searched for the right words. Finally, he just said, "Welcome home."

And those two words were the most powerful, heart touching words I'd heard in a month of Sundays. It had been nearly two years since I'd last seen Ma and Pa. And standing there on that porch, I realized how long it had been since I felt like I belonged anywhere at all.

Pa squeezed my hand and stepped aside so I could come in.

Ma rested a hand on my back and gave a gentle nudge. "Come wash up, supper's nearly ready."

I stepped over the threshold like I was walking into a memory. The floorboards creaked the same, the air smelled of stew and woodsmoke, and for the first time in a long while, I didn't feel like a stranger.

We sat down to supper like we'd done a hundred times before—plates warm, coffee hot, Jasper stretched under the table like he'd never left. The house looked smaller than I remembered, but just as full of comfort. The meal was simple—beans with salt pork, collard greens, applesauce, and soda biscuits—but I swear it was the best meal I'd had in a long time. Pa said grace and I dug in like a horse bound for the barn after a long day on the trail. Ma watched me with a smile, but she was eating slowly. I could tell something was brewing by the quiet, careful way she looked at me when she was worried but trying not to crowd.

After a few bites, Ma set her fork down and asked, "How's Eddie?" She paused. "And the kids?"

Pa glanced over, too, his brow furrowed. He didn't speak, but the question was there in the silence between us. I swallowed hard and wiped my mouth on a napkin. "Eddie and I aren't together anymore. She's with the kids in Duff. Been living over the livery barn with Sam and Mary since spring."

Ma's eyes softened with both relief and concern. "And you've been with them?"

I nodded. "Every Sunday since June. Got a job up north in Long Pine breaking horses. Rode down to see them every week. We went swimming, shot tin cans, skipped stones. George carved his initials into a driftwood log. John napped with his head on my leg. William tried to teach Jasper to fetch. Fern—" I stopped, throat tight. "Fern grew so much, Ma. She's walking now. Got this little way of holding your thumb like she's never going to let go my."

Ma reached across the table and set her hand gently over mine.

"Eddie let you visit?" Pa asked, watching me closely.

"Yeah. At first, she wasn't sure. But we found a rhythm. It was working...until it wasn't."

I saw the flicker of understanding in Ma's eyes before she spoke. "What happened?"

"I lost my temper," I admitted. "Didn't swing at anyone. Didn't break anything. But I said things I shouldn't have. Let jealousy get the better of me. Made a scene."

No one spoke for a long while. Only the ticking of the wall clock and the scrape of Ma's thumb against the rim of her mug.

"She still loves you?" Pa asked finally.

I thought of her laugh outside the saloon, the way she didn't look back.

"I think she did," I said quietly. "Maybe part of her still does. But I don't know if that's enough anymore."

Ma looked down at her plate. "Sometimes love ain't about being enough. It's about what you do when you ain't."

Pa gave a grunt—something between agreement and sympathy. Then he reached for another biscuit and passed it down the table, the way he always had, like the world hadn't shifted beneath us.

I took it with both hands and said, "Thanks."

Not just for the biscuit. But for letting me back in the door.

A few days later, I was out behind the barn, shooting tin cans off the fence posts. I hit every can I aimed at. I might not've been as good as Eddie, but I was better than most.

Guy watched me in his quiet, curious way, then asked, "How'd you get to be such a good shot?"

"A lot of practice." I smiled as I hit another can.

"What do you shoot besides cans?"

"Deer and rabbit for food. Wolves to protect the cattle."

"You ever have to shoot a horse?"

"Sometimes, when a horse is too injured to save." I paused. "That's one of the hardest things a cowboy ever has to do."

He was quiet for a moment, then asked, "You ever shot a man?"

He said it like he was asking if I wanted water at high noon—matter-of-fact, no judgment in his voice.

I hesitated, then set down my rifle. "I've thought about it. Back in Duff, when I saw that cowboy with Eddie, it took everything I had not to blow a hole in his chest."

"Couldn't blame you if you had," he said with a shrug.

"The sheriff was standin' nearby," I said. "If I'd pulled the trigger, I'd be rottin' in a jail cell in that two-bit excuse for a town."

Guy looked at me steady. "But have you ever pulled the trigger on a man?"

I looked at him—still so young, still full of questions. I didn't want to lie. "Sometimes a man does something he'll carry with him forever."

"I don't get it."

"Sometimes you're just doing your job. When I was your brother's age, some rustlers stole our horses. Three of us went out to get 'em back. Shots were fired. I hit one of 'em."

"Did he die?"

I nodded. "Yeah. He did. And I've regretted it ever since."

"Would he have shot you if you hadn't?"

"Most likely."

"Then you'd be the dead man."

I nodded again. "Maybe. But I still wish I'd shot him in the leg. Or the shoulder. Anything but a kill shot."

"Did they put you in jail?"

"No. They never figured out who did it. And I doubt they ever will."

"If they did, would they string you up?"

"Probably not. Horse thievin' don't sit well in cowboy country. But even when it's justified, takin' a man's life ain't something you ever want to do." I looked him in the eye. "You understand that?"

Guy was quiet, then nodded. After a while he said, "Unless you're protectin' your family."

I put my arm around his shoulder. "You're right. Unless you're protectin' your family."

That was the last time I ever talked to anyone about that killing. And I hope I never have to again.

That winter, I stayed. And then I stayed the next. The days blurred, and before I knew it... two years had passed. Drought stole the crops. Prices fell through the floor. Hope thinned like the soil beneath our boots. We were broke—down to patching boots with twine and watering beans with prayer. I was lost, too stubborn to leave, too tired to dream.

As each year passed, it felt like I drifted further and further from my kids. Once a year, I rode the train up to Duff for a week or two. The kids welcomed me, but Eddie ignored me. Sam and Mary kept an eye on me like I was a criminal. George still wrote in between visits, but I never heard a word from Eddie. We were still married, but only in name.

In late May of 1910, with the ground cracked and the barn near empty, a chance came riding up like salvation. A rancher down in Sulphur Springs, Texas needed hands to move a small herd north—three hundred miles to the Osage Reservation, just shy of our homestead. It wasn't much, but it was honest pay and just maybe enough to pull us through the summer.

I saddled Nancy. She was getting on in years—eighteen now, with a little stiffness in her bones and gray hairs around her muzzle. She didn't have the fire she used to, but she still moved with the certainty that comes from miles and memories. I didn't ride her hard anymore, not unless I had to. But she knew the rhythm of a drive, and when I swung into the saddle that morning, she took the weight without complaint. We'd been through a lot together. She carried me like she always had—steady, willing, and without a hint of doubt.

Erroll mounted beside me, nineteen and ready for the trail.

Tall and lean, with Pa's shoulders and a look in his eye that said he was ready to carry more than his share. Guy trailed behind on a shaggy pony he proudly called Lightning—fourteen now, strong as an ox, with the first hints of manhood showing in his voice and the stubborn set of his jaw. We rode south under a hard sky, chasing dust and whatever luck we still had. Jasper trotted alongside, ears perked, tongue lolling.

We reached Sulphur Springs after eight days—saddle-sore, sunburned, and hungry for some good food. The town sat low against the horizon, its brick buildings weathered by heat and time, it's Main Street a site for sore eyes.

As we rode in, dust clung to our boots and sleeves. Jasper stuck close to Guy's stirrup, tail low but wagging. He gave the porch of the Broadway Boarding House a good sniff, where the smell of fried chicken and apple pie hit us like a warm welcome and made our mouths water.

But first we had to check on the herd—a stringy mix of fifty head, mostly longhorns with a few black baldies thrown in. The rancher met us at the stockyard, handed over part of the pay up front, and tossed in a coil of fresh rope, a bag of jerky, and a warning about water scarcity past the Red River. Said if we got them north in two weeks, there'd be a bonus.

We stabled the horses, filled our canteens, and headed into the boarding house to fill our bellies. We hadn't planned on staying in town, but the ride south had worn us thin. Figured we'd earned a night under a roof. Besides, there was a dance at the grange hall, and the thought of a little fun and music was too tempting to pass up. So we washed up as best we could and let ourselves forget—just for a while—how broke we were and how far we still had to go to get back home.

The grange hall sat just across from the boarding house, its windows glowing warm against the dusk, fiddle music spilling out into the street like laughter after a long silence. We stepped inside just as the band struck up a waltz, the notes swirling through the lantern-lit room like wind through wheat. The place smelled of floor wax, tobacco, and perfume. Erroll straightened his collar and scanned the crowd like he'd been born for it—tall and sure, that thick brown hair catching the light. He was already picking out girls who'd been watching him walk in. Seemed like every girl in the county had their eye on him—and judging by the glint in his, he aimed to dance with every single one of them.

Guy, on the other hand, froze in the doorway, wide-eyed and fidgeting with the sleeves of his cleanest shirt. He'd never been to a proper dance before. Shy and gentle, he wasn't built for crowds or noise—he preferred books, animals, and the quiet certainty of chores. I gave his shoulder a quiet pat and nodded toward the food table, where boys his age clustered with tin cups of lemonade and nervous grins. He drifted that way, moving slow and careful like he wasn't sure the floorboards would hold.

The place was packed wall to wall, lanternlight catching dust in the air and turning everything a little more golden than it probably was. Erroll was already in his element, spinning one partner after another across the floor like he'd been born doing it. He danced every song, always with a different girl, laughing loud and drinking just enough to keep the swagger loose in his step. By the time I caught up with him near the lemonade, he was wiping sweat from his brow like he'd been bucking hay on a hot August afternoon.

"I didn't realize you were such a ladies' man," I said, raising an eyebrow.

He just winked. "I'm just popular."

Across the hall, Guy stood with his back to the wall, watching like it was a story he hadn't been invited into. His shoulders were tight, eyes always moving—scanning the band, the dancers, the cat that slipped under the food table to lick up the crumbs. He never chased attention. But he didn't miss a thing.

Outside, Jasper lay curled beneath the porch, ears flicking at every burst of laughter or fiddle cry that spilled through the grange hall windows. He'd lift his head whenever Guy came near the door for air.

I scanned the room again, not really looking for anything—just letting the music and the warmth sink in—when movement near the center of the floor caught my eye. And that's when I saw her.

She wore a pale blue dress with a high lace collar and pearl buttons down the front—simple, but elegant in the way it fit her frame and moved when she turned. A cream-colored sash cinched her waist, and the hem brushed just above polished boots that tapped lightly on the wooden floor in time with the fiddle. Her light brown hair was pinned up in a loose twist, with a few soft curls falling around her ears. There was something calm about her—like a prairie at dusk, quiet and open.

She didn't show off. Didn't laugh too loud or spin wild like the other girls. She just moved with a steady rhythm, graceful and sure, dancing with a clean-shaven cowboy in a white shirt and silver belt buckle. When she turned, her gaze brushed mine. And for half a second—maybe less—she held it. Just long enough to make my chest tighten.

My heart beat harder than I wanted it to. I tried to slow it down, to look away. But there was something in the way she carried herself—gentle, thoughtful, like she could carry the world on her shoulders, and it wouldn't weigh her down. I felt myself drawn in without meaning to be. Drawn in and scared, too. The last girl I met at a dance had stolen my breath, then broke my heart clean in two. So I looked away.

But a few songs later, I saw her again—this time across the hall near the food table, where an older woman had tripped and fallen hard. Someone had stepped on the hem of her dress in passing and kept walking, too caught up in the music to notice. Another man swore at her and called her clumsy. The crowd veered around her. Nobody helped her.

But the girl in the pale blue dress did.

She knelt beside the woman without hesitation. Helped her sit up slow, brushed the dust from her sleeves, and offered a glass of lemonade with both hands like it was something sacred. Then she stood, linked arms with the woman, and walked her to a bench near the stove—never drawing attention, never asking for thanks. It wasn't the kind of moment anyone else would remember. But I did. She didn't do it to be seen. That's what impressed me most.

Later, while I stood near the back wall watching Erroll kick up a storm, she caught my eye. Her dance partner had gone off to smoke, and she walked toward me, as a cloud drifts across a lazy afternoon sky.

"You from around here?" she asked, voice soft but clear.

I straightened, caught off guard. "No, ma'am. Just passing through."

She smiled—not the flirty kind, just kind. "I thought so. You've got the look of someone who's been out in the wind a while."

I gave a small nod. "Name's Allen Stephens. I'm from up near Fairfax, in the Osage."

"You're a fair spell from home."

"My brothers and I are herding some cattle north at first light."

"I'm glad you stayed for the dance."

"So am I."

"Era Leewright," she said, offering her hand. "My family lives just west of town."

I shook her hand gently, surprised at how small it felt in mine—and how steady.

"I saw you help that older woman."

She blushed. "It was nothing."

"I thought it was something."

"It was the right thing to do."

"Not a lot of people do the right thing," I said.

"Next time you're in town," she said, "I'd be glad if you'd ask me to dance."

"I just might do that."

She smiled and turned to join her friends by the piano.

I watched her go, knowing I'd remember the sound of her name long after the music faded.

That night I couldn't sleep. The boarding house was too warm, the straw mattress too lumpy, and my mind wouldn't quit turning. I kept seeing her face—soft and thoughtful beneath the lantern glow—kept hearing her voice asking where I was from, like it truly mattered. There was a lavender scent on the air when she passed me, and somehow it lingered longer than it had any right to.

She was sweet, innocent, and refined in a way that didn't try to prove anything. Just the opposite of Eddie Dailey, who lit every room on fire and dared you not to get burned. Era didn't burn—she calmed. And that scared me even more.

I told myself it was nothing. Just a moment. Just the nice memory of a friendly smile and a kind heart. But as I lay there staring at the shadows on the ceiling, listening to Erroll's steady breathing and Guy's occasional snore, I knew better.

There was something different about this girl—something special. I knew it sounded crazy—so crazy I hardly wanted to admit it to myself. But feelings can warm you from the inside, same way the sun warms the back of your neck. And deep down, in a place I didn't like to poke around too often, I knew I'd already fallen for Era Leewright.

By morning, the night before felt like a dream I hadn't meant to have.

I was halfway through buttoning my shirt when Erroll pushed open the door to our room at the boarding house, a cocky grin on his face. "I got something I think you'll want," he said, leaning in the doorway like he owned the place.

I glanced at him, groggy and still working the sleep from my eyes. "And what would that be?"

He held up a folded scrap of paper between two fingers. "An address."

I stared at him, confused. "What?"

"The girl you had eyes for last night."

"I didn't have eyes for anyone," I said, reaching for my boots.

"Don't lie to me," Erroll said. "I saw the way you looked at her. Like you forgot how to breathe."

He stepped into the room and set the paper on the washstand beside me.

"How'd you get it?"

"From the lady who runs the boarding house. Got up early for coffee and told her my brother was smitten and too proud to say anything. She laughed and said she had a soft spot for shy cowboys."

I picked up the paper and tucked it into my pocket without a word. For a second, I swore I could still catch a trace of lavender—like the memory of her had been stitched into the fold.

Erroll stretched and turned to leave. "You're welcome, by the way."

He walked off toward the kitchen, whistling low and tuneless, leaving the door half-open behind him. I stayed there a moment longer, thumb resting against the crease of that folded note in my pocket.

The sun was already high when we saddled the horses behind the boarding house. Guy was still yawning, and Erroll was humming a bit of that waltz from the night before, grinning like he'd had his pick of the girls—which, knowing him, he probably had.

I kept my head down, checking Nancy's cinch twice more than I needed to. Across the street, the grange hall stood quiet now, windows shuttered, dust settled along the steps like the night had never happened.

Part of me wanted to ride by Era's house, tip my hat, maybe even say goodbye.

But I didn't. I couldn't.

We turned the herd north and rode out slow, the wind at our backs and silence between us. I didn't look back—but I thought about her the whole way home. As the miles passed and the prairie opened up wide again, I couldn't shake the picture of her—Era Leewright in that pale blue dress, steady and kind. I knew she was more than I deserved. But that didn't stop me from hoping the good Lord might still see fit to bless a broken-hearted cowboy with one more chance at a dream.

BITTERSWEET

It felt good to be back home.

Ma and Pa were waiting on the front porch with a pitcher of lemonade, the glasses sweating in the heat. Pa gave me a nod; Ma pulled me into a quick hug. It was one of those late August days when the porch boards were too hot to touch, and sweat clung to your back before noon. Cicadas whined in the cottonwoods, and the air tasted like sunburned earth and old sorghum. I came back from the cattle drive a little richer, a little dustier, and more smitten than I cared to admit.

We'd earned enough to keep the family going for six months if we were careful—more than I'd hoped for when we set out. But it wasn't the pay that stayed with me.

It was Era.

I thought about her every morning I swung into the saddle, every night when I rolled out my bedroll under the stars. I replayed our dance, our conversation, that trace of lavender that never seemed to leave my coat. I'd written her every week since we parted, long letters full of stories and confessions I couldn't say out loud.

Back home in Fairfax, things felt different. Nancy was going lame, so I turned her out to pasture behind the house. I bought a four-year-old buckskin mustang for twenty-five dollars from a ranch not far from the homestead. I named him Texas—'cause that's where I still felt I was meant to be. Jasper spent most days sleeping under the porch or trailing after Guy like a shadow. I kept telling myself I should be content there. But the truth was, part of me was already halfway back to Sulphur Springs.

But the days didn't stand still. The heat began to ease, just enough to whisper that summer was losing its grip. And before I knew it, we were saddling up again—headed south with another herd and a whole lot more on my mind than cattle.

We hit the trail in early September. Same route, same sunbaked hills—but everything felt different. I wasn't just chasing a paycheck this time. I was chasing a feeling.

Sulphur Springs came into view like a mirage—dusty streets, weathered boards, and that wide, forgiving sky. The town hadn't changed, but something in me had. It felt like the beginning of something.

She was waiting at the stockyard, brushing a curl behind her ear and smiling like she'd been expecting me all along.

"Dinner tonight?" she asked.

I nodded, heart thumping. "Wouldn't miss it."

Her house stood just beyond the edge of town—a tall Victorian with wraparound porches, lace curtains in the windows, and a manicured garden that stood defiant against the Texas dust. Her father, Will Leewright, greeted me with a firm handshake. He wore a clean shirt, silver-rimmed glasses, and the posture of a man used to giving orders. A Santa Fe Railroad pin gleamed on his vest. Her mother, Florence, was gracious, sharp-eyed, and clearly adored her daughter.

After dinner, Era walked me out. We sat on the front porch talking like a pair of schoolchildren.

"Thank you for the letters," she said softly. "They've meant more to me than I can say."

"I'll keep writing," I said. "Every week."

That night, we headed back to the same grange hall where we first met. It was lit up again—lanterns glowing, fiddles playing, laughter spilling out the open windows. Inside, the air smelled like fresh-cut pie and old leather. Folks clapped along to the music, and little kids chased each other between hay bales at the back of the room.

Era and I danced slow, swaying in a corner where the shadows softened everything. Her head rested easy on my shoulder at first, and I let myself believe—for just a minute—that maybe this could be something. Something real.

We moved together like we'd done it a hundred times before. Her hand found mine, and her breath brushed my neck as she laughed softly at something I said—I don't even remember what. The world felt quiet around us, even with all the noise.

It was the perfect evening—right up until the music stopped. With our fingers still intertwined, she eased back just enough to meet my eyes. Her smile faded.

"Have you ever been married?" she said, her face serious.

The question caught in the quiet like a splinter. I hesitated.

"Once," I swallowed hard. "A long time ago."

Era was quiet. I waited for her to yell, to hit me, or just walk out the door without looking back. It's what I deserved, and I knew it. But she didn't do any of that. She didn't even let go of my hands. She just took a deep breath and looked up at me—eyes glassy with tears.

"Why didn't you tell me?"

She said it so calm, it cut deeper than any shouting could've. Guilt and shame burned in me until my face blazed red, and my mouth felt as dry as a shallow well at the end of a hot spell.

"I was afraid I'd lose you."

"So... are you divorced?"

"Not really."

She tilted her head just a little. "Not really?"

I nodded, swallowing hard. "She took the kids. We were living in Montana, and she moved them to Nebraska. I haven't seen them in two years."

"How many kids do you have?"

"Three boys and a girl."

"So why can't you see them?" she asked—not angry, just curious, maybe even concerned.

"I got jealous when I saw her with another man. Lost my temper. Said things I shouldn't have. Things I regret."

"Do you still love her?"

"Not anymore," I said, though the sadness in my voice surprised me. "Too many years, too much hurt, too little trust."

"Then why aren't you divorced?" she asked.

"I just... never got around to it. I didn't wanna stir things up or upset her. So I let it be."

"My parents won't be happy about this," she said quietly.

"I get that," I said. "And I'm sorry. I should've told you."

She looked at our hands, still joined. Then, gently, she pulled hers away. Not in anger—just enough to make the distance known. "I like you, Allen. I really do. I think I might even love you. But this—this changes things."

"I didn't mean to lie," I said quickly, my voice catching. "I just... when I'm with you, it feels like maybe there's still a chance for something good. Something hopeful."

Era's smile was faint, wistful. "Maybe there is," she whispered. "But if even a part of you is still tied to her... I can't be the one you lean on while you untangle it."

We stood in the corner of that crowded hall, the space between us growing wider than the room itself.

I got a letter from Era a few weeks later. She said she'd told her father everything—about me, about how she felt. Said she told him she had strong feelings for me. He didn't take it well.

She wrote that he just stood there for a long time, staring at the floor. Then finally, he shook his head and said, "This is not acceptable. How can you be involved with a married man? What are people going to say? This isn't right. I don't want you to ever see him again."

And she nodded and said, "All right. I can do that."

Then she told me they were moving to Denver after the holidays. Her father had been offered a better position with the Santa Fe—a desk job, steady pay. A big opportunity.

She ended the letter with: "I love you, and I will never forget you. But my father is right."

I stared at the letter for a long time, the words blurring. It felt like something inside me came loose. Like one more dream had slipped through my fingers. I'd only just begun to imagine a future with her—just started believing I might deserve it. And now, all of it was unraveling. I walked around for a few days with a hollow chest and a tightness in my throat I couldn't shake. It was the kind of heartbreak that made you wonder if you'd ever felt anything real to begin with.

But then, something changed.

A few days later, Mr. Leewright sent word that he wanted to speak with me himself—to look me in the eye, ask his own questions, and decide for himself if I was the kind of man his daughter could trust.

I didn't waste a minute. I saddled up Texas and rode alone straight back to Sulphur Springs as fast as he would take me.

The closer I got, the more the anxiety set in. My mouth was dry. My hands wouldn't stop sweating. I ran through answers in my head, but none of them felt good enough—not for a man like him. It felt like I was headed for a high stakes poker game with a seasoned gambler, and all I had was a pair of twos. But I knew I was a good man— sometimes foolish—but still a good man. And I loved his daughter more than anything in this world. I was willing to do whatever he asked to prove it to him.

We sat in the parlor of that tall Victorian house, lace curtains drawn against the low October sun. He was steady and exacting— the kind of man who'd built his life on grit and God and wasn't about to hand over his daughter's future without knowing exactly who he was dealing with.

He asked me hard things. About Eddie. About what had gone wrong. About whether I was still tied to that life. About my children. About what I truly hoped for. And whether I had the courage to see it through.

I didn't flinch. I told him the truth—that I wasn't proud of what had happened, but I was trying to set it right. That I would move forward with divorce proceedings as soon as I could.

He sat back in his chair, quiet for a long while, then said, "I can't give you my blessing. Not as things stand. But if you follow through— if you make yourself free and come to Denver—I'll help you find honest work. That much I can offer."

I thanked him. It was more grace than I'd expected.

Later that evening, I found Era waiting on the porch. Her arms were crossed, but her eyes were hopeful. I told her everything her father and I had discussed. She lit up—stepped forward and kissed me quick, like it had slipped out before she could stop it—then pulled back with pink cheeks and whispered, "I really shouldn't have done that."

I smiled. "But I'm glad you did."

I stayed in Sulphur Springs for a few more days. October had settled in by then—the air crisp, the leaves turning brittle gold and rust. We rode out past the edges of town, down quiet country roads lined with hayfields and sagging fences. She showed me where the wild blackberries used to grow, and I told her about the time Nancy threw a shoe crossing the Cimarron. The days were short, and the light turned golden early. We didn't talk much about the future.

But we didn't have to.

Winter came early that year. After I left Sulphur Springs, the days grew colder and quieter. I spent the next few months back in Fairfax, working odd jobs, keeping my head down, and trying to make sense of what came next. I thought often about the divorce—knew it had to happen, knew what I'd promised—but I couldn't bring myself to take that step. Not yet. Not without speaking to Eddie first. It didn't feel right to make something final without giving her the truth straight and plain, no matter how hard it might land. So I waited. I wrote to Era when I could, short letters full of ordinary things—frost spreading like lace across the barn windows, Jasper digging after moles behind the well, the quiet ache of a house that no longer felt like home. Her replies came steady as snowfall. By the time the crocuses began to push through the mud, I knew it was time.

In March, I packed my things—just the essentials. A few shirts, my bedroll, the worn Bible Ma had given me when I left home the first time, and the photograph of my children that John had sent me last spring. Jasper watched from the doorway, head tilted like he could sense change in the air.

Nancy was too stiff in her joints for a trip that long. I turned her out behind the barn, kissed her nose, and whispered goodbye. She nickered softly and walked off slow, her tail swishing like she understood. Jasper followed me to the gate, tail low. When I bent to hug him, he licked my cheek once, then padded over to Guy. Guy beamed and scratched behind his ears.

Jasper trotted after me to the wagon steps, then stopped short, watching with those knowing eyes. He didn't whine or fuss—just sat down, like he understood goodbye.

That morning, I loaded my bag in the family's old wagon. The boards creaked and the wheels groaned like always, but it held together. Ma packed a small basket of biscuits and jerky for the road. Nobody said much as we rode to the station—the air between us full of everything we couldn't bring ourselves to speak aloud.

When we arrived, I hugged Ma a little longer than I meant to, her cheek pressed against my collar, her arms still strong despite the years. "You write when you get there," she whispered. I nodded, not trusting myself to speak. Pa shook my hand the way he always did— firm, steady—but his eyes gave him away. "Make something of it,"

Pa said gruffly, his grip lingering just a moment longer than usual. "Don't waste what's ahead."

I slapped Erroll on the back and told him to keep his boots dry and his mouth cleaner than mine.

He just grinned. "You always were the sentimental one."

"Maybe," I said. "And that's why I'm leaving Texas with you. He's a good horse, and I expect you'll take care of him."

"That's mighty generous of you."

"Well, I probably won't need a horse in Denver."

"I thought every cowboy needed a good horse."

I shrugged, then turned to Guy. He was only half-grown but already taller than I'd been at his age.

"Take care of Jasper for me," I said. "He's family."

Guy nodded, serious as a preacher. "I will. I promise."

Jasper leaned into my side one last time, his body warm and steady against mine. I buried my hand in his fur, wishing I could explain. I scratched behind his ears and gave his ribs a final pat.

Then the train whistle blew. I picked up my bag, climbed aboard, and didn't look back.

Two days later the train hissed into Duff just past noon, wheels screeching against the rails like they didn't want to stop. I stepped down onto the platform with my bag slung over one shoulder, the spring sun warm on my face but doing little to ease the tightness in my chest. The town looked the same—same lousy saloon, same crooked hitching posts, same smell of hay and old wood smoke on the breeze. I walked slow, boots scuffing the dirt as I made my way toward the livery stable at the edge of town. My heart beat faster with every step.

I hadn't seen Eddie or the kids in two years, and I didn't know what kind of welcome I'd get. But I had promises to keep—and the kind of truths that couldn't be softened or put off any longer. The livery came into view, and before I could call out, William spotted me. He sprinted across the yard like a wild colt, arms flailing, straw stuck in his hair.

"Pa!" he yelled, crashing into me with a full-force hug. I dropped my bag and caught him mid-leap.

"Hey, buddy," I said, holding him tight. "You been behaving?"

"Nope," he said proudly.

George, nearly twelve, followed at a slower pace, taller now, with that serious look he'd picked up somewhere along the way. He gave me a solid handshake, eyes scanning my face like he was taking stock of the man who'd left and come back different.

"You look older," he said.

"You too," I said. "You shaving yet?"

"Almost."

John hung back a few steps, arms crossed, watching from under the brim of a too-big hat. I opened my arms to him, not sure what he'd do. After a pause, he came in for a quick, tight hug—then backed away just as fast.

I let the moment settle, stepping back to look at them—my boys. Taller, tougher, older than they had any right to be. My chest ached with both pride and regret.

We sat down on a bale of hay and ate cold meat sandwiches that Eddie had made for us. Nobody said much at first. William talked with his mouth full. George asked what books I'd read lately. John just watched, chewing slow, eyes flicking between me and the barn door like he wasn't sure how long I'd stay.

Then we cut across the pasture behind the livery and spotted an old tin can half-buried in the grass. George picked it up and tossed it in the air once. "Reckon you still got your aim?" he asked, a challenge in his voice.

"Reckon I might," I said.

So we lined up bottles and cans on a split-rail fence and took turns plinking them with John's .22. The sound of metal ringing out across the field brought the younger two to life—William bouncing on his heels every time he hit something, John squinting down the barrel like a soldier on patrol. George stood back at first, arms crossed, then stepped up and shattered the last bottle with one clean shot.

"That's my boy," I said.

They beamed. All three of them. And for a moment, it didn't matter how many miles or months had come between us. We were just a father and his sons, together in the sun, doing something simple and good.

We walked back slow, the light turning amber as it filtered through the cottonwoods. The boys carried the .22 between them, still arguing good-naturedly about who was the better shot. I let them talk, hanging back just a little, trying to memorize the way their voices rose and fell—their laughter, the way William's arms swung too wide when he walked, the quiet confidence in John's stride.

At the edge of town, Fern came into my thoughts—small and pink-cheeked, barely able to speak the last time I held her. I wondered if she'd remember me at all. If one day she'd look up and ask Eddie where I'd gone. The thought twisted something in my chest. She had turned five already, growing up while I'd been trying to put the pieces of my life back together. I'd missed most of her life—and was about to miss even more.

We stopped in front of the livery, the warmth of the afternoon already starting to fade. I dropped my bag in the dust and turned to the boys.

"I've gotta head back to the station soon," I said. "Train doesn't wait."

George nodded, jaw tight. He stuck out his hand again, and I shook it firm.

"You'll write, right?" he asked.

"I promise," I said.

John gave me a stiff nod, same as before, but this time his eyes lingered on mine a little longer. I put a hand on his shoulder.

William blinked up at me. "Will you be back for my birthday?"

I swallowed hard. "I'll try, bud. I'll sure try."

He leaned in and hugged me again, tighter this time. I held him close, then let go before it broke me.

"I'm proud of you," I said, looking at all three of them. "Each of you."

They didn't say much. Just nodded, shuffled their boots, looked off toward the horizon like they didn't want to watch me walk away.

"But now I need to talk to your mother," I said.

I looked over toward the livery stable, and there was Eddie—leaning against the door, arms folded, her scowl cautious, like she wasn't sure whether to brace for a lie or a goodbye.

"Can we talk?" I asked, my voice low, uncertain.

She didn't answer right away. Just turned her head, eyes fixed on something far beyond me. "No," she said finally.

My mouth went dry. I shifted my weight, thumb hooked in my belt like it might anchor me. "We need to," I said, though the words felt small and clumsy in my mouth. I wasn't sure where to begin—wasn't sure if anything I could say would matter.

"Why would I want to talk to you after the way you treated me last time you were in town?"

"That was two years ago."

"It feels like yesterday. If Sheriff O'Brien hadn't stepped in..."

"I know," I said. "I was wrong. I lost control."

She looked at me with something colder than anger. "So if you did it once, how do I know you won't do it again?"

"I don't want to fight."

"Then what do you want?"

I took a breath. "A divorce."

She laughed—short, bitter. "Is that all?"

"I didn't want to hurt you any more than I already have."

"Do I look that fragile to you?"

"No," I said quietly. "You never did." I wanted to also tell her she was the strongest person I'd ever known. But the look in her eyes stopped me. She wasn't asking for comfort—she was asking for honesty.

She looked down, then back at me. "What else?"

"I want to see my children."

She crossed her arms. "And how's that going to happen?"

"I'm moving to Denver and I figured we could work something out."

"Denver is a long way from Duff."

"It's closer than Oklahoma."

"Still four hundred miles away."

I looked down. "I'm sorry it didn't work out."

"It wasn't all your fault," she said. "But we had some good times."

"We did."

She hesitated, then exhaled through her nose, shoulders sagging just slightly. "Draw up the papers," she said. "I'll sign."

She turned without another word. A breeze caught the edge of her dress, lifting it just slightly, then letting it fall. I watched her disappear into the stable's shadow, and the ache behind my ribs bloomed sharp. It wasn't how I'd hoped things would end—but maybe it was the only way they could. I wiped my eyes on my sleeve and climbed aboard the westbound train for Denver.

This new beginning filled me with excitement, but it came with a cost. It wasn't the fresh start that hurt—it was everything I had to leave behind to reach it. Bittersweet, I guess. But that's the only kind of freedom I've ever earned.

Still, as the train pulled into Denver, something stirred in me— nerves, hope, even a flicker of wonder I thought I'd lost. Maybe it was foolish, but I couldn't shake the sense that this city held the next chapter I'd been chasing all along. Whatever waited for me there, I knew I was stepping into it with eyes wide open.

I stepped off with a suitcase in my hand and the weight of it all on my shoulders. It was the biggest place I'd ever seen—streetcars rattling by, smoke drifting over red-brick rooftops, saloons pressed up against opera houses. You could catch a symphony at the Tabor Grand and lose your boots outside a brothel two blocks away. A mix of grit and polish—just like me, I supposed. Worn by hardship, still trying to stand tall. Still believing, somehow, in something finer.

I rented a room in a narrow boarding house on Curtis Street. Started work as a brakeman for the railroad the following Monday. It was dangerous work—coupling cars, riding high, watching for signals—but the pay was the best I'd ever had.

As soon as I was settled, I hired a lawyer. Papers went out the next week. Eddie signed and sent them back without a word. By the end of April, I was a divorced man.

Era was more excited than I'd ever seen her. I took her to the city park one warm Sunday, and we sat on a bench beneath a cottonwood just beginning to bud. At thirty-three, I wasn't the boy who'd ridden away from home under a flower moon with cornbread in his saddlebags and nothing to lose. I'd lost things now. But I still had enough hope left to ask the question anyway.

"Will you marry me?" I asked, heart thudding like it had in Sulphur Springs that first night.

She didn't say anything at first. Just reached out and took my hand. Her fingers were cool and steady, but her thumb brushed mine like she'd already made up her mind. The city buzzed around us, but in that moment, everything else went quiet. I held my breath, waiting for the world to turn on me again.

Then she smiled. "Yes." She squeezed my hand, and for the first time in years, I believed in second chances.

MID-DAY

(1911–1925)

ERA

December Twenty-Ninth

A Hard Blizzard

The White Plague

Another Beginning

The Better Man

A Ranch in Ruckles

A Man Does What He Must

It's Just Fifteen Miles

A Little Cough

Every Sunday

A Plain Wooden Cross

DECEMBER TWENTY-NINTH

Mr. Leewright didn't like me. Oh, he was kind—generous, even—and carried himself like a gentleman ought to. But he didn't like me. Not for his daughter. Not one bit.

He never said so outright. That would've been too crude, too inelegant for a man like him. But I saw it in the way his lips stayed tight when I entered a room. In how he looked past me like I wasn't even there. And when he did speak, it was cold and clipped, like we were discussing cattle futures or the cost of freight—never feelings, never family.

But I didn't care, not at first. I was in love—madly, completely. So was Era. We wanted to get married right away, to seal it up quick and proper before anything could go wrong. We didn't want to miss one minute of a marriage we knew would be as beautiful as a sunset over the mountains west of Denver. But that's not how it worked out.

Mr. Leewright was a good man, reminded me a lot of Mr. Rhodes back on the JR Bar Ranch. And he loved his two daughters more than life itself—I'd wager he'd take a bullet for either one. Era was the older of the two and was getting past what most folks called marrying age. Esther was only sixteen, but looked and carried herself older than that. The family was close knit, and neither girl would've done anything to defy or disappoint their daddy.

The Leewrights had high expectations—prim and proper ones. No eloping in the night, no hasty promises under starlight, no ordinary wedding. They wanted a church, a dress, a gathering of folks with polished shoes and upright manners. And more than that, they wanted assurance. Her father, especially.

To them, I was a risk. A rambling cowboy with a past and too little to show for it. They didn't believe I'd follow through on the divorce. Didn't think I'd last long in a city job or make a steady life of anything. I respected Mr. Leewright. But I couldn't help wondering if he'd ever believe I was truly good enough for his daughter.

He was a railroad man to his bones—strict, precise, obsessed with timetables and deadlines. Everything in his world ran on the click of gears and the whistle of on-time departures. He ironed his shirts with military corners and aligned the silverware just so at supper. Era told me he once fired a man for being two minutes late.

No surprise he looked at me and saw delay, derailment, disaster. But he also saw how damn stubborn I was. I think that deep down he truly respected me for that.

One morning I received a note that I was to meet him at 10:45am. And you can be assured that I was plenty early. It was a bright spring day, blue sky outside his office window at the railyard. He was dressed to the nines in a gray European-cut suit and a red silk tie. His mustache was neatly trimmed, the ends twisted and waxed. The room smelled of his English Lavender cologne—clean and manly. I came in wearing my best shirt, boots polished near clean. He didn't ask me to sit. Just looked me over like a man sizing up a broken plow he didn't trust to cut a straight furrow on level ground.

"If you are serious about marrying my daughter, you need to prove it. I've already got you a job with the Santa Fe—no problem there. But you'd better be ready to meet my other conditions. Four of them. No excuses. No exceptions."

I nodded, caught between fear and excitement. Truth be told I'd have done just about anything that man asked me to do. Then he laid out his terms—clear as daylight and solid as a fence post.

I had to be divorced for a full year.

I had to work for the railroad for eighteen months straight.

I had to have five hundred dollars in an account at First National Bank.

And I had to swear—plain and clear—that Era would be my first priority from that day forward.

He didn't raise his voice. Didn't threaten. Just laid it all out and said, "If you haven't met these conditions by the last day of 1912, you'll return to Fairfax and never speak to my daughter again. Do you understand?"

My throat felt dry as bone. I wanted to say something—anything— but all I could manage was, "Yes, sir."

He frowned. "Let's see if you're up to this."

That was it. No handshake. No farewell. Just the challenge, handed over like a rusted set of keys.

I walked out of that office with my boots heavy and my chest burning. I wasn't mad. I knew he was doing what he thought was right. But I also knew he was dead wrong about me. I'd been a lot of things in my life, but I wasn't a liar. And I wasn't a quitter. So I went to work.

The months that followed were hard. Brakeman work was no easy thing—long hours, dangerous climbs, freezing nights riding atop freight cars in the high mountain passes. I saw men lose fingers, legs, even their lives. But I kept showing up. I cashed every paycheck, sent a little home to Ma and Pa, and stashed the rest at First National Bank.

I counted the months on a folded piece of paper tucked in my pocket. Drew a line through each milestone as I hit it. Twelve months divorced. Eighteen on the job. Five hundred dollars earned by sweat and steel. And through it all, I saw Era every Sunday for three hours— never a minute more.

We met in the Leewright parlor, drinking tea and reading books. If the weather was right, we walked the garden—roses, poppies, hollyhocks when in bloom. I lived for those visits. And in the days between, we wrote letters—dozens of them—full of love and dreams for the life ahead. We were wildly romantic.

When November of 1912 rolled around, I'd met every term he'd laid down. I was excited—so was Era. She met me outside the depot one evening, her whole body trembling as she pressed herself against me. "We're finally getting married," she said, eyes shining brighter than I'd ever seen.

That night, her mother hugged me so hard I nearly lost my breath. And Mr. Leewright? He gave me a single nod. But that was all I needed. He was a man of his word. And he kept it—even if it broke his heart to do so.

Era and her mother got straight to planning. Even her younger sister got involved. Cake tastings, fabric swatches, whispered talk of flowers and songs. I stood back and watched it all unfold. I didn't care about any of that. All I cared about was the smile on Era's face and the quiet pride rising in my chest. I'd earned her hand the hard way. And I wasn't letting go.

It was the week after Christmas, and Denver still shimmered with leftover magic. Wreaths clung to doors, lamplight flickered through frost-bitten windows, and the air smelled of pine, coal smoke, and the last crumbs of holiday cheer. The streets had quieted—gifts unwrapped, guests gone home, the city settling into that soft, slow breath before the new year. But not for us. We were counting down to something more.

We got married on a Sunday afternoon, four days after Christmas in a small church on the edge of town. It wasn't grand—just a simple white building with fog on the windows and a potbelly stove glowing in the corner—but it was proper, and it was ours.

Era's mother had hoped for something elegant—satin gloves, pressed flowers, a string quartet. Her father wanted his daughter happy, though he never did look me straight in the eye that morning. Era and I just wanted to be married. She looked beautiful that day— soft and certain in her quiet way.

She wore a long-sleeved ivory gown, modest and well-made, with a high collar and a row of small pearl buttons down the back. Her hair was swept back with a silver comb that once belonged to her grandmother—engraved with tiny wildflowers, worn smooth at the edges from special occasions. Her cheeks were pink from the cold, her hands like ice in mine—but her eyes didn't waver. They held no hesitation, only trust. I met them knowing I would never want to hurt her or let her down.

Esther stood beside her sister at the front of the church, holding a small bouquet of roses and baby breath. She looked up to Era like little sisters do—with wide eyes, quiet awe, and the hope that someday she might be a bride that looked just as beautiful. She did everything she could to help that day—brushing the snow from Era's shoulders, adjusting the silver comb in her hair, whispering something sweet that made her sister laugh—just the two of them for a moment, as if no one else was there.

But I was there, smiling with the two of them. When the minister asked if I took her to be my wife, I said 'I do' a little too loud—like those words had been echoing in my chest since the moment I met her.

There was a quiet stillness after that—like even the cold outside had paused to listen. I looked at her and she looked at me, and for just a second, the whole world felt sacred and secure—like everything was just the way it ought to be. We kissed once—soft and sure—and the handful of folks there clapped loud like they'd been waiting for it all winter.

It wasn't the wedding her parents had pictured. No grand hall, no china or white lace. But it was ours—humble and quiet and true. Watching her laugh, watching her shoulders ease like she'd finally stopped bracing for something, I knew we were exactly where we were meant to be. And in that small warmth, in the hush between snowflakes, it felt clear as day—we'd done something good.

None of my family could come. Too far, too cold, too close to the holiday. But Pa sent a letter, folded sharp and neat: *Make her laugh. Say what you mean. Don't run when it gets hard.* Ma tucked a handkerchief inside, along with a sprig of dried lavender. I kept both in my coat pocket that day, held close as a reminder of home.

Afterward, we all squeezed into the kitchen of her parents. The cook's niece had baked a spice cake, and someone passed around mugs of warm cider. Era and I stood near the stove, our fingers laced together, watching snow slide down the windowpanes. She leaned into me like she'd found a place to rest, and I couldn't stop smiling.

The days that followed felt like a dream we didn't dare speak aloud, afraid it might vanish if we named it. We shared everything—coffee in the mornings, stories at night, quiet smiles passed across the supper table like secrets. Some nights, I'd catch her watching me over the rim of her cup, her eyes half-curious, half-smiling, and I'd feel more grateful than I deserved. Even the city, so big and strange when I'd first arrived, seemed to soften around us. I'd come home to her every evening with the scent of smoke on my coat and her arms ready to wrap around me. We both worked hard—Era at the telephone exchange and me for the Santa Fe. We didn't have much, but we had each other—and in those first weeks, it felt like more than enough.

But looking back, there was a hint of restlessness, not in her, but in me. It was a soft unraveling I couldn't yet feel, a shift I never saw coming.

I loved working for the Santa Fe. Living in Denver was better than I ever imagined. The whole city felt like it was breathing in time with the trains—more than a hundred rolling through each day from six different railroads. It was a transportation crossroads, sure—but for me, it was something more. Trains became my obsession. Every engine felt like a promise, whispering freedom and adventure. They weren't just massive machines—they were a way out, a way forward.

A straight line toward something better. A fellow brakeman once told me, "Endless rails, endless chances." I never forgot that.

A steam engine's faster than the fastest horse and ten times more forgiving than a saddle. Stronger than any bull I ever saw, and louder than a thunderstorm right overhead. It could cover two hundred miles in a day without lagging. I loved that chugging rhythm—the way the whole world rattled to life when the wheels caught the rail. Even the sulfur smoke seemed to carry a story—like the scent of something unstoppable carving its way through the world.

I used to tell Era that someday I wanted to ride all the way to the end of the line, buy a little land, and start over—no boss, no past, just wide-open sky. She'd always smile and nod, resting her head on my shoulder.

"Someday," she'd say.

And I believed her.

Life settled into a quiet rhythm after the wedding—morning coffee, work, supper, a deep sleep. Then we'd do it all again. It was steady. Almost too steady.

Several months after we got married, I was sittin' on a bench outside Union Station, coat collar turned up against the wind, watchin' the 4:15 disappear into the foothills. Smoke hung low over the tracks, and the air tasted like soot and iron. Folks hurried past with satchels and suitcases, eyes fixed on wherever they were headed. But I just sat there—still as a stone in winter.

Mr. Leewright must've known I was the restless sort, because before he gave us his blessing, he made me promise not to leave Denver for at least a year. Said Era needed stability. I gave him my word. But truth be told, I'd been countin' down the days ever since.

Funny thing is, five years ago I wouldn't have looked twice at a train. They were background noise back then—just something that cut across the edge of town when I was a boy. But somewhere along the way—after the cattle drives, the fights, the long nights in Butte after Eddie left with the kids and the house went quiet—I started to fall for 'em. Not just the sound or the size, but what they stood for. Trains don't get stuck. They're always moving. I reckon that's what I came to admire most.

I've sat on these benches a dozen times now, and it's always the same. That whistle cuts through the air, and something in me lifts. I find myself wonderin' about the people on board, and what they're runnin' to—or runnin' from. There's a kind of hope in that motion. A quiet promise that life keeps going.

So there I sat in Denver, watchin' the last car vanish into the haze. I didn't move for a long while. Just watched the smoke fade and the station settle. Part of me wanted to stay planted right there. The other part wanted to grab Era's hand, hop the next train, and ride 'til we ran out of track.

Later that night, I told her. She listened without interruptin', then took my hand and said, "I support your dreams—but remember your promise to my father. We must stay until January."

I smiled a little and shook my head. "No," I said. "We promised your father a year—that gives us until December twenty-ninth. Not a day more."

She chuckled and said, "We'll see."

I didn't press her. But I started watching the calendar like a man watches the sky for rain.

A HARD BLIZZARD

"I have a surprise," Era said one evening, her face glowing.

"I'm too tired for surprises." I sank into the kitchen chair and let out a long breath.

A few months earlier, we'd rented a small flat in Curtis Park—a second-story walk-up over a tailor's shop, just a half-hour walk from the train yard. The floors creaked with every step, and the radiator knocked like a tired ghost on cold nights. It wasn't much, but it was cozy and caught the morning light. Era had added her touches—lavender in the drawers, lace on the windows—and somehow, it felt like home.

"Ten-hour days in this cold are wearing me down." I rubbed my hands together, oil still sunk deep in the lines.

Era sat beside me and took my hands in hers. "And I appreciate every minute of it."

"Starting out on your own isn't easy," I said. "But you're working just as hard as I am."

"A telephone operator sits in a warm room connecting calls. It's not exactly backbreaking."

"So what's this surprise?" I leaned over and kissed her cheek.

She smiled. "You're going to be a father."

I blinked. "What? Are you sure?"

"Sure as frost in November."

I stared at her, the weight of it just starting to settle. "When are you due?"

"The doctor says we'd best have a cradle ready by early spring."

I sat there, not knowing what to say, staring at the wall behind her like it might give me an answer. My heart thudded slow and heavy, like a train easing into the station. A father. The word felt too big to speak out loud.

Era squeezed my hand, and I looked down to find her watching me—calm, steady. I saw the glow in her eyes, the hope in her smile, and I knew I should be glowing too. But I hadn't thought this far ahead. Not really. I wasn't sure how this fit into the shape of my dreams. She waited, saying nothing, letting me catch up. Letting it sink in—quiet and certain, like snowfall in the early dark.

I squeezed her hand back and said, "I suppose I'd better start building that cradle."

A month later, on Monday, December 1st, the snow started. It came slow at first, then heavier, then heavier still. By Friday, Denver was buried under nearly forty-six inches of wet, heavy snow—the kind that bent trees, collapsed rooftops, and soaked straight through your coat if you stayed out too long. Trains couldn't get in or out. Streetcars froze on their tracks. Wagons sat abandoned in the middle of the road, wheels buried up to the hubs. Life didn't just slow down—it screeched to a stop.

For a whole month, the city felt like it was holding its breath beneath a blanket of white. And in that stillness, Era and I hunkered down in our little flat above the tailor's shop, listening to the radiator knock and the wind rattle the windows. The pipes froze twice. We boiled water on the stove just to keep the air warm enough to breathe. I couldn't reach the yard—not even on foot. Era was less than a mile from the telephone exchange, but once lines iced up, the switchboard went quiet and there wasn't much reason to show up at all.

We spent our days bundled in layers, rationing coal and playing cards at the kitchen table. Era had just begun to show, and I worried every time she coughed from the cold, every time the wind howled louder than the night before. But she never complained. Just pulled my coat tighter around me when I came in from shoveling the stairwell and kissed my knuckles warm.

By the end of the second week, the snow had piled higher than the windowsills. The city started hauling it off by wagonload, dumping it anywhere there was space. Folks were going stir-crazy, but not us. I read *Riders of the Purple Sage*, *The Lonesome Trail*, and every *Wild West Weekly* I could get my hands on. Era, who wasn't quite the same kind of reader, worked through *Anne of Green Gables*, patched my clothes, knitted me a wool sweater, and baked a cake for us every Saturday.

We talked, too. Long talks about how a child would change everything, and what kind of future we wanted. That month was the first time since we'd married the year before that the world stood still long enough for us to simply be—no rushing, no scraping, no survival, just time. And in that stillness, something settled between us. Like the snow itself—falling slow and sure until it covered everything. This came to be called The Great Blizzard of 1913.

By the new year, we both knew Denver wasn't where we wanted to stay. The city was too cold, too busy, too full of smoke and noise and cars. It was a good place to begin—but not to grow roots or raise children. We were ready for something else. Something greener.

Soon, I was asking around about railroad jobs farther west. Within a week, I heard the Southern Pacific was hiring car inspectors in Eugene, Oregon. The work wasn't all that different from what I was doing, and the pay was about the same. Eugene was a small timber town with wooden sidewalks and about ten thousand people. A fraction the size of Denver, sure—but bigger than Fairfax. It sat right on the edge of wild country, and something about that felt right. I took the job on the spot. Two weeks later, we packed up and moved.

Era's mother was upset—didn't like the idea of her daughter moving so far away, especially so close to the baby's due date. If that wasn't enough, Esther went and muddied the waters even more. She turned twenty and suddenly she became as restless as me. Where the sisters had always done whatever their father had asked, Esther now saw his control as a lasso trying to limit her freedom. And when she saw open country ahead, she was hell-bent on riding into it.

When she learned we were bound for Oregon, she decided right then she was coming too. She loved her father, but no one was going to wrangle her to the ground. That was the last straw for their mother—losing one daughter was bad enough, but losing both to the same far off wilderness was more than she could bear. Her tears came like a torrent, like rain off a tin roof.

Her father didn't take it any better. He was as mad as a nest of hornets a greenhorn has used for target practice—but not at his daughters. He aimed every bit of that anger square at me. He said I was ungrateful for the job he'd given me at the Santa Fe. That stung. It wasn't true. I'd worked hard and kept my word. He also accused me of being untrustworthy for breaking my promise to stay in Denver a full year. But I'd stayed a year and two weeks. Still, none of that could dim what Era and I felt. We were genuinely excited for a fresh start. Just the two of us, and her younger sister, starting over on the edge of civilization, chasing something that might finally be ours.

After the move, I sent a letter to Ma and Pa to let them know where we'd landed. Told them Era was well and the baby was due in a few months. I kept it short—just the facts, mostly. Figured they'd be glad to hear we were starting over somewhere green, somewhere with rain and promise.

A few weeks later, their reply came—six pages thick, full of questions and worry. Ma was over the moon about the baby—hoping for a girl, praying for an easy birth. But beneath all that joy, I could feel the sting of disappointment in her words. Oregon was too far. Too far from Oklahoma, too far from them. They were scared they might never see us again.

They also filled me in on the boys.

Erroll had joined the Marines a year earlier and shipped out to the Philippines in May. Pa didn't say much—he never does—but Ma did. Said Pa shook Erroll's hand like he was sending off a soldier, not just his son. When the train pulled away, he didn't look back—just stood there, staring down the tracks like he could still see him. They're proud of him—so proud you could hear it in every word Ma wrote.

Guy was seventeen and helping Pa on the farm, but Ma said he had that restless pull in him. Said he paced the fencelines with that far-off look, like the prairie itself was whispering his name. Too much fire in his blood, just like I had. Pa was slowing down—more than he'd admit—and without Guy's help, he didn't know how much longer he could keep the place going. The sorghum fields didn't care if your back ached or your knees gave out. They needed tending, or they gave nothing in return.

It was a good letter. Full of love, but not sugarcoated. Just like Ma. Just like Pa. They missed me. And I missed them something fierce.

Then came the letter from Eddie.

I hadn't heard from her in over two and a half years—not since that last visit to Duff. George still wrote now and then—almost every month at first. But his letters had grown short and stiff. No more drawings, no questions, no little stories from the younger boys or Fern. Just the facts: school, chores, crops. Over time, it felt like I was more of a stranger than a father.

After we settled in Oregon, I sent Eddie a letter—just to update her. Told her I'd married Era, that we were expecting a baby, and that I missed the kids. Told her I still loved them. That I hoped to see them again as soon as I had the time and money.

Her reply came three weeks later.

I opened it at the table, not expecting much—maybe a word from George, maybe even a photograph. But the first sentence hit like a hammer.

She was furious about the wedding. Furious about the baby. Said I'd replaced them—her and the children—with some new life out west. Said I had no right to call myself their father. That I'd walked away, and I didn't get to come back to see them just because I felt like it. She didn't want to see me. The kids didn't want to see me. She asked why I couldn't just leave them be. Worst of all, she wrote that she'd do everything in her power to make sure I never laid eyes on them again.

I must've read that line a dozen times, hoping I'd misread it. My hands were shaking. The page fluttered in my grip like it might fly away. Tears came, same as when a west wind throws dust in your eyes. I stood there frozen, the whole room too quiet. I didn't know what to say. I didn't even know how to breathe.

Era came up behind me and laid a hand on my shoulder. Asked what it was. I couldn't answer. Not right away. I just handed her the letter and stared at the wall like it might give me something— an answer, a way out. She read it slowly, her eyes narrowing, then softening. When she finished, she set it on the table, turned to me, and wrapped her arms around my chest like she could hold all the broken pieces together. I let my head fall to her shoulder and closed my eyes. The wind beat against the window. The silence wrapped around us.

There were no words that could fix it. Just the truth—quiet, awful—that something had torn wide open again. And this time, I didn't know how to patch it. It reminded me, all over again, how different Era was from Eddie.

Eddie was like wildfire—quick to laugh, quick to rage, her eyes always sparking with something you couldn't quite catch. She burned hot and bright, consuming everything in her path. Being with her felt like running full gallop—thrilling, dangerous, and impossible to hold for long. She could be sweet as honey one minute and cut you to the bone the next. Her love had sharp edges, and she never tried to soften them. You either took her as she came, or not at all. She lived for the fire—for the feeling. And when that feeling faded, so did she.

But Era—Era was like cool water after a long ride. The kind that seeps into your bones and washes off the dust. She reminded me of the parts of myself I'd long forgotten: patience, gentleness, hope. She didn't arrive with fanfare or fireworks. Just a quiet steadiness. Like shade at midday. Like home after a hard trail. When she was near, my shoulders dropped. My breath came easier. And for the first time in a long while, I believed my dreams had a place to land.

That night, after Era had gone to bed, I sat alone at the kitchen table with a blank sheet of paper and Eddie's letter beside me. The lamp glowed softly, casting yellow shadows across the page. I picked up the pen half a dozen times, only to set it down again.

What could I say? "I'm sorry" felt too small. Telling her I still loved the kids felt like shouting into the wind. I'd already said it a hundred times. And she didn't believe me. Maybe she never would.

I scratched out a line. Rewrote it. Tore the page in half. Tried again. "Dear Eddie," I wrote—and sat there staring at it like it might finish itself. But nothing came. Just a hollow ache behind my ribs and the weight of everything I couldn't undo.

I didn't know how to fight her anger without making it worse. Didn't know how to prove I still deserved to be their father—not with words. And I sure as hell didn't know how to live with the thought that I might never see them again.

Eventually, I folded the blank page, slid it into an envelope, and tucked it in the drawer. Not mailed. Not even sealed. Just there.

I thought of Era sleeping in the other room, the soft rise and fall of her breath. I blew out the lamp and stood there in the dark, listening to the house settle—trying not to think of George, or John, or William, or Fern.

But I did. I always did.

THE WHITE PLAGUE

Eugene was a quiet, comfortable town, tucked between the Cascade Mountains and the Coast Range, about sixty miles from the Pacific. From the moment we arrived, Era and I felt like we belonged. The town rested beside the Willamette River, in a fertile valley along the Southern Pacific line that ran from Portland to San Francisco. It was wetter and warmer than Denver, and the frost didn't cling to the trees quite as long. There was a sense of wildness here, too—something untamed and hopeful—that matched exactly what we'd been looking for.

We lived in a boxy little house just two blocks from the depot—small and square, built from fir timber with a low-pitched roof and a lean-to kitchen out back. The whitewash was peeling from the siding, and the windows rattled whenever the freight trains thundered past, which they did day and night. A narrow porch faced the dirt road, sagging a little on one side, but still wide enough for two wooden chairs. The air was fresh, and the country around us all rough edges and a shifting sky. We'd sit out there for hours and watch the world go by.

Era worked to make it feel like home—lace curtains at the windows, rag rugs on the cold floorboards, a quilt over the bed that her grandmother had given her back in Sulphur Springs. She even hung little bundles of cinnamon and cloves from the rafters to soften the smell of soot and smoke.

By then, she was seven months along—uncomfortably big with the baby and moving slower every day. Money was tight, but we agreed she wouldn't work until after the baby came. I hated leaving her alone, but the trains didn't pause just because a baby was on its way. I worked ten-hour shifts, sometimes longer, inspecting couplings and brake lines in the cold damp mornings while the whistle echoed off the river. Most days I came home too tired to talk, with coal dust in my hair and grease deep in the lines of my hands. But Era always met me at the door, one hand on her back and the other offering me a hot cup of coffee or a plate of beans.

Sometimes, after dinner, we'd sit out on the porch—Era with her feet propped up and me with my boots off, both watching the sky change colors. She'd rest her hand on her belly and say, "Do you think he'll like the sound of trains?" I'd smile and nod. Truth was, I hoped he'd hear the same kind of music in it that I did—in the rumble, the smoke, the steel.

All went well those first two months out west. We were excited about the baby—truly excited. Era wouldn't stop talking about it, naming every flutter, every craving, every little hope for who the baby might become. I built a cradle out of pine and rubbed it smooth as satin. She set up a nursery in the back room, hanging little white curtains and folding tiny clothes into the drawers. Ma and Pa sent a baby gift—knitted booties and a quilted blanket that smelled like home.

The only difficulty was how much Era missed her mother. She talked about her constantly, especially their Saturdays at the Grand Atrium, where they'd sit over tea and talk about whatever women talk about—hopes, dresses, futures. They weren't just mother and daughter. They were each other's closest companion.

Florence Leewright was slender, with silver-streaked hair always pinned back and pale gray eyes that missed nothing. She moved with quiet grace and dressed with modest care. Everyone respected her. She worried about Era's tender heart—thought she was too impulsive, too dreamy, too quick to love. I always figured that's why Florence never fully took to me. She didn't think I was enough. And truth be told, I couldn't blame her. But Era adored her and admired everything about her. The bond between them ran deeper than most—steady, constant, unshakable.

Since Florence was so far away, at least there was Esther. At first, I wasn't too happy with her living with us. The house felt too small to share with another adult. But she landed a part-time job with telephone exchange, and that helped cover the rent. More than that, she was there for Era. With me working such long hours and her mother so far away, the two of them grew even closer. I'd smile each time I found them leaning over the kitchen table, heads bent together, giggling over some old childhood story from Texas. Or shuffling cards, teasing each other like only sisters can. They were good for each other, and Esther eased my guilt about not being there for Era myself.

When I stepped through the gate on a blustery March afternoon, I saw Esther standing on the porch, wringing her hands. "She's been calling for you," she said, her voice tight. "The midwife's already here."

I hurried past her into the house, the sky outside hanging low and gray—the kind of gray that seeps into a man's bones. The wind slammed the door behind me, rattling the thin walls. Era's groans rolled through the rooms—raw, relentless, the sound of someone fighting with everything they've got.

The midwife met me in the hallway. "She needs you," she said.

I rushed to the bedroom. Era was half-sitting against the pillows, her skin slick with sweat, eyes half-closed and glassy. She reached for me without a word, her hand trembling in mine. I wiped her brow and tried to steady my voice.

"Push harder," the midwife urged.

Moments later, our child was born—a tiny boy. But something

was wrong. He was pale blue and limp in the midwife's hands. He didn't cry. He barely breathed. The midwife moved fast, clearing his nose and mouth, rubbing his chest. Still—nothing.

"What's wrong?" Era gasped. "Let me hold him."

"He needs air," the midwife said, but her face told another story.

By then Esther was trying to sit up, reaching out for her baby, her face ashen white. "Why isn't he crying?" she asked.

"He's struggling," the midwife said quietly.

I sat on the edge of her bed and wiped Era's brow. I gripped her hand, feeling useless—frozen in place while the midwife worked. I wanted to say something—to reassure her, to comfort her—but my well was dry. So we watched in silence as the midwife wrapped him in a blanket and rocked him gently. Still—no sound, no movement. No breath.

"I'm so sorry," she whispered.

"No!" Era cried, pushing herself up despite her pain. "Give him to me."

The midwife placed the tiny bundle in her arms. We all wept.

He was five pounds, one and a half feet long. We named him Daniel Sickles Stephens, after her great uncle—a Union general and hero at Gettysburg. It was the only gift we had left to give him.

Era broke completely. She cradled Daniel to her chest, rocking him and whispering words only she could hear. Esther knelt beside the bed, her hand on her sister's back, murmuring through her own tears. Era wouldn't let him go. Not for hours. Not until midnight, when the midwife finally took him away. She pressed his head to her cheek like she could will him to stay. Her arms trembled, but she wouldn't loosen her grip. And all I could do was watch.

Era collapsed back against the pillows, empty and silent. Her skin was pale, her lips cracked, dark circles etched deep beneath her eyes. Her tangled hair framed her face like a shroud. When she looked at me, it was like staring through fogged glass—her grey eyes vacant, unreachable.

She didn't eat. She didn't speak. She didn't move. For the next week, she lay in bed, curled in on herself like a shadow. Here, but not. Alive, but barely.

She needed me—to hold her, to grieve with her, to keep her tethered to this world. But I wasn't there. I couldn't be. I tried like hell, but I just couldn't. I hated myself for letting her down. I turned inward and disappeared. I told myself I was giving her space. That she needed quiet. But the truth was, I couldn't even look at her without breaking. I failed her. I left her alone in the dark with her pain, while I lost myself in mine. I worked. I drank. I slept. And I drank too much.

Every day after my shift, I stopped at the Corner Saloon and stayed until they closed. I didn't want to think, so I drank. I didn't want to feel, so I drank. I didn't want to go home to silence and sorrow—so I stayed longer, and drank even more. But the bottle didn't help. It just numbed me enough to get through one more night.

I wanted to be the man she needed. But the hurt was too raw. Too familiar. It tore open the same wound Robert had left behind—and I couldn't face it. Not again. Not so soon. Robert's death was ten years back and 700 miles away in Kalispell. But it might as well have been yesterday. A hurt will take a man down, just as certain as a slug to the gut—don't matter if it happened today or way back when.

Since I wouldn't speak, and I wouldn't stay, she called her mother.

A week later, Florence arrived in Eugene to be with her daughter. She'd taken the three-day train trip without hesitation the moment she heard what had happened. She could feel Era's pain—her devastation—and was willing to do anything to help her through the loss. Florence was determined to be strong, but the journey had taken a toll. She'd spent most of it seated beside an older woman with a severe cold, coughing and choking for hours on end. When we met Florence at the station, she didn't look well. Her face was pale, her body slumped with fatigue, and she was burning with fever.

Florence had always been strong and healthy, but ever since moving to Denver three years earlier, she'd struggled with stomach problems. She'd lost twenty pounds, suffered from severe cramps in her middle, and didn't have any energy. It worried her, but she never let it slow her down—especially not when her daughter needed her.

When I drove the sisters to the train station. Era burst into tears the moment she saw her. She clung to her mother like she was the only thing left keeping her upright.

But over the next few days, Florence got worse. She coughed constantly during the day, and by night she was drenched in sweat, gasping for breath. Within days, she couldn't get out of bed. The doctor came and examined her. "She needs rest, fresh air, milk, and dandelion tea," he said.

Esther and Era did everything they could, but nothing helped.

"She has galloping consumption," the doctor told us.

"What's that?" I asked.

"Tuberculosis. A fast-acting form. Many call it the White Plague."

"There must be something else we can do."

"Sometimes cod liver oil and turpentine can slow it down."

"We've already tried that."

He shook his head. "I'm sorry. All you can do now is make her comfortable and say your goodbyes."

Soon she was coughing up blood, drifting in and out of consciousness. Her strength slipped away little by little.

Three days after she arrived, she gripped my hand and whispered, "You'd better stop drinking. And take care of Era. She needs you."

"I promise," I said.

Her daughters surrounded her—holding her hand, praying, telling her how much they loved her, how they needed her, how they couldn't live without her.

"I'm so cold," Florence said.

They piled thick wool blankets on her while I fed more wood into the stove. But she still shivered, and the chills only grew worse.

"Please, Mother..." Era's voice trailed off, not knowing how to finish.

I stood there feeling as helpless as a barn kitten caught in a coyote's teeth. Florence was dying. Era was crying. Esther pressed dandelion tea to her mother's lips, but nothing helped.

Then Florence coughed up blood. Her head sank back into the pillow, her chest rising once...twice...and then not at all. The room went quiet except the stove's low crackle. She lay perfectly still. She didn't move. She didn't breathe.

We all knew it was over.

Era hid her face in her hands. "How could this happen? She was only forty-nine. One week I lost my son, the next my mother. What did I do to deserve this? I would've gladly given up my life to save theirs."

Era's heart broke in a way I'd never seen. She wept uncontrollably. But this time, I stayed by her side. I held her, grieved with her. I didn't disappear. I'd done that before—and I swore I would never do it again.

We shipped Florence's body back to Denver. Mr. Leewright met the train in a black coat and gloves, but all his usual polish was gone. His tie was crooked. His shoulders sagged. The man carved from order and precision had unraveled. Every trace of control he once wore like armor had slipped away.

Mr. Leewright had always seemed untouchable—tall and lean, hair silvering at the temples, his suits pressed and boots shining, a pocket watch ticking in his vest like the beat of a perfect schedule. But when Florence died, grief cracked him open. I saw the man underneath for the first time: not stern or distant, just broken. Tired. Heart-sick. Trying to hold it together for his daughters. But he couldn't.

We buried her in Fairmount beside the chapel, where the cottonwoods grow tall and quiet. As we stood there, Mr. Leewright placed a hand on my shoulder—just once, and only for a moment— but it was enough. A quiet kind of forgiveness passed between us.

Era made her decision that same week. "He needs me," she said. "He can't be alone in that house." Her voice was steady, but her hands trembled. I didn't argue. I knew she was right. And I knew what I had to do, even if it meant letting go of the quiet life we'd just begun to build in Eugene.

But Esther made up her mind to stay in Oregon. Heading to Denver felt like going backward. Her father and sister tried their best to talk her into moving, but Esther was stubborn as a freight train on an uphill grade. She loved them, sure enough, yet she figured her future was out west. She found herself some friends and a job, and even a fella—handsome, hard-working, a few years older. She wasn't sure if it would amount to anything. Still, she was hoping, willing to play the hand she'd been dealt and find out if the cards would fall her way.

I looked around our little house one last time—the lace curtains, the empty cradle, the porch where we'd watched the sky change. It hadn't been much, but it had been ours. A place we thought we might finally rest. But some things mattered more than rest. Three months after we arrived, we packed up again and headed east.

I found work with the Union Pacific. That made three railroads in four months. The hours were long, the pay steady. It wasn't what I wanted—but it didn't matter. What mattered was standing beside Era. This time, I wasn't running. I wasn't drifting. I was staying put, even if staying hurt.

The trains still howled through the night, but I wasn't chasing them anymore. I was chasing something better—love, and the kind of selflessness that puts someone else's needs before your own.

ANOTHER BEGINNING

Denver greeted us with wet streets, thawing gutters, and coal smoke hanging in the spring air. It wasn't the warmest welcome. The last of the snow melted into the city's cracks, and the train yards groaned back to life after a hard winter.

Era didn't say a word as we stepped off the platform. I could see the weight of it all in the way she held herself. There was a lot on her mind—but I knew she wasn't ready to talk about it, and I respected her too much to ask. She clutched our suitcase like it was the only thing keeping her upright—eyes fixed ahead, face pale from too many sleepless nights. Florence was gone. And with her went the light in Era's eyes—that bright, hopeful spark that made even hard days bearable.

The move hadn't been easy, but it mattered to Era—and that was enough to make it matter to me. I'd transferred from the Southern Pacific to the Union Pacific—still a car inspector, but now out of the Denver yard. The hours were steadier, the pay a little better, and for once I could come home to Era at a decent hour each night. It wasn't glamorous, but it was solid work, and it gave us something close to a rhythm again.

But the house on Logan Street felt empty. The silence that followed Florence's passing hung in every room, and even Era couldn't ignore the weight of it. Her father drifted through those rooms like a man clinging to routine while everything familiar slipped away.

We moved in—not just to keep him fed and organized, though

that was part of it. We did it because the house felt too lonely, too full of ghosts and echoes of better days. And Era couldn't bear the thought of him facing it alone.

It was a proud old home on a quiet stretch of Logan Street, just a few blocks from the golden dome of the Capitol. A three-story Queen Anne with a steep gabled roof, a rounded turret on the northeast corner, and a wide wraparound porch. The white railings had weathered, ivy curled up the brick unchecked, and the flower beds along the walkway had gone wild since the funeral.

Inside, the house continued to hold the weight of Florence's presence. Lace curtains hung crisp and white in the front windows. A china hutch stood untouched in the dining room, every dish exactly where she'd left it. But the rooms felt too still. The mantle clock ticked through the silence, keeping time for no one.

Mr. Leewright had taken to cold dinners in the study, papers scattered across the desk, his spectacles left askew. He moved through the house methodically, but untethered. Something in him had gone quiet—shut away—someplace even Era couldn't reach at first.

She put on a brave face, unpacked our things upstairs, and began filling the space with small signs of life—warm meals, fresh linens, daffodils on the dinner table, soft conversation over tea. It was no small thing. But it felt right.

One evening, not long after we'd settled in, I found Era sitting alone in her mother's sewing room. The door was half-closed, lamplight spilling into the hallway. I hadn't meant to intrude, but there she was—sitting calmly, hands folded neatly in her lap. The room hadn't changed. A half-finished quilt lay draped over the rocking chair, fabric spread smooth, needle still tucked in the edge like Florence might return at any moment to pick up where she left off. The air smelled faintly of lavender and starch—the way Florence always liked to keep it.

Era didn't turn when I stepped inside. She just looked at the wall, at a little frame holding a photograph of her mother in younger years—smiling beside a flowering dogwood, one hand shading her eyes from the sun. It had been taken in Sulphur Springs, in the garden behind their old house, where the dogwoods bloomed wild every spring and Florence used to hang laundry in the breeze. Era had once told me that was her favorite picture—the one where her mother looked most like herself.

"She used to sit right there," Era whispered, nodding toward the rocking chair. "Every afternoon after lunch. She'd hum old hymns, work her fingers raw piecing together scraps from dresses I'd outgrown. She said a good quilt tells a story."

I sat beside her on the edge of the bed—not touching her yet. Just listening.

"She never let anything fall apart," she said softly. "Not the hems, not the house... not any of us."

Her voice caught. She turned into my shoulder and let the tears come—quiet, steady, almost apologetic. I held her close and said nothing. There was nothing to say. Only the sound of the old house settling around us, and the slow creak of the wind nudging the shutters.

Looking back, I was surprised by how well that first year held together. My new job with the Unions Pacific suited me—I liked the rhythm of the Denver yard, the crisp mornings, the solid feel of honest work done right. Era found comfort in routine too. She lingered over breakfast with her father, strolled with him beneath the elms lining Logan Street, and rekindled old conversations by the parlor fire each evening. The flower beds that had once wilted with grief came alive under her care, spilling with marigolds, daisies, and snapdragons until the whole yard seemed to hum with color.

And as the days stretched out into something steady, I found myself growing close to Mr. Leewright in ways I hadn't expected. We weren't just sharing a roof—we were building a solid friendship, shaped by mutual respect and pleasant mornings that began to feel like ritual. We'd talk for hours. I'd tell him about cowboy life and he told me about his childhood in Indiana.

One Saturday in early autumn, I found him out on the porch with his sleeves rolled and a copy of *The Denver Republican* folded under one arm. A thin column of steam rose from the teacup beside him. He didn't say much when I sat down—just passed me a second mug and nodded toward the sunrise.

"Looks like the country's leaning toward Wilson again," he said, thumbing the edge of the paper. "Don't know if that'll be good for railroads or bad. Hard to tell anymore."

I sipped the tea and shrugged. "Long as they keep laying track and paying wages, I'll vote for whoever keeps the trains moving."

He gave a short, dry chuckle. "Practical. I like that."

A breeze stirred the ivy along the railing. We sat for a while without speaking, just watching the light change over the rooftops.

Eventually, he leaned back and crossed one ankle over his knee. "You still reading that Zane Grey book?"

"Finished it last week," I said. "Traded it for *The Virginian*. Figured it was about time I read the one everyone talks about."

Mr. Leewright nodded. "You do have a soft spot for cowboy novels."

"They're the best," I said, smiling.

"You ever miss those days out on the trail?"

I leaned back, watching a pair of sparrows dart through the ivy. "There's a wildness on the prairie—and a kind of peace too. Sitting on a horse with the wind in your face, the smell of sage all around— that's about as close to heaven as I've ever been."

"Sounds like you're a bit nostalgic?"

"Sometimes." I stared into the morning. "But it's a hard life. Cold mornings, long stretches without anyone to talk to but your horse, and nothing waiting for you at the end of the trail but more dust. I don't miss all that."

He nodded slowly. "The railroad can also be a hard life, in its own way."

"That's true. But I haven't been happier in years. There's something settled about this life—honest work, a warm house, Era waiting when the day is done. I never thought I'd get that."

"It's a good life," said Mr. Leewright. "Not always what I expected, not always happy, but it's still good."

"Yes, it is." I paused. "And Era's the best woman I ever met."

"I can't disagree with that." Mr. Leewright smiled, the lines at the corners of his eyes softening. "If her mother could see her now..." His voice caught just slightly, and he glanced toward the parlor where Florence's rocker sat by the window. "She'd be proud. So proud."

We talked a while longer—about business and politics, about the new electric streetcars being proposed for Capitol Hill, even about Florence. His voice softened when he spoke of her, and for once, the weight in his tone felt less like grief and more like memory.

When we finally went back inside, he clapped a hand on my shoulder—just once, firm and quick—and said, "I'm glad you're here, Allen."

It was the first time he'd ever said anything like that. And in that moment, it was all I needed.

By Christmas, Mr. Leewright was doing much better, and I was starting to feel restless. That first year had gone more smoothly than I ever could have expected. The grief was still there, of course, but the routines had softened its edges. Life had taken on a shape again. But, I couldn't shake the sense that the longer we stayed in that house, the more likely something might unravel.

That winter gave way to a cold, clear January when the idea first took shape—unexpected, but promising. We'd managed to save a fair bit over the past nine months, thanks to steady work and not paying rent. Mr. Leewright, feeling stronger and more grounded then he had in a long time, began talking about the future in a way he hadn't since Florence passed. One evening over supper, he said he'd been thinking about putting his money and his time into something we three could build together. Before long, the talk turned into a plan—buy a building, start a business—and he'd come in as a half owner.

I'll admit, the thought caught me off guard, but it set something in me to stirring. The more I turned it over, the more it gathered momentum, until I could see the whole thing in my mind—clear as a fresh trail in new fallen snow and just as irresistible.

The idea was simple: buy a property with ground-floor retail space, start a used furniture store, and live in the apartment above it. We'd call it North Side Furniture Exchange. Era would run the shop during the day while I worked at the train yard, and I'd help on the weekends. It was a way to build something of our own—something that felt a little more rooted than iron rails and open schedules.

The building we found was at 1503 Boulder Street, in the Lower Highlands neighborhood—about two miles northwest of Mr. Leewright's house. It was a sturdy, three-story brick structure built back in 1891, with a storefront below and apartments above. The streetcar ran right past it, through a neighborhood full of churches, schools, saloons, cafés, and small shops, surrounded by rows of Victorian homes. Most of the families were working class—Irish, Italian, German, English—many of them first- or second-generation immigrants. It was the kind of place where people knew their neighbors and watched out for each other.

Era and I were excited. For the first time, it felt like we were creating something truly our own. A home. A business. A future.

Yet, not everything came easy. Era had her heart set on starting a family again. She tried to hide it, but I could see it plain as day. Sometimes I'd find her sitting quietly in the garden at her father's house, or curled up alone in our old bedroom, tears on her cheeks. The memory of Daniel still haunted her. It haunted me too. It always would.

But she believed in this new beginning. She said it was the kind of place where a family could grow—where life might feel a little safer, a little more stable than what the railroad offered. And for the first time, I started to believe that too.

Setting up the store took more work than I'd expected. The space had good bones—wide front windows that let in morning light, a pressed-tin ceiling that echoed with every step, and oak floorboards worn smooth by decades of customers. But it needed cleaning, sanding, painting. The fixtures were outdated, and the back wall had a crack that let in cold air on windy days. I spent every spare hour after the train yard scraping, hauling, and fixing—sometimes until long after the streetcar stopped running. My hands were raw from sanding counters, my shoulders sore from moving armoires up narrow staircases. But I loved it.

There was something deeply satisfying about taking a place that had been half-forgotten and giving it new purpose. Mr. Leewright helped where he could—mostly with bookkeeping and haggling over inventory. He knew his numbers, and he knew how to deal with wholesalers who tried to push junk for too much coin.

Era handled the storefront design. She had a knack for arrangement—knew just how to group an oak dresser with a worn rocker and a mirror with beveled edges so it all looked like it belonged together. She hung lace curtains in the windows and placed a bowl of dried lavender on the counter. Said it smelled like comfort.

We opened North Side Furniture Exchange on the first Saturday in March of 1915. The bell above the door rang all morning. Locals wandered in out of curiosity at first, then came back with cash in hand. A schoolteacher bought a writing desk. A new couple picked out a dining set with mismatched chairs. People talked, lingered, smiled. It was modest, but it was ours.

Upstairs, the apartment was small—two rooms and a kitchen nook—but Era made it feel like home. She painted the bedroom walls a soft green and unpacked the quilt her mother had started but never finished. She folded it at the foot of the bed without a word.

At night, when the lamps were turned low and the street below had gone quiet, I'd find her standing by the window, one hand resting on the sill, watching the shadows of the trolley wires stretch across the rooftops. She didn't say much those first few weeks. She moved carefully, as if waiting for something to break.

One evening, I came in to find her sitting on the floor beside the crib we'd set up in the corner of the bedroom. She wasn't crying— not exactly. But her eyes were red, her hands clenched in her lap. "I don't know if I can do this again," she said without looking up. "I want to. More than anything. But I'm scared."

I sat beside her, rested my hand on her back. "You don't have to do it alone," I said.

She nodded, and for a long while we just sat there in the stillness, listening to the city breathe beneath us.

On the anniversary of Daniel's death, we received a letter from Ma and Pa. They usually wrote every month, and it was always Ma's handwriting on the page—neat, steady, and somehow full of warmth. She had a way of finding the silver lining in anything. As a kid, she used to tell me, "The worst storms water the best grass."
She offered her condolences first.

Time don't stop the ache—it just teaches you how to carry it quieter. I know he's been gone a year, but come this day, it still feels as raw as a new wound.

Then came the harder news.

We all thought Erroll was doing so well in the Marines. To us, he was a hero—serving in China, protecting American lives and property. But things haven't gone as we hoped.

Turns out he'd been in and out of trouble—nothing too violent, but definitely reckless. Drunk and disorderly. Street brawls. Skipping duty. Mouthing off to officers. And then there was something they called "the rickshaw incident." No one's said exactly what happened—just that he either stole one or wrecked it, and wound up in the brig. Sixteen charges in all. They held him at some military garrison in Peking for a month or two.

I know Erroll's a good man, but even the best of us can be dumb as a post and stubborn as an old mule.

Last January, they'd shipped him back to Mare Island, California. Word was he was looking at a dishonorable discharge—but we hadn't heard a thing from him in months. Then Ma added:

Your Pa's wearing thin, but Guy's been picking up the slack.

That was all she wrote about it. But I could feel the heaviness between the lines. I could see Ma pacing the kitchen, hands, twisting in her apron, praying for Erroll and worrying herself sick. I wished I could do something—anything—but I didn't have the first notion what.

I folded the letter and set it back in its envelope, but the words stayed. I couldn't shake them. Erroll had always been the bold one— quick with a joke, quicker with his fists. He'd fight anybody who looked at him sideways, but he'd also give you the shirt off his back if you needed it. When we were boys, he once stood up to a group of older kids picking on Guy, even though it meant getting a black eye and a bloody nose. That was Erroll. Wild, but loyal. Reckless, but full of heart.

I guess I thought the Marines would knock some sense into him. Give him purpose. Structure. Something to be proud of. And maybe it did, for a while. But now all I could picture was him pacing a cramped cell in Peking, knuckles scabbed, eyes hollow, stuck halfway between defiance and shame. I wanted to believe it was just a rough patch. A few bad decisions. But part of me knew better. The part that remembered the fights with Pa, the stolen bottle of whiskey, the nights he didn't come home until dawn. And still, he was my brother.

I thought about writing him—thought about it more than once— but I didn't know what I'd say. "I'm sorry"? "Get it together"? "We're pulling for you"? None of it felt like enough. And what if he didn't write back? So I didn't write. Not then.

Instead, I sat there by the window with the letter still warm in my hand, watching the city go about its business, wondering how many more chances a man like Erroll got.

Didn't hear much about Erroll for a while—just that he'd been discharged from the Marines and, somehow, all the charges had been dropped. I swear, that boy's got more lives than a jackrabbit in a coyote den. Ma said he'd settled in California, working on a horse ranch east of Fresno. Sounded like he was trying to follow in my boots, doing his best to be a cowboy for a change.

Then, out of the blue, I got an invitation in the mail. Erroll was getting married—June 10th, 1916, in Fresno, to a girl named Nellie Hagar. No note. No explanation. Just a neatly printed card with his name on it like nothing had ever gone sideways.

I wasn't sure how to feel about it—relieved, maybe. Surprised, definitely. But mostly, I hoped it meant he was turning a corner.

I set the invitation on the table and stared at it awhile. Part of me wanted to toss it in the drawer and forget about it. After everything that had happened—the brig, the silence, the shame he left behind—I didn't owe him anything. He hadn't written, hadn't apologized. Just disappeared into the smoke like he always did.

But he was my brother. Maybe not always reliable, maybe not always right, but blood all the same. And if this was him trying to turn things around, trying to start fresh, maybe he deserved someone in his corner when he said "I do."

I read the card again, just to make sure I hadn't missed anything, then slid it back into the envelope. I wasn't sure yet if I'd go. But I didn't throw it away either.

That had to count for something. We all needed another beginning. The good Lord had already given me my share of fresh starts—maybe this was his.

THE BETTER MAN

I was torn. Part of me didn't want to go to the wedding. I was still mad at Erroll—for what he'd done, for falling out of touch, for letting so much time pass without a word. But another part of me—the part that remembered those long rides to Sulphur Springs, driving cattle and swapping stories under the open sky—knew he was still my brother. And that still counted for something.

I had the store to run and a railroad job that didn't much care for time off. But in the end, I knew I'd regret it if I didn't go.

June marked a turning point for him—one of those rare moments when a man stands at the edge of the life he's been living and steps into something better. He'd been drifting for years, chasing work and outrunning trouble—though more than once, it managed to catch up with him. Now he was settling down, staking a claim on something that I would only hope would calm his restless streak. Getting married meant more than a ring and a promise—it meant putting down roots, facing the days ahead with someone special by his side. I knew what that had done for me, and I figured it might do the same for him—provided he let it.

So I set my mind on being there for my brother—standing beside him, shaking his hand, telling him I'd have his back, and warning him that he'd better treat his wife as good as Pa treated Ma. Mr. Leewright offered to watch the shop while we were gone. He even bought our train tickets, since we could ride the whole way on the Santa Fe. Three days of traveling west—just me, Era, and the steady rhythm of the iron wheels, the whistle's lonely cry, and plenty of time to think.

We pulled into Fresno under a sky already starting to bake. The platform shimmered with heat, and I spotted him right away—leaner than I remembered, but standing tall with his hands stuffed in his pockets. We both looked at each other, and for a second, neither of us spoke.

Then he grinned. "You look older."

"You look thinner," I said, shaking his hand firm and sure—the way a man does when he means it.

He nodded toward Era. "You must be the one that stole my brother's heart."

Era smiled. "And you must be the legendary Erroll."

"That's not always good," he said.

"So I've heard." She grinned.

"I'm trying to live that down," he said with a half-laugh, scratching the back of his neck. "Thanks for coming."

"We wouldn't have missed it," I said. "So, tell me about this girl you're ready to marry."

Before he could answer, a voice called out from behind him. "Erroll? You just gonna stand there all day?"

We turned to see her walking toward us—strawberry-blonde hair catching the light, a bunch of wildflowers in her hand. She was slender but strong, the kind of strength that comes from working under open skies. Sun had kissed her skin to a warm gold, and there was a bright energy in her step, halfway between a playful laugh and a birdsong riding the morning breeze. Her eyes—clear and lively— missed nothing, and her smile was quick and unguarded, bright enough to soften any edge. Even from a distance, she carried herself with the easy confidence of someone who knew where she stood in the world. As I watched her come closer, I figured right off this was just the sort of girl Erroll needed.

"This is Nellie," Erroll said, his voice quieting like a man who knew just how lucky he was. "Nellie Hagar."

She held out her hand. "You must be Allen. And you must be Era. I've heard so much about you both."

"All good, I hope," Era said, returning the handshake.

"Mostly," Nellie teased. "I'll be the judge of that."

She turned toward Erroll and tucked her hand into the crook of his arm like she belonged there.

He looked at me then, his voice lower. "If she'd met me two years ago, she wouldn't have given me a second look."

"Good thing you changed your ways," I said.

"I agree. And I'm sorry I lost contact with you."

"It's been a while."

"Not the most productive while. But when I met Nellie, things started to make sense. She might only be nineteen, but she's as level-headed as someone twice her age."

I nodded. "That was how old I was when I married Eddie."

And just like that, the years between us started to fade. Erroll was grinning ear to ear when he showed us the small ranch he'd bought just east of Clovis, ten miles outside Fresno. The land wasn't much—dusty pasture, neat rows of cotton and alfalfa, and a weathered barn that stood five times taller than the modest farmhouse—but it was his, and that made all the difference.

He raised and bred horses for farm work—strong Quarter Horses he sold to cotton and alfalfa growers across the valley. These weren't just for show. They worked hard, same as the man who raised them.

The place was already turning a profit, and you could see the pride in his eyes. He'd cleaned up since his Marine Corps days—no more drinking, no more brawling, no more run-ins with the law. He walked straighter now, spoke softer, listened more.

Ma and Pa were proud of the changes he'd made—said they hardly recognized the young man who used to come home with a busted lip and a chip on his shoulder. He wasn't chasing trouble anymore. He was building something. He looked like a man who'd figured out what mattered—and meant to hold onto it. That's why it cut a little deeper that they couldn't be here to see it for themselves—to watch him take this step and stand beside the woman he meant to spend his life with.

Pa hadn't been feeling well for a spell, and the trip clear across the country would've been too much for him. Guy was tied up in the middle of planting sorghum, and there's no walking away from that when the ground's ready. Ma didn't take to the idea of making the journey on her own—said it wasn't safe, and truth be told, she'd never been one to wander far without Pa by her side. So, for all their wanting to be here, it just wasn't in the cards. Erroll and Nellie were disappointed, and so was I—it had been five years since I'd seen them.

The wedding itself was simple but moving, held under a canopy of cottonwoods behind the farmhouse. Nellie wore a pale beige dress and carried a bunch of daisies tied with twine. Erroll stood tall in a borrowed suit, his hands shaking just enough to show how much the moment meant. When she reached him, he took her hands and didn't let go.

After the vows, Erroll kissed his bride like he knew he'd never do better. There wasn't music or dancing—just pie, strong coffee, and enough laughter to bring brothers back together. Folks lingered at the tables—trading stories, telling jokes, drinking whiskey, and singing old, cowboy songs. Now and then I'd catch Erroll looking at Nellie like he couldn't quite believe she was real, and her smiling back like there was magic in the air. I'll admit, it got to me—it was one of the sweetest sights I've ever laid eyes on.

We stayed one more night, talking late with them on the front porch as the lamps burned low and crickets filled the quiet between our words. Come morning, we packed our things and loaded up. Era and I had work waiting back in Denver, and the train didn't care about goodbyes. Erroll walked me to the train, his coat slung over one shoulder. The girls followed, lost in their own conversation. We stood beside the train for a moment, neither of us saying much. Then he reached out his hand.

"Let's not wait another five years," he said.

I shook it firm. "We won't. You write, I'll write back."

He nodded once. "Deal."

As the steam engine pulled away, I watched him standing beside Nellie on the platform, one hand raised in a quiet wave. He had his life, I had mine. But we'd promised—no more years lost to silence, no more letting the miles turn us into strangers. Not this time. Not again.

I wrote to Erroll almost every month, and he always replied within a few weeks. It felt good—like I finally had my brother back. Era and Nellie started writing too, sharing recipes, bits of news, and talk about families they aimed to have someday.

Six months after their wedding, just before Christmas, Era received another letter. But this time, her reaction was different. She sat at the table staring at the paper, unusually quiet.

"Are you alright?" I asked.

"I'm not sure," she whispered, wiping away a tear.

"What's wrong?"

"Nellie's with child. I should be so excited for her, but..." She paused and looked away. "It just reminds me of Daniel—and how much I want a family. What's wrong with me? Why can't I have a child?"

She'd tried to stay strong, but I could see it breaking through—the ache she didn't always say out loud. Some nights, I'd find her folding and refolding the same tiny blanket we'd once bought for Daniel. Other nights, she'd stand at the window, staring out like maybe something was supposed to arrive on the breeze. She never asked for sympathy, only silence. But I knew how badly she wanted what she couldn't have, and how every new life born to someone else only made the absence louder.

"Just be patient," I said gently. "We'll have children soon. And you'll be a wonderful mother."

"That's easy for you to say," she snapped. "You already have four."

"But I never get to see them." My voice dropped.

Era saw the darkness pass over me. She reached across the table and took my hand. "I'm sorry. I shouldn't have said that."

"But it's true. I miss them so much. George is seventeen now, and little Fern is almost eleven. The hardest part is knowing they've moved to New York. They're living with Eddie's parents."

I kept every letter George had ever sent—creased, smudged, and full of things he wasn't sure how to say. He always signed them "Your son, George Allen Stephens," like he was trying to remind himself of who he came from. I didn't know what Fern's voice sounded like anymore. I didn't know if John was still a good shot, or if William remembered the songs I used to sing to put him to sleep. They were drifting further from me with each season, like shadows stretching across a prairie sunset—still there, but out of reach.

"At least George still writes to you." Era interrupted my thoughts.

"But only every six months," I said, shaking my head.

"Maybe someday they can visit us in Denver. Or we can take the train to New York."

"Even if we went all that way, Eddie would probably refuse to let us see them."

"But they're your children too."

"Eddie's wild and stubborn. Once she sets her mind on something, there's no changing it."

Four months later, in April, Erroll and Nellie welcomed a healthy baby boy—Erroll Jr. I could hear the smile in my brother's voice clear through the telephone line, bright as a spring morning. I'd never known him to sound so proud, so tender, and so full of life—and it was the first time I'd ever gotten a telephone call from him. Era knitted a pair of tiny socks and tucked them into a care package with soft blankets, sweet-smelling soaps, and a note that read, "Hold him close for me." We were over the moon for the new parents, and I found myself grinning for the rest of the day.

The months drifted by, gentle and steady as a river current. I kept at my work on the railroad while Era and I poured our hearts into the furniture store, watching it grow busier with each passing week. Sundays belonged to Mr. Leewright's dinner table, where Era would slip her hand into mine under the linen as conversation and laughter flowed. That summer, we stole away for a week, riding Appaloosas side by side up Boulder Canyon to Cripple Creek, the mountain air cool on our faces. At night, we camped under an endless stretch of silver stars, her head resting against my shoulder while I told her stories of prairie nights and wide-open country. One afternoon, out at the great red sandstone monoliths, I kissed her with the wind in our hair and the sun warm on our backs, thinking I'd never known a moment more perfect. She was everything I'd ever wanted, and I thanked the good Lord—right there and then—that I'd been lucky enough to stumble into Sulphur Springs when I did.

In April and May of 1918, we started hearing whispers of a fast-spreading illness overseas. They were calling it the three-day flu, and it was tearing through Europe with symptoms of fever, headache, and fatigue. It still felt far away. And nothing to worry about.

By midsummer, there were rumors it had reached Boston. Then Chicago. A few weeks later, Denver saw its first case. From there, it spread like wildfire. They were calling it the Spanish Flu now—and millions had already died.

On the first Sunday of October, the mayor closed all schools, churches, theaters, and public halls. People were urged to stay home and avoid contact. If you had to ride the train or streetcar, you were required to wear a face mask. The whole city seemed to fall silent. We closed the store for a week—not that it mattered since we didn't have any customers. The streets lay empty, quiet as a graveyard at midnight.

When we did see someone, the flu was all anyone talked about. There had already been five million deaths around the world. The newspapers reported that in October alone, 200,000 people in the U.S. had died. They warned it was just the beginning. I didn't believe them—but they were right.

By November, folks were calling the Spanish flu an epidemic and I was beginning to feel troubled. This was spreading faster and taking more lives than I ever thought possible. Sleep was hard to come by, and when it did, the nightmares came with it. Still, I had no notion that November was fixin' to be the worst month of my life.

Since Pa had been feeling strong, he and Ma took the train across the country to Fresno to visit Erroll and Nellie. They were excited to finally see little Erroll Jr.—now a toddler—and to lend Nellie a hand, who was due with her second child. But when they arrived, Erroll was already sick, showing every sign of the flu. On Wednesday, he was burning with fever. Ma laid cool cloths across his forehead, hoping to draw it down. On Thursday, he slipped into silence, non-responsive. Still, Ma and Pa stayed close, praying, talking, doing anything to bring him back. By Thursday, he was gone.

Nellie was beside herself, her grief spilling out in waves that none of us could stop. She clutched at Erroll's still body, begging him to wake, begging him not to leave her with a child at her knee and another on the way. Her cries rattled the windows and cut through the house like a winter storm that wouldn't let up. She tore at her hair, called his name over and over until her voice was raw, then collapsed against Ma's shoulder, trembling and gasping for breath. Nothing could console her. Not Ma's gentle words, not Pa's quiet prayers, not the thought of the baby she carried. She rocked back and forth on the edge of the bed, holding onto Erroll's hand long after it had grown cold, as if she could pull life back into him with sheer will.

Then Ma and Pa both came down with the Spanish flu. Terribly ill. It took the strength clean out of them so neither could rise from bed. Nellie, heavy with child and worn thin from grief, did what she could—moving between their rooms, tending fires, trying to keep the place from falling apart. On November 18th, with her body worn out and her heart dulled with sorrow, she gave birth to a baby boy, Leslie Raymond. It should have been a day of joy, but joy had no place there. The very next day, Pa slipped away.

When Ma finally began to recover, weak as a whisper but alive, she sent me a telegram. She wrote that she knew she ought to call me on the telephone, but she couldn't bring herself to form the words out loud, nor bear to hear the shock in my voice. So she put it down on paper, plain and hard, and sent it to me.

I sat on the edge of the bed that night, the telegram still trembling in my hand. Just weeks before, Erroll had been alive—laughing with his boy in the yard, waiting for another child to arrive. And now he was gone. So was Pa. He taught me how to shoe a horse. How to hold a rifle steady. How to keep my word even when it hurt. Now he was gone, and I hadn't seen him in years. I should've gone back to Oklahoma to spend more time with him. Should've written more. Should've let him know how much I respected him. But all I could do now was sit with the weight of it. The silence in our house wasn't just quiet. It was more than I could carry.

By some miracle, Ma recovered. The fever broke just when it seemed she might slip away, and within days she was back on her feet—pale, but steady. She stayed in Fresno to help Nellie with the children, cradling the newborn in one arm and wiping tears from the other boys' cheeks with the other. She lost her son and her husband less than two weeks apart, but kept going. Maybe that was just her way—pouring herself into whoever was still standing.

When I received the news, I was in shock. I couldn't believe it. None of it felt real. But everywhere I turned, someone was mourning.

In just two months, the global death toll had soared to nearly twenty million. A wave of grief and fear swept through every home, every street. Era and I stayed healthy, somehow, but Mr. Leewright had been in bed for a week. He'd been mighty sick—but he pulled through.

And then came more terrible news. Eddie had died. The flu had taken her too. I hadn't spoken to her in years, but that didn't mean I'd stopped caring. We'd been through too much—loved too hard, fought too loud. I still dreamed of her some nights—always walking away, with Fern in her arms.

I was thankful her sister, Mary, and her husband, Sam, were there to comfort the children. But I still ached for them—for what they were going through, and for what I could no longer give.

I pictured George trying to hold everything together—shoulders squared, jaw tight, doing what I once did when my own world came undone. Maybe he kept Fern close that night, let her cry into his chest the way she used to cry into mine. I imagined John pacing the hallway, asking questions no one could answer, and William retreating into silence, sitting in the corner with his fists clenched, trying to pretend it didn't hurt. He was fourteen—old enough to understand what had happened, but not old enough to know what to do with the weight of it. And Fern, sweet Fern, still young enough to hope it was all a mistake. I wasn't there to hold them. I wasn't there to explain. That's what tore me apart the most—not just that Eddie was gone, but that my children had to face it without me.

The world was losing too much, too fast. And somewhere in all that loss, I was trying to remember what it meant to keep going.

A RANCH IN RUCKLES

There are times in one's life, you have to move on. You don't really have a choice. The place you've been holds too many memories—of life and death, of joy and disappointment, of laughter and loss.

In the March after Pa died, Ma sold the farm in Oklahoma and moved to Denver. Without him, the place couldn't hold her. Even Guy had other dreams, and when Ma decided to let go of the land, he finally felt free to chase them. By May, she was living in Denver.

She found a small house just a few blocks from the furniture store—modest and neat, with a tidy porch and a single cottonwood out front. She settled in like she'd lived there a lifetime—found a church, joined a sewing circle and a garden club, made friends with the neighbors, went to the library every Thursday afternoon.

I'd walk over to her new home most mornings before work, sometimes just to check in, sometimes to sit with her over coffee and talk about Pa. She didn't cry often, but I could see the grief in the way she moved. Still, there was strength in her too. She filled that little house with quilts, sunflowers, and the smell of fresh bread. It wasn't the farm, but it was home in its own way. And it meant the world to me to have her close again.

That summer, in June of 1919, William and Fern came to visit us in Denver. I was thrilled—it had been eight years since I'd last seen them back in Duff, Nebraska. George and John were grown by then and had moved on with their lives. George had joined the Navy and John took work on a ranch out in Kansas.

We had a summer full of moments I'll never forget—some easy, some hard. When William, who was seventeen, and Fern, thirteen, arrived the house felt alive. But come September, their aunt and uncle—Sam and Mary—insisted they return to New York to attend school. I thought about fighting to keep them with us, but I couldn't bring myself to do it. They loved Sam and Mary. Since their mother's death, that bond had only grown stronger. New York had become their home. I didn't want to rip them from it.

Fern and Era got along especially well. She was bright and full of joy. They laughed together, went shopping together, cooked side by side. They bonded like sisters. One afternoon, I came to our apartment from the railyard and found the two of them at the sewing table. Scraps of fabric, dried lavender, and spools of thread covered the table.

"We're making drawer sachets," Fern said brightly. "Smells better than coal smoke."

Era laughed and reached over to brush a strand of hair from Fern's cheek. "You're a natural."

Fern fell quiet for a moment, threading the needle again. "Do you think my mother would like the way I'm growing up?"

Era looked over at her, steady and sure. "I think she'd be proud of you. Every single part of you."

Fern smiled, a little softer this time. "I hope I'm like her."

"I'm sure you are," Era said gently. "The light in your eyes, the spark for living, the way curiosity dances with charm—that's all Eddie."

I nodded in agreement.

Fern smiled, holding a sachet up. "This one's for your socks, Daddy."

I grinned. "That's what every rail man wants."

I tucked it in my shirt pocket.

William was different, more difficult. He wore a scowl whenever he saw me. Pain kept him trapped in the past. He resented my absence from his life, my leaving, my remarriage. Some days I think he hated me. Not truly me—but the hole I'd left in his world. I understood. I carried that guilt every day. He especially couldn't forgive Era for taking his mother's place with me. No matter how hard she tried—with kindness, patience, gentleness—nothing seemed to reach him. He wouldn't let her in.

It was past midnight on the night before the kids were returning to New York, and I'd finally put my book down. The floors creaked under my steps as I moved through the dim apartment. The furniture store below us was silent now—the scent of lacquer lingering in the air, the faint tick of Era's wind-up clock marking the quiet.

I noticed the front window cracked open. A breeze fluttered the curtain, and the faint glow of a streetlamp spilled across the floor. William was sitting on the fire escape just outside, his legs dangling over the edge, shirt sleeves rolled up, cigarette smoldering between his fingers.

"You can see more stars out here than you'd think," I said, sliding open the window.

He didn't look at me. "Still not enough to make this place feel like home."

I stepped out beside him, careful not to make the old metal groan. "I know it's not New York."

"It's not anywhere. It's just the middle of nowhere."

We sat in silence for a moment, the neighborhood hushed around us. A dog barked in the distance, crickets sang their lonesome song, a train whistle called from far off.

"You ever wonder how it would've gone if you hadn't left us?" William asked, his voice low.

"All the time."

He took another drag, the smoke curling around his face. "Was it that you wanted an easier life—one without us in it?"

"I didn't leave because it was easy."

"No," he said. "But you did leave."

He stubbed the cigarette out on the ledge and stood, brushing off his pants. "Trying to make things right doesn't erase what's been done."

Then he climbed back inside. The curtain swayed for a moment, then settled. I stayed out a while longer, listening to the whistle blow again, and thinking how much louder silence can feel when it comes from your own son.

The next morning I noticed William wearing one of my nicest shirts.

"Is that mine?" I asked.

"Maybe," he replied with a smug look.

"Are you taking it with you?"

"I figure you owe me," he said. "If all I get from you is an old shirt, so be it."

"I'd give it to you if you just asked."

"I'm not asking for anything from you," he said. "If you want your stupid shirt, take it."

"No," I said calmly. "I'd like you to have it."

"Then why were you having a fit about it a minute ago?"

I shrugged. "I don't know. I just love you, son. And I hope one day we can have a real relationship."

He muttered, "Maybe next summer."

Fern kissed us both on the cheek. "Ignore William," she said. "He's in a mood. But I've had the best time, and I can't wait to come back next summer."

William stood near the platform, suitcase at his feet, hands in his coat pockets. Fern waved from the train window, her face bright and tearful.

He didn't say goodbye, not in so many words. But just before he climbed the steps, he turned back to me. His eyes met mine—just briefly—and I saw something flicker there. Not forgiveness. Not yet. But something softer than before.

He tugged at the collar of the shirt he'd taken from my closet that morning and gave a half-smile. "Thanks for the shirt."

His voice was guarded. It wasn't an apology. It wasn't forgiveness. But it was something.

That afternoon they were gone, and I had all the time in the world to miss them. But time moves on and by April I'd worked five years on the railway in Denver. It earned me a fancy pocket watch—brass casing, clean white face, Union Pacific engraved on the back. I carried that watch for the rest of my life. But the best gift was a free trip anywhere along the Union Pacific line. It might not have been much, but I was glad to take it.

So in the second week of that month, Era and I went to the station, boarded the train, and traveled as far west as the tracks would take us. I had a week off work and was ready for an adventure.

The line ended at a tiny station called Ruckles in a remote corner of southwestern Oregon. It wasn't a town, nothing but a platform where workers unloaded rail and timber. No stores, no houses, no saloons. Just the end of the line. The only passengers on that train were Era, me, and a few construction men, broad and sunburned from days laying steel.

We stepped off the train and stood alone on the platform.

"This place is beautiful," I said, taking in the quiet hills.

"There's nothing here," Era replied.

"Maybe that's what I like about it."

We left our bags at the station and walked a narrow dirt road north to the Clarks Branch River—more of a stream, really. It wound gently through the hills, clear and slow-moving.

After a few miles, we stopped for lunch—bread, cheese, and a slice of carrot cake Era had packed. We sat in a field of pink and yellow wildflowers, surrounded by ancient oaks and elms. The air was crisp and sweet after a spring rain.

This was paradise. Not the dusty prairie of Nebraska, the humid flatlands of Oklahoma, or the cold highland of Colorado. This was the garden of Eden that Ma had told us about when I was a kid.

"I think this is it," I sighed, letting the moment settle in my chest.

"It is peaceful."

"It feels like home."

"Home is in Denver," Era said gently.

"We went there for your father. He's retired now, after forty years with the Santa Fe. I doubt he'll stay in the city much longer."

"I thought we were going to visit Eugene—where we lived when you worked for the Southern Pacific?"

"I've been thinking. That's where Daniel died. That's where your mother passed, too. Maybe we don't go back."

"But there's nothing here," she said again.

"That's the point," I replied. "It would just be us. Something new."

"What would you do here?" she asked, arms crossed.

I looked out across the hills. "I'll be a farmer. Like my pa."

"You've been a cowboy, a railroad man, and now you want to be a farmer?"

"I started life as a farm boy. And later on I helped Pa plant and harvest in Nebraska and Oklahoma. I can do it again."

She picked a wildflower, smiling despite herself.

We ate slowly—chewing the bread, savoring the cheese, each bite of carrot cake sweet and nutty. Era leaned back, her eyes half-closed in the sun.

"This reminds me of that summer in Sulphur Springs," she said. "Before everything got so complicated."

"Are you saying that marrying me made everything complicated?"

"No," she giggled. "It's just moving to the big city with all its noise and crowds and hecticness takes its toll. The city has expectations."

"Too many for a person to just relax and be themselves."

"I agree," she said. "There's something simple and gentle about sitting here."

"What do you think your mother would've said about a place like this?"

"She'd complain there's no clothing store."

We both laughed.

"But she'd understand," Era added. "She always told me to choose the kind of life that lets you sleep soundly."

I looked around—at the trees, the grass swaying in the breeze. "Do you think this might be the place?"

Era didn't answer right away. She plucked at the petals of the wildflower, her eyes distant.

"It's lovely," she said finally. "But I wonder what it would feel like after the novelty wore off. No neighbors. No stores. No church bells or trolley whistles."

I studied her face. "You think you'd miss all that?"

"Maybe not at first," she said. "But maybe later."

The railroad was selling off parcels near the tracks to help fund construction. As Era and I walked along the muddy road, I kept stealing glances at the open ground, already weighing what it might mean to own a piece of it. It wasn't much now—just weeds and dirt alongside the rails—but I couldn't help picturing a house, a barn, maybe even a corral full of horses, set there someday. By the time we reached the platform, the thought had taken root. I turned to Era and said I wanted to buy it.

She smiled and said she knew from the look in my eye I wasn't about to let go of this one.

"Are you with me on this?" I asked.

"I'm with you," she said softly "No matter where your dreams take us."

The agent sat outside the depot with a red ledger spread open on a crate, his bowler brushed clean and tipped back on his head. He gave me a long look, licked the end of his pencil, and said, "You sure you want this ground? It's not worth much yet."

"It's worth plenty to me."

"But what about your job in Denver?"

"I'm sending them my resignation."

Era glanced at me, surprised. "You're really leaving the railroad?"

I nodded.

"It's stable work, Allen. And we just got on our feet again."

"I know. But I'm ready for something different. Something that belongs to us."

She didn't argue. Just turned toward the hills and let the wind tangle her hair.

"I just sell the land," said the agent. "So which parcel are you considering?"

"The one a few miles north on the hillside east of the tracks."

"That's forty acres."

I nodded my approval.

The agent marked the coordinates, noted the price, and handed me a form to sign.

"At two-fifty an acre," he said, "that puts you at a thousand even."

I carefully removed a leather wallet from my coat and handed over the bills. I picked up the deed with both hands and stared at it, barely believing that this land was mine. The ink was still wet. It smelled like glue and dust and everything I'd ever hoped for. It was the prettiest land I'd ever seen.

The nearest town was Myrtle Creek, six miles south. A small logging town with a dry goods store, two churches, three saloons, and a hotel. We caught a ride to the hotel and stayed the night. Early the next morning, a farmer sold us two horses, and we rode out to survey our new land.

We sent word back to Mr. Leewright, asking him to sell our half of the furniture store and ship our belongings to Ruckles. He agreed—said he was retiring and heading to Seattle, where Esther and her husband, Ira, had settled. But he promised to visit us on the way through. A month later, Mr. Leewright arrived in Ruckles. Era and I were still living in a rough little shack on the property, nothing more than boards and tar paper. He took one look and decided he'd be better off renting a room at the hotel in Myrtle Creek.

"I had to see this land you plan to live on," he said. "And since I was passing through, I figured I'd personally deliver your possessions."

It took me three trips to get all the crates to our property. After helping me load the last reminders of our life in Denver into the Model T, he brushed the dirt off his coat and looked me square in the eye.

"Where'd you get the automobile?"

"At the auction in Roseburg," I said with some pride. "Only five years old, and I got it for a hundred and fifty."

He gave a small nod. "Sounds like you're a shrewd negotiator."

"You taught me a lot," I said quietly. "I'll always be grateful for that."

His eyes stayed on me. "How are you treating my daughter?"

"Like I love her," I answered without blinking.

"But you brought her out into this wilderness."

"We made the decision together."

He studied me for a long moment.

"I suppose she's old enough to decide what she wants."

"That she is." I nodded.

"Era's a strong woman. And stubborn."

"That's what I love about her."

He softened then. "She's as faithful as they come. Treat her right, and she'll give you everything she's got."

"I've noticed," I said, a half-smile tugging at me.

He reached into his coat pocket, pulled out a small silver case, and placed it in my hand. I turned it over, puzzled.

"This was Florence's," he said. "She kept peppermint leaves in it."

I looked at him, struck silent by the meaning and thought behind the gift.

"She'd want you and Era to have it," he went on. "To remember that not everything sweet comes easy."

"Why not move to Ruckles with us?" Era asked him later in the day.

"Ruckles isn't even a town," her father replied. "It's where the tracks stop. They've got a post office and a train platform. That's it."

"But it's a start," she said.

"It's too small for me, too rugged. I've lived my life in cities. Seattle's a big town—and besides—Esther needs me."

"And so do I," Era said, her voice catching.

"But she's got Everett. And a two-year-old needs a grandfather."

The look in Era's eyes stopped me cold. Sudden. Deep. She'd been struck where it hurt most. The reminder of her being childless crushed her spirit, and I couldn't do a damn thing about it. She turned her face away.

"Seattle's a lot closer than Denver," her father said.

Era lifted her gaze back to him. "It's still three hundred and fifty miles away."

"That's nothing with that Model T Allen just bought," he said.

"I'm sure someday, we'll come up to visit."

Then she left to find a private place to shed her tears.

Over the next few months, Era and I built a small, two room house. The first wall went up crooked. I cursed under my breath and nearly split the plank trying to realign it.

Era stepped over with a level. "Maybe measure twice next time?"

"Maybe you want to swing the hammer?"

She raised an eyebrow, took the hammer, and drove in a nail with three clean strikes.

I handed her another board. "I'll cut. You build."

We laughed and got back to work. By sundown, the frame was up, and I was already imagining which window would catch the morning light. Era was planing a porch where we could sit in the evenings and listen to the river.

A few weeks later we raised a barn big enough for chickens, goats, pigs, two horses, and a milk cow. We were exhausted, which meant that we slept more soundly than we had in years.

One morning I stood on the hillside, hoe in hand, breaking the soil where we'd plant prune trees in the fall. The earth here was soft, rich, black. And it smelled so good. I thought of Pa. Of that first row of wheat we planted together in Oklahoma, how he showed me to press the seed with care, not force.

The breeze carried the scent of rain and pine. Era waved from the porch, a cup of coffee in her hand, sunlight catching in her hair. I turned back to the earth and dug. I couldn't have been happier. We had a place to belong. It might be remote and quiet and wild, but it was ours.

I was content, but Era wasn't. I could see it in her eyes. Life was good, but something was missing. We both knew what it was.

In July, William and Fern took the train out to see us. Fern was all smiles the moment she stepped off the platform—eyes bright, eager to take in every inch of the countryside. William, on the other hand, kept his shoulders stiff and his words clipped. He wasn't happy to be there, that much was clear. Still, I was grateful they came.

They stayed two months, and it went better than I'd expected. William and I spent the early mornings together, hunting deer and pheasant in the cool hush before the sun crested the hills. His aim was sharper than mine, and more than once, he brought down the bird while I was still lining up my shot. We brought the game home, and Era and Fern turned it into suppers we'd talk about for days— roasts, stews, and flaky meat pies with herbs from the garden.

During the afternoons, William helped me expand the barn. He worked hard—quiet, focused—and I showed him how to drive the Model T, easing the clutch like he'd been doing it for years. He caught on fast, and for a few days, we almost felt like father and son again.

Era and Fern sewed together on the porch, heads bent in

concentration. They tended the garden in the mornings—rows of potatoes, corn, tomatoes, green beans, zucchini, and peas— all thriving as long as we gave them a good evening soak. Their laughter floated through the open windows, light and steady, the kind of sound that makes a house feel like home.

On hot days, we all cooled off in the river. None of us were swimmers, but we didn't care. We splashed in the shallows by a grove of oaks, dunking each other and hollering like kids, water glinting on our arms as the sun burned gold above the hills. Even William smiled then, wading out waist-deep before tossing Fern over his shoulder with a laugh.

But the good days ran out too fast. On the morning they were set to leave, we walked together down the dirt road toward the Ruckles station. The summer grasses rustled in the breeze, and the silence between us felt heavier than it should have.

"What are you carrying in that burlap sack?" I asked William.

He shifted the bag and looked away. "Something I found of my mother's."

I frowned. "I don't have anything of Eddie's here—just a few old pictures."

"I found her sewing machine."

I stopped walking. "That's Era's machine."

"No—it's Mother's. I know it," he snapped, holding the bag tighter to his chest.

Era and Fern stood behind us, quiet, watching it unfold.

"I'm telling you the truth, son. Your mother never had a sewing machine, not while we were together. That wasn't her way."

"She told me she had one. In Kalispell. Said you still had it."

"If she did, it got left behind. But this one—it isn't hers."

"You're lying," he said, the words bitter on his tongue.

My chest tightened. "William—"

"I don't care what you say. This is my mother's, and I'm taking it with me."

There was a second—just one—when I could've let it go. But he shoved past me, and something snapped. We were grappling, rolling in the dust like we still had something to prove. I wrestled the machine from him—he stormed off, yelling back over his shoulder as he marched to the station. "I never want to see you again!"

I stood there alone on the road, bruised and breathless, watching the boy I'd raised walk away from me for the last time. Wished I'd held my tongue. Wished I'd let him take the damned machine. Wished I'd kept my temper. That moment has haunted me ever since.

In the fall I planted 2,000 saplings. Rows upon rows of young trees stretching toward the horizon, fragile and full of promise. Mr. Leewright loaned me the money to get started. The hard part, of course, was waiting. It would take three to five years before they bore fruit—if they survived at all.

That Christmas was quiet. Just the two of us. Snow blanketed the orchard in white, softening everything it touched. The windows of the ranch house glowed with firelight, and the tree Era had decorated stood proudly in the corner, its branches hung with bits of red yarn, pinecones, and a star cut from an old tin can.

We ate roast venison by the hearth—thick slices with rosemary, carrots, and mashed potatoes. Era had baked a spiced apple pie from the last of the cellar fruit, and we poured each other coffee sweetened with molasses. We didn't speak much, not at first. There was a stillness between us, made of all the things we'd lived through this year—the move to Oregon, the fight with William, the planting, the grief, the hope. It sat in the room like another presence, a presence that brought us closer.

After a while, Era leaned her head on my shoulder. "You did good this year," she whispered.

I looked into the fire. "Some days, it feels like all I've done is hold things together with twine and prayer."

She smiled softly. "Things might be hard, but I'm still here."

I reached for her hand and gave it a gentle squeeze. "Sometimes I wonder if William will ever write. Will he ever come back."

"I think he will." She paused. "One day."

I nodded. "I hope so."

"You've built us a home here," she said. "And I'm as happy as I've ever been."

We sat there a while longer, the fire dying down, our hearts holding to the hope that the good Lord might keep us in his thoughts.

Outside, the wind pressed gently against the windows, and somewhere in the distance a coyote called into the dark. I listened to it fade, then closed my eyes.

"I never thought peace would look like this," I said. "Just you and me. A warm fire. A roof that doesn't leak."

She smiled, her hand steady on my chest. "Sometimes peace is just surviving what tried to break you."

I looked into the fire, its glow softening the edges of the room. Her breath was warm against my collarbone.

And for that moment—with the wind at the windows, the orchard sleeping beneath snow, and her hand in mine—I let myself believe it was true.

A MAN DOES WHAT HE MUST

I didn't know how we were going to make it. We were dead broke. Nothing on the horizon but dark clouds and rolling thunder.

Why did I quit a perfectly good job with the Union Pacific? The orchard was planted and looked beautiful. But it would be two more years until it would produce any fruit and we'd make any money from it. Besides I owed Mr. Leewright money for helping buy the saplings. He was patient, but I hated owing anyone money. It felt like they'd have control over me. We had a hardy garden, so we didn't starve. A solid house, so we stayed dry. A car—but nowhere worth going.

Era was positive and worked hard making our little house feel like a home. I didn't want to worry her by letting her know we were in such dire straits. The dry goods store in Myrtle Creek gave me credit for needed supplies. I spoke to some of the guys in town and they said that in March crews would go out logging. I figured that would be my best bet to dig us out of this hole. So I signed up with the South Umpqua Timber Company to become a logger. It wasn't what I ever aimed for, but a man's got to provide.

Era was nervous about me being gone so much. The place felt too quiet, too far from anyone, and the loneliness was wearing on her. So when the dry goods store owner mentioned a farmer with a one-year-old dog to give away, I said I'd take a look.

She was a sweet-natured mutt—part cocker spaniel, part German shepherd, maybe a bit of golden retriever. When I brought her home, she ran straight to Era, tail wagging, and licked her hand like they already belonged to each other.

Era knelt and laughed—really laughed—for the first time in days. She hugged the dog close and whispered, "You're a little lady." And that's what we called her—Lady.

From then on, they were inseparable. Lady followed her everywhere, curled up at her feet while she shelled peas or read by the window. It wasn't just company—it was comfort. And knowing Era wasn't alone gave me more peace than I could admit.

The crew started on a wet, rainy day in March of 1921. There were ten of us loggers, working two miles west of town up Rock Creek Canyon. This was a rugged land—steep hills, deep draws, thick underbrush, muddy narrow roads. The forest was thick with old growth Douglas fir—two hundred feet tall, seven feet in diameter. I was one of two fallers. It took Jack McDonald, a life-long logger, and I a full day to take down one of these giants. We used double-bit axes, two man crosscut saws, carbon steel wedges, and brute strength. This sort of work wasn't easy. It would have been hard in my twenties, but at forty-two it was a back breaker. I was constantly tired and aching, but I never complained. Complaining don't drop trees, and it sure don't pay the bills. I'd put in my time as a cowboy, a railroad man, and a farmer. They all required hard work, but the hardest by far was the life of a logger. At times I wondered whether $3 a day was worth it, but it brought in enough to put clothes on our back and boots on our feet.

Sun's up, saws up—no excuses. Twelve hours a day, six days a week. I counted off each day until I could make it home to sleep in my own bed, next to my good-hearted wife. Saturday nights I'd roll onto the farm about nine—dirty, dog tired, stiff, beat to hell, and slightly corked. Prohibition had just begun, but that didn't mean anything. After a brutal week in the woods, the crew stopped at the Roaring Ranch Roadhouse just off the main highway where we could get as much moonshine as we wished. I'd keep it to just a couple swigs, but it still hit me fierce and fast. Era would rush out to the front porch when she heard me drive up, greeting me with the sweetest embrace I could ever imagine. She never mentioned the alcohol on my breath. She just held me like she was so proud of me and I was the only thing that ever made her proud.

That June was sunny and bright—a welcome change from the long, soaking rains of spring. But there was sorrow in the sunshine. William didn't come to visit that year; he wouldn't come near me. I missed him sorely, and I missed the older boys too. Fern, bless her heart, made the journey alone—three thousand miles by rail—and arrived cheerful as ever. She brought light into the house, especially for Era, who'd been lonely with me only home on Sundays. The two of them took long walks, kept each other company through the daily chores, and talked deep into the evenings. Fern only stayed a month, but in that time she struck up a friendship with a young man named Grant Smith, five years her senior. He and his brother worked their family homestead a few miles upriver. Their father had passed when Grant was just a boy, and he'd grown into a quiet, steady sort. Fern seemed taken with him, and I could see why. When she left, she promised to write him as often as she could. I said to Era I reckoned Fern had found the man of her dreams. Still, when the train pulled away, my chest ached more than I let on. I only wish I'd had more time with her.

August was uncomfortably hot and dry as a desert wind, with fire danger hanging over every ridge and hollow. Our crew had gotten close in the six months of working ourselves down to the ground, but never giving up. The ten of us did everything together for six days a week and we got to know each other pretty good. But August nineteenth is a day I'll never forget. It was the kind of day where the heat settles in your bones and the sweat don't dry. The flies were thick, and the air hung still, except for the whine of the crosscut saw and the occasional caw of a jay in the timber.

Me and Jack McDonald had been working the same slope for near two weeks—tight stand of old-growth fir, thick with rot and shadows. There was one tree we called "The Monster." She was the biggest damn fir I'd ever seen. You could feel her hum when the wind touched her crown. But we were determined to take her down. All day long we'd been cutting on her.

Jack drove the wedge in slow and steady, the sweat running off his brow. His hands were rough and calloused. He might have been ten years younger than me, just thirty-two, but he had the experience of a man who'd known trees his entire life.

"You ever think about quitting?" I asked, wiping sap from my neck.

He gave a low chuckle. "Every damn day. But this is all I know. This is what my pa did and this is what I knew I'd do."

"Does your wife want you out of it?"

"Course she does. She wants a cabin up near Glide with chickens and hogs and a whole lot of land. She wants a place with peace and quiet where we can raise the boys."

"How many kids do you have?"

"Three boys, all under eight." Jack smiled. "But Lily is expecting another in December."

"Congratulations! Era would be tickled pink if she were expecting."

"Lily is praying for a girl. And she says that the family needs me closer to home. So I promised her that this season's the last. Once we hit November, I'm off the crew and not returning."

"What do you think you'll do?"

"Anything but logging."

And we both laughed.

"You're a good man, Allen," Jack said after a beat. "You don't talk much, but you show up. That counts for more than you think."

I shrugged. "Just trying to do right by my family."

"Ain't that what we're all after—leavin' behind something our kids can be proud of?"

"You ever get a feeling?" Jack asked, pausing mid-saw. The long blade stilled between us, teeth buried in the heartwood of that massive Douglas fir.

I glanced over, surprised. "What kind of feeling?"

He didn't answer right away. Just stood there, one hand resting on the saw handle, the other rubbing the back of his neck. The morning sun filtered through the canopy, catching the dust in the air, and for a moment, everything seemed to hold still with him.

"I don't know," he finally said. "Like something's off. Not wrong exactly—just... off."

I let out a dry chuckle. "It's logging, Jack. Something's always off."

He gave a weak smile, but it didn't reach his eyes. Then, like shaking off a bad dream, he reset his grip. "Let's get it done."

"This is a tough one," I muttered.

"But she oughta come down easy."

"Nothing about this tree is easy," I said.

He gave me a look. "Ain't that the truth."

I nodded and looked up at the tree. There was something about her that made me nervous. She looked rooted, stubborn, and unwilling to let anyone take her down.

When the saw bound up, Jack stepped back to wedge it. Jack was humming again—he was always humming something. But then the tree groaned. Real deep. The kind of sound that sinks in your chest before it hits your ears.

"Timber!" he shouted.

Only she didn't fall right. Something twisted in her gut—maybe wind, maybe rot, maybe we just ran out of luck at the wrong time.

The tree kicked back fast. No warning. Just a blur of bark and splinters, the ground tearing apart like lightning struck the earth. I was on the safe side, Jack wasn't. He turned to run, but she caught him mid-step—hit like a freight car, took him to the ground, and pinned him with a painful cry.

The crash echoed through the canyon like a rifle shot. Then everything stopped. No birds. No wind. Just silence. I stood frozen, the saw still in my hands. All I could hear was the ringing in my ears and the blood thudding in my chest.

I yelled and ran to him faster than I'd ever run in my life. But death had claimed him. His body was crushed, the flannel of his shirt already dark and wet. His eyes were open wide, locked on something far beyond the canopy. One hand was curled like it had tried to reach out. Blood seeped into the forest floor beneath him, red as autumn leaves.

I grabbed his hand—it was still warm. I held it like maybe I could keep him here, like if I just held on tight enough, he'd come back. But he was gone. I stared at those deep brown eyes, not believing what I was seeing. It had all happened so fast it didn't feel real. I bowed my head and whispered the kind of prayer Ma used to say when nothing made sense and there wasn't much left to hold on to.

Then the rest of the crew was surrounding Jack. Nobody said a thing. We just stood there. After a while several of us cut a length of canvas from the gear bag and covered him the best we could. Then we just sat there till the sun set and the forest grew as dark as our thoughts. We all knew logging had its risks. It's dangerous work. You swing steel, you sweat blood, and some days the mountain decides it doesn't want you no more. And there ain't a damn thing you can do about it.

The next morning, just after sunup, the boss gathered us by the gear pile. His face looked like it hadn't seen sleep. He pulled off his cap and held it to his chest.

"We're shuttin' it down, for the rest of the week" he said, voice low. "It ain't right to send men back up that hill like nothin' happened. Too dry, too dangerous. We'll settle up pay next week."

No one said a word. There wasn't anything to say. We just nodded and went quiet, packing our kits with slow, heavy hands. Jack's saw still leaned against a stump where he'd left it. No one touched it.

By late morning, we loaded his body into the back of the boss's flatbed. The pine box was plain, nailed together from camp lumber, and covered with a worn canvas tarp. Someone tucked a pair of leather gloves beneath the tie-down rope, a quiet gesture of respect.

We rolled down the canyon road in silence, the wheels slipping now and then in the loose dirt. Myrtle Creek was only a few miles east, but the ride stretched long under the hot sun. The firs gave way to pastureland, fences running straight as a plowed field, and fruit orchards heavy with late summer apples.

Jack's house sat on the north edge of town—a modest white place with a tin roof, a few chickens in the yard, and a porch swing that creaked in the wind. Lily was waiting on the steps, hands folded over the swell of her belly. The boys were just behind her, still as fenceposts.

The boss stopped the truck out front. For a moment none of us moved. The engine clicked as it cooled. Then I climbed down, took off my cap, and walked around to the back.

"Lily," I said. "We brought him home."

She nodded, jaw tight. "Thank you."

The crew helped carry the box up the walk. We set it down beneath the shade of the maple tree beside the porch—Jack had built that porch himself, just last spring. Lily watched, dry-eyed, one hand resting on her stomach. The box thudded onto the ground with a finality that made Lily flinch, though she didn't cry out. The breeze lifted a corner of the canvas before settling again.

The youngest boy stepped forward and touched the canvas, his fingers tracing the shape of the wood underneath. Lily knelt and pulled him close. "It's alright," she whispered. "Papa's home now."

We stood in the yard a while, caps in hand, boots shifting in the dirt, not one of us knowing what to say. Lily disappeared inside and came back with a patchwork quilt—faded reds and blues, worn at the corners. She draped it over the box herself.

"It was his favorite," she murmured.

Then she sat beside it, her skirt gathering dust, her eyes fixed on some far-off place beyond any of us.

We stayed long enough to know she wouldn't be alone. Then, one by one, we tipped our hats and walked back to the truck. The drive out of town was even quieter than the way in.

And I kept thinking about the way she sat there—not crying, not breaking—just still, with her hand on that quilt and her boys close beside her, like the only thing left to do in this world was hold steady.

By the time I got home, the sun was starting to dip behind the ridge. The hills glowed with that late summer haze—orange and dusty gold—and the gravel popped under the tires as I pulled into the drive. The house stood quiet, the garden rows neat and green, and Lady lifted her head from the porch and gave a low whine. She knew something wasn't right.

Era stepped out before I'd even turned the engine off. She had a dishrag in one hand and flour on her apron. Her hair was pulled back loose, wisps clinging to her cheeks in the heat. "You're home early," she said gently.

I nodded, climbing down from the car like every bone in me had turned to stone. "Job's shut down for the week."

She looked at me for a moment, her eyes scanning my face like she could read the story there. "It happened, didn't it?"

I just lowered my head.

Era stepped forward and wrapped her arms around me. Not quick or frantic—just firm and quiet, the way she always did when something heavy needed holding.

"It was Jack," I said into her shoulder. "Tree came down wrong. Hit him clean. There wasn't a thing any of us could do."

I felt her breath catch, but she didn't pull away. She just held me tighter.

"We took his body to Lily this morning," I went on. "She didn't cry. She just sat beside him with her boys and laid that old quilt over the box like she was tucking him in for the night."

Era didn't speak, but her hand came up to the back of my neck, steady as ever.

"I keep thinkin' how he'd just told me this was gonna be his last season. Said he was done. Promised Lily he'd come home for good by November. Now he's laid out under a maple tree and she's got three mouths to feed and one on the way."

We stood there a while, the evening breeze tugging at her apron, the sound of crickets just beginning in the grass. She finally looked up at me.

"You did right by him," she said. "And by her. Sometimes all a person can do is show up."

I swallowed hard, my throat like sandpaper. "He said that, you know. Yesterday. Said I was a man who showed up. That it counted for more than I thought."

She smiled then—soft, tired. "He wasn't wrong."

I looked out past the garden, toward the hills where the timber stood silhouetted against the sky. "It could've been me. Just as easy."

"But it wasn't," Era said, drawing me back inside. "You're here. And I'm grateful."

We sat at the kitchen table in silence after that, the smell of baked bread lingering in the air, the lamp casting gold light across the worn wood. I didn't have the appetite for supper, but I took her hand and held it. And in that stillness, with dusk settling in and the ache still in my bones, I realized there were worse things than hard work and empty pockets.

"I'm finishing out the season," I said, taking her hand. "But once November comes and I get my last paycheck, then my career as a logger is done."

I kept that promise and thanked the boss for the opportunity, but told him I needed to be back on my farm with Era. I'd made enough money that if we were careful it would last us until the orchard started producing.

That Christmas, we sat together in our little cabin, the fire crackling in the hearth, and thanked the good Lord we'd made it through the year.

"I appreciate everything you went through to keep us going," Era said softly, her hand resting on Lady's head as the dog dozed beside her.

"Logging was... an experience," I said, stretching my legs toward the warmth. "One I hope I never have to repeat."

Era smiled, her eyes glowing in the firelight. "I think life's going to get better. In fact, I've got a feeling that 1922 might be our best year yet."

I looked at her—really looked—and saw hope where there had been fear. Strength where there had been silence.

"I hope you're right." I reached down and scratched behind Lady's ears. She stirred and let out a soft sigh.

Outside, the wind stirred the pines, but inside, we were warm, fed, and together. We didn't have much—not money, not certainty—but we had peace. I kissed her hand. She leaned her head on my shoulder, and for the first time in a long while, everything felt right.

Maybe Era was right. Maybe 1922 really would be our best year yet.

IT'S JUST FIFTEEN MILES

We walked the orchard just after sunrise, the air crisp and fragrant with spring. Every branch was cloaked in white blossoms, their petals catching the light like snowflakes that refused to melt. The hillside above the cabin was alive with color—pink trillium, purple iris, and bright orange poppies spilling toward the river.

In the garden, neat rows of carrots, onions, beets, and broccoli were already pushing through the soil. We'd planted more—lettuce, peas, radishes, squash—hopeful the rich earth and steady rain would see them through. The whole place felt like it was waking up from a long sleep.

The barn, too, was full of new life. Tiny goats wobbled on unsteady legs. Chicks chirped from a crate near the wall. Piglets squealed whenever anyone stepped inside. A striking young colt, all legs and wide eyes, stood close to its mother in the straw. And the kittens—tucked into corners and hay bales like hidden treasures—seemed to multiply by the week.

More than once I found Era out there, her dress dusty at the hem, crouched low to feed the animals or scratch their ears. Her face softened with them. She'd whisper to the baby goats, stroke the colt's neck, cradle a kitten like it was sacred. I'd stand in the doorway, just watching her. Something about the way she moved—the calm patience in her hands, the tenderness in her eyes, the easy smile on her pink lips—made me believe life couldn't be finer.

We'd been through a lot—more than most—but this spring felt

different. There was a quiet between us now, the kind that comes after a long storm. I felt it every time she laughed, brushed past me in the kitchen, or rested her head on my shoulder in the evening. I loved her more than ever—not just for who she was, but for everything we'd come through. For what we were building, day by day. After nearly two years on the farm, she seemed lighter, steadier—happier than I'd ever seen her. Last year had been hard, but her prediction for 1922 was proving true.

On a bright April afternoon, we walked down by the river with Lady trotting at our side. Era stopped, bent to pick a daisy, and held it to her chest. She closed her eyes and breathed deep, lost in thought.

"Are you okay?" I asked.

She smiled softly, then looked out over the water as if searching for something just beyond the horizon. "More okay than I've ever been."

"So what makes you so happy?"

She took my hand. "I've had a feeling for a while."

"A feeling?"

"A very good feeling."

"For how long?"

"A while, but I was afraid if I said it out loud, it might just blow away." Her face brightened. "I didn't want to say anything until I was absolutely sure."

"Sure of what?" I asked, not quite following.

She placed my hand on her belly. "Sure the good Lord's blessed us with a baby."

"A baby! We're going to have a baby?"

"Yes." She grinned, her whole face lit up. "Lily McDonald says I'm probably due in late August. She even offered to be my midwife."

"Does she have any experience?"

"She had four of her own, and her mother was a midwife. Lily's been helping at births since she was a girl."

"You're sure?"

"You don't sound as excited as I'd hoped." She squeezed my hand, studying my face.

"I'm excited," I said, then glanced out at the water. "I'm also just a little jumpy."

"Because of Daniel?"

I nodded and looked away.

"That's why I want a midwife," she said, steady as ever. "I've talked to some of the women in town. They say even if you've lost a child, the next one is usually perfectly healthy."

"I hope they're right."

"You're going to be a fine father."

"I figure I've learned a thing or two from my mistakes."

"You have." She smiled.

"I just want it to turn out right this time."

"My mother used to say, 'Don't borrow trouble. Let tomorrow take care of itself.' I can't let myself go to that place. I'm choosing to believe the best."

"You're right." I pulled her into my arms. "Pa used to say, 'Worryin' don't plow the field any faster.'"

"Lily says I'm strong and healthy, so that's what our baby should be too."

"I'm sure she's right." I paused. "How's Lily doing? It's been eight months since Jack died."

"As well as can be expected. She had her baby in December—a girl, just like she hoped. She named her Jacklyn."

"That would've made Jack happy. I miss him. He was a good man. And even though I only knew him for six months, I considered him a close friend."

"I've already been thinking about names for our baby."

"Aren't you getting ahead of yourself?"

"Maybe. But if it's a girl, what do you think of Elizabeth?"

"That's Ma's name," I said.

"And if it's a boy, we can name him after you—Allen John Stephens."

I chuckled. "I have to admit, I'm hoping for a boy."

"I don't really care either way," she said. "I'm just looking forward to being a mother—rocking a sweet little baby in my arms."

"Then I think we should celebrate."

"I'm already celebrating."

"I know, but let's dress up in our Sunday best, go down to the roadhouse, and let someone else do the cooking for once."

Era laughed and kissed me. "You just want some moonshine."

"Just a swig or two."

A few days later, we received more good news—Fern had written to say she was getting married.

"Well I'll be," I said, staring at the letter like I wasn't sure I'd read it right. "How'd this come about?"

Era was already smiling. "She and Grant have been writing back and forth every week since last June."

"But they only spent a month together."

"Sometimes that's all it takes," Era said softly. "Love's a strong and mysterious thing."

I leaned back in my chair, still letting it sink in. "So when's the wedding?"

"She finishes high school in May. They're planning to marry in June."

I raised my eyebrows. "Sixteen years old and getting married. Lord, she's still just a kid."

Era reached for my hand. "I know. But she's steady. And sure of herself."

"Is this happening in Roseburg?"

Era nodded. "And she wants you to give her away."

I set the letter down and rubbed my jaw. "Glory be, my baby girl's getting married!"

"They'll be living up river, at the Smith homestead. Grant's adding on a room so it'll be ready in time."

I chuckled. "Well, I'd say we just found ourselves some help with the baby."

Era laughed too, her eyes shining. "And a bit more family close by."

In May, I built two extra rooms onto the cabin—one for the baby, and one in case any of my older kids ever decided to visit. I even made a new cradle, just like I had years ago for Daniel.

Each day, Era's belly grew more rounded. In the late afternoons, we walked along the river, her hand resting in mine to steady her steps. We smiled as Lady splashed in the water and chased rabbits along the muddy shoreline. I gathered bouquets of wildflowers, which Era arranged in a milk bottle and set on the kitchen table.

We talked about the days ahead, dreaming of a little boy running over the hillside, his laughter carrying on the wind. We pictured ourselves teaching him to read by lamplight and showing him how to milk the cows at dawn. I imagined riding horses side by side with him and wading barefoot in the creek to catch crawdads. Mostly, we dreamed of how he would fill our lives in ways we could hardly put into words.

After dinner, we sat side by side in old wooden chairs, watching the sun dip behind the trees and the stars scatter across the sky. The sweet scent of lavender and jasmine filled the air. She'd insisted on planting flowers around the cabin, even though I'd thought it a waste of time and money. But on evenings like those, I was glad she hadn't listened to me.

When the cabin slipped into darkness, we went inside to play cards and cribbage by lamplight, often laughing until we were giddy with exhaustion.

On Saturday, June 3, under a heavy stretch of gray afternoon clouds, Era and I arrived at the First Christian Church near the edge of Roseburg. It was a modest white building with a steeple that leaned ever so slightly and windows that let in the soft light like a blessing. The wedding was small—just ten of us gathered inside—but it was full of warmth.

Grant's older brother John and his wife Nancy brought fried chicken and potato salad packed in wicker baskets, planning a simple picnic at the park just a few blocks from the church. Era had bundled red roses and sprigs of lavender from her flower garden that morning, which she gave to Fern as a bouquet, the scent clinging to her dress as we walked up the steps into the chapel. Era looked as beautiful as the day we were married. She wore a pale pink gown—a simple, graceful piece she'd ordered months before from the Sears and Roebuck catalog. And I couldn't take my eyes off of her.

None of Fern's brothers could be there. George and John were both married now, living in California and Kansas, and William had just taken a seasonal job on a farm near Fresno. Still, Fern didn't let their absence dampen her spirit. Her uncle Sam and aunt Mary had come all the way from New York, and that helped fill the empty space her brothers had left.

Mary had brought along the white blouse and long brown skirt Eddie had worn at our wedding so many years ago. Fern put them on with pride, and I'd never seen her look more alive. She glowed with quiet joy, graceful and composed, like she knew she was exactly where she was meant to be. When I walked her down the aisle, I barely made it three steps before the damned tears started. I wiped them away, but they kept coming.

Standing at the front of that little church, I placed her hand into Grant's and met his eyes. The boy looked like he'd just watched the sun rise for the first time—steady on his feet, but full of awe. You could tell he was overwhelmed, but to his credit, he didn't waver. The minister smiled kindly and spoke the vows with warmth. When he declared them husband and wife, Fern looked up at Grant with so much love it nearly broke me in two. Soft cheers and laughter followed—gentle, joyful, and just right for a day like that.

After the ceremony, I kissed her on the cheek and held her a moment longer than I should've. "If you find even a fraction of the happiness that Era and I have," I said, my voice catching, "your life will be a beautiful one."

That evening, after the picnic and goodbyes, Era and I returned to our cabin. The house was quiet but felt full somehow, like the day had left a kind of blessing over everything. We lay in bed with the windows cracked open, letting in the scent of pine and earth and distant river water. Era's head rested on my chest, her fingers gently tracing circles on my arm.

"She was radiant," she whispered. "And so calm."

"She's got her own fire," I said, kissing her hair. "Strong, soft, and sure as grit."

Era chuckled, and I felt the laugh deep in my ribs. "I hope they build something good up there at the Smith place. A home. A family. Something steady."

"They will," I said. "He loves her."

Silence settled between us, but it was a warm, contented kind. I stared at the low ceiling beams, remembering Fern as a little girl chasing chickens, singing to the goats, always barefoot and wild-hearted. And now—married.

"We've had a good life," I said softly.

Era tilted her head to look at me, eyes reflecting the faint glow from the oil lamp on the dresser. "And it's not over yet."

"No," I whispered, pulling her close. "Not by a long shot."

This had been a perfect day, but by mid-July, I began to notice small things. Era would sit longer than usual after chores, catching her breath. One morning, she winced climbing down the porch steps. "Just tired," she said. But I could tell her smile didn't reach her eyes.

I told myself it was normal. A baby growing will take it out of you—but deep down, something itched at the back of my mind.

As the weeks passed, my concern grew. So did Era's belly. And yet I couldn't figure out what was wrong—not until the first week of August. That's when everything changed. She got sick. So sick she couldn't get out of bed. Every time I brought her food, she'd push it away. Her skin turned pale, her strength drained. She'd become a shadow of herself.

"I can't lose my baby," she cried. "Please don't let me lose my baby."

I held her hand and promised I'd do everything I could. Lily McDonald came by every day to check on her. She said the baby still seemed to be growing. But Era wasn't getting better.

The days blurred together. I sat beside her bed, wiping her forehead with a damp cloth, whispering the same quiet reassurances over and over. Outside, the summer sun beat down on the hills, but inside the cabin everything felt still and heavy. Too quiet.

Lily did what she could. She brought tonics and broth, checked the baby's position, listened to Era's breath—slow, shallow, and sometimes wheezy.

"The baby's hanging on," she'd say, trying to sound sure of it. "And that's a good sign."

But Era was struggling. Her cheeks had hollowed. Her hands trembled when she tried to lift a cup. She barely spoke, and when she did, it was all frantic whispers and jumbled dreams. Some nights I'd wake to find her soaked in sweat, her nightgown clinging to her like fevered gauze. Sometimes she'd reach for me in the dark, not even fully awake, just murmuring, "Don't go. Please don't go.."

And so I stayed. I slept on the floor beside her—holding her hand, rubbing her back—barely sleeping at all.

I kept thinking of Daniel. How fast he'd gone, before I even had the chance to hold him. I remembered the aching emptiness, the way my prayers fell flat against the silence. And now here I was again, staring at the same edge, the same darkness, the same damned helplessness. Only this time, it wasn't just a baby I might lose.

I was worried sick it might be her. During that hot, humid month of August, she didn't get better—but she didn't get worse either. She just lingered, somewhere between strength and surrender.

On a Sunday afternoon, Lily said, "The baby is getting ready to come."

"So what do we do?" I asked, glancing at Era. She lay helpless on the bed, barely able to move.

"She doesn't have the strength." Lily raised Era's hand—it fell limply to the side. "I've never helped birth a child when the mother was this sick."

"But you have to!" I said, panic tightening in my chest.

"This is beyond me," she said calmly. "You need to get her to a hospital."

"A hospital? I've never been to a hospital."

"Mercy Hospital in Roseburg," she said. "There are doctors there who know how to handle cases like this."

"I don't trust hospitals."

My pa never trusted hospitals. Said they were places folks went to die. I used to laugh at that when I was younger—but now, with Era limp in Lily's arms, I couldn't shake the thought. It clung to me like sweat.

"You don't have a choice. If you don't get her there as quickly as possible, I'm afraid of what might happen."

I looked at Era again—pale, soaked in sweat, barely breathing—and I knew Lily was right. I just didn't want to believe it. "Okay." I wrapped Era in a blanket and carried her to the Model T.

"You can do this. It's only fifteen miles away."

"What if something happens on the way? Please—come with us," I begged, more desperate than I'd ever been in my life.

Lily climbed into the backseat and held Era's head in her lap. Lady jumped into the front beside me, as if she knew something was wrong and wasn't about to be left behind. I ordered her out, but she refused to move. I didn't have time to argue. I pushed her out and hit the gas.

I drove wildly down the hill toward the main road. Lady chased after us, running hard until I hit the open stretch and left her in the dust. The road to Roseburg was a two-lane gravel track, rough and winding. I shoved it into high gear and drove as fast as I dared. Halfway there, Lily shouted over the wind, "Faster! You've got to go faster!"

"I'm going as fast as this car will go!"

"She's passed out—and I can't wake her up!"

We hit a patch of rough gravel and the whole car rattled like it might come apart. I gripped the wheel tighter, eyes fixed on the road ahead, but everything was blurring—sky, trees, dust, panic.

Behind me, Lily was trying to rouse her. I didn't dare look back.

"Come on," I muttered. "Just hold on a little longer."

The wind tore past us. The road stretched on. Behind me, Lily kept calling her name, but Era didn't stir.

I gripped the wheel so hard my knuckles ached. I kept my eyes on the road and muttered, "Just a little longer. Please." But something inside me shifted. Quiet. Cold. Like a lantern going out in a room I hadn't known I was in. I'd never been this scared. Not when Daniel died. Not even as a boy riding out on my own for the first time. Back then, I believed grit was enough. That if you held on hard enough, you could pull anything back from the edge.

Now I wasn't so sure.

The road kept winding. And for the first time in my life, I couldn't see how this was going to end in anything but loss.

A LITTLE COUGH

By the time we made it to the hospital, Era was still breathing. Just barely.

I paced the hospital halls for hours. Back and forth past the same pale walls, the same chipped linoleum, the same nurses whispering behind the desk. No one told me anything. Just that she was "in good hands" and "they were doing all they could."

But all I could think of was the way she'd looked when they wheeled her through those double doors—so small against the white sheets, her skin too pale, her lips pressed tight with pain.

Lily had driven the Model T back to Myrtle Creek after dropping us off, promising to return in a day or two. I'd barely noticed her leave. My whole world was inside that room.

I tried to pray, like Ma taught me long ago. But the words wouldn't come. So I walked. Hands clenched. Heart pounding. Every tick of the clock a hammer. I pressed my ear to the door more than once, hoping for some sign—crying, footsteps, anything. But all I heard was silence.

I thought of all the things that could go wrong. Fever. Bleeding. The baby not breathing. Her not waking up.

And then—there was a cry. Not Era's. A baby's. Sharp, loud, and angry.

I stumbled back from the door, breath caught in my chest. A nurse rushed by me with a smile, and I nearly grabbed her by the arm. "Is it a boy?" I asked. My voice cracked.

She nodded. "Strong set of lungs, that one."

Three days after we'd arrived—on August 30, 1922 at eleven in the morning—our son was born. A.J. Stephens.

When they finally let me in, Era was lying in the bed, damp curls sticking to her forehead, skin still pale, but eyes glowing. She looked up and smiled—like she'd just climbed a mountain and found a meadow beyond.

"Allen," she whispered, holding out the bundle swaddled in her arms, "we did it."

I sat on the edge of the bed and touched the boy's tiny fingers. He wrapped one around mine, fierce and warm.

Era looked down at him, her voice thick with emotion. "I don't care if I made it or not, as long as he was healthy."

I tried to protest, but she was already kissing his forehead, already counting his fingers, already laughing—soft and breathless.

And let me tell you, he was healthy—as healthy as a corn-fed calf fresh on his feet. And he even had a set of lungs on him that could be heard a mile away.

They let me hold him later that afternoon, once they were sure he was warm and breathing steady. The nurse showed me how to support his neck and cradle his back, but my hands trembled anyway. He weighed almost nothing, and yet he felt like the heaviest thing I'd ever carried.

I looked down at his scrunched little face, red and blotchy, his mouth slightly open as he slept. "You're alive!" I whispered. "You're really alive!"

He shifted, frowned, then stretched one arm like he'd already had enough of the world. I couldn't help but laugh.

"You take after your mama," I said. "Strong from the start."

On Sunday, a week after we'd first arrived, I drove them both home. The Model T rattled along the road, Era bundled in the passenger seat, A.J. nestled in a blanket beside her. The early September sun was warm on the hills, and everything felt touched by gold—dust lifting behind the tires, trees flickering light through their leaves, the first hints of autumn sneaking into the morning air.

When we pulled up to the cabin, Lady was waiting on the porch, tail thumping like a drum. She didn't bark or run—just stood and watched, ears up, like she knew something sacred had just entered her world.

Era climbed out slowly, holding A.J. tight to her chest. Lady stepped forward and sniffed the bundle gently, then leaned her head against Era's knee with a quiet sigh, as if all was finally right again.

Inside, the house felt smaller, warmer. I swept the floors, aired out the linens, made up the bed fresh, and tried to cook something— though nothing I made ever tasted like Era's Sunday roast. Still, it felt good to have them home.

We sat on the porch that evening, the baby asleep in Era's arms, Lady curled at her feet. Era leaned against me, her eyes soft with exhaustion and peace.

"I still can't believe he's ours," she whispered.

I wrapped my arm around her and kissed the top of her head. "Me neither," I said. "But I'm glad you're both here."

For a while, things felt almost normal. She nursed him with ease, hummed lullabies I didn't recognize, and called him "my little thundercloud" every time he let loose that powerful wail of his. Her cheeks had color again, her hands steady as she buttoned his tiny shirts.

But then came the little signs. She started sleeping in. Not just tired—exhausted. I'd bring her breakfast, only to find it untouched by midmorning. She'd get winded climbing the stairs or hanging laundry. I tried not to mention it, but it gnawed at me. And the cough—it never left. A soft rasp in the mornings, a deep rattle at night.

Early one evening, while I was chopping kindling out back, I saw her through the kitchen window. She was leaning over the sink, one hand gripping the counter, the other holding a handkerchief tight to her mouth. When she turned and saw me watching, her face softened—like nothing was wrong at all.

I stood there a long moment, the ax heavy in my hands, the kindling half-forgotten. I'd seen that kind of smile before—thin and brave and hiding the truth. I told myself it was nothing. I told myself a lot of things.

Later, I asked her about it. She reached for my hand and squeezed it. "Stop your worrying," she said gently. "It's just a little cough."

But even Lady knew better. She followed Era from room to room like a shadow, curling beside her feet while she rocked the baby, whining at the foot of the bed if Era stayed asleep too long. Some nights, I'd wake to hear Lady pacing the hall, her claws clicking softly on the wood.

And in the quiet moments, when the baby slept and the house went still, I'd catch Era staring out the window, her hand resting over her chest, as if she felt something dark stirring deep inside her which she couldn't quite name.

On a cloudy morning in late October, I found her at the kitchen table with a blanket wrapped around her shoulders and a letter half-written in front of her. The baby was napping, and steam rose gently from the teacup by her elbow. Her handwriting was slower than usual, and she paused often—gathering breath, collecting thoughts.

She looked up when she saw me watching and gave a tired smile.

"I'm writing to Papa," she said. "Just... letting him know I've been under the weather."

I nodded, sitting down beside her. "That's good. I'm sure he'd want to hear from you."

She reached for my hand. "I didn't tell him everything. Just enough to make him curious. I asked if he might consider coming down for Christmas. It's been almost two years, and I'd love for him to meet A.J. before he gets too big."

She looked down at the page again, blinking slowly. "I don't want to worry him... but I miss him. And maybe having him here would make things feel a little easier."

I kissed the back of her hand. "You're not alone, Era."

"I know," she whispered. "But sometimes, it helps to hear it."

A few days later, I walked with her down to the mailbox at the end of the lane. She was bundled in her coat and scarf, A.J. tucked in against her chest, and Lady trailing close at her heels. The air was sharp with the scent of fir and woodsmoke, and a thin fog clung to the hollows near the trees. Era held the letter tight in her mittened hand, pressing it to her lips before she dropped it in.

"What'd you write in the end?" I asked gently.

She smiled. "That I missed him. That the baby's beautiful. And that I'd love to see his face again if the Northern Pacific would carry it down this way."

We stood there for a moment, just listening to the wind. Then we turned back toward the house, Era's pace a little slower than it had been earlier that morning.

The weeks passed, and the weather turned. Frost clung to the porch railings each morning, and smoke curled constantly from our chimney. Era had good days and bad ones—days where she laughed and hummed while baking sweetbread, and days when she barely got out of bed.

Then, in mid-December, a postcard arrived from Seattle. The handwriting was firm, almost formal, but the message was short and sweet:

The train arrives at the Roseburg Station December 22nd. I hope there's room at your place for an old man and a sack of gifts. —Papa.

Era read it twice, then pressed it to her heart and closed her eyes.

"He's coming," she whispered. "He's really coming."

I saw something lift in her then. Not just joy—something deeper. Relief. Like a weight had been shifted, even if just for a little while.

We cleared out the guest room, swept the porch, strung pine boughs along the mantel. A.J. watched with wide eyes as Era hung paper snowflakes from the window and tied a ribbon around Lady's collar. Her cough still lingered, but her spirit burned bright that week, as if she was willing her body to keep pace with her heart.

On the morning of the 22nd, I drove the Model T down to the Roseburg Station, and there he was—tall, gray-bearded, and straight-backed, wearing a long coat and a wool cap, suitcase in one hand, and a bundle of wrapped gifts in the other.

When we got back to the house, Lady barked once, then wagged herself silly. Era opened the door and just stood there, tears shining in her eyes.

"Papa," she breathed.

He stepped forward and wrapped her in his arms, careful not to crush her, but holding her like she was still his little girl. And for the first time in months, she let herself be held—no smile, no brave front. Just a daughter, in her father's arms.

We kept the fire burning through Christmas. Papa sat near the hearth most evenings with A.J. cradled in his arms, rocking him gently while Era rested nearby. He brought a wooden railroad whistle for A.J. and a Zane Gray western, *The Mysterious Rider*, for me. Then he handed Era a small box. Inside was a silver locket with a pressed violet inside—one he'd found near the Cascades two summers ago and kept in waxed paper.

The house felt full in a way it hadn't in months. We shared warm bread and venison stew, played checkers by lamplight, and listened to the wind outside. Era managed to sit by the fire now and then, bundled in shawls, her head resting against Papa's shoulder while he hummed a hymn she hadn't heard since childhood.

On Christmas morning, she smiled as she watched him cradle A.J., brushing the boy's soft curls back with a trembling hand.

"He's stubborn," she whispered. "Like his daddy. But he's got a Leewright heart."

Papa chuckled, never looking up from the baby. "He's got your eyes, girl. That's what'll carry him through."

Two days later, I drove Papa back to the Roseburg station. The sun was just rising, a pale gold mist stretched over the hills. He sat quiet beside me, suitcase at his feet, his cap folded in his lap. "I could stay," he said softly. "If you think she needs me longer."

"She's stronger for having you here," I said, "and she's thankful you stayed as long as you did."

He nodded, looking out the window. "There's something in her— same as her mama had. That quiet kind of grit."

We sat a moment longer after I parked near the platform. He turned to me. "Take care of her, Allen. And that boy—he's worth fighting for."

"I know," I said. "And I will. With everything I've got."

He clapped a hand on my shoulder, gripped it hard, then stepped out into the cold.

I watched the train pull away, steam trailing like a breath held too long. He stood at the rear until the trees swallowed the tracks, one hand lifted in farewell.

Back at the house, Era was rocking by the window, A.J. asleep in her arms, Lady curled at her feet. She looked up when I came in, and though she didn't say anything, I saw the peace settle in her eyes like falling snow.

Through the spring and summer, Era faded—her color, her strength, even her words. I did what I could, but it was no more use than trying to stop an avalanche with a snow shovel. She no longer walked with me down to the river. No longer gathered wildflowers for the kitchen table. And she didn't laugh like she used to—with that magic twinkle in her eyes that could light up a room.

Most days, she just sat in the rocker by the fireplace with A.J. in her arms—rocking him, feeding him, humming soft lullabies into the thick brown curls above his forehead. Lady at her feet, always close.

Lily came by every Sunday afternoon. She and Era would sit together for hours, whispering and sipping tea, while I split wood or tinkered with the car just to keep from worrying too much.

It was Lily who finally pulled me aside one Sunday in August. "You need to take her to a doctor," she said. "In Roseburg. Soon."

"She just needs rest," I told her. "She's still nursing. That takes it out of a person."

Lily shook her head. "You almost lost her last year. Don't forget that. The doctors saved her. Do you really want to wait until it's too late this time? What happens to A.J. if she…" Her voice caught. "If she doesn't get better?"

I stared at the floorboards, jaw tight. I didn't want to hear it. But I knew she was right. I took Era to Roseburg the next morning.

Dr. Adair met us at the clinic. I was surprised to see she was a woman—mid-forties, sharp but kind eyes, a firm handshake. I felt uneasy at first, but she was gentle with Era, and after a few minutes, I stopped caring about her being a woman doctor.

She listened to Era's chest for a long while, her face growing more serious by the second.

"What is it?" I asked.

"Her lungs," she said quietly, stethoscope still pressed to Era's back. "There's a lot of crackling—popping sounds. Congestion. Let's run a few tests. I want to see what's going on in there."

She gave her a skin test, then sent her down the hall for a chest x-ray. "Come back next week," she said. "We'll go over the results then."

I nodded, but my chest felt tight. Like I was already bracing for something I didn't want to hear.

When we returned the following Friday, I knew something was wrong the moment Dr. Adair stepped into the room. She didn't smile. Didn't sit.

"It's tuberculosis," she said. "I'm sorry. She needs to be admitted to the State Tuberculosis Hospital in Salem—immediately."

I'd made promises once—promises to never leave, to stay steady, to always be at her side. But now it wasn't me walking away. It was the world threatening to take her. And I didn't know how to fight it. I felt like the air had been knocked out of me.

"No," I said. "Absolutely not."

"She's very ill," Dr. Adair said, her voice firm. "She needs constant care—rest, nutrition, isolation. That hospital could save her life."

"I'm not sending her away," I said. "I can take care of her."

"She's contagious."

"Then we've already been exposed—me and A.J. both. And we're fine. We'll be fine."

Dr. Adair sighed, but she didn't argue further. "I can't force you," she said. "But if you're going to keep her home, she needs complete rest. No exertion. Fresh air and sunlight every morning. Warmth. Good food. And isolation as best as you can manage it."

"I can do that," I said. "I will do that."

"Do you understand how serious this is?"

I nodded.

"Her prognosis is not good," she said firmly. "If anything gets worse, take her to Salem."

But as we walked out into the pale afternoon light, doubt twisted deep in my gut. Was I making the right choice? Should I have let her go? What if she got worse? What if I couldn't fix this? No. I couldn't think like that. I wouldn't. There are some thoughts a man just can't afford to dwell on—not if he wants to keep it all together.

In the next few weeks, Era seemed to hold her own. She didn't get better, but she didn't get worse. Then we got word that Mr. Leewright was dead—a heart attack in his sleep. It came out of nowhere.

I was taken aback by the news. Mr. Leewright was a kindhearted man—steady, sharp, and full of quiet grace. He'd been a good friend to us, especially back in Denver. At Christmas he'd seemed so strong, so full of life. But nothing surprised me much anymore. Life's a hard trail, and you never really know what's waiting around the bend. He'd lived his seventy-two years well. Still, it reminded me how little we control—and how fast everything can change.

I didn't want to tell Era. I knew it would make things worse, but keeping it from her felt wrong. She would take this hard—and it would make her worse. She would also want to go to the funeral, but that was something she just couldn't do. I tried to lay it out, slow and gentle, but it made no difference. When Era heard, it was like her spirit gave way.

She wouldn't eat, wouldn't drink, wouldn't even look at A.J. She just lay there coughing up blood.

The next Sunday Lily looked at me with fear in her eyes. "If you don't take her to Salem right now, I'm afraid she won't last more than a few days."

"But I can't just leave her alone in a strange hospital, in a strange town, where she doesn't know anyone."

"Then she'll die."

"I can't keep her away from A.J."

"You don't have a choice."

"If she's going to be in Salem, then so will A.J. and me. I'll find a place near the hospital. I'll get a job in Salem. I love her—I won't abandon her."

That very afternoon, I packed a suitcase for her, one for me, and one for A.J. I strapped them to the luggage rack on the back of the Model T and left the ranch in Ruckles behind. Lady chased the car to the main road. I gave a wave and called, "Don't worry, girl—we'll be back when Era is well."

I drove a hundred and fifty miles north to a four-story building perched on a hill. The sign said in bold letters: OREGON STATE TUBERCULOSIS HOSPITAL

I stared at it with Era sleeping beside me, A.J. cradled in her arms. Time seemed to stop. I knew what had to be done, but I felt frozen.

As the sun set and the world turned dark, I looked up at the massive white building, every window lit, and whispered, "Help me. Dear God, make my Era well again."

Then I looked over at her—peaceful, pale, perfectly still—and whispered, "I knew it was never just a little cough."

EVERY SUNDAY

I watched Era walk slowly up the stairs, alone, her suitcase in hand. My heart broke. She paused at the top, one foot still on the last step, and turned to look at me. The light caught in her hair, and for a split second, I almost thought she'd come back. But she didn't.

She knew I couldn't join her, though I wanted to with everything in me. I raised my hand in a wave just as a young nurse stepped forward and gently took the suitcase from her. Era offered a tired smile—brave, distant, with just enough fear in it to break my heart. Then she slipped behind the heavy wooden door and was gone from sight.

I didn't drive away. I just sat there staring at the tall, three-story brick building as if by sheer force of will I could make her reappear. They called it a sanitarium, but it looked more like a prison to me— one with flowers in the windows, manicured lawns, and a silence too heavy to be peaceful.

That night I slept in the front seat of the Model T, my coat bunched up under my head and A.J. curled up on the floorboards with a blanket tucked around him.

The rules at the sanitarium were strict. Visitors were allowed only on Sundays, and even then just for two hours in the open-air pavilion. It would be a full week before I could see Era again, but I didn't want to leave town. I needed to be close—just in case.

The next morning, after getting A.J. some warm milk and bread from a grocer, I asked around and found a room for rent about a mile from the sanitarium. It was a small, tidy space in a whitewashed farmhouse on the edge of a peach orchard, owned by a widow named Mrs. Alice Nickerson. She was 35, warm-voiced, and neatly dressed, with chestnut hair pinned back in a bun and an air of quiet confidence that came from having no one left to fuss over but herself. Her husband had been a banker and part-time farmer—killed in an automobile accident the year before on the road between Albany and Salem. They had no children.

She agreed to rent me the room and care for A.J. during the day for ten dollars a week—eight for board, and two for the boy. It was more than I ever made in a month back at the JR Bar Ranch, but it was warm, honest living, and I was grateful.

She told me to call her Alice. Her farmhouse was clean and modest. Lace curtains filtered the afternoon sun. A braided rug warmed the floor. The parlor smelled faintly of lemon oil and woodsmoke. She had a milk cow out back, which meant there was always cream for the coffee and fresh milk for A.J. In the evenings, once he was asleep in the little bed she'd tucked near the stove, Alice and I would sit in the parlor, a cozy room with bookshelves stacked high and a green velvet settee that had worn thin at the arms.

Sometimes she read aloud from her husband's old books—mostly history or poetry. Her voice was low and sure, turning even the driest passages into something melodic. Other nights we played cribbage or dominoes by firelight, sipping coffee and trading small talk.

She had a way of asking about my day that felt genuine, not just polite. And sometimes her questions came with a glance that lingered just a second too long, or a laugh that seemed too friendly. But I thought nothing of it. Because no matter how kind she was or how calm the house felt, I loved Era and missed her more with every passing day.

A few days after settling in, I got a job at the Oregon State Mental

Hospital over on 23rd Street. They took me on as a security guard and transport officer. It wasn't the kind of work I'd imagined for myself, but it was steady—seventy dollars a month, plus mileage when I used my own car.

Most days I was stationed near the front gate or patrolling the men's wards. Other times, I was sent out across western Oregon—Portland, Eugene, Tillamook, even as far south as Coos Bay—to pick up patients committed by court order or physician's recommendation. I'd load them into the Model T, sometimes with a nurse, sometimes alone. Some came quiet as lambs. Others fought like hell. A few just stared out the window the whole way, too numb to speak.

One evening, after I'd tucked A.J. into bed, I found Alice in the parlor folding linens near the stove. She glanced up as I came in.

"How was your first day?" she asked, setting the stack aside.

I eased down into the armchair with a sigh. "Tiring. Sad, mostly."

She waited, not pushing, just listening.

"I picked up a girl from a little farm near Tillamook," I said after a moment. "About twenty-five. Couldn't eat. Wouldn't speak. Her folks said she hadn't gotten out of bed in weeks."

Alice folded her hands in her lap. "And when you got there?"

"She barely looked at me," I said. "Didn't fight. Didn't cry. Just let me help her into the car like she'd already left the world behind."

Alice's brow furrowed. "That must be hard to see."

"It is," I said quietly. "Makes you wonder how a person gets so far down they stop reaching for the light."

The fire crackled between us, and for a while neither of us spoke.

"She's in a good place now," Alice said gently.

"I hope so," I murmured. "God, I hope so."

A few days later, Alice asked as we sat near the fire, "How did it go today?"

I think she was really interested. I leaned back in the armchair, rubbing the back of my neck. "Sent to Portland. Had to bring in a big fellow—must've weighed a hundred pounds more than me. Mean as a bearcat and didn't want to come."

She gave a soft chuckle. "How on earth did you manage that?"

"With a towel and a strong arm," I said. "No one's too much to handle, not if you know how to move quick and hold firm."

Her brow lifted slightly. "You must've been something to see."

I shrugged, not catching her tone. "Just a job. Get 'em in the car, get 'em to Salem, keep 'em safe along the way. That's all."

Alice reached over and poured another cup of coffee. "Still," she said, her voice softer, "not many men would take that kind of work."

"I didn't have a choice."

She didn't answer, just handed me the cup with a faint smile, her fingers brushing mine.

Every Sunday, I put on my best clothes and walked the mile to the hospital. I'd comb my hair in the reflection of a storefront window and wait under the slatted roof of the pavilion for Era to be brought out.

Sometimes she smiled. Sometimes she didn't. But every time, she reached for my hand. And I held on like the world might end before I got another chance.

That first Sunday, the sky was light blue, with clouds clinging to the western horizon like they didn't want to leave. The nurse from before met me at the front steps and led me through the gardens—roses just beginning to fade, dry leaves crackling underfoot. The pavilion was small, paint peeling at the corners. Era lay in a narrow bed, propped up on pillows, with a chair close enough that I could hold her hand.

She looked smaller than I remembered. Her shawl was pulled tight over her shoulders, and her hair had come loose in the wind. She stood twisting the hem of her dress, eyes fixed on the ground. When she looked up and saw me, she reached out. "Allen."

Her hands were cold. Her voice was thin. But she still smiled.

"I missed you," I whispered.

She looked up at me, eyes shining with tears she hadn't yet let fall. "I thought about you every day," she said. "Every hour, some days."

I brushed a strand of hair from her cheek. "I wish I could be here more."

"I know," she said. "But you came today. That's enough."

She held my hand tightly—tighter than I expected from someone who looked like a breath might break her. I kissed her knuckles, one by one, and didn't care who was watching.

"A.J.'s here," I said softly. "He's back at the nurses station."

A small smile tugged at her mouth. "My boys," she said. "I dream about us, the three of us. Walking by the river. Laughing. Like we used to."

"We'll have that again," I told her, though I wasn't sure if I believed it. "We will."

Fern wanted to visit too—she drove up nearly every week. She missed Era deeply and always sent something along: a note in her careful hand, a jar of blackberry jam, a scarf she'd knitted in the quiet hours after supper. But the sanitarium only allowed me and A.J. inside. It was hard on Fern, being so close and still kept at arm's length. She once told me if it were up to her, she'd be there every Sunday. And I knew she would.

"Tell Fern I think about her, too," Era said softly, her eyes drifting toward the trees. "I wish I could see her."

When she felt stronger we'd sit in wicker chairs, and I pulled the blanket over her lap. She leaned into me, her head resting on my shoulder like she used to on long train rides, back when the world still felt full of wide-open futures. The scent of pine drifted through the cold air. Somewhere across town, a bell rang. Her breathing was shallow. Each inhale sounded like it came at a price. I held her hand the whole time—her fingers so thin and fragile. But her grip never faltered. She was still here. Still fighting.

And that—just that—was enough to keep me going another week.

Ma wrote to me nearly every week—folded pages in her careful hand, always full of prayers and Scripture, sometimes a pressed flower from her garden in Denver. They came like clockwork—short, sweet, steady things that reminded me she was still out there believing in me. They were also filled with questions—about Era, A.J., and Fern—questions that were hard to answer. But I did the best I could, mostly in the quiet hours after A.J. fell asleep and Alice had gone off to bed, the fire in the parlor fading to embers.

By late October the wind had a sharper edge to it, and the trees around the sanitarium were nearly bare. Fallen leaves skittered across the pavilion floor like tiny messengers with nowhere left to go.

We sat side by side, the blanket pulled tight around us. Era's head rested lightly on my shoulder, and I could feel how thin she'd become. The silence between us was comfortable, the kind that came after everything worth hiding had already been said.

"I try to make it back to the cabin once a month," I murmured, watching a few last leaves drift down from the sycamores. "If my schedule allows."

Era didn't answer right away, just let her fingers play with the edge of the blanket.

"Fern took Lady to her place," I added. "She's probably letting her sleep on the good furniture."

That drew a faint smile from her. "Good. Lady deserves it."

"Fern and Grant come by every morning to feed the animals and milk the cow. I let them keep the milk—no sense letting it go to waste."

Era looked up at me then. "Good. I'm glad somebody is watching the place."

"They keep an eye on the ranch. And I keep an eye on you."

"And you'll never know how much I appreciate it."

I paused, tightening my arm around her shoulders.

"No matter where I am—on the road, in the orchard, even sitting in the quiet of Alice's parlor—I carry you with me."

She turned her face toward mine, eyes soft and searching.

"I hear you in the wind," I said. "In the leaves. I feel your hand in mine even when I'm alone." I looked down. "I feel it like when we walked the streets of Denver or sat beside the river at the ranch."

Era blinked quickly, but a tear slid free anyway. She didn't wipe it away.

"I don't want to be a memory, Allen," she whispered.

"You're not," I said. "You're my wife. And you're still here."

The wind had picked up by the time I started walking back to Alice's. Leaves blew across the road in restless swirls, crunching under my boots. Her words kept rolling through my mind: I don't want to be a memory. She wasn't. Not to me. She was still here—still breathing, still fighting. And I wasn't giving up. Not now. Not ever.

I pictured the three of us back at the ranch one day—Era in the kitchen window, A.J. chasing chickens through the yard, and me on the front porch with a book about cowboys while Lady slept at my feet. We were all smiling, and I was thinking that I must be the luckiest man on God's green earth. That picture was what I held onto with each step I took.

It was the Sunday before Christmas.

We sat in the pavilion beneath a pale sky, bundled against the cold. I brought Era a small parcel wrapped in brown paper and tied with twine—a pair of wool mittens and a peppermint stick A.J. had picked out. She laughed and kissed my cheek, then held my hand between hers to keep warm.

"What are you and A.J. doing for Christmas?" she asked. Her voice was light, but there was something under it—thin as frost on glass.

I hesitated. "Alice is fixing a special dinner. Ham, I think. An apple pie, too. She's even making stockings for the boy."

Era smiled, but once again it didn't quite reach her eyes. "That's thoughtful of her."

"It is," I said softly.

She looked down at our hands. "I just wish I was there. It feels like being trapped here, I'm missing out on life—on building special memories with A.J."

I didn't know what to say. I squeezed her hand gently.

"She's just helping out. That's all."

Era nodded slowly, but her eyes stayed fixed on the garden path beyond the pavilion. "It's nice of her. Really." But the words were thinner than her smile.

A gust of wind kicked up through the trees, rattling the last of the leaves. I pulled the blanket tighter around her and rested my chin against her hair.

She didn't bring it up again.

It was a week or two after Christmas.

The road to the sanitarium felt longer that Sunday, even though I knew every turn of it by now. I drove slow, one hand on the wheel, the other resting on the worn seat beside me—where Era used to sit. A.J. was back home with Alice, and the silence in the Model T left too much room for my thoughts.

The fields were bare and brown, trees stripped down to bone. A flock of starlings lifted off a fence post and drifted into the sky like smoke. Everything felt still. Like the whole countryside was holding its breath.

When the sanitarium finally came into view—brick rising behind the winter branches—I pulled over and sat for a minute, watching my breath fog up the windshield. Then I stepped out and walked the gravel path toward the pavilion.

Era was already there, wrapped in her red shawl, sitting in the wicker chair that creaked when she shifted. She stood as soon as she saw me and smiled—so bright, it stopped me in my tracks.

"You're early," I said, crossing the last few steps to her.

"I couldn't wait," she said, eyes dancing. "Allen, I have something to tell you."

She reached for my hands and gripped them tight. Her breath came fast, and her cheeks were pink—not from the cold, but from something glowing underneath.

"We're going to have a baby," she whispered.

I blinked, staring at her, not quite able to take it in. "What? But we've only been together once."

"Once is all it takes."

"I don't know what to say." I just sat there dumbfounded.

"The nurses don't much approve. I suppose they've guessed what we've been up to when left alone."

"Are you absolutely sure?"

She nodded. "The doctor saw me yesterday. Said I'm about two months along. I've been waiting all week to tell you. I wanted it to be in person."

I stepped forward and pulled her into my arms. She came easily, burying her face against my coat. I held her close, trying to steady the feeling rising up in my chest. I was stunned—so full of love and fear and hope, I couldn't speak.

"I don't even know what to say," I murmured.

"Say you're happy."

I leaned back and looked into her eyes. "I'm more than happy, Era. I'm grateful. And scared. And so excited I feel like I might come apart."

She laughed through tears and held my face in her hands for a moment. Then we sat down together, close under the old blanket. Her fingers laced through mine, and she laid our hands gently over her belly.

The wind moved through the trees. A bell rang from the far side of the hospital. And for a little while, we just sat there, quiet and still.

"You're still sick," I said at last.

"I know," she replied softly. "But I'm still here."

And in that moment, with her beside me and the promise of new life between us, I remember thinking that somehow, despite everything, we were being given a new beginning.

Winter gave way to spring, and Era seemed to be getting stronger with each passing week. Then early on a Saturday morning, just before dawn, a heavy knock came on the door of the house. A moment later, Alice called me out of my room. A worker from the sanitarium stood at the door. "Sorry for the interruption. But your wife needs you."

"What's wrong?"

"She's about to give birth," he said. Then after a pause, "Twins."

"Twins?" I repeated, blinking hard as if that would make the word make more sense.

The man just nodded, hands shoved deep in his coat pockets. I handed A.J. to Alice and was halfway down the porch steps before my boots were on.

The road blurred under my tires. All I could think was: hold on, Era. I'm coming.

A PLAIN WOODEN CROSS

The car skidded into the narrow drive beside the sanitarium. I killed the engine and sprinted up the steps to the main building—heart pounding, face flushed, sweat clinging to my collar.

"Where's Era?" I asked breathlessly.

"She's in delivery," said the young nurse who'd welcomed us the first time we'd arrived at the sanitarium. She placed a firm hand against my chest. "I'm sorry, but I can't let you see her yet."

"She's having a baby," I said, my voice shaky. "Two babies."

"You'll have to wait."

So I waited—pacing the porch, watching the clouds drift past the rooftop, trying to pray.

Then, just before noon, I heard them—two strong, healthy cries lifting through the hallway window like sunlight breaking through stormclouds. I stood with one hand pressed against the wall, eyes closed, letting those cries settle into my chest like answered prayer.

They let me in about thirty minutes later. The young nurse opened the door and nodded me through, and there was Era—sitting up in bed, pale but glowing, her hair tucked behind her ears and her eyes shining bright. We'd been visiting every Sunday for almost a year in the open-air pavilion, but nothing could compare to this. She looked like herself again. Her cheeks were flushed, eyes dazzling with something I hadn't seen in months—joy. Or maybe hope. More than herself—like someone made new.

Both babies were bundled in a cradle beside her, small and perfect. Era was speaking quietly with the head nurse.

"Please," she said, her voice thin but urgent, "please let me keep the twins."

"I'm sorry," said the nurse gently. "Infants can't stay here."

"But they need their mother."

"Your husband can bring them every Sunday."

"They need to be nursed."

"Then he'll need to find a wet nurse. Or bottle-feed them."

"Please don't take them away."

"You're contagious. And you're too weak."

"Please," she said again, barely above a whisper.

The nurse hesitated, then nodded. "You can keep them for a day or two. But no more."

Era breathed out slowly and grabbed the nurse's hand. "Thank you so much."

"Remember," said the nurse, "only a day or two." Then she looked at me and smiled. "You've got two beautiful babies, a boy and girl."

I smiled back and sat down on the bed next to Era. "You're looking wonderful."

"Even though I just had two babies, I'm feeling better than I have since I got here."

"What should we name them?" I asked.

"I was thinking of Arle and Arlene."

"We can name them anything you'd like."

Era reached into the cradle, lifting Arlene with trembling hands and holding her close. For a moment, the sanitarium walls disappeared. The sickness, the silence, the rules—all of it faded. There was just her and the babies and a look in her eyes I would never forget.

That evening I kissed her forehead and left quietly, promising to return on Sunday.

The next day I put on my best shirt and drove through the orchards and farmland to the hospital. The young nurse met me at the door and led me around back to the garden path. I found Era on the pavilion bench, a blanket across her knees, both babies sleeping in her arms. I sat beside her, and we didn't speak much—just watched the breeze dance through the trees and counted tiny breaths.

On account of the circumstances, the sanitarium allowed me to stay longer that day. The nurses could also see how the babies brightened Era's mood, so they let her keep them an extra night.

I came back early Monday morning and packed their things in silence. A nurse helped wrap them snug and safe. Era kissed each baby on the forehead, then leaned back against the pillow, spent but peaceful. I lifted them gently—one in each arm—and carried them out through the front doors. She watched me from her window upstairs, her hand resting on the glass.

I nodded once before stepping off the porch.

I drove home with the twins tucked into a padded crate beside me on the front seat. The sun was still rising over the hills, casting long golden streaks across the orchard rows. Every few minutes I glanced over to make sure they were still breathing. They hardly stirred—just the softest movements beneath the blankets and those little sounds babies make, part sigh, part murmur, part whimper. All I knew was, they melted my heart.

When I pulled into the drive, Alice was already standing on the porch, apron on, drying her hands on a dish towel. She must have seen the Model T coming. She met me at the car door and leaned in without a word, lifting Arle gently into her arms while I gathered Arlene.

"Well, look at you," she whispered to the baby, pushing back the blanket. "You've got your mama's nose."

Inside, she had already set up a makeshift nursery in the front room—clean linens, a cradle from the attic, a basin of warm water on the stove. I didn't ask, and she didn't offer a speech—just moved through the space like she'd been preparing for this moment all along.

"I made broth for you," she said quietly. "And there's bread in the oven."

I stood in the doorway, suddenly too tired to speak. My legs felt weak. My arms were still holding Arlene, but it was like my whole body had just realized what we'd made it through.

Later that afternoon, A.J. came toddling in from the yard, cheeks pink from the sun, hair tousled and sticking up like a rooster. He stopped short when he saw the cradle. His eyes got wide.

"Babies?" he asked, pointing.

I knelt down beside him. "Yes, son. Your brother and sister."

He crept forward carefully, standing on tiptoe to peek into the blankets. Arlene stirred first, yawning with her whole face. A.J. blinked, then looked at me, like he needed permission to believe what he was seeing.

"Little," he whispered.

I nodded. "So were you, once."

He turned back and reached out, just barely brushing her foot with one chubby finger. Then he sat down cross-legged on the floor and didn't move. Just watched them breathe, eyes wide with wonder.

I looked over at Alice, who stood in the kitchen doorway with a dish in her hand and a knowing smile on her face.

"Looks like he's taken to them," she said.

I exhaled slowly and sat down beside my son. "

One way or another," I said softly, "we'll figure it out."

Summer and fall passed quickly. Every Sunday, I took A.J. and the twins to see their mother. For a while, it looked like Era was getting better. And that the twins had brought her back to life. My work at the State Mental Hospital kept me busy during the week—driving all over western Oregon to transport patients.

Alice was wonderful with the twins. She never charged me extra for watching them, and the five of us settled into a quiet rhythm.

Each evening, after the kids were asleep, Alice and I would share dinner, play a few hands of cards, read by lamplight, and talk about our days. She was good company—kind, steady, and quick to laugh—and I'm not sure how I could've made it through those months without her. She knew my heart belonged to Era, but sometimes I wondered if part of her hoped that might change.

But right around Christmas, Era worsened. It was sudden—like all the progress she'd fought so hard for these past six months vanished overnight.

When I saw her the first Sunday of February, she wasn't even aware I was there. Her eyes were closed, her breathing shallow, her hand limp in mine. She never opened her eyes again. But I wouldn't give up. For the next week, they let me visit every day. The young nurse—kind, gentle, with sorrow in her eyes—told me quietly, "She's nearly at the end. You should come while you can."

So I did. I came each morning and stayed until they made me leave. I brought flowers from Alice's yard, fresh ones each day—wild lilac, white narcissus, a branch of apple blossoms I found blooming too early. I placed them by her bedside, though she never stirred to see them.

Her skin had gone so pale it seemed to blend with the bedsheets. Her breathing was shallow, barely lifting her chest, each breath spaced by long silences that made me hold mine without realizing. I spoke to her anyway—quietly, gently—telling her stories about A.J. collecting stones and lining them up along the porch rail, about the twins learning to hold spoons. I told her how the rain had returned, how the river had risen, how much Lady missed her. I don't know if she heard me, but I spoke like she did.

Each night, I kissed her forehead before leaving, held her hand in both of mine, and whispered, "I'll be back tomorrow."

And I was.

By Friday, it was clear things would not improve.

Her breathing changed—long pauses, then short gasps, as if her body was deciding whether to keep going. I sat beside her in silence, unable to read, unable to pray. I just listened, eyes fixed on her chest, measuring every movement.

Late that afternoon, as I was preparing to leave, the nurse laid a hand on my shoulder. "You should get some rest," she said gently. "We'll let you know if anything changes."

Then, early Saturday morning, just after sunrise, a worker from the sanitarium knocked on our door. I didn't move. I couldn't. I just sat there, frozen. I knew what that knock meant. And somehow I believed that if no one opened the door, it wouldn't be true. But the knocking continued—steady, persistent—until I had no choice but to rise and face it.

The man stood quietly in the doorway. I just stared at him—his short hair, his tired eyes, his hands that fumbled a piece of paper. He cleared his throat, looked at the ground, and mumbled, "She's gone" like he couldn't get the word out fast enough. He handed me a paper. "These are the details."

I fell apart. He apologized and walked back to his car, the gravel crunching beneath his feet, then drove off and disappeared into the morning fog.

Alice appeared behind me, a child on each hip. "Who was it?" she asked softly.

"A worker from the sanitarium."

"Oh no." She stepped closer, setting the babies down and guiding me gently inside.

"She's gone," I said, staring out the window. "Only thirty-seven."

"I'm so sorry." She wrapped her arms around me as I wept uncontrollably.

"Seven forty-five this morning," I choked out. "She passed in her sleep."

Alice held me tighter. "She fought as long as she could."

"She was in that sanitarium for a year and a half, almost five hundred days," I said.

"She fought hard," Alice repeated, her voice soft. "But now she's at peace."

"And I'm here. Alone. With three kids."

"You're not alone," she said, brushing her hand gently down my back. "I'm here. I'll help however I can."

"You've already done so much."

"I wish I could've done more," she whispered.

"I had a dream about her last night," I said. "We were back at the ranch. She was young and full of life again. We fed the chickens, and she petted the goats. We walked by the river, and she picked wildflowers for the kitchen table."

"What a sweet dream."

"I didn't want it to end. I knew it was a dream. But we were happy. And I just... I didn't want to wake up."

My voice broke. Sobs shook me. Alice held me close, rocking me gently like I was a child. And for that moment, in her arms, I felt safe. I felt loved. And I didn't want her to let go.

A week later, there was a simple graveside service at a small cemetery on the east side of town—barely marked on the map, just past the train tracks and down a muddy lane lined with bare cottonwoods.

The sky hung low and heavy, gray with rain. A cold wind pressed against our backs as we stood beside a narrow, freshly dug grave. The ground was soft and slick, and our shoes sank into the grass. The only sound was the drizzle tapping against the black umbrellas, and the minister's voice—measured and low—offering words of comfort that didn't quite reach me.

A plain wooden cross stood at the head of the grave, bearing her name in careful handwriting. No marble. No inscription. Just her name, her dates, and a world of meaning in between.

The twins were only eight months old, they didn't understand what was happening. A.J. clung to my leg, his eyes round and silent. I held him close, my other arm around Fern, who hadn't said a word since she arrived. Lily stood beside her, lips trembling, gloved hands holding a single carnation. Alice held the twins when I couldn't. She stood firm, steady, the only dry-eyed one among us, quietly carrying what she could of my grief.

When it came time to lower the casket, I had to look away. Something inside me broke with that sound—the soft thump of ropes sliding, the dull thud of wood settling into earth.

A.J. tugged gently at my coat sleeve. "When's Mama coming back?" he whispered. His two-and-a-half-year-old voice was small, uncertain—like he already knew something wasn't right but didn't know how to say it.

I opened my mouth to answer but nothing came. I looked down at him—his eyes full of worry and rain, his cheeks pink with cold— and I felt my throat close. I knelt beside him and pulled him close, wrapping my arms around him. He leaned into me, still waiting.

"She's... not coming back, son," I finally said. "But she loved you very, very much."

He didn't say anything after that. Just nodded once and held on tight.

After the minister prayed, I stepped forward and placed the silver locket her father had given her four Christmases ago on the casket. Then I set a lilac sprig from the ranch beside the locket. It was already damp from the rain and its scent reminded me of Era— everything we'd done together. I could barely stand to let it go.

I bowed my head and whispered into the wind, "God...if you're listening, take me too."

I shut my eyes and tried to see her—the Era from my dream. Barefoot in the grass, hair dancing in the breeze, laughing as she strolled the river's edge with wildflowers in her hand. I reached to touch her face, to draw her against my chest, but she slipped away like smoke on the wind. When I opened my eyes, there was nothing but a plain wooden cross—mocking me, reminding me of the truth, stripping away every last piece of hope.

I turned away from the grave and walked into the rain.

Then, behind me, I heard A.J. chasing after me, calling my name.

SUNSET

(1925–1958)

MATTIE

Adoption

As Far Away as Possible

A Big Lie

Three Strikes Out

What More Can We Do?

Goat's Milk

The Sweetest Baby

Too Close For Comfort

Aunt Esther

Brazil

Two Weddings

Not What I Thought

One More Chance

Cut the Damn Thing Off

A Closing Thought

ADOPTION

How could I live without Era?

It didn't seem possible. She'd been all I'd known for thirteen years—the best thirteen years of my life. I couldn't go back to the ranch—just too many memories. Planting the orchard, herding cattle, walking along the river, picking wildflowers, scratching Lady's back. Many nights I lay sleepless in my room, staring at the shadows on the ceiling and wondering how I could go on. And why I'd even want to.

February was dark and gray, with a steady rain. But I got up each morning and moved numbly through the routine—greeted the kids, ate breakfast, listened to Alice, drove to work, did whatever needed doing. Then the next morning I'd do it all again.

On a Monday afternoon in early March, I got an emergency call from Ward C. When I arrived, there was a violent case raving something awful. A thin man in his forties—shaved head, crooked nose, no teeth—was gripping a young nurse's aide, twisting her arms until she winced in pain. She looked terrified. I saw it in her eyes, though she tried her best not to show it.

"She's poisoning the food!" he shouted. "Controlling my mind!"

"I'd never hurt you," the girl said calmly. "Everything's going to be alright."

His eyes were wild, jerking from side to side like he was scanning for enemies. "She needs to be taught lessons," he said. "Hard lessons. Hard-boiled lessons—with boiled eggs. She's a hard-boiled dame and she's not gonna control my eggs!"

A crowd of nurses and orderlies stood frozen, afraid to get too close to him.

"If anyone takes one step closer," he warned, "I'll tear her arms right from their sockets."

"You don't want to hurt this girl," I said, stepping forward, slow and steady.

"Yes, I do!" he snapped, twisting her arms harder. Tears spilled down her flushed cheeks.

"The government sent her! She's a spy—they've got her watching me with an evil eye. A poison eye. And now I've got an eye on her."

"Why would they do that?" I asked.

"They want to control us, hurt us, drive us crazy."

"But not this girl," I said. "I bet you don't even know her name."

"I don't care about her name. She's evil and poison and hard-boiled."

"I don't think so." I took another step forward, keeping my voice cool and easy. "Look at her. She's pretty."

"That's the worst kind! Poison's always pretty."

"Just look," I said. "Blonde hair..."

"She's got shades of red!" he interrupted. "She's a Bolshevik, sent to take my freedom and lock me up forever!"

"Look at her," I said again. "She's half your size. And as innocent as a calf in a hailstorm."

He hesitated. "But hailstorms are hellstorms. They fall on the good and the bad. Someone has to stop them."

I turned to the girl. "What's your name?"

"Mattie Rozar," she said.

"And what's that I hear in your voice? An accent?"

"Yes, sir. I'm from Georgia. Dublin, Georgia. My best friend and I came out here—just the two of us. I've only been here five months."

"And how old are you, Miss Mattie?"

"Twenty-six."

"You hear that?" I said, turning back to the man. "Does she sound like she's trying to hurt you?"

He blinked. "I... I don't know. Could be a trick. Bolsheviks are full of tricks."

"Well, she looks more like a Southern belle than a Bolshevik, if you ask me."

He wavered, glancing down at her. "Maybe," he muttered.

While I kept talking, two orderlies crept up behind him. I nodded for them to grab his arms and strap him down. Mattie dropped to the floor in tears.

I knelt beside her. "You're safe now. He can't hurt you." I paused. "But your arm's starting to swell. You'd better get it checked in the infirmary."

"Thank you," she whispered, looking at the floor. Then, suddenly, she threw her arms around me. "You saved my life."

She caught me completely off guard. I wasn't sure what to do so I chuckled—it was the first time in a long while. I looked her in the face, her lips trembling, and said, "He was a scary-looking guy, sure. But he wasn't going to kill you. Might've snapped an arm or two, but not kill you."

"I still owe you," she said, not letting go. "You were so calm, so collected."

"It's just part of the job." I patted her gently on the back and helped her to her feet. "Dealing with disturbed and unmanageable patients is a daily routine."

"Sounds dangerous."

"Risky, not dangerous." I smiled. "Besides, it's kind of nice saving damsels in distress now and then."

"Well, I owe you for your courage and assistance," she said, holding my hand to keep her balance. "Maybe I could repay you by inviting you and your wife over for dinner next week?"

"That would be nice." I paused. "But my wife passed away last month."

Her face softened. "I'm so sorry. I didn't know."

"Well, I'd never turn down a free meal," I said. "If the offer still stands."

"Of course it does," she said, brushing back her hair. "What about a week from Friday?"

"That sounds perfect."

That night, after the kids had gone to bed, Alice and I sat at the kitchen table with freshly baked cookies and coffee. She listened to my day and told me about the local gossip. It was a warm and comfortable conversation, no different than a hundred others we had shared. After she'd retired to her room, I sat alone nursing a cup of coffee that had long since gone cold. The rain was steady against the windows, ticking like a slow watch, and the lamp above cast a soft glow over the worn table and the stack of unpaid bills sitting in the corner.

I should've felt bone-tired after the day I'd had. Ward C was never quiet, but that scene with Mattie—that man's wild eyes, the pressure in the room, her tears—ought to have wrung me out. But instead I felt... something else.

Excitement? Anticipation? Guilt?

Why had I said yes to dinner with a girl I barely knew? A girl with strawberry blonde hair and a Georgia drawl, who reminded me of the world outside grief for just a few moments. And now here I was, sitting in the dark, replaying the way she'd held my hand and the way her voice softened when she invited me to supper.

I set the cup down and leaned back with a long sigh. What was wrong with me? How could I be thinking so warmly of this southern girl? I didn't really know anything about her. What I did know was that I was lonely, and I was not the type of man who could live without a woman by his side. Yet thinking like this felt disloyal and as if I was not being properly respectful to Era. Yet deep inside I knew she'd understand. That's just the type of woman she was.

Era had only been gone a month. Yet, it felt so long since I'd stood in the red clay of that hillside cemetery and watched them lower her into the ground, my heart breaking like dry wood under a heavy boot. I kissed her forehead one last time. I'd held her hand until it went cold. I'd promised myself I'd never forget how her voice sounded when she read to A.J. or how her hair curled behind her ears when she was working in the garden.

And now, barely four weeks later, I was thinking about another woman's smile. I hated that part of me—this part that still wanted something, even now. But I also knew grief could crack a man open. Sometimes what poured out wasn't just sorrow. Sometimes it was hunger—for life, for warmth, for something to look forward to again.

I ran a hand down my face and walked to the back door. I opened it and stepped out onto the porch. The rain had quieted to a mist, the air clean and cold. I looked up at the dark sky.

"I'm sorry, Era," I whispered. "I didn't plan this. I didn't ask for it. I'm not even sure I want it."

Somewhere deep in the trees, an owl called out. I stood there a while longer, listening to the silence. Letting it hold me. Letting it judge me—or maybe forgive me.

A week later I pulled the Model T to a stop in front of the little boarding house on Elm Street and cut the engine. The porch was painted pale green, with clean white trim and a crooked swing that creaked in the wind. A.J. sat beside me in his short pants and scuffed leather boots, clutching a ragged toy horse. I'd scrubbed him up best I could and combed his hair with the back of my hand. He looked sharp. Sharper than me, maybe.

I'd dressed in my Sunday best—clean shirt, brown vest, the one good pair of trousers I hadn't worn since the funeral. A tie too, though it hung crooked no matter how I tugged at it. In my hand was a bouquet of wild daffodils I'd picked that morning—nothing fancy, just something cheerful, bright like spring trying to push its way through all this rain.

"You ready, cowboy?" I asked.

A.J. nodded solemnly and reached for my hand.

Mattie answered the door herself, hair pinned back with a few loose curls framing her cheeks. She wore a plain blue dress with a little apron around her waist and smiled wide when she saw us. "Why, don't y'all look like a postcard," she said.

"These are for you," I said, holding out the bouquet like a boy at a barn dance. "In exchange for a good meal."

"Well now," she said, cheeks pinkening. "Ain't nobody brought me flowers since I left Georgia. Thank you kindly, Mr. Stephens."

"It's just Allen," I said, stepping inside. "And this here's A.J."

She bent down. "Well hello there, little man."

A.J. stared for a moment, then mumbled, "Hi," and tucked in close to my leg.

Mattie led us through the front hall and into the modest kitchen where a second young woman stirred something on the stove. She had short dark curls and a quick smile.

"This is my best friend, Evelyn. We came out from Dublin together. We worked there at the state asylum," Mattie said. "She's the better cook."

"I only know how to fry things in bacon grease," Evelyn said with a wink. "You must be Allen."

"Guilty," I said, hanging my hat by the door.

The table was already set—four chipped plates, a bowl of green beans, a cast iron pan full of skillet corn bread, and something bubbling in a baking dish that smelled like heaven. I caught the scent of butter, onions, and something that reminded me of Sunday suppers back home.

"We've got chicken and dumplings. Hope that suits you."

"It suits just fine," I said. "Better than anything I've eaten in weeks."

A.J. climbed up on the wooden bench beside me while the women brought over the dishes. Mattie poured sweet tea into mason jars and

Evelyn slipped a pat of butter onto A.J.'s bread with a practiced hand.

Mattie watched him quietly for a moment, her smile lingering as he reached for the cornbread with both hands. "He's precious," she said, almost under her breath.

"Do y'all say grace?" Evelyn asked.

"That's what my ma taught me," I said. "Though lately the prayers have been a bit rusty."

I bowed my head. "Lord, thank you for these good folks and this good food. Thank you for steady hands and warm kitchens and new friends. Amen."

Dinner passed easily enough once my nerves settled. The women talked about the hospital—nothing too grim—and Evelyn told a story about a patient who tried to trade her socks for a stray cat. Mattie laughed until she snorted, which made A.J. giggle, which made her laugh even harder. I hadn't seen laughter like that in a long time.

A.J. ate two helpings of dumplings, wiped his mouth with his sleeve, and laid his head in my lap halfway through Evelyn's story about their first winter in Oregon. He fell asleep there, warm and safe.

"I've never seen a little one eat so much," Mattie whispered, lifting the edge of a blanket to drape over him.

She brushed his hair back gently, like she'd done it a hundred times before. "He's got the sweetest face when he sleeps."

"Yes, he's a good boy," I said softly. "Quiet, but strong."

We sat like that for a moment—the three of us—while Evelyn cleared the dishes and whistled some southern tune I didn't recognize. Mattie's soft hand brushed mine once when she reached for the butter dish, and neither of us moved right away.

Evelyn slipped quietly out of the room, humming as she went, and suddenly it was just the two of us at the table, A.J. asleep under the blanket beside me.

I cleared my throat. "Would it be alright if I saw you again sometime?"

Mattie looked down, then back up at me with a shy smile. "I'd like that," she said. "I'd like that a lot."

"There's a western—*The Trail Rider*—playing down at the Grand Theatre," I said. "I hear it's got a real cowboy in it. Thought maybe we could go."

Her cheeks flushed a little pink as she nodded. "That sounds lovely."

The windows were fogged from the warmth inside their little boarding house, but the moonlight pushed through, soft and clean. I didn't want to leave, but it was past A.J.'s bedtime.

A week later we went to the Grand Theater. It was a wonderful night. Afterwards I drove to her house on Elm Street. Sitting in the Model T as the rain drummed lightly on the car, I told her that this was the first movie I'd ever seen and how exciting it was to see a man who knew how to keep in his saddle.

"You sound like you wish you were a cowboy."

"I used to be. Back in Nebraska." I smiled.

"You were a real life cowboy?"

"I sure was," I said. "It was a hard life, but it had a certain honesty about it that I wouldn't trade for anything."

"And now you're a guard for the State Mental Hospital."

"No, this is just a temporary job so I could be close to Era while she was in the sanitarium."

"That must've made it easier for A.J. to see his mother."

"Yes. A.J. and the twins."

"So you have twins?"

I nodded. "A boy and a girl. Ten months old. The lady I rent a room from watches them for me."

"They need a mother."

"I know," I said. "My kids got saddled with a raw deal, and it ain't their fault."

"That's so sad."

"It would break Era's heart. But I can't give them the proper care they need."

"So what are you going to do?"

The rain traced long lines down the windshield. I just stared through it. "A woman from the children's welfare society is looking for a good family for the three of them. She knows a wealthy family in Portland that wants a baby girl. And she's sure she can find homes for the boys. It just might take a little longer."

"That's nice for the twins." She paused. "But A.J. really looks up to you. It's probably going to be hard to let go of him."

"It will," I said with a shrug. "I hate to do it, truly. But I don't see that I've got much of a choice. I've had about all the sorrow I can stomach, so let's not dwell on it any longer."

"I'm sorry for asking so many questions. My mother always said I had a knack for sticking my nose where it didn't belong."

"Don't be sorry. I like your questions. Some are just harder to answer than others."

"Then can I ask one more question?" she said.

"Most certainly."

"If the hospital is just a temporary job, what is your permanent job?"

"I've got a forty acre ranch a few hours south of here—cattle, horses, goats, chickens. Once I've finished my business in Salem, that's where I'm headed."

"I'll sure miss you if you leave the city."

The rain beat softly against the roof, and her eyes found mine in the hush that settled between us. I leaned over and kissed her—I wasn't planning on doing it, but it just happened. I apologized for being so forward.

She blushed and said, "I'd hoped you would."

I laughed. "Then I'm glad I didn't let you down."

She smiled. "You didn't. Not one bit."

The next month was full of life and sunshine. I saw Mattie almost every day. The relationship was moving mighty fast, but neither of us complained. On a bright morning in early May, I took her on a day trip to the ranch in Ruckles.

As we left Salem, I said, "Yesterday they took the twins."

"That must've been hard." Mattie placed her hand gently on my shoulder.

"Yes and no," I said, eyes fixed on the road ahead. "They placed Arlene in Portland and Arle in Coos Bay—good families, I'm told."

"What about A.J.?"

"I've been thinking a lot about what you said. And I can't let him go. At least not yet. Maybe not ever."

"He's awfully attached—you can see plain as day that he thinks the world of you."

I was quiet for a while, thinking about what she'd said about A.J. He was old enough to remember Era—her voice, her touch, the way she used to hum when she brushed his hair or tucked him in. I could tell he felt her absence like a hole torn straight through his little world. And when he reached for my hand at night, or curled up beside me without a word, I knew what it meant. He didn't have the words for his grief, but I could feel it in every quiet glance, every trembling sigh, every time he clung to my shirt like it might hold him together.

He needed me. And if I was honest, I needed him too. He was the last piece of her I could still hold. How he tilted his head when curious, how he laughed with his whole body—those were Era's gestures, Era's spark. Letting him go would've felt like burying her all over again. Most nights, after I'd carried him to bed, I'd sit there in the dark, watching him sleep. His little chest rising and falling. The faintest trace of her in his face. And I'd think: This is what's left. This is what matters. I couldn't lose him. Not to the state, not to strangers, not even to anyone. He was my son. My boy. My anchor. And no matter how broken I felt inside, I couldn't let him go.

"I know it must be hard letting go of the twins," Mattie said quietly. "But I think you did the right thing."

A few hours later, I took a right off the main road and followed the old gravel path up the hill to the ranch. I hadn't been there since before Christmas. I'd forgotten how peaceful it was—the orchard in full bloom, clouds of white blossoms glittering in the sun.

"What a wonderful place," Mattie said as we stepped out of the car.

Lady bounded out from behind the barn with her tail wagging and that same high-pitched bark she used to save for Era. She ran straight for Mattie, circling her with joyful hops like they'd been friends for years. Mattie knelt to scratch her ears, laughing as Lady licked her chin.

"Well, someone's made a fast friend," I said.

"She's beautiful," Mattie replied, smoothing Lady's coat. "What's her name?"

"Lady. She's been with me through it all. Loyal as they come."

We passed the chicken coop—hens clucking and scratching in the dirt, a few pausing to eye us before going back to their feed. Mattie offered a handful of corn and smiled as one took it from her palm.

"You've got a regular farm going," she said as we moved on to the goat pen. One of the smaller goats nudged her hip, sniffing for treats.

"Don't let him fool you," I said. "He's only friendly when he thinks you've got something to eat."

Mattie laughed and scratched behind his ears anyway.

In the pasture, two chestnut horses lifted their heads at our approach. One of them—Dusty—whinnied and trotted over. Mattie leaned on the fence rail while I rubbed his nose.

"And the cattle?"

"Up near the west fence. Grant moved 'em to better grass."

Everything looked just as I'd left it—the fences sturdy, the barn roof patched, tools hanging neat in their places.

"Grant and Fern have done a good job keeping the place up. Real good. Better than I could've hoped. The animals are fed, the fields planted. They've honored this place."

Mattie paused by the fence, running her fingers over the weathered wood. "I can see why you love it here. It's perfect."

We walked on, the grass brushing our ankles, warm sunlight flickering through the cottonwoods. Mattie knelt in a patch of wildflowers, plucking a few of the purple ones. She held one to her face, breathed in deep, and closed her eyes. "They smell like sunshine," she whispered.

That's exactly what Era used to say. I stood there, stunned for a moment, hearing her voice in my memory like it hadn't faded at all.

We made our way down to the river, where the current sang against the rocks. Mattie came up beside me and took my hand. "This place feels like it has a soul," she said. "Like it remembers."

"It does," I said. "We built it with love. Me and Era poured every hour we had into that house. Nailed every board ourselves, hauled every beam up that hill."

We turned toward the rise where the house stood—weathered but still strong, the porch sagging just a little, the shutters hanging crooked. Mattie stepped up slowly, one hand trailing along the post as she climbed the steps. She paused near the door and rested her palm against it, like she was listening to the memory inside. "It's lovely," she said. "I mean it."

I didn't answer right away. She reached into her handbag and pulled out one of the wildflowers she'd gathered earlier, lifting it gently to her face. That same peaceful smile spread across her lips. For a moment, the ache in my chest loosened.

Maybe it was the place. Maybe it was the quiet. Or maybe it was just Mattie—breathing life into corners I thought had gone cold forever.

As the light faded, we sat on the porch as the sun dipped behind the hills, the sky turning lavender and gold. Mattie leaned against my shoulder, a flower still tucked in her hand.

"It's getting late," I said quietly. "Suppose we should head home."

She turned toward me, her voice soft. "Can't we stay a little longer?"

So we did—saying nothing, just letting the quiet settle around us.

"How could you do such a thing?" Alice stood in the parlor, hands on her hips.

"I didn't have much of a choice," I said quietly. It was late in the day, and I'd just gotten home from work.

"I've been caring for the twins for nine months," she said, her voice breaking. "I did it out of the goodness of my heart. I loved those babies. And now they're just—gone."

"But they are in good homes."

"This was a good home."

"I'm sorry," I said. "I didn't realize how much they meant to you."

"That's the problem!" She paused, blinking back tears. "You don't see what's right in front of you."

"So tell me—what don't I see?"

"How long have you lived under my roof?"

"Nearly two years," I said. "Since I first came to Salem."

"And how have I treated you?"

"Better than I ever could've hoped for. You did my laundry, cooked my meals, cared for my kids. And every evening we'd sit and play games, talk about everything under the sun. I'll never be able to repay you for all you've done."

"I didn't do it for repayment. I did it because I truly cared—for A.J., for the twins, and especially for you."

"For me?"

"Yes. I've been smitten with you since I first met you. But I'd have never interfered with your marriage. Yet when she passed away, I thought that maybe..."

"I'm so sorry." I nodded slowly. "You've been more than good to us, but I had no idea."

"And I'd hoped..." She took a breath. "I'd hoped you might come to feel even a little of the love I've felt for you."

"You're wonderful, Alice. I mean that. But I don't know what to say."

"That says it all." She turned away. "And now I've made a complete fool of myself."

"No, no—you haven't." I stepped forward. "I'm the fool. You've been one of the kindest, most gracious people I've ever known. I don't think I could've made it through these past two years without you. And now I've hurt you."

"I was just hoping..." Her voice trailed off.

"I know," I said gently. "You've been the truest of friends. And in my blindness and stupidity, I led you to believe we could become something more. I'm sorry."

She stood there a moment, silent, her back still turned. Then she crossed the room to the fireplace, her shoulders tight, movements sharp. She looked into the fire and reached for the poker, but didn't use it—just gripped the handle with both hands and stared into the fading flames as if trying to hold herself together.

"I never expected anything in return," she said finally, her voice low and trembling. "But I did hope. And I suppose that's what hurts the most—that I let myself believe there might be something real between us."

I swallowed hard. "You're not wrong for hoping."

She turned just enough for me to see the shine in her eyes. "Then why does it feel like I've lost something I never really had?" Her face flushed, jaw tight with the effort of not breaking. "It's a foolish thing, loving someone who doesn't love you back."

"I never meant to mislead you," I said, barely above a whisper.

"I know," she said, wiping at her cheek. "That's what makes it worse."

She didn't wait for a reply. "Supper's in the oven," she murmured, almost like an afterthought, and walked upstairs, her footsteps slow and heavy on the risers. A moment later, her door clicked shut.

I stood there for a long minute, staring at the closed door. What had I done? How had I gotten into such a messy situation? How could I have hurt Alice so badly, and not even been aware of it? I looked around the room. It had fallen still, the warmth of the fire swallowed up by the simple truth—this wasn't home anymore. I had to move on, for everyone's sake. I rubbed the back of my neck and let out a breath I hadn't realized I was holding.

Then I turned toward the kitchen, opened the oven, and pulled out the casserole dish she'd left behind—scalloped potatoes with bits of ham baked into the top, still warm and smelling of rosemary and cream. I set it on the table and poured two glasses of milk. The only sound was the soft clink of silverware.

A.J. walked in from the hallway, rubbing his eyes. "Where's Alice?"

I knelt down beside him. "It's just you and me tonight."

"But Alice always eats with us."

"I know."

He looked at me sleepily, then climbed into his chair. I spooned food onto his plate and sat across from him.

We ate in silence—both of us sensing something had shifted, though neither of us quite knew what it meant. He swung his legs beneath the table and hummed a little lullaby that Alice sang to him when she tucked him into bed. I watched him, this boy who'd already been through so much... and who would soon go through even more.

When he finished eating, he leaned over and rested his head on the table. I reached out and ran a hand through his hair. Outside, the wind stirred the leaves. Upstairs, all was quiet.

A week later, I took Mattie on our second day trip to the ranch. This time we brought A.J. along. He slept soundly in the back seat of the Model T as we followed the old highway, the hills rolling past like waves.

"I need to move," I said, more abruptly than I intended.

"Move? Down to the ranch?"

"No. I need to move out of Alice's boarding house."

"Why? She seems like a good woman—and she's done right by A.J."

"She has. She's been a friend. But I reckon she hoped for something more and now I've hurt her. The longer I stay under her roof, the more painful it gets—for both of us."

"There's a spare room at the house next to where Evelyn and I stay."

"If I moved in there, I suppose it'd make seeing each other easier. But... would that be too forward?"

"It's the 1920s, after all. We're both adults—we can do what suits us."

"Maybe so. But I'm still a bit old-fashioned."

"That's right—you're a cowboy. And a gentleman."

"And a rancher," I added.

She grinned. "Whatever you are, I'd say the nearer you live, the better."

I smiled and took her hand, keeping my eyes on the road.

"You know a fair bit about me now, but there's so much I don't know about you—aside from the fact you and Evelyn came from Georgia."

"Well, where do I start?" She took a breath. "I'm the youngest of nine. We grew up on a cotton farm that had been in our family for three generations."

"That sounds mighty respectable."

"Not really. We were dirt poor. Half the time, we barely had enough to eat."

"I know what that's like," I said, quietly.

"Then the boll weevil came through—about six years back—and ruined what was left of the crop. My daddy... well, he'd always had a temper. But after we lost the crop, he turned downright mean. Took it out on whoever was near. And I was the only one left at home."

"What did your mother do?"

"She tried to step in. But when Daddy hits the bottle, there was no stopping him."

"So what did you do?"

"I stayed longer than I should've. Then one day, I packed my things and ran. Took the road to Milledgeville, fifty miles away. Found work at the Georgia State Sanitarium."

"What kind of work?"

"Nurse's aide. Paid twenty-five dollars a month and a hot meal for each shift. That's where I met Evelyn. She'd left her people for similar reasons."

"So that's where you learned to care for the disturbed."

She nodded. "I've never been easily rattled. Not by madness. Not until last March when that man on Ward C attacked me."

"He was touched in the head," I said. "But how'd you and Evelyn end up all the way out here in Oregon? That's quite the distance."

"Nearly three thousand miles. Took us the better part of a week by train."

"But why Oregon?"

"I needed to escape. To start over. To live a life of freedom. Georgia was behind me, and I didn't want to look back. It held too much hurt. So I went to the station and the man at the counter asked, 'Where to, Miss?' I told him, 'As far from here as possible.'"

"That took real moxie."

"It wasn't bravery. Just something I had to do. A one-way ticket cost seventy-five dollars. I'd been saving for years. So I bit my lip, gave him the money, climbed on board, and didn't look back."

"Mercy," I breathed. "That's one hell of a journey."

Mattie nodded. "And I think it was one of the best things I've ever done. I'm here and I'm happy."

I looked at her—not just for what she'd survived, but for how she'd carried herself through it. Strong, honest, unafraid. There was a simple grace to her, the kind you don't find often. And something in me stirred—quiet, but sure.

An hour later, as the mid-morning sun filtered through the oak trees, we drove the old gravel path up the hill to the ranch. Lady ran out to meet us, barking with her tail wagging, and nearly knocking A.J. off his feet. "Big dog." He laughed as Lady licked his face.

"It's even more lovely than I remember," said Mattie, kneeling beside the toddler. The hillside was ablaze with bright yellow and purple wildflowers. The orchard was heavy with green fruit, still at least six weeks from harvest.

Suddenly the chickens scattered in a flurry of dust, squawking and screeching, as someone walked across the pen.

"Fern, good to see you," I called out.

She walked toward us with a pail of feed in one hand and a baby balanced on her hip.

"Let me introduce you to Mattie," I said. "And Mattie, this is Fern, who feeds the animals and takes care of the house."

"I've also been staying in the house the last couple of nights."

"And why's that?"

"Grant and I had... an incident."

I raised an eyebrow. "An incident?"

"It only happens when he's drinking."

"But it's Prohibition. Alcohol's illegal."

Fern gave a small shrug. "That doesn't stop anyone if they know where to get it."

"Fair enough."

"Anyway," she said, her voice flatter now, "last Saturday night, he was drinking—and he hit me. Hard. That's one thing I won't take."

"You shouldn't have to," said Mattie.

"I packed up my little one and we moved into your house." Fern hesitated and looked away. "I knew you wouldn't mind."

Mattie stepped closer and touched Fern's arm. "You did the right thing," she said, her voice low but firm. "Some men don't change unless someone takes a stand."

"There's no excuse for a man hitting a woman unless it's self-defense." I sighed and turned to Mattie. "Would you mind taking A.J. into the barn to play with the goats so Fern and I can talk?"

"Of course," she said, taking the boy's hand. A.J. followed her without hesitation.

I looked into Fern's eyes. "Would you tell me what's really going on?"

"I love Grant," she said. "But whiskey isn't good for his disposition. I ignored it the first few times he hit me. After he sobered up he felt real bad. But this time, I told myself, 'Enough is enough.'"

"And what does Grant say about what happened?"

"It's been four days, and I haven't heard a word from him."

"That's not right," I said.

"Grant has a stubborn streak. And if he thinks he's justified, he doesn't budge."

"How does he think he's justified?"

"He says I wasn't being properly respectful."

"Hitting a woman is just not right."

Fern nodded. "I just told him that if he couldn't handle his whiskey, he shouldn't be drinking. Then he went crazy—throwing punches and swearing like a demon with a toothache."

I nodded slowly, a tightness forming in my chest. I'd seen what a bottle could do to a man—and what silence could do to a woman. The first strike was never the last—not unless something changed.

"Do you mind if I talk to him?"

"Not at all," she said. "But you might want to wait until the afternoon."

"Why's that?"

"He hasn't been getting out of bed lately until half the day is gone."

I nodded, jaw set. I didn't like the thought of her hiding out while he lay in bed nursing his pride. Something needed saying—and I aimed to be the one to say it.

By noon, the sun was high and warm, but a steady breeze off the hilltops kept it pleasant. The three of us started in the orchard, where the plum trees cast long patches of shade across the grass. A.J. darted between the trunks, laughing, while Mattie called out from behind a row of apple saplings.

"Where'd that little rascal go?"

She peeked around a tree and caught him mid-giggle, crouched behind a stump with his hands over his face like that might make him invisible. When she grabbed him and spun him around, he shrieked with delight.

"My turn to hide!" she said, setting him down and running in the opposite direction. A.J. looked up at me, wide-eyed and thrilled.

"You gonna count or chase her?" I asked.

He didn't answer—just took off after her as fast as his little legs could carry him.

After a few rounds, we slowed things down and walked the length of the barnyard. Lady trotted ahead of us like she was giving a tour. A.J. insisted on greeting every single animal—the goats first, then the chickens, then the old barn cat who stretched in the sun. Mattie knelt beside him to show how to feed the mare a cube of sugar from his palm. The mare took it gently, and A.J.'s eyes went wide with wonder.

"She likes me," he said, beaming.

"She does," Mattie replied. "Animals can tell when someone has a kind heart."

We made our way down to the river by way of the lower pasture, Lady bounding ahead and back again like she couldn't decide who to follow. At the bend in the river, where the cottonwoods arched low over the water, Mattie spread out the checkered blanket she'd brought from town. She unpacked the lunch she'd made that morning in Salem—cold roast chicken, a loaf of brown bread wrapped in wax paper, pickled beets in a glass jar, and a peach pie wrapped in a flour sack.

"Figured we might work up an appetite," she said with a wink.

We sat in the grass and ate with our hands, the river whispering nearby and a pair of dragonflies humming above the reeds. A.J. nestled close to Mattie as she handed him a torn piece of crust, brushing the crumbs from his chin with her sleeve.

After lunch, we lay back in the shade. A.J. curled up on the blanket between us and dozed off, one hand still holding tight to a crust of bread.

I glanced over at Mattie. Her eyes were on the boy, soft and thoughtful.

"You're good with him," I said quietly.

She smiled but didn't look away. "He makes it easy."

The wind stirred the leaves above us, and somewhere downstream, a bird called out—clear and bright. Then all was quiet. With the sun warming my boots, my son asleep between us, and Mattie's hand resting just inches from mine, I felt that life had hope again—not just for healing, but for something more.

A BIG LIE

Two crows circled above the cabin, black arrows in a blue sky. Suddenly they shot downward with loud, harsh cries. A red-tailed hawk sailed on wide wings away from the crows' territory. But the black birds chased it anyway, their cries growing sharper until the hawk vanished into the tall oaks along the river.

Fern and I sat on the porch of my cabin and watched in silence. I sipped the warm lemonade she'd fixed while she nursed her baby. We could hear Mattie and A.J. playing tag in the orchard, with Lady barking in the distance.

"She's so good with your son," said Fern.

"She's been good for both of us."

"Then why didn't you introduce me to her properly?"

"I did." I sounded more defensive than I intended.

"You introduced me as a neighbor and a caretaker, not as your daughter."

"Well, I didn't want to complicate things."

"How would that have complicated anything?" she asked.

"I don't want her to know I have a daughter just eight years older than her."

"Why? What's wrong with me?" Fern looked confused.

"Nothing! Absolutely nothing. You're the perfect daughter."

"Doesn't sound like it."

"I'm just trying to keep things simple."

"But it is simple." Fern looked me directly in the face. "I'm your daughter, and you're my father."

"I know. I'm sorry if I hurt you."

"Hurt me? You made me feel like you don't want me." She looked down at her baby, brushing a finger over his brow. "Sometimes I wonder if anyone does."

"That's not true."

"But that's how it feels—like you don't want me, and now my husband doesn't even want me."

"Grant's a fool," I said. "But he loves you and wants you. He promised me he'll never hit you again. He feels a lot of shame for what he's done."

"It would be nice if he told me that."

"He said he'll talk to you tomorrow."

"We'll see. It'll depend on how much he drinks tonight."

"When I was talking with him, we dumped out all his whiskey."

"That's a good start." Fern was quiet for a moment, then asked, "Why does it bother you so much if she knows I'm your daughter?"

"Because then she'll know how old I really am. She's twenty-six, and I'm forty-six. She thinks I'm a lot younger."

"You do look younger than that. But why should age make a difference?"

"I might be smitten with her."

"I can see why." Fern had an impish grin. "She's attractive and sensible."

"But I'm twenty years older than her."

"Why should that matter?"

"It just does." I sipped my lemonade.

"But it shouldn't. Just be honest with her and see what happens."

"I can't." I set down the lemonade and folded my hands. "I've lost too many things—Eddie, Era, the kids I couldn't hold onto. I don't think I can bear one more goodbye."

"So what are you going to do?"

"She thinks I'm only ten years older than her. I'm just going to let her believe that."

"But it's a lie."

I looked out at the hills, where sunlight brushed the edge of the orchard, turning the leaves a soft gold. "Yes. But I don't know what else to do."

Fern didn't answer right away. She just looked at me—steady, quiet—like she saw more than I wanted her to. Then we heard laughter drifting through the trees, light and windblown, followed by the rustle of leaves and the thud of small feet on sunbaked ground.

A moment later, Mattie stepped out from between the trees, her cheeks flushed, hair damp at the temples, with A.J. skipping close behind her. He held a firm green plum in one hand and bit into it with a determined crunch, puckering at the sour taste.

"We were hiding," he declared proudly, his voice still breathless from the game. "And I found this!"

Lady bounded up the hill after them, barking once before flopping down beside Fern, her chest rising and falling with quick, happy breaths. Mattie laughed as she climbed the porch steps, brushing at a smudge of dirt on her skirt. She lowered herself to the floor beside me with a soft sigh, her shoulder grazing mine, and tucked her knees to her chest. A.J. wandered over to Fern, intrigued by the baby nestled in her lap.

Mattie looked from Fern to me, her eyes warm but curious. "What are the two of you talking about?"

I turned to look at her—dirt on her knees, hair falling loose, cheeks pink from the sun. She looked so alive, so easy with my boy, like she belonged here without even trying. I wanted to tell her everything. But instead, I just smiled and said, "Nothing too serious."

A month later, on a hot Saturday afternoon, I was as jumpy as a jackrabbit at a June dance. I went downtown for a haircut and a clean shave. Back home, I wiped the sweat from my neck and dressed in my Sunday best. I stared into the mirror at my weathered face and tight jaw. I hadn't felt this nervous since rushing Era to the hospital in Roseburg.

My shoes felt too tight as I walked to the boarding house next door and knocked. Evelyn opened the door and smiled. "I've seen plenty of men dressed up before, but never like this. You cut a mighty fine figure."

I nodded—more confidently than I felt.

"Is this the night?" she asked.

"I hope so."

Then Mattie came down the stairs, and everything stopped. My mouth went dry. My heart stuttered. Her bright blue dress shimmered with each step, the hem just below her knees. The waist dipped low, trimmed in delicate lace. A bell shaped hat hugged her strawberry curls, and a string of pearls rested just above her collarbone.

But it was that coy smile that undid me. I stood frozen, staring at her like she was the first breath of spring after a long, hard winter. She was fresh and radiant, and I suddenly felt every year I'd lived. My dark suit looked outdated. My pants too tight. My burgundy tie, dull as dishwater.

She looked down and smoothed the front of her dress.

"Is it too much?" Her voice was quiet. I could've told her no— that it was just right, that she'd never looked more beautiful—but the words got caught somewhere behind my ribs. So I did the only thing I could—I offered her my arm.

Her hand slipped into the crook of my elbow—light as a sigh, warm as morning sun—and I felt like I was holding something too good to be real. I escorted her to my old Model T and opened the door for her.

"What a gentleman you are," she said.

"I aim to please."

I drove Mattie to a fancy restaurant on State Street. It was more expensive than I could afford, but I wanted the night to be special.

I'd only known her for five months, but the way she turned to look at me when the wind caught her hat—that small, unguarded smile—I knew. She was the one for me.

We ordered our meal, though I could hardly taste a thing. My nerves had gotten the better of me. I moved my food around with my fork and watched her instead—how she took small, deliberate bites, how she dabbed the corner of her mouth with her napkin like she'd grown up knowing how to do that sort of thing. She looked calm, but her fingers toyed with the edge of her water glass.

I drank a glass of water myself, wishing there wasn't Prohibition so I could knock back a shot or two of whiskey. Just something to steady the shaking in my hands. But instead I sat up straighter, nodded when I ought to, and tried not to make a fool of myself.

We finished eating just as the streetlamps flickered on outside, casting a soft glow across the sidewalk. I paid the bill with the twenty-dollars I'd been saving for three months and held the door open for her like a proper gentleman.

The evening air had cooled, but the sidewalks still held the last of the supper crowds—couples strolling arm in arm, boys weaving their bicycles between streetcar tracks, the glow of the Capitol dome watching over it all. Shopkeepers were locking up, movie posters flapped in the breeze outside the Grand Theatre, and somewhere down the block, a jazz tune drifted from an open upstairs window. We walked slow, side by side, letting the noise fall behind us as we reached the quiet of the courthouse square. Under a maple tree just beginning to turn, I stopped. A few dry leaves skipped across the sidewalk at our feet.

"I've been trying to find the right time," I said.

Mattie turned to me, curious. "For what?"

I reached into the inside pocket of my jacket and pulled out the small velvet box I'd been carrying for weeks. I held it in my hand without opening it. "For this."

Her eyes widened, but she didn't speak.

I took a breath. "You already know I ain't perfect. I'm a rancher, a widower, and a father. Life hasn't always gone the way I hoped—but somehow, you make me believe it still can. You bring joy where there used to be silence. And love where there was just... loss."

I opened the box. The ring wasn't much. Just a modest gold band with a speck of a diamond. But it said that I was serious.

"I want to build something with you, Mattie. A life, a home. Will you marry me?"

She didn't say anything at first. Just stood there with both hands covering her mouth. Then she nodded once, then again, her eyes shining. "Yes," she whispered. "Yes, I will."

I slid the ring onto her finger, and her hands were trembling as much as mine.

The next morning, I headed down to the ranch. I needed to tell Fern myself—before she heard it from someone else. She'd moved back in with Grant, and he was on his best behavior. The kitchen smelled of tomatoes and onions, something he'd been stewing in the back room. Fern was wiping down the table with one hand, baby Ray balanced on her hip, when I stepped in from the porch with my hat in my hands.

"I asked Mattie to marry me," I said.

Fern froze. She turned slowly, eyes wide with disbelief. "You did?"

I nodded.

She smiled a little, almost in spite of herself. "Well, that's something. What did she say?"

"She didn't say anything at first. Just covered her mouth with both hands. Then she nodded. Twice. And whispered yes."

Fern leaned her hip against the table and shifted Ray higher. "She's kind," she said. "And she loves that boy of yours."

"She makes this place feel like a home again," I said.

She looked at me for a long moment. "So... when are you going to tell her?"

I didn't answer right away.

She let out a quiet sigh. "Dad..."

"We've been over this."

"No," she said softly, "we really haven't."

I pulled out a chair and sat, resting my hat on my knee. "She knows about Era."

"And Eddie?" Her voice wasn't sharp—but it landed like a stone in a still pond.

"She doesn't know about Eddie. And I don't see why she needs to."

"Because you were married to her. Because she's my mother." Fern's voice cracked, just barely. "Don't you think Mattie deserves the truth?"

I rubbed my hands together, staring at the worn wood grain of the table. " Yes. But I don't want to scare her away."

"Just think about it," she said finally, her voice lower now. "If you love her like you say you do... she should get the whole story. Not just the parts that make you look good."

I nodded once, not promising anything.

Ray let out a sleepy yawn and nestled under her chin. The kitchen felt warm, almost too warm, and I looked toward the open door. Dust hung in the sunlight like suspended time. I rose, placing the hat back on my head. "Thanks for hearing me out."

Fern didn't answer, just brushed a crumb off the table and kissed her son's forehead.

We got married on a Friday evening in September, just five days before Mattie's twenty-seventh birthday. It was a small gathering— no more than twenty people—in the Baptist Church on Liberty Street. Evelyn came with her boyfriend. Fern brought Grant and their baby. A few folks from work, the boarding house, and the farms along Clarks Branch River filled the rest of the pews.

When Mattie walked down the aisle, it nearly took my breath away. I just stood there, staring, all the blood draining from my face. Her strawberry blonde hair was pulled back in a silver clip, falling neat against a satin dress of moonlit ivory—simple, stunning. When I took her hand I could hardly get my words out. Lucky for me the pastor kept it short so I didn't make a fool of myself.

Afterward, we served cookies and cake from Smith's Bakery on Commercial Street, and that's when Fern came up to me. She leaned close and whispered, "I saw your marriage certificate."

"Yes, the pastor just signed it," I said, smiling.

"But it's not true."

I glanced at her. "What do you mean?"

"It says you're forty."

I exhaled. "I almost wrote thirty-six."

She glanced down, then met my eyes again. "Why not just tell her the truth?"

"We've talked about this."

"And you put down that this is your second marriage." Her voice wavered. "What about my mother?"

I swallowed. "Mattie doesn't know about Eddie—and I'm keeping it that way."

Fern's eyes filled, but she blinked the tears away. "It makes a difference to me."

"Can't you just let us be happy?" I said, a little too sharply. "Did you see how beautiful Mattie looked tonight?"

"She'd still be beautiful if she knew who she was marrying," Fern said softly.

I paused, struggling for words. "So what if I'm forty-six, and this is my third marriage? This is the happiest day of my life."

She gave a faint shake of her head. "I won't say anything to her.

But lying—on your wedding certificate, of all things—" She looked up at me with red-rimmed eyes. "I don't think that's how you start a real marriage."

Before I could respond, I felt a small hand tug at the edge of my jacket. A.J. stood beside me in his little navy suit, cheeks sticky from frosting, a crushed paper napkin clutched in one fist. "Papa," he said, beaming. "I gave her flowers. She put 'em in her hair."

I knelt beside him and straightened his tie. "She looks mighty pretty, doesn't she?"

He nodded, eyes shining. "Like a princess."

"Yes, she does."

I kissed the top of his head and stood again, but Fern was already walking away, holding her baby close as she crossed the church lawn. I watched her go. A.J. had already skipped ahead toward Mattie, grinning like nothing in the world was wrong. For a long moment, I just stood there—half smiling, half sick—and told myself the truth could wait.

THREE STRIKES OUT

It was a cloudy morning in late March, six months after our wedding. I was as happy as I'd ever been. We lived in a small, one-bedroom bungalow just a few blocks from the State Hospital. The place was modest—white walls, squeaky floorboards, a porch swing that creaked in the wind. But Mattie had made it cozy with soft rugs, lace curtains, and shelves lined with books and photographs. There were wildflowers in jars on every windowsill, and the smell of coffee and oatmeal clung to the morning air.

I'd just come in from splitting kindling for the stove, my boots tracking in damp earth from the corner of the yard where Mattie had planted tulips and daffodils.

"Daddy, it's breakfast time!" A.J. called, climbing up into his chair at the kitchen table, his legs swinging under the bench.

I nodded and brushed off my sleeves before sitting beside him. "Well, if my boy says it's breakfast time, I'd better not keep him waiting."

Mattie handed me a steaming cup of coffee and kissed my cheek. Her hand lingered on mine for a moment—warm, soft, familiar. I smiled and asked, "What are the two of you doing today?"

"Learning my numbers!" A.J. said proudly, puffing his chest out. "I'm a big boy now."

"You certainly are," I said, ruffling his curls. "Biggest boy in Salem, I'd wager."

"He's three and a half now," Mattie said, setting a bowl of oatmeal with cinnamon and raisins in front of me.

I took a bite and looked at her. "Mattie, I've been thinking."

She gave me that amused look I'd come to know so well. "Allen, you're always thinking."

I smiled, but my voice turned more serious. "I figure it's about time we move to the ranch." I took a sip of the hot coffee, savoring it as the words hung in the air.

Mattie blinked, then her smile returned, easy and genuine. "It's about time. I've been hoping to move out of the city. Salem's just too hectic. I'm more of a country girl."

"There's nothing as sweet as the ranch in spring," I said, reaching for the sugar jar. "The wildflowers in bloom, the river running full from the snowmelt. And that breeze through the orchard trees—I can almost smell it from here."

"I love it there," she said softly. "It's so calm and peaceful. The perfect place to raise A.J."

"He loves the goats and the chickens," I said, grinning at the memory of him toddling through the pen in his boots, trying to catch a hen by the tail feathers.

"He's such a good kid," Mattie said, watching him scoop oatmeal into his mouth with both hands. "Happy no matter where he is. But the ranch—it feels more like home."

I nodded. "I've been thinking about it for a long time. It just didn't seem right before."

"So why now?"

"Fern wrote me last week. Says the orchard's thick with blossoms. Five years since we planted those trees—now it looks like they'll finally give us enough fruit to make something of it. Maybe more than just prunes for ourselves this time."

Mattie came to stand behind me, wrapping her arms around my shoulders. "Let's go home, then." She leaned in and rested her chin gently against me. "I knew from the very start—we could build something beautiful together."

I reached up and touched her hand. "And now it's time to build it."

A week later, I filled the Model T with everything we owned. Mattie folded linens into old apple crates while I loaded tools and blankets into the car. We wrapped our wedding china in newspaper and tucked A.J.'s favorite toys in a box marked IMPORTANT in Mattie's careful handwriting. It took all morning to get it just right—every inch of the vehicle packed tight, even the running boards stacked with bundles tied in rope.

Mattie stood by the front door, holding A.J. by the hand and a patchwork quilt under the other arm. "You sure we've got everything?"

I nodded and pulled her close, brushing my lips against her forehead. "Got the two of you, everything else is extra," I whispered.

We drove south beneath low clouds, the kind that hang like wool and carry the scent of rain. Behind us, Salem faded into memory—narrow streets, hospital shifts, the rhythm of town life. Ahead of us lay the open road, the budding hills, and the ranch in bloom.

It was time to begin something new.

As we drove up the dirt path to the cabin, Lady came bounding out from the orchard, barking joyfully, her tail wagging like a banner in the breeze. She circled the Model T twice, then pressed her nose to the passenger door, as if she somehow knew that we were home for good.

Mattie wasted no time making the cabin ours. She swept out years of dust, scrubbed the windows until sunlight danced across the floor, and stitched new curtains from leftover wedding fabric. I patched the holes in the barn roof and rehung the gate that had sagged on its hinges. The orchard was as thick with small green plums as Fern had promised. Five years of waiting, and it looked like we'd finally have a true harvest.

That spring, in May of 1926, Mattie told me she was pregnant. It was a warm Sunday afternoon, and we were having dinner at Fern and Grant's place. The table was set out under the trees, pink petals drifting down like confetti in the breeze. She leaned in close and whispered, "Allen—I'm late. Fern says there's no question about it."

I blinked. My fork paused midair. "Are you sure?"

Her face lit up, all wide eyes and trembling excitement. "Yes. Really sure."

I didn't know what to say. I wasn't sure I was ready. But I didn't want to be the weight against her joy. So I just stood, pulled her into my arms, and kissed her like I had on our wedding day—gently, fully, with everything I had.

Later that week, Mattie told A.J. he was going to be a big brother. He grinned ear to ear and declared, "It's gonna be a boy! I'm sure of it."

In September, the prune harvest was better than I'd ever seen. We sold enough to carry us comfortably through the year. I used the profits to buy ten sheep—"more friends," A.J. called them—and the ranch felt full and alive again.

Then, on a foggy November morning, Charlie was born in our cabin with Lily McDonald by Mattie's side. A small, quiet baby, but perfect in every way. We wrapped him in a quilt Fern had sewn and laid him gently against Mattie's chest.

That afternoon, Fern and Grant came by to see the baby. Fern leaned close, grinning, and whispered, "I'm pregnant too. Imagine that—our little ones growing up side by side."

But something wasn't right with Charlie.

He cried with a soft, strained whimper, barely louder than a breath. He wouldn't nurse, no matter how Mattie shifted or coaxed him. He'd root for a moment, mouth open and searching, then pull away and wail in frustration. He rejected the bottle too, twisting his head and fussing until he wore himself out. His skin stayed pale, almost bluish, with deep shadows under his eyes. And he never seemed to sleep.

His body never filled out. His limbs stayed thin and wiry, his hands limp when I held him. Once, I lifted him from his crib and felt how impossibly light he was—like holding a bundle of feathers wrapped in linen.

At first, I told myself he just needed time. Some babies were slow to take to feeding—that's what I'd heard. But by the second week, I began to feel the quiet edge of panic creeping in. I promised Mattie I'd do everything I could—every remedy, every trick, every prayer— but the truth was, I didn't know how to help. I watched helplessly as she tried again and again, her voice gentle, her hands steady, even as her eyes filled with worry. And I felt useless. Powerless. Like less than a man.

"I'm failing him," she whispered once.

"No," I said, reaching for her hand. "We'll figure it out. I swear to you, we will."

But we didn't.

Most nights, I'd wake in the dark to find her in the rocker by the fire, holding Charlie close, humming lullabies through cracked lips. She'd whisper prayers, beg him to eat, make promises she couldn't keep.

"Come on, sweetheart," she'd murmur. "Just a little sip. Just one for Mama."

Sometimes she'd cry, but only when she thought I was asleep.

We tried everything—cow's milk, warm compresses, and Lily's old folk remedies made from peppermint, sugar, catnip. I even drove into town and bought a new bottle with a softer nipple, hoping maybe that would make the difference. Nothing worked. Charlie stayed small, silent, and fragile—slipping further from us each day.

I hated how useless I felt—standing there with rough hands and an empty heart, watching the woman I loved unravel while the son we'd prayed for faded before our eyes. I couldn't fix it. Couldn't fix him. Couldn't fix her. And that crushed me.

A.J. slept soundly in the loft most nights, unaware. We never told him anything was wrong. I don't think I could've said the words even if I tried.

By February, we were out of ideas. Out of time.

That night, the wind picked up and rattled the shutters. The fire had burned low, casting long, flickering shadows across the walls. I sat at the table for hours, listening to the creak of the rocker and the soft rhythm of Mattie's voice.

Then the world went silent. I stepped quietly into the front room and saw her there, still cradling Charlie in her arms. Her face was pale, streaked with silent tears. The baby lay still, his tiny chest no longer rising.

"No," she whispered, swaying gently. "No, no, no…" She pressed his face to her neck and rocked faster now, as if the movement might stir him. Her whole body trembled.

I dropped to my knees beside her and reached for Charlie, but she held on tight, her grip firm and trembling.

"I just wanted one more night," she said. "Just one more."

I touched his chest. I tried to find a heartbeat, even though I already knew. The room was unbearably quiet. Even Lady didn't make a sound. She lay curled near the fire, watching us with soft, knowing eyes.

Outside, snowflakes drifted down from a gray sky, gathering on the windowsill like ashes. Inside, we held our four-month-old son and wept—because there was nothing else left to do.

We buried Charlie at the top of the hill, beneath the cottonwood trees that overlooked the orchard. It was the coldest day of the year—gray skies, wind like needles, and a silence so thick it felt like a burden too heavy to bear. Mattie and I stood in silence, A.J. between us, each of us holding one of his hands.

The earth was hard and stubborn, but I dug the hole myself. My fingers ached, my shoulders burned, but I didn't stop—not until the last shovelful was done. We placed him in a small pine box lined with flannel and stitched with Mattie's own hands.

A little white cross, plain and uncarved, marked his grave. No preacher. No hymns. Just wind and snow and our breath fogging in the bitter air.

Mattie said nothing—not on the hill, not on the way back down, not even when I reached for her hand as we crossed the yard. She didn't pull away, but she didn't hold on either.

Inside, the cabin was too warm. The fire popped in the hearth, the smell of woodsmoke clinging to everything. A.J. sat quietly in the corner, hugging his stuffed horse, eyes wide and searching. "Where's Charlie now?" he asked.

I crouched down beside him. My throat tightened. "He's in heaven, son. With the angels."

"Is he cold?"

I swallowed hard. "Not anymore."

That night, Mattie curled up on Charlie's quilt and fell asleep on the floor. I tried to move her to the bed, but she wouldn't budge. She held one of his tiny socks in her hand, and every few minutes she'd press it to her cheek like it still carried his warmth. Lady lay beside her, protective and still, her eyes never leaving Mattie's face.

I sat alone at the kitchen table, staring at the lamp's flickering flame. I couldn't remember the last time I'd felt warm. Not in my bones. Not in my chest. Not in my hands.

Grief doesn't announce itself. It seeps in slowly—through the floorboards, through the quiet, through the ache behind your eyes when you wake in the dark and forget, for one fleeting second, that anything's changed. And then you remember. And your heart breaks all over again. It all comes crashing back.

I couldn't stand it any longer. So I pulled on my boots, went to the barn, and saddled up the biggest horse. I rode up the creek and into the hills, following what folks on the prairie call the hungry moon. I didn't know where I was headed, I didn't care much. Just needed to get into the wide open spaces where I could shout and swear and let off a little steam.

My horse took me where I needed to go and brought me back when I was ready. It was nearly sunrise in my night wanderings and a hard saddle reminded me there was still a cowboy alive inside me. Beyond the hills, the first light came mean and bright, like it didn't care what I'd lost. I thought about riding further and building a campfire. But I knew Mattie and A.J. needed me. So I gathered the reins and turned toward the cabin, ready to face whatever waited for me. After all, that's just what cowboys do.

Two months later, when spring was in full bloom, Fern had a healthy baby boy named Donald. Mattie celebrated the birth as if it were her own. She crocheted a blue blanket and baked lemon scones for the occasion. But in her heart, Donald reminded her of everything she'd lost with Charlie.

1927 was a dark year. Mattie drifted through the days like a ghost in her own skin. She cooked, cleaned, milked the cows—did what needed doing—but the life had gone out of her. Her face was unreadable, her voice quiet. Lady stayed close by, but Mattie rarely acknowledged her. Every afternoon she sat on the porch alone for hours, staring down the slope toward the orchard as if waiting for something that never came.

One morning, as A.J. and I fed the chickens, he looked up at me with serious eyes. "What's wrong with Mommy?"

"She misses Charlie," I said.

"So do I," he whispered.

"We all do, son."

"Sometimes I dream of him," he said, tossing a handful of feed. The hens gathered, clucking around his boots.

"What do you dream?"

"I dream my other mommy—the one in heaven—is rocking baby Charlie to sleep."

I knelt beside him. "That's a beautiful dream."

The wind stirred the straw. A hen clucked loudly, then quieted.

He frowned, thinking hard. "What can we do to make Mama smile like she used to?"

I sighed and rubbed the back of my neck. "I don't know. I've tried everything I could think of. Guess we just wait. Sooner or later, her smile will come back."

"Maybe we should bake her a cake. Or cookies," A.J. said brightly. "Cake and cookies always make me feel better."

Summer turned to winter. I managed the ranch the best I could, kept up the chores, kept A.J. fed and loved. But the air felt heavy, like the whole place had fallen under a hush. Even Lady moved slower, as if she, too, felt the weight of sorrow.

Then in April, just as I was beginning to wonder how long we could all hold on, we got the news: Mattie was with child again. And just like that, the color returned. Her eyes lit up, her cheeks flushed pink. She sang as she cooked, laughed at A.J.'s stories, picked wildflowers for the table, and walked the riverbank with Lady at her side. There was hope again. It filled the house like sunlight spilling through open windows.

It was a warm August night in 1928, when Mattie gave birth to another baby boy. We named him Jack.

But Jack came early—too small, too quiet, his skin pale like Charlie's. When I first saw him, my gut went cold. It felt we were riding straight into a nightmare—like cattle breaking toward a cliff, and no matter how hard I spurred my horse, I couldn't move fast enough to head them off.

We watched him struggle to breathe, his little chest rising and falling like the wings of a trapped bird. Evelyn came down from Salem and Lily McDonald traveled up from Myrtle Creek. They tried everything. He gasped for every breath, fighting to hold on to that fragile thread of life that was unraveling with each passing moment. Mattie held him, rocking gently, whispering to him, but nothing helped.

Jack struggled for two months. One morning in October, he slipped away in Mattie's arms. We all saw it coming. No one said it out loud. Hope is a stubborn thing—it keeps you going long after the odds have turned against you.

It was raining when we climbed the hill again. On that late afternoon, the vibrant yellows of the cottonwoods marked the ridge against the pale mist. Jack's small body was wrapped snuggly in a red and white quilt Fern had made for him. We laid him beside Charlie. Two small white crosses now stood in the earth, just a few feet apart. A.J. gathered the last of the wildflowers and laid them gently at the base of each cross. Then, with his eyes closed, he whispered a prayer for both his brothers.

I wrapped my arms around Mattie, but she didn't cry. She just stared at the trees, her face pale and still. My heart broke again for her. I wanted to comfort her, but I didn't know what to say. My head spun with words, yet they all sounded stupid and shallow. I was afraid if I opened my mouth, I'd just make things worse. So I said nothing. Then she looked up at me, and I realized she didn't want my words—she just wanted my presence. And she was thankful I was there.

Moments passed and she said quietly, "Take A.J. back to the cabin," she said. "I need to grieve alone."

A.J. hesitated, glancing from me to the crosses. Then he reached for her hand. "I don't want you to be sad alone."

She held it tight, then kissed his knuckles as the rain stopped and the sun set and turned us into shadows.

I lit the lantern and set it on an old stump, casting gold across the crosses. We stood there together, the three of us, in silence. The air was cool, and above us, the stars began to appear—one by one—as if the sky itself was mourning with us.

That night, we didn't speak much. Mattie sat by the hearth, rocking slowly with Lady curled up nearby. I tucked A.J. into bed and kissed his forehead. He fell asleep clutching a folded scrap of paper—a picture he'd drawn of two angels holding babies in their arms.

Outside, the wind stirred the cottonwoods. Inside, the fire crackled. Grief had returned, but this time, we faced it together—close and quiet, one hour at a time.

And by morning, we would have to set it down, because life doesn't stop and the work would begin again.

A year to the month after Jack's death, baby Irene was born.

By then, I'd sworn to myself—I wasn't going to lose another child. Not if there was anything I could do about it. I'd already started talking to doctors in Roseburg and Salem while Mattie was still only six months along. I bought every tonic, every medicine, every folk remedy any old midwife or pharmacist swore might help. I even tracked down an herbalist in Eugene who gave me something bitter-smelling in a green bottle. I didn't know if any of it would work, but I bought it all anyway.

Two weeks before her due date, I packed our bags and drove Mattie north to Portland. We checked into a clean little hotel near Good Samaritan Hospital, and I hired the best doctor in the city. Money was tight, but I told myself nothing mattered more than this child. Nothing.

We left A.J. with Fern and Grant. Sometimes I wondered whether he liked it at their place, playing with Ray and baby Donald, more than with us. Fern also fed our animals and Grant kept an eye on the ranch.

One night, while Mattie was sleeping, I called Ma in Denver from the payphone downstairs. Her voice crackled through the line like a whisper through dry leaves.

"I'll have the whole church pray," she promised. "And I'll pray every night myself. This little one's going to make it, Allen. I believe that."

I wanted to believe it too.

Irene was born on an early rainy morning. The sky outside the hospital window was a dull gray, but inside that delivery room, everything felt washed in light. They must've felt sorry for me, because they broke the hospital rules and let me hold Mattie's hand as she pushed through the pain, sweat beading on her brow. And then the baby arrived.

When the nurse handed me that baby girl—so tiny, so new—I held her close against my chest and cried like a thirsty cowboy who thought he was dead, but found a spring bubbling up in the desert.

She was the most beautiful thing I'd ever seen. Rosebud lips, soft cheeks, bright blue eyes that blinked up at me like she was already trying to understand the world. Her fingers curled around mine, barely the width of a blade of grass. She looked perfect. Whole.

"She's strong," the doctor said, smiling as he checked her over. "And healthy."

For a few days, we believed him.

But a week later, Irene stopped eating. Her cries grew weaker. The nurses tried everything—warm compresses, gentle feeding tubes, special formulas. We stayed in Portland, renting a room above a bakery, the scent of rising dough and wood smoke drifting in through the windows each morning. I spent my days pacing the hospital halls, asking questions no one could answer.

Some days, she rallied. Her eyes would open wide, and she'd grip my finger like she meant to hold on forever. I'd read to her from a book of Psalms Ma had sent in the mail. Mattie would sit beside her crib and hum southern lullabies.

But then came the bad days. Days when Irene barely moved at all. When even her breathing was a faint flutter, like a moth caught behind glass.

Six months passed that way. Half a year of hope and heartbreak braided together like barbed wire. And then one cold February morning in 1929, while Mattie slept in the cot beside her, Irene slipped away.

The nurse found her first. She didn't cry or call out. Just walked in, checked the tiny form beneath the blanket, and gently reached for the button to summon the doctor.

I held her again that day. Still warm, still soft. My tears fell onto her blanket like rain hitting dry earth, too late to save the crop. I whispered all the things I'd hoped to teach her. All the places I wanted to take her. All the ways I had tried to love her enough to keep her.

But she was gone. We had done everything we could. And it hadn't made a bit of difference. Damn it all.

It took eight hours to drive back from Portland to the ranch. We didn't speak a word. Our silence said it all. It felt like the longest drive I'd ever made. My eyes were tired, my body numb, the road blurry. I thought about pulling over somewhere, just to scream or throw something. But the road kept pulling us forward. And maybe I was afraid that if I stopped, I wouldn't be able to go on.

We had tried three times. And each time broke us a little more. As we packed Irene's tiny body in a small box to lay beside her brothers on the hill, we felt hollow. Lost. Hopeless.

Mattie held her feelings in—cold and quiet. As for me, I was mad as hell. Never liked baseball, never been to a game, never cared to go. A contest that didn't involve horses, cattle, lassos, or guns never seemed like much of a sport—leastways, that's how I saw it. But I had to admit, with three strikes you're out—and I was out for good.

WHAT MORE CAN WE DO?

We buried Irene beside her brothers, three tiny crosses on the hill beneath the cottonwoods. A.J. set a bouquet of white winter jasmine on her grave. It was a cold February afternoon, with the wind cutting through our clothes and freezing our tears halfway down our cheeks.

"Can we go back to the cabin?" A.J. rubbed his hands together to make heat.

"I suppose there's nothing more to achieve by standing out here," I said.

Mattie didn't say a word. I reached for her hand, and she let me take it—passive, unresisting. Other than that slight movement, she was still as a stone. It was as if she feared that the slightest motion might break her open, unleashing a flood of grief so fierce it would wash us all away.

The collar of her thick wool coat hid her mouth. A black scarf covered her strawberry blond hair, showing only her blue eyes and rosy cheeks.

"Mattie, you're going to freeze to death out here."

There was a subtle shrug, and she buried her hands deep in her pockets. If I didn't know her so well, I might've missed it. Her eyes stayed on the newest cross. They squinted, and her forehead furrowed. It was too much for her. I gritted my teeth, wishing I could carry the burden for her. She leaned against me, and I felt her body tremble. I slipped my arm around her waist as Lady nestled up against her left leg.

"Ma sent a verse," I said, pulling a letter from my pocket. "'I will lift up mine eyes unto the hills from whence cometh my help. My help cometh from the Lord, which made heaven and earth.'"

"Thank her for the scripture," Mattie said. "I need all the help I can get—from heaven or earth."

"Can we go now?" A.J. tugged on my hand.

"Not until Mommy's ready."

"I'll never be ready," Mattie said softly, then turned and walked toward the house, with A.J. and me scurrying to keep up.

"How can I help you?" I asked later that day as Mattie stirred the stew pot. The smell of onions and beef filled the kitchen, mingling with the soft clatter of the wooden spoon against the cast-iron pot.

"You can't," she said softly. "No one can."

I leaned against the doorframe, watching her shoulders stiffen. "I know I can't take the pain away," I said. "But maybe we can try again. Start fresh."

"I've had enough," she whispered.

I nodded slowly. "It's been a hard four years."

She turned her face toward the window, the waning light catching the edge of her cheek. "I can't keep trying. If God wanted us to have more children, He would've let us."

"But I know how much you wanted them."

"I did." She set the spoon down and walked over, reaching for my hand. "But if I have to put one more cross on that hill... it'll kill me."

"So... no more babies?"

She nodded. "That's right."

I looked down at our joined hands. Her fingers were pale and raw.

"At least we've got A.J.," I said.

"You're right," she murmured, managing a faint smile. "And he's such a good boy."

Lady padded into the kitchen just then and laid down by our feet with a soft sigh. Outside, a gust of wind rustled the bare branches against the side of the house.

The next morning dawned clear and cold. While Mattie packed A.J.'s lunch, I helped him button his coat and adjust the strap of his school satchel.

"Do I really have to go to school?" he said with a sigh, like he was headed off to war.

"You'll do just fine," I told him. "Mind your manners. Don't talk back to Miss Granger."

He nodded, then trotted down the lane toward the Ruckles schoolhouse, boots crunching through the frost-covered grass. Lady followed a few paces behind, escorting him halfway before circling back.

By the time the sun crested the eastern ridge, I was out mending the north fence where last week's storm had brought down two posts and stretched the wire taut as fiddle strings. The ground was still half-frozen, and my breath rose in little clouds with every hammer strike. Lady sniffed along the brush, ears alert.

Back at the house, Mattie had moved her sewing table near the front window to catch the light. She'd laid out soft squares of fabric—muted blues and worn plaids, pieces cut from old shirts and feed sacks—and was already stitching the first rows of a new quilt.

"Who's this one for?" I asked, stomping snow from my boots and warming my hands by the stove.

She kept her eyes on the needle. "A woman over at the Bound's place. Lost her baby girl last week."

I didn't say anything right away. Just watched her work—slow, careful, each stitch placed with graceful purpose. I stood amazed at her compassion toward a neighbor when she'd just experienced the same loss. This was one of the many things I loved about Mattie: she could turn the deepest grief into generosity.

Outside, the wind had stilled. The hills looked washed clean in the pale light. Nothing was fixed, not yet—but the world kept turning. And so did we.

Weeks passed, and life settled back into a regular rhythm at the ranch. We didn't speak of the three crosses. We just worked harder and longer, praying for the strength to make it to spring. On a windy Thursday afternoon I found a letter waiting in the mailbox at the bottom of the hill. The envelope was postmarked Denver. I tore it open.

Dear Allen,

I regret to inform you that your beloved mother, Elizabeth Skinner Stephens, passed away peacefully in her sleep. A memorial service will be held at 11 a.m. on March 1st in the year of our Lord 1930 at the First Baptist Church of Denver on Stout Street.

Our thoughts and prayers are with you and your family during this time of sorrow.

At the bottom of the page was a signature I didn't recognize.

The words blurred. I stood in the still morning air, letter trembling in my hands. I held it for a long while, as if the weight of my gaze might change what it said. But it didn't.

One more loss. This cruel world was hitting me hard—maybe too hard for this beat up cowboy. A slug to the gut when I'd just taken a punch to the face. Ma had sounded fine a month ago, but now she was gone.

I thought about the train to Denver, about what it would mean to sit in that old church on Stout Street where I'd once watched the light catch the stained glass behind her favorite hymn. But I couldn't leave Mattie. Not now. Not with the days as heavy as they'd been and her heart just starting to heal. The grief we carried was piled too high for either of us to bear alone.

So I folded the letter and slipped it back into the envelope. I didn't tell her right away. Instead, I walked back up the hill slow, like each step was some kind of prayer.

Later that evening, as I split kindling out behind the cabin, I said a few words to the cottonwoods—words Ma would never hear but ones I needed to say. I told her thank you. For the lullabies, the black coffee, the steady strength. For every goodbye she waited patiently through and every homecoming she welcomed without question.

I didn't need a pew or a preacher. She knew I loved her.

Death had become a regular visitor these past few years. I'd stopped asking why. It's just the way life is—things bloom, things fade. And somewhere in between, you hold on as best you can. Ma had always taught me to face the truth head-on—like the prairie wind blowing sand in your eyes. It might be hard, but you do what you need to do. So that's what I did.

With both Ma and Pa gone, I found myself growing reflective. Spring and summer had always been my favorite times of year. The sun lingered longer, the work came steady, and there was comfort in the rhythm of the season.

I stayed busy—mending fences, thinning branches in the orchard, tending the animals—but something inside me had begun to settle. Sure, there was sadness if I looked back at the long trail behind me. Regret, too. I'd made my share of mistakes. But I'd also known adventure, and love, and the kind of lessons a man only learns with time.

One morning, I sat alone on the porch with a tin cup of coffee, watching the sun climb over the ridge. The breeze carried the smell of ripening prunes from the orchard. It was quiet but full of life— birdsong in the distance, the soft creak of the porch boards beneath my boots. I felt thankful. Not just for the peace I had now, but for the whole trail behind me. The peaks and the valleys alike. And I couldn't think of that trail without thinking of the women who'd helped shape it—each one just right for the season she belonged to.

Eddie was like a wild prairie fire—lighting up the horizon and scorching you if you got too close. She was intense, unpredictable, unforgettable. Leaving her was hard—but it had to be done.

Era was as gentle and graceful as a river, flowing past meadows of wildflowers. Losing her broke something deep inside me. But no amount of love can stop the current when it's time to let go.

And then there was Mattie. Not as dangerous as Eddie, not as romantic as Era—but exactly who I needed for the life I had now. She was as solid as the hillside our cabin was built on, and as steady as the orchard at harvest. As each month passed, I appreciated her more—not for who she used to be or who I imagined she might become, but for who she already was.

The screen door creaked open behind me. Mattie stepped onto the porch holding a plate of freshly fried bacon and eggs, steam rising into the morning air. She smiled without saying a word. I stood and wrapped my arms around her, pulled her close, and kissed her full on the mouth. "Thank you," I whispered. "For being here with me."

Mattie was a good wife, a loving mother, and a decent soul through and through. But the past five years had worn on her. I wanted her to know how much A.J. and I appreciated her—truth was, I wasn't sure how we would've managed without her.

When the prune harvest brought in more money than I expected, I decided to give her a gift she'd never forget. I knew she hadn't been back to Georgia since leaving six years earlier, and I figured a trip home to see her kin might lift her spirits. So, on our fifth wedding anniversary, I gave her a round-trip ticket to Dublin. I would've gone with her if I could, but one ticket was all I could afford.

At first, she said she didn't want to go unless I went too. But after a few days, she changed her mind. By the time we saw her off at the station, she even seemed excited. A.J. and I stood on the platform waving as the bus pulled away. She leaned out the window with a wavering smile, blew us a kiss—and just like that, she was gone.

When she returned, she told me the following story.

After five days of traveling she stepped off the bus at the corner of Bellevue Avenue and Jefferson Street. The worn strap of her satchel digging into her shoulder, Mattie squinted beneath the Georgia sun. The Greyhound pulled away in a hiss of brakes and dust, leaving her standing in the same heat she'd once called home. Six years gone, and still the air in Dublin smelled like dry cotton, woodsmoke, and warm syrup drifting from the cane mill just beyond the depot.

She was bone tired. Too many days on that rickety bus, riding through hills and flatlands and towns that blurred together. Some folks could sleep through the bumps and chatter, but not her. Every jolt startled her half-awake. Every cry of a baby, every snore, every rattling bridge—they all tugged at her nerves like loose threads. By morning, her eyes were dry and stinging, her limbs leaden with fatigue. She hadn't had a proper rest since she'd left the ranch.

The streets looked smaller than she remembered. Main Street had narrowed with time. Some of the storefronts were empty now, their windows streaked with dust and "FOR RENT" signs fading in the sunlight. W.H. Jones Mercantile still stood, though the awning sagged and the red paint had peeled down to gray. She paused at the window, remembering the way her mama used to press a gloved finger against the glass and point out fine china they could never afford.

Turning down Jackson Street, she stared at the First Baptist Church with its tall white steeple. Then the bell rang—once, then again—bright and solemn. It made her pause mid-step, the sound stretching across the rooftops and settling somewhere deep in her chest.

She passed a row of clapboard houses, many sagging at the porch or boarded at the windows. Laundry fluttered on the line behind one of them, and two barefoot boys chased a dog through a yard of red clay. She smiled at the sight, then looked away. Those children could've been her own if the world had turned out differently.

The old schoolhouse came into view, red brick with tall windows and a slate roof dulled by time. She remembered standing on those steps in a blue dress her mama had sewn, clutching a slate and a sandwich wrapped in wax paper. The same oak tree still grew in the yard, though its branches hung lower now, like an old man's shoulders.

She kept walking until she reached the cemetery hill, where the grass grew wild between tilted headstones. Her mama was buried there. So was her sister. She hadn't brought flowers. She hadn't brought anything, really, except herself. She stood at the gate a long while, hands gripping the rusted iron fence, her breath catching in her throat.

"Home," she whispered. "It's just not the same."

The breeze shifted, rustling the pecan trees overhead—the same breeze that used to lift her hair when she ran barefoot through the back pasture, and the same one that dried her tears the night she left town with nothing but a suitcase and a heart full of hope.

Mattie turned south toward the family farm to see her daddy. She hoped he wasn't drunk. And that he'd be glad to see her. But with Daddy, you never really knew. That was what made her nervous.

She walked the two miles down the dusty road, kicking up grit with each step. Eventually, she saw it—the old farmhouse where she and her eight siblings had been born. The picket fence was falling down, hidden among switchgrass and pokeweed. The white paint on the house had faded and peeled, curling off like birch bark. The wood-shake roof was patched with random strips of tar paper and rusted tin. The place looked deserted. She climbed the porch steps, weaving between broken boxes, crumpled newspapers, and the shards of a shattered plate. The front door hung open.

Inside, the air was thick with dust. It floated in the sunlight and settled over every surface like a forgotten memory. Each step creaked beneath her shoes. The whole house seemed steeped in silence and neglect.

Her daddy was slumped in his worn-out chair in the front room, fingers wrapped tight around a bottle of moonshine. His shirt was sweat-stained, his dungarees stiff with grime. He snored and snorted, reeking of piss and puke. She stood there for a long moment, unsure what to do. Afraid of what might happen if she did anything at all.

Then he woke with a jolt, eyes wild and unfocused. He clutched the bottle tighter and stared at her like she'd crawled out of a grave. "What the hell are you doing here?"

He scared the living daylights out of her, but she collected herself enough to look him in the eye and say, "I came home to visit you."

"This ain't your home." He rubbed his eyes, scratched himself. "What do you want?"

"Just to visit."

"Liar," he spat. "You came to steal my stuff."

"Daddy, I don't want your stuff."

"I ain't your daddy."

"Don't you recognize me?" she said with a sick feeling in her gut.

"Why would I recognize some city girl lookin' to rob me blind?" He pushed up from the chair, stumbled toward her. But she stepped out of the way. He crashed into the wall and crumpled to the floor.

"I'm Mattie. Your daughter."

"Liar," he muttered, groaning. "You don't look nothin' like Mattie. She's dead. I killed her myself. Buried her out back. Stupid kid didn't even deserve a plot on cemetery hill."

"Daddy....I'm not dead."

"Get away from me," he barked. He reached for the shotgun propped in the corner and swung it toward her, hands shaking so bad he couldn't have hit a buffalo at five feet.

She should've been scared, but all she felt was pity. "Please, put down the gun. I'm Mattie. I came all this way to see you."

He pulled the trigger. The blast shattered the front window and knocked him flat on his backside. She rushed in and pulled the gun from his grasp while he groaned on the floor.

"This is the welcome I get?" By this time, her pity was turning into downright aggravation. "After traveling five days just to see you and my family?"

"You ain't Mattie," he growled. "If you were, I'd have to kill you again."

"Why would you say that?"

"You're after my stuff."

"I told you—I don't want anything."

"Then leave. Leave my property right now!"

"Where are the others? Where's the rest of your kids?"

"Gone," he muttered. "All gone far away. Stole from me. Every last one of them."

"Daddy... what happened to you?"

"Get outta here!" he roared. He staggered to his feet and lunged again. She stepped aside, and this time he hit the wall hard—something cracked. Maybe the wall. Maybe a bone. He collapsed, cussing and groaning and spitting threats that cut to the bone.

Mattie didn't wait to see what came next. She left the house in tears, shedding more than she cared to admit, her shoes pounding the same dusty road that had brought her there. She walked the two miles back to town without stopping, without looking back. Why had she come back home? What had she been hoping for? She was a plain fool and nothing more.

When she got to the station, she bought a ticket for the next bus to Oregon—and didn't even care where it stopped along the way. she just wanted to get out of there as quickly as she could.

The bus rumbled through the outskirts of town, past cotton fields and crooked fence posts, past everything she used to know. Mattie sat near the back, forehead resting against the cool glass, arms folded tight across her chest. She didn't cry—not anymore. The tears had dried somewhere between the front porch and the cemetery. All she felt now was hollow. Hollow and tired. She had come looking for family, for some piece of herself she thought she'd left behind. But this wasn't her home anymore. These weren't her people. Home was in Oregon, with the orchard and the river and the quiet hills. Family was Allen and A.J.—the ones who loved her, who saw her, who believed in her. She closed her eyes, leaned into the rhythm of the road, and let the miles carry her back to where she truly belonged.

That's what Mattie told me when she came back after only a week. I was mighty surprised and asked how the trip went. She just said, "I learned a lot." I pressed for more, but she shook her head and told me she couldn't talk about it—not yet.

About a month later, she finally told me the whole story.

"I'm so sorry," I said when she finished.

"No, no," she smiled gently. "You gave me a precious gift."

"A precious gift?" I didn't understand.

"Yes. You showed me where I truly belong." She reached for my hand. "And that the only place I'll ever be happy is beside you."

The next two years were as good as any I can remember.

The prune harvests were bountiful. I joined the Eagles Lodge in Myrtle Creek, where we played poker and told tall tales late into the night. A.J. did well in school—reading, writing, arithmetic. In the evenings, I'd sit beside the fire or out on the front porch and read aloud to him until Mattie poked her head in and reminded us it was well past bedtime. The two of us could get lost in a good story. His favorites were *Treasure Island* and *Swiss Family Robinson*.

Mattie started going to the little white Baptist Church with Fern about once a month. It was on a hill overlooking the river. It was a simple building with a modest steeple, a stained glass window, and a meeting room with twelve pine pews. She'd ask if I wanted to join them, but I always claimed I was too busy with ranch work. Still, I liked seeing her dress up and head out the door. It reminded me of Ma. And somehow, it seemed to add to the peace and strength she carried so well.

Now and then, I'd drive all three of us into Roseburg to the Majestic Theater. We'd sit together in the velvet seats, sharing popcorn and watching the latest picture show. I especially liked the Westerns—*Born in the Saddle*, *The Lone Rider*, *The Big Trail*—films that made me feel like a boy again, riding fast with the wind in my hair.

Life was peaceful, steady, full of laughter. Nothing grand or remarkable happened, but we found joy in the simple things. Looking back, those two years were some of the best we ever had. And I had no idea that things were about to get even better.

Thanksgiving Day, 1931, was one of those crisp, golden afternoons that made you thankful just to be alive. We spent it at Fern and Grant's farm, tucked between rows of frost-bitten orchards and woodsmoke curling from the chimney. We brought the turkey— plump and golden brown, fresh from our own coop. They provided everything else: mashed potatoes, sweet yams, green beans in cream, cornbread stuffing, and two kinds of pie.

Ray was six now, Donald four, and the two of them tore around the yard in wool sweaters and muddy boots until the food hit the table. A.J., nine years old and trying his best to act grown, ran with them for a while but eventually ended up playing the referee. Still, he laughed right along with them, his face bright and flushed from the cold.

Inside, the table was packed with food and surrounded by warmth. Ray carried a toy wooden truck and parked it beside his plate. Donald had to be talked into washing his hands. A.J. settled between Mattie and Fern, sneaking bites of cornbread when he thought no one was looking.

Before we ate, we all joined hands and went around the table, each of us offering a short blessing—thanks for harvests, healthy children, steady work, and gentle nights.

When it came to Mattie's turn, she paused. Her eyes sparkled. "I have the biggest blessing of all," she said.

The room went still.

She smiled wide. "I'm going to have a baby."

For a moment, no one moved. Fern's hand froze halfway to her glass. Grant leaned back, blinking like he hadn't heard her right. A.J. looked up, startled, his mouth still full of bread.

Then the silence cracked into a chorus of smiles and surprised laughter—some of it joyful, some a little uncertain. After everything we'd been through, it was natural to feel a bit nervous. But I'd been reading—medical books and journals, anything I could get my hands on. And deep down, I believed this time would be different.

"This baby's going to make it," I said. "This is the one we've been waiting for."

Mattie reached for my hand under the table. Her grip was firm, her eyes steady.

We didn't say much more after that. Just smiled and passed the dishes around. Ray insisted his toy truck get its own napkin. Donald asked for pie before finishing his potatoes. A.J. leaned in close to Mattie, quieter than usual, like he was already imagining life with a little brother or sister.

Outside, the apple trees rattled in the wind. Inside, the house was full—with food, with laughter, and with the kind of hope that maybe, just maybe, we'd made it through the hardest part. The past two years had been good—better than we ever imagined—but what lay ahead promised to be even sweeter.

At least that's what I hoped for.

GOAT'S MILK

Mattie loved Christmas. She dreamt of it, planned for it, and cherished every one she'd ever known. She acted like it was bigger than birthdays, Thanksgiving, and the Fourth of July all rolled into one. I've never seen anything like it—and I never saw Mattie so happy. For this holiday she made gifts for A.J. and me, wrapped them with ribbon and butcher paper, and set them neatly beneath the Douglas fir in the front room. On Christmas Eve, the house filled with the smell of baking—cinnamon bread, honey cakes, and apple pies. A.J. said it smelled so sweet he thought he'd died and gone to heaven.

Two weeks earlier, A.J. and I had cut down the perfect eight-foot tree on the hill east of the ranch. We set it up across from the fireplace, and Mattie turned it into something magical—strands of popcorn, bows of red and white ribbon, bundles of cranberries, and a shining tin angel I'd cut from a leftover scrap of roofing.

That evening, we sat around the tree and sang holiday songs—"Jingle Bells," "Silent Night," "O Little Town of Bethlehem." Then we opened our presents. Mattie gave me a work shirt and a package of my favorite cookies. I gave her a coral cameo necklace that Ma had passed down to me years ago. Together, we gave A.J. a bone-handled hunting knife and a shiny mouth organ.

He was so excited he played it nonstop. After a couple hours of wailing and wheezing, I started to regret the gift. Mattie patted my shoulder and handed me two small balls of raw wool. "He's just a kid," she said. "Put these in your ears and try to ignore it."

Around noon on Christmas Day, we packed up the Model T to spend the afternoon with Fern and Grant. We brought enough food to feed a whole cattle drive twice over.

"We don't need this much," Mattie said as we climbed in.

"I know, but Grant's been struggling to make ends meet. I just want to make sure they don't go hungry."

"You certainly have a soft spot for those two and their boys."

"They're good people." I started the engine, and Lady jumped into the back seat beside A.J. "I just want to be neighborly."

"You're more than just neighborly when it comes to Fern. If she weren't so much younger, I might've started to wonder."

I leaned over and kissed her cheek. "You've got nothing to worry about."

"I hope not."

Half an hour later, Mattie was out in the pasture behind Grant's place playing tag with all three boys while Lady darted after them, barking playfully and zigzagging between their legs. Grant had wandered off to the barn, while Fern and I stood together in the kitchen, putting the finishing touches on Christmas dinner.

"How's Mattie doing?" she asked.

"She's due in three, maybe four months. She's excited."

"After the last three, I'd be terrified."

"We've got a new plan," I said. "The doctors think goat's milk might help."

"Goat's milk?" Fern raised an eyebrow. "That's unusual. But if it works..."

"They said if a baby can't digest normal milk or formula, sometimes goat's milk works. That's what the doctors say and I'm counting on it."

"Is Mattie as confident as you?"

"She's got Ma's kind of faith. She believes this baby's going to be strong and healthy."

"I pray she's right."

"She's as steady as they come."

Fern nodded, then looked me directly in the eyes. "She's strong enough that you should tell her the truth about me—and about how old you really are."

"Christmas isn't the right time."

"There's never a good time," Fern said gently. "She's smart and sooner or later she's going to start asking questions."

"She already has," I said.

"I've been her friend for six years, and I feel like I've been lying to her."

"You've only done what I asked."

"It's still a secret I've kept from her. And I've respected your wish to be the one to tell her."

"You're right. This hasn't been fair to you. I've put you in a hard spot, and I'm sorry. I'll tell her—I promise. Maybe tonight."

A.J. spent the night with his cousins Ray and Donald. After the boys had gone to bed, Mattie and I drove home under a full moon. Lady sat in the back seat and pushed her cold nose between us to nuzzle Mattie's shoulder.

"You were asking about Fern earlier," I said, eyes on the narrow road that followed the river toward our cabin.

"Yes."

"Well... I've got something to confess."

"The pastor at First Baptist says confession is good for the soul."

I pulled off onto the gravel shoulder and took her hands. "I haven't been fully honest with you about Fern."

"In what way?"

"She's not just our neighbor..." I swallowed. "She's my daughter."

"I know," Mattie said softly. "I've known for a while."

"How?"

"It's the way you look out for her. The way you protect her. You treat her like I always wished my father had treated me."

"There's more. She's from Eddie—my first wife."

"I figured that out too. I knew Era wasn't her mother, so there had to be someone else."

"I should've told you all this a long time ago. You deserved to hear it from me, but I was afraid you wouldn't marry me. I'm twenty years older than you. I just didn't want to lose you."

"I'd have married you anyway," she smiled. "You're the best thing that's ever happened to me. It just makes me sad that you didn't think you could be honest with me."

"I'm so sorry."

She didn't answer right away. Instead, she reached up and touched the cameo at her neck—the one I'd given her the night before. Her fingers lingered there, slow and thoughtful, like she was remembering something sweet—and deciding something, too.

"Let's just promise—no more secrets. From now on."

"I promise." I wrapped my arms around her, not ever wanting to let go.

We sat in the cold car, wrapped in each other's arms, letting the full moon pour through the windshield, filling us with quiet confidence that things were going to be better—and our family would soon grow.

Winter gave way to spring. As the days lengthened and the wildflowers began to bloom, Mattie grew more anxious. The closer we got to her due date, the quieter she became—checking and rechecking the baby things, folding the same blankets over and over, watching the sky like it held the answer.

To help ease her worry, I gave A.J. a job. He was in charge of milking the goats and, once the baby came, checking on him first thing each morning. A.J. took his job serious and swore he'd be the best big brother in the whole county.

And then—right in the middle of April—our baby boy came into the world. April 19th, 1932, to be exact. We named him Erroll, after my little brother who'd died during the Spanish Flu pandemic.

Lily McDonald and Fern both served as midwives that day, calm and steady as ever. When Erroll let out his first cry—strong, loud, and full of life—we all froze for a moment. His color was good, his breathing clear, his little fists clenched and kicking. He looked so healthy, we were almost afraid to believe it. Mattie held him for a long while and just cried. But then, just like the other three, he wouldn't take her milk.

"Allen, I guess this is where we try your idea," said Fern.

"I'm ready," I told her. "A.J. milked the goats this morning, and nothing is going to take this baby from us."

Over the next couple of weeks, Erroll grew weaker and lost weight. But every three hours, day and night, we fed him goat's milk—just as much as he'd take. He seemed to like it, and more importantly, it seemed to help. Slowly, he regained the strength and weight he'd lost. Then he started growin' like ragweed after a spring rain. And once little Erroll began to grow, nothing was going to stop him. Within a year, he was as tall and handsome as the healthiest kid in the county.

A.J. did just what he swore he would. He told Mattie and me more than once that it was his job to keep Erroll alive and safe, and he meant it. Every morning, he checked the bottles, helped warm the milk, and kept an eye on his little brother like a hawk circling a mouse. If Erroll so much as whimpered, A.J. was the first to his side, patting his chest or whispering soft things he'd heard Mattie say. Sometimes we'd catch him sitting by the cradle with a picture book in his lap, showing the baby the pages like he understood every word. That kind of love—steady and unshakable—gave us a quiet confidence that everything was going to be okay.

Mattie, for her part, blossomed in a way I hadn't seen since the early days of our marriage. She sang while she worked and rocked Erroll for hours, even when he wasn't fussing. She'd kiss the top of his head and whisper, "You're my strong boy, you're my miracle." Sometimes I'd find her just watching him sleep, her hand lightly resting on his chest like she was afraid he might drift away if she let go. Lady often lay curled at her feet, her head on her paws, eyes half-closed but always alert, as if she'd taken it upon herself to guard the baby.

And she never forgot A.J.'s part in it all. "I couldn't have done this without you," she told him one night as they folded diapers together at the kitchen table. A.J. beamed, sitting a little straighter in his chair. That boy had taken on the job like a soldier, and Mattie made sure he knew it hadn't gone unnoticed. We were a team—seasoned by all we'd been through, but stronger because of it. And for the first time in a long while, our little house didn't just feel warm—it felt full of life, and full of excitement for whatever came next.

With the secret out and the lie forgiven, the friendship between Mattie and Fern strengthened like fence posts set in firm prairie clay—planted solid, upright, and steady no matter how hard the wind might blow.

They'd been close before, but now there was something unspoken between them. A kind of knowing. A softness in their voices when they spoke to each other. They walked together most days in the summer, usually down by the river, talking about whatever it is mothers talk about—babies, recipes, chores, and sometimes things that went deeper. Mattie would carry baby Erroll on her hip, while the other three boys wandered ahead in a noisy pack, throwing rocks and chasing dragonflies. Both women dreamed of more children, filling their homes with even more laughter, even more love.

That summer, Mattie found something tucked away in an old cigar box in our bedroom. It was a silver ring I'd given Eddie years ago, back when we were young and hopeful. When she left Montana with the kids, she left behind a few things—mostly junk she didn't want—but she must've forgotten about that ring. I'd held onto it for reasons I still can't explain. Maybe I just wasn't ready to let go of that part of my life. But when Mattie found it, she had plenty of questions. I answered them as honestly as I could. Then she held the ring up to the light, polished it clean, and said, "Since this belonged to Fern's mother. It ought to go to her."

I didn't disagree.

A few days later, Mattie handed the ring to Fern. "This was your mama's," she said. "And now it's yours."

Fern stared at it for a long moment, her eyes wide, her voice caught somewhere between surprise and gratitude. "Are you sure?"

Mattie smiled and nodded. "It's where it belongs."

Fern slipped it on her middle finger, right next to her wedding band. It fit like it was made for her. From that moment on, she never took it off.

They spent the rest of that summer as if they'd always been family. They made strawberry jam and apple butter together, their aprons dusted with sugar and flour. They canned peaches, tomatoes, green beans—anything that grew. When the weather turned wet and cold, they sat by the fire sewing quilts, stitching patterns so fine it made your eyes ache to follow them. They made quilts for every new marriage and birth in that part of the county, and their hands worked in rhythm like they'd been doing it side by side for a lifetime. Watching them grow closer warmed my heart like sunrise on a cold prairie morning.

Our two families spent every holiday together and many a Saturday night. The kids played until they dropped, and the grownups told stories or sang songs or just sat in the comfort of one another's company.

Fern had grown into a woman I was mighty proud of. She was the prettiest girl in the county, no doubt about that, with short silky hair—fashionable back then—and a smile as contagious as measles. But more than her looks, she had the kind of character that only comes through hardship. Though just past her mid-twenties, she had the wisdom and work ethic of a woman twice her age. She was gentle, faithful, and full of grace—just like Ma had been. I often wished Ma could look down and see what a fine granddaughter she had.

And Fern was a good mother, patient and kind. A steady wife, too. Grant had finally seen that and changed his ways before he lost her for good. He'd been a different man these past few years—not a drink, not a raised hand since I'd had words with him before Mattie and I were married. It took some doing, but he'd become the kind of husband Fern deserved.

All of this made what was about to happen even more heartbreaking.

A week before Christmas in 1933, Fern got real sick. She said it was just her stomach at first—something she ate, maybe—but by the next morning, she couldn't get out of bed. Grant didn't know what to do. He paced the floor, wringing his hands and whispering prayers like he didn't know which end was up. I've never seen a grown man so desperate.

With Prohibition just ended, I half-expected him to go back to the bottle. And if I'm being honest, I wouldn't have blamed him. But he didn't. He stayed sober and scared, watching the woman he loved twist in pain and not knowing how to help.

Mattie sat by Fern's bedside for three days straight. She bathed her forehead with cool cloths and whispered encouragement when the pain came in waves. But it only got worse. By the third night, Fern was too weak to speak—just curled in on herself, trembling and pale.

Late that night, Grant finally loaded her into the truck and drove her to Mercy Hospital in Roseburg. The wind was howling, and the roads were slick with ice. I stood on the porch and watched the taillights disappear into the dark. I didn't say it out loud, but something in my chest told me she wouldn't be coming back.

She never did.

At first, the doctors didn't know what was wrong. But I could see—if they didn't act soon, it'd be too late. And I was right. By the time they figured it out, there was nothing left to do. They said it was an ectopic pregnancy. I'd never heard of such a thing. Fern moaned and sighed from somewhere deep inside her. I held one hand and Grant held the other. Mattie stood in the corner, praying with more fervency than I'd ever seen. But it was too late. An hour later Fern died. It was mid-January, just twelve days after her twenty-eighth birthday.

Just like that, she was gone. I hadn't hurt that bad since Era died.

And all the quilts, the laughter, the apple butter, and the summer walks by the river—they lived on in memory. But Fern herself—the girl with the short, silky hair and that contagious smile—was no longer part of this world. It didn't seem fair. Not after everything she'd survived. Not after how hard she'd loved, and how much she'd grown.

I went out into the cold and climbed to the top of the hill with my rifle clutched in hand. The wind blew hard, stinging my face, but I didn't care. Losing Fern was like losing Eddie, and Era, and Ma, and the three babies beneath the crosses. It felt like a stampede of cattle, and I was flat on the ground with their hoofs, pounding my chest, my face—every part of me. Damn it all! I aimed my gun and started shooting. I reloaded and shot again. I wasn't aiming at anything in particular—I was just shooting. Didn't really make any sense, but somehow pulling that trigger made me feel better. I stayed on the top of that hill for hours.

Mattie wept for days. A.J. didn't speak for nearly a week. And Grant—well, Grant sat on the edge of his porch with his head in his hands and didn't move for hours at a time.

Ray and Donald didn't understand at first. They kept asking when their mama was coming home. Grant tried to explain, but how do you make sense of something like that to two boys still small enough to believe in bedtime prayers and Christmas angels?

We buried Fern under the cottonwoods, near the bend in the river where she used to walk with Mattie, where the boys once chased dragonflies in the sun. And after the crowd left and the wind died down, I stood there alone and whispered, "I hope you knew, Fern. I hope you knew how loved you were."

Because she was. God help us, she was.

THE SWEETEST BABY

Hard times—that's what we called it all up and down the South Umpqua River, from Roseburg to Myrtle Creek. In the big cities they called it the Great Depression. We lost money on the prune harvest of '33. Nobody was buying our milk. The cattle and hogs we hauled into town didn't even fetch enough to cover the feed we'd used to fatten them. We were flat broke—but so was everybody else.

After Fern's death, I turned to the one thing I still had in plenty: trees. I became a woodcutter, selling firewood on the west side of Roseburg. It gave me something to do. Nothing works on sorrow like breaking your back from dawn till dusk, splitting oak alone in the cold. The wood was hard as any I'd ever cut, but there was something gratifying in it—something steadying about putting all a man's hurt into work and watching the wood pile grow. Besides, I figured folks still needed heat to get through the winter.

They needed it—but no one had the money. It took me a full day to cut and stack a good cord of oak. I'd haul it into the city, where a cord used to sell for eight dollars. I offered it for five. In the end, I gave it away to three families, each of them promising to pay me when times got better.

It was a long time before times got better.

A month after we buried Fern, Mattie told me she was with child once again. We were both so excited. But we kept it quiet for a long while—partly because we were still mourning Fern, and partly out of respect for Grant, who hadn't been the same since she passed. Looked like he'd let loose of the reins and didn't give a damn where the trail took him.

He tried to act like he was holdin' it together, but anyone worth their salt could see he was carryin' a hurt so heavy, his back was about to give out. Mattie went down to his place once or twice a week to cook a meal and watch the kids. The boys were glad to see her, but Grant hardly said a word.

Every once in a while, I went down there myself, just to sit with him and try to draw him out. But I did most of the talking while he just stared off toward the hills. I told him I hurt too, that I missed Fern, and that it was the coldest trick in the book to take a girl like that from this world. He acted like he didn't hear a word I said—like I wasn't even there. I'd have done near anything to help, but nothing seemed to reach him.

Sad thing was, Grant's grief drove him back to the bottle. Most days he'd sit on the front porch, starin' out at the fields and whittling odd shapes out of busted up pieces of kindling. But two or three nights a week, he'd leave the boys with us and head down to the Roaring Ranch Roadhouse, just off the highway to Myrtle Creek. The whiskey was cheap, and the music was loud enough to drown out the cry of your own heart.

Spring of '34 passed in a golden hue. Mattie was as happy as a chattering flock of chickens, waiting for that first scatter of feed to hit the dirt. She hummed while she worked, hung laundry with a lightness in her step, and baked more than we could eat just for the joy of it. Some afternoons, I'd find her out on the porch, stitching a colorful quilt with the sun on her face, smiling at nothing in particular. It was the kind of bright anticipation that only comes from a strong faith and a heap of optimism.

As for me, I worked most days clean through sunset, barely stopping long enough to eat. By the time I dragged myself through the door, I was dog-tired—back aching, hands raw, muscles burning from the day's labor. Most nights I collapsed into bed and was out cold before my head even hit the pillow. A.J., meanwhile, kept an eye on Erroll—teaching him how to walk, throw rocks, chase chickens, and pull weeds. Those two were thick as thieves, always up to something, always underfoot. But Mattie and I were more grateful than irritated by their boyish mischief.

Near the end of July, we knew Mattie's time had come. Lily McDonald came out to the ranch to make sure all went as smoothly as possible. And so it did—no complications, no scary silences, just a strong cry and a healthy little body wrapped up tight in a cotton blanket.

We were all surprised she was a girl. Mattie had been so sure it would be another boy, she hadn't even picked out a girl's name. But when she held that baby close and looked into her blue eyes, she smiled in a way I hadn't seen in a long time. Then a brightness flickered across her face. "I know it," she said suddenly.

"Know what?" I asked.

She turned to me, eyes shining. "Let's call her Mary. Mary Elizabeth Stephens."

I took her hand and nodded. "That's perfect. I couldn't imagine a better name."

Then Lily placed the bundle in my arms. She was so small I hardly dared breathe. The weight of her was no more than a ten pound sack of sugar, yet it felt like I was carrying the whole world. Her skin was soft as milkweed fluff, her breath warm against my shirt. She blinked up at me, blue eyes wide and steady, as if she'd known me all my life and was just now letting on.

I glanced at Mattie. Her face glowed with a softness I hadn't seen in months—since before Fern's passing. Tears brimmed in her eyes, but they weren't the heavy kind. They were bright, trembling like sunlight caught on water. She reached out and brushed the baby's cheek with her finger, lips moving in a silent prayer.

"Look at her," she whispered. "She's ours." Her voice broke on that last word, and she pressed her face into her quilt, shoulders shaking with a joy she could barely hold.

I kissed her tiny forehead and whispered, "Mary Elizabeth." The name settled over her like a blessing, soft and certain.

Mattie reached for my hand, squeezed it tight. "This is what I prayed for," she said. "A fresh start. A full table. Children laughing in every room." Her eyes flicked to mine, steady and shining. "We've got all that now."

A.J. and Erroll were beside themselves with excitement. They kept peeking into the cradle, whispering to her like she understood every word. A.J. gave her a feather he'd found and saved, and Erroll tried to hand her a carrot he'd pulled from the garden—dirt and all. Lady stayed close by, curled at Mattie's feet, ears perked and tail thumping every time the baby made a sound.

And as I stood there, looking down at that tiny bundle in Mattie's arms, I couldn't help but think—God had taken one little girl from me, and given me another.

A few weeks later, Grant dropped his boys off at our house right after supper.

"Could you watch them for a few hours?" he asked.

"Where you headed?"

"You know where I'm headed." He looked at the ground. "Just need somethin' to lighten the load."

"Whiskey's not the answer."

"Maybe not," he said, shuffling his boots in the dirt. "But it doesn't hurt."

"I'm not so sure. You been spending a lot of time at the Roadhouse lately."

"You're probably right, but..." He gave a shrug as the boys climbed down from the truck. "I'll pick them up by eleven."

"Don't drink too much," I called as he pulled away.

"No promises," he said, waving as the dust swallowed his taillights.

Just after midnight, Mattie got out of bed to feed the baby.

"Where's Grant?"

"Running late," I mumbled, half-asleep.

Two hours later she woke me again. "He's still not here. The Roadhouse closed an hour ago. This isn't like him."

"If he's not back in an hour, I'll go look."

At first light, I grabbed the flashlight and headed out in the Model T, driving slowly down the main road toward the Roadhouse. The sky was clear and full of stars, the kind of still night where sound carries. About two miles from the ranch, I spotted his truck. It had run off the road into some thick brush, angled nose-first but still upright. The headlights were on. The engine ticked as it cooled.

I jumped out of my car and found Grant slumped over the wheel. "Grant!" I yelled, yanking the door open. "Wake up!"

He groaned and tried to push me away. A bottle tumbled from the truck and shattered on the rocks. "Come on," I said, lifting him out of the cab. His breath reeked of liquor.

"Leave me alone."

"I'm takin' you to the ranch to sleep this off. We'll talk in the morning."

At breakfast, Mattie handed him a cup of black coffee. Grant sat hunched over the table, rubbing his head, eyes bloodshot. "Sorry about last night," he muttered. His words were thick, barely clear.

"You were lucky," I said. "If you'd gone off the road closer to the river, we wouldn't be having this conversation."

He nodded slowly. "I know. I probably wouldn't've survived if I'd gone over the cliff."

"And what about your boys? They already lost their mama. You want them to lose you too?"

He shut his eyes. "No. God, no." He took a shaky breath and finished his coffee. "Thanks," he said.

I nodded.

"But I got something more I need from you." He looked me straight in the face. I know I got no right to ask, but please don't tell anyone about this. I just got a job driving school bus. If this gets out, I'll lose it."

I leaned back in my chair. "I won't say anything—this time. But if it ever happens again, I'm going straight to the school board. No hesitation."

"I understand," he said. "My boys deserve better than what I gave 'em last night."

"Yes, they do."

That afternoon, I watched him haul a wooden crate from the back of his truck. He carried it behind the barn, boots heavy in the dirt, the boards creaking under the weight of glass and liquor. The slosh of whiskey was loud in the still air.

He set the crate down hard against the fencepost, jaw tight, sweat shining on his forehead. For a long moment he just stood there, staring at the bottles, chest rising and falling like he was working up the courage to take the first swing. His hands shook as he pulled one out. Then, with a sudden roar, he hurled it against the post. Glass shattered into a hundred pieces, sunlight catching the shards as they rained down into the weeds. The smell of whiskey filled the air— sharp, sweet, and rotten all at once.

One after another, he smashed them. His arms swung like hammers, each crash louder than the last. Alcohol streamed down the wood, darkening the dirt, soaking into the grass. But he kept throwing, yelling as he let go of each bottle. When nothing was left, he wiped his face with the back of his wrist, leaving a streak of dirt across his cheek.

I leaned on the corral rail and said nothing. Some reckonings a man has to fight out alone.

At last he stood over the wreckage, chest heaving, glass glittering at his boots like ice. His face was set hard, but I could see it—just behind his eyes—the tears he was biting back. He bent down, picked up the empty crate, and slammed it down one final time. The sound echoed across the pasture, clean and final, like a door slamming shut.

He didn't look at me as he walked back toward the house, but his shoulders weren't slumped anymore. They were squared. And in that small, quiet way, I knew he'd made a choice that might just save his boys—and himself.

I never saw him take a drink after that night. He stopped going to the Roadhouse. He started fixing meals for his boys and going fishing with them down at the river. One Sunday morning, I saw him walking down the road toward the little church, the boys on either side of him in matching button shirts. That's when I knew he'd turned a corner. And my respect for him grew deeper than I ever expected.

September came, and we didn't even try to harvest our prunes, except for what Mattie canned in mason jars and lined along the dirt wall of our cellar. We let the rest fall to the ground, where swarms of yellow jackets sucked up the sweet nectar. The winter that followed bit hard, and we were as broke as church mice. If we were going to make it through another year, I had to act—and act decisively, like our survival depended on it.

Joy had returned to our house, but the bills kept coming. I couldn't ignore what the land had taken from us the year before. So in March of '35, with Mary only nine months old, I took a job at a work camp in Annie Springs, about a hundred miles east of the ranch. Mattie wasn't happy about it. She was used to me being close, and she figured if I was nearby, I'd be safe—and she'd be safe. She'd heard enough about my time as a faller up Rock Creek Canyon back in '21, and what happened to Jack McDonald to make her uneasy. The thought of me that far from home—in a strange place with folks she never met—didn't sit well with her.

I did my best to reassure her, told her I'd be a supervisor this time and not be in harm's way. But I don't think she believed me. She said the mountains were full of dangers—seen and unseen— and she wasn't keen on being a widow at thirty-six with three children and a ranch to manage.

"I promise you," I said, "you've got nothing to worry about."

She didn't answer right away, just stood there looking at me like she could already see the worst. Then she stepped forward and held on tight, like I was a soldier headed off to war. I kissed her—hard and long—and pulled myself free. I hated to leave her like that, but there was no way around it. I had a job to do and a schedule to keep. I'd been hired to supervise a group of young single men. Most were good guys—worked hard and earned their keep. Our job was to repair and widen the road up to Crater Lake. Each man earned thirty dollars a month, sending twenty-five back to his family. I got forty-five and sent forty to Mattie.

I left home in March, when the snow was still patchy along the ridge and the air carried that raw edge of winter. The work started slow—clearing fallen trees, sharpening tools, setting up camp—but by May the days were long and the dust hung in the sunlight like smoke. I tried to write when I could, short notes to let Mattie know I was all right, but letters had a way of getting lost between here and the ranch. Nights were cold, mornings colder, and most evenings I'd sit by the fire thinking about home.

By July the crew had settled into a rhythm: work, eat, sleep, and do it again. It was hard, honest labor that wore a man down to the bone, but in that rough, cowboy way that left you proud of the ache. Nobody complained. We all got along well enough—laughed when we could, shared what we had—and before long it felt less like a job and more like a big, dust-covered family. Most days passed without trouble—just heat, dirt, and sweat—but every now and then the mountain would remind us who was in charge.

One hot afternoon in August, we were out exploring an isolated stretch south of the lake. Those boys were thirty years younger than me, and though I was strong and stubborn, I was struggling to keep up. Six miles into the backcountry, we came to a deep, rugged ravine—thick with pines, hemlocks, and manzanita. The boys slid down the bank and scrambled up the other side quick as jackrabbits with coyotes on their tails. I stayed behind, catching my breath.

The ravine looked to be about twenty feet deep. Going down was the easy part—it was the near-vertical climb back up that had me rattled. I studied the slope. Not far off, a thick Douglas fir had fallen across the draw. I had decent balance, and figured that was my best way across.

Slow and steady, I inched my way along the log. My heavy boots dug into the bark. A slight wind kicked up, and I leaned into it. Wind never bothered me much—my legs were strong from holding steady in the stirrups and working long days in the fields. I felt sure of myself, maybe a little too sure. A few more steps and—my feet slipped. That's when I knew I was in trouble.

I flung out my arms, gasping for air, but it was too late. I fell in slow motion. The world rushed past me, the trees blurring, air whistling sharp in my ears. I hit hard on a rock shelf. The jolt shot through my spine. Then came a sudden crack deep in my back, like a dry branch snapping beneath a heavy boot.

A burst of white pain tore through me, so fierce I thought I might scream, but all that came out was a rasp of breath. The back of my head thudded against the dirt. I blinked up at the sky—blue, uncaring—and tried to figure what the hell had just happened.

I lay at the bottom of the ravine, flat on my back, breath shallow and scattered, the pain echoed endlessly across my middle. I tried to move—but I couldn't. My arms lay heavy at my sides, no strength left to lift them. My legs were numb. The ground was cold and damp beneath me, but my skin felt like it was on fire. Everything around me started to spin—trees, sky, sound, light—swirling like ashes in a cold wind.

Pebbles pressed into the back of my skull. I could taste grit and blood at the corner of my mouth. My own groan seemed to vanish into the pines. Above me a hawk circled slow and easy, its piercing cries slicing the steel sky—mocking my pride, my strength, the man I thought I was. The sunlight was bright and merciless, slanting through the branches, warm on my face though the earth beneath me felt like ice.

Faces flickered in my mind—A.J. teaching little Erroll how to throw rocks at tin cans, both of them laughing so hard they nearly toppled into the weeds. Mattie on the porch, humming as her needle danced through a quilt, eyes shining the way they did when hope was close. And Mary—sweetest baby in the world—her blue eyes staring up at me, her fist clutching my finger, her cry soft as a meadowlark in tall grass.

"Lord," I whispered inside myself, though no sound left my lips. "Is this where my trail ends?"

I wasn't afraid. I wasn't angry. The pain was still there, sharp as barbed wire, but even that was fading fast. What filled me was a strange calm, like a wide river current carrying me away. The trees stood silent. The sky didn't care if I stayed or went. In that silence, the sorrow cut clean through me—knowing I'd never see Mattie's smile again, hear my boys shouting in the yard, hold that baby girl against my chest.

I could hear water rushing somewhere close, but I couldn't tell where. I wanted to shut my eyes. I wanted to sleep. But I was scared I'd never wake up. Damn it—this ain't the way I wanted it to end.

TOO CLOSE FOR COMFORT

A thick, silvery fog filled the window across from my bed. I stared out at it, but everything was hazy and obscure. The fog felt like it surrounded me. I tried to sit up, but I was strapped into a metal-framed bed so tight I could barely move. The room was bright, with tall ceilings. Strangers in white came and went. Nothing around me made any sense. I closed my eyes and tried to figure out what was happening, but I couldn't—I couldn't think straight. Everything seemed turned around in my head. Was I crazy, or sick, or already gone? It was too much to sort out, and truth be told, I wasn't sure I cared anymore.

I fell back asleep, but my dreams were full of falling. When I woke, it was black outside. I had a strange, fuzzy memory of a long trip—Mattie crying and saying goodbye, me lying on my back as a car drove over winding roads, people asking me questions I was too weak to answer. And now I was here.

"Where am I?" I mumbled.

"I'm the night nurse," a woman said softly. "You're in the hospital."

"In Roseburg?"

"No. You're at St. Mary's in San Francisco. You broke your back, and we're the best hospital on the West Coast for that sort of injury."

"But San Francisco? How did I get there?"

"They put you on a stretcher, loaded you into a railcar, and shipped you down here."

"Oh!" My mind spun. "I thought I was a goner."

"You almost were," she said. "But a lot of folks pulled together to save you. The crew got you off that mountain, the doctor up there worked on you half the night, and by the time you made it here, you were only hanging on by a thread. I just did my best to make sure you stayed with us."

"Well, I'm still here, so I suppose you did a good job. Saying 'thank you' doesn't seem like enough."

"I'm just glad you made it this far." She paused. "But to be honest, you still have a long way to go."

"Mattie," I murmured. "Where's Mattie... and the kids?"

The nurse leaned closer. "They're all right. They know you're here. And your wife sends you her prayers. You just need to rest now, Mr. Stephens."

A hundred questions raced through my head, but all I could manage was, "Will I ever walk again?"

"Well," she said, "that depends on you."

Then I drifted back asleep, and the fog surrounded me once more.

For the next year I lay in traction on a stiff bed, my body bound in metal braces and cloth bandages, unable to move. I lay perfectly still—reading for short periods, staring at the ceiling, praying to get out of that god-awful hospital, but mostly sleeping. I'm not complaining; the nurses and doctors were some of the kindest folk I'd ever met. Still the smell of medicine and bleach in that place was about to kill me. Reading, or being read to, was what kept me from going mad. I mostly liked westerns like *Robbers' Roost* and *The Drifting Cowboy*, but there were only so many books I could get my hands on—and most of them weren't westerns.

A sweet little nurse read me *The Maltese Falcon*. It was a detective novel, not my usual style, but I liked the main character. Sam Spade was a tough man with a strong code of ethics, a sense of loyalty, and big dreams. Yet my favorite line came from a lady named Brigid, who reminded me of how I'd felt since being trapped in this hospital. At one point she said, "Oh, I'm so tired, so tired of it all, of myself, of lying and thinking up lies, and not knowing what is a lie and what is the truth." They told me I'd be there for a month or two, and I believed them. I was sure that any day now I'd be home with Mattie and the kids. But in the end, it was nearly a year and a half.

Then there was a novel called *The Good Earth*. It was about a farmer in China who loved the land. I guess farmers are farmers, no matter where they live. It talked about how he belonged to the land, and how nothing felt as real as having the soil beneath your feet—planting in the spring and harvesting in the fall. I would've done anything at that point to get back to Ruckles Ranch—walk through the orchard, feed the chickens, watch the corn grow tall, and sift the soil through my fingers. That had been my home for fifteen years, longer than I'd lived anywhere. And all I wanted was to get out of that hospital and get back to the land.

But I had too much time to think—and that was the problem. As I lay there, looking at the ceiling, I thought of a hundred things. Since I couldn't do anything, I was stuck thinkin' about everything—successes, regrets, loves, losses. I even thought about death. What if I never get out of this hospital? What if I never see Mattie again? What if my kids end up without a dad? What if I can't ride a horse or manage my ranch or make love to my wife? Thinkin' too much can get your soul more tangled than a wagon wheel in blackberry brambles.

Thinking about missing someone is even worse. And I missed Mattie just as much as any man ever missed a woman—the color of her hair, the softness of her skin, the way she looked at me when she thought I was wrong. I missed it all. But money's money. A one-way ticket to San Francisco cost fifteen dollars, and with me not working, we just didn't have it. Paying the doctor's bills and feeding the family took every penny we had. Mattie sold milk, eggs, jelly, honey, quilts—anything she could. She even sold some of our goats and cattle, but it was never quite enough.

Since there wasn't a thing I could do about it, I learned to wait. I didn't see Mattie, A.J., Erroll, or little Mary for fifteen long, lonely months, and that just about killed me. Some nights I'd close my eyes and see them by the fire—Mattie sewing, the boys whispering, Mary on her lap. The only thing that reached me from home was their voices on the telephone—ten minutes a week to remind me what I was missing.

A.J. was now thirteen. He and Grant shouldered the grit and grunt work of ranch life while Mattie milked the cows and Erroll fed the chickens. I felt like a no-good son of a gun, layin' on my back four hundred and fifty miles away while the others did all the work—the work that should've been mine. I wasn't pullin' my weight, and that don't sit right with a man. So I promised myself that the day I could stand again I'd work twice as hard to make things right.

I kept that promise in my heart through every slow, painful day of healing. The months dragged on, but little by little I got stronger. I pushed myself harder than I ever thought I could, learning to walk again—at first as unsteady as a newborn foal, all legs and no balance. But I wasn't about to be a cripple the rest of my days. With steady work and a fair amount of cussing, I found my footing. Maybe I didn't walk as smooth or as sure as before, but it was progress.

By December of '36, the hospital finally let me loose. The doctor said to be careful and not do any work without wearing a body brace. I rode the Southern Pacific Railroad on a five-hour trip back to Roseburg. Grant picked me up at the station with Mattie and the kids. It was the finest reunion I'd ever known, and I couldn't stop grinnin'. My heart was stretched full with more joy than I knew what to do with—more than I could shake a stick at. We hugged and laughed and cried for nearly an hour before getting back to the ranch. That Christmas was the first I'd been home for in a year and a half. And it was beautiful.

I loved that old ranch, even when the roof leaked and the west winds howled down the chimney. The place was home, and most of it felt just the same as when I'd left it—the gentle slope of the land, the sound of the river, the rush of the chickens at feeding time, the three white crosses at the crest of the hill. But some things had changed. A.J. and Grant had added a room to the house for Mary. Grant said that even though she was only two and had slept with her mama while I was gone, there'd come a time she'd need privacy from her brothers. He had a solid point.

And there were other changes—the boys were taller, the garden had been enlarged, the old oak tree on the south end of the property had fallen down, and a small wildfire started by lightning had scorched a few acres north of the ranch. But the hardest change for me was the death of Lady. She was the most loving, loyal dog I'd ever known. She'd been a comfort to both Era and Mattie, and the kids adored her. She welcomed us when we were away, walked along the river with us, stayed close in sad times, pranced about when life was sweet, and lay at our feet at the close of the day. She'd lived longer than any dog I'd ever known—some sixteen years. We'd all miss her something fierce, but life in this ragged world don't sit still for no one. If a man can't stomach change, he'll wind up in a mighty sorry state—like tryin' to wade upstream when the river's ragin'.

That January, the Model T broke down after runnin' like clockwork for sixteen years. I bought a used Model A truck that was only five years old for two hundred dollars. It was a little beat up, but it got the job done. I needed something to get me to Crater Lake and back. Near the end of April, as the snow was meltin' in the mountains, I drove up to the work camp at Annie Springs. All the guys welcomed me, and we reminisced around a campfire about my fall from the log that snapped my back like a twig. Some thought for sure I was a dead man. Others swore I'd never walk again. Every one of them was shocked when they saw me drive up to camp twenty months after the accident. Several even thought they were seein' a ghost.

"Yeah, it was too close for comfort. But you can't get rid of this cowboy that easy," I laughed. "I figured I was a goner, sure as sunrise. But don't count me out just yet—I'm tough as nails, and it'll take more'n that to plant me in the ground. Truth is, I came face to face with my Maker. Asked Him if it was my time, and He said I'd better clean up my act some if I wanted through them pearly gates. I told Him I'd try a heap harder. And I reckon He believed me—'cause He gave me a second chance. So here I am."

For the next six months, I worked as a powder man widening the thirty-three miles of the ring road around Crater Lake. Now I'll admit, that was something Mattie wasn't too keen about. She looked me in the eye, and said, "I just about lost you once, you old fool, and I'm not about to lose you again."

But I told her I'd promised myself I'd worked twice as hard to get us back on our feet. We owed some folks in town from the hard times we'd been through, and I wasn't about to rest until every cent was paid.

I worked hard, but there was a beauty around that lake, which made you want to take your hat off and stand quiet for a spell. The vistas around the caldera were spectacular, lookin' two thousand feet down into the deepest shades of blue—turquoise, indigo, sapphire. The water glowed with an intensity that knocked my hat off. I could sit on a ledge starin' at that clear surface for hours. There's a magic to that place that's beyond words. I felt privileged to be part of makin' it accessible to more folks so they could marvel at its majesty.

My job was simple—and dangerous.

I drilled holes deep into volcanic rock to set black powder and dynamite. Then I'd light the fuses, plug my ears, and run like hell— faster than a jackrabbit in a brush fire. 'Cause when that spark hit the powder, the whole earth shook, throwing dirt and rock high into the air with an explosion louder than a freight train rollin' through a canyon at midnight.

It was a good job that paid well. I worked it until the first snow hit the mountains in late September. That's when I packed my gear and headed back to the ranch. Mattie greeted me with a kiss and I couldn't have been happier to be home.

It was a fine fall day, late in October. The hillsides burned with color—maples blazing orange-red, oaks holding to their golden amber—set off against the steady dark of the cedars and pines that lined the road. The whole scene seemed to blur together as I rode along Dole Road, a patchwork of fire and shadow, too pretty to pass without taking notice. I'd picked up Erroll from school in Ruckles. He was so excited about first grade that nothing could keep him quiet. We were going down a steep hill about a half mile from the ranch when the truck started acting strange. The steering wheel was hard to move and I had to put all my strength into it to keep us on the road.

I was headed down the hill a little faster than I should've. Truth is, I usually drove faster than most—but it had never caused trouble. Not until now. There was a sharp curve at the bottom of the hill. I pulled the wheel as hard as I could, but it only moved the Model A half of what she needed. Part of the steering mechanism must've come loose and I knew I couldn't make the turn. "Hold on tight," I said to Erroll.

He looked at me, confused. "What should I hold onto?"

"Anything you can! This truck is going off the road." I slammed on the brakes and we skidded hard through the gravel, tires howling. A moment later we rolled over a bank and smashed against some oak trees, which kept us from bouncing further down the side of the hill and into the river. The truck rolled over—two, maybe three times— and we got flung about like feed sacks off a runaway wagon. I pulled Erroll to my chest, trying to protect him from the chaos. We stopped with a sudden jolt, but we were upside down. My head hurt and my body ached.

"Son, are you okay?"

"I think so." He let go of my shirt which he had gripped hard.

I looked around. Windshield gone. Roof caved in. Everything was upside down. What got me most anxious was we were both pinned under the truck. Luckily, when it rolled, I ended up sideways in the seat, which cushioned the blow a little. But I couldn't move and I remember thinking that my back was just healed, and I hope I didn't break it again.

Erroll was bendy as a green switch—looked like he could squeeze through a keyhole if he had to. I don't know how he managed to wriggle out of that truck, but he did. Somehow the floorboards came loose, and he pushed them aside just enough to wiggle out through the frame.

I told him to make his way up to the main road and wave down any car he saw. "Tell them your Daddy is pinned under his truck and he needs help real bad."

A few minutes later I heard A.J. sliding down the bank toward me, screaming my name over and over again. His friend Jerry Bounds followed him.

When I heard A.J.'s voice, I felt a flicker of hope. I was mighty weak, but I conjured up enough strength to whisper, "I can't breathe, help me."

From what I saw through that shattered window, I'll tell you—fear really does give a man strength he didn't know he had. A.J. and Jerry grabbed the back of my truck bed and lifted it off the ground.

"That helps a lot," I whispered. "I can breathe better."

A.J. said, "Hold on Dad, it's going to be okay. We're getting you out of there."

"How's Erroll?"

"A few scratches and a bit shook up," A.J. said.

"How'd you find me?"

"I was riding home on the school bus when I saw Erroll standing in the middle of the road waving his arms, crying his eyes out, and yelling, 'Daddy's under the truck.' The driver let us off the bus, and here we are."

"That was mighty brave of Erroll."

"I yelled 'Where?' and he pointed down the hill to your upside down truck buried in the manzanita bushes."

"Thank God you two came down here." I tried to smile, but winced instead. "Where's Erroll?"

"The driver took him into town to get some help for you."

A.J. propped up the truck with whatever wood he could find, just enough to keep the weight from pressing down on me. He kept talking to me to make sure I didn't pass out. I hurt like hell, but I kept my eyes open. He found a rusty crowbar in the back of the truck and shoved it deep into the passenger door. He did everything he could—groaning, swearing, pounding with his fist—but the door wouldn't budge.

I was trapped and it appeared that nobody could do anything to get me free.

About an hour later, it seemed like half the town came pouring down that hill to help. They turned the truck back on its wheels and pulled me out. I was pretty beat up with scratches and bruises, but nothing was broken. I did have a cut on my forehead that bled down the side of my face. Grant Smith wiped it clean with his handkerchief and gave me a big old bear hug. The crowd cheered and whistled and slapped me on the back. I was so moved by that bit of human kindness, it near brought a tear to my eye—and that don't happen easy.

Grant drove A.J., Erroll, and me home, where Mattie was sitting on the porch with little Mary. She stared at me. "What happened to your head—and why are you limping?"

A.J. told her the whole story, and she clung to me like she wasn't ever gonna let go. "You must've had some sort of a guardian angel riding in that old truck with you and Erroll."

"Maybe so," I said as I held my side.

AUNT ESTHER

A week later, I was talking to A.J. from a hospital bed in Seattle. "The doctors in Roseburg said that my auto accident did more damage than I thought."

"You were limping a lot," said A.J. "And Mom was worried about your back as soon as she saw you."

"Mom worries about everything."

"After over a year in San Francisco, can you blame her?" A.J. was fifteen years old and nearly six feet tall, with jet-black hair. Cocky as a young rooster learning to crow. "And now here you are back in the hospital."

"You've got a good point, son." I was laid out in an uncomfortable bed at Harbourview Hospital, strapped in traction. My back was beat up again—couldn't move, pain running deep. I wasn't happy about it, but I wasn't complaining either. Fact is, I was just thankful it wasn't broke this time.

"How long do we have to be up here?"

"Longer than either of us want to," I told him as I gritted through the pain.

"I don't mind, except for all this rain."

I smiled at that, not because it was funny, but because I knew exactly what he meant. Every time I looked out the window, all I saw was rain—and I missed the sun too. I found myself yearning for the wide-open skies of Nebraska, Oklahoma, or even Montana. A cowboy gets used to whatever the wind blows in, but truth is—we like it dry. The rain in Seattle was like the good Lord had opened up the heavens, pouring steady as a horse trough filling in a storm. Seemed to me it might be time for Noah to start building his ark.

"The doctors say I'm stuck here till January, maybe even longer," I said. "I'm not thrilled about it. Mattie isn't either. She's got her hands full with the younger kids. So she thinks I oughta send you back home."

"Dad, I'm staying right here by your side. A boy needs time with his dad."

I looked at this boy and saw the stirrings of a young man—loyalty, determination, maybe a bit of wisdom. I smiled. "But Mattie told me plain and simple: 'That boy belongs in school, not sitting in some hospital room.'"

"I'm not knockin' school," he said, "but I don't need it—not like this. Being up here in Seattle with you feels like an adventure. Way better than sitting in some stuffy classroom all day."

I closed my eyes and nodded, knowing there was no use arguing with him. Truth was, I admired that kind of loyalty. And I sure wasn't one to preach about schooling—not when I'd only made it through sixth grade and I can read and write just fine. Mattie always said I spelled like a cowboy. She was probably right, but that never slowed me down. I might not stack words like a schoolmarm, but I could read the sky, mend a fence, and do what needed doin' to take care of my family. The world was bigger than words on a page. I picked up what matters out on the prairie, up in the mountains, and workin' the homestead. I might not have been polished—but I got the job done just the same.

I didn't much like hospitals. They reminded me too much of San Francisco—of time wasted away from my family. I must admit that having A.J. here made things not feel so lonesome. Other than being tied down, the biggest aggravation was that I slept so much. The doctor said that that was a good thing because my body needed rest so it could heal.

But A.J. was patient and never complained. He checked out books from the library—Hemingway, Steinbeck, and some westerns—which he spent hours reading to me. At other times we'd talk about my cowboy days, the railroad, and his mother. That kid had more questions than a night sky had stars.

After one long talk I said, "Since we are in Seattle, you should visit your Aunt Esther?"

"Aunt Esther?" he said. "Who's she?"

"Your mother's little sister."

"I didn't know she had a sister."

"I haven't seen her in a long time, not since you were just a baby."

"So she lives in Seattle?"

I nodded. "Last I heard she was living over on 12th ave, west side of the city, not far from downtown."

The next day A.J. didn't come to my hospital room. I knew right off where he was, and I didn't begrudge him for it. The day after, he came bouncing in, nervous as a jackrabbit in a cornfield.

"Guess where I was yesterday?"

"At your Aunt Esther's place," I answered with a smile.

He blinked in surprise. "How'd you know?"

"Because that's right where I'd have gone, if I were you."

"Her and Ira are good folks, glad as could be to see me."

"Esther loved your mother," I told him. "They were close. I never knew her husband, Ira, all that well, but when your grandpa got older, they looked after him."

"So I heard." A.J. smiled. "Esther said you and Grandpa didn't get along at first."

"That's right. He never did trust cowboys. But once he saw how much I loved your mother, he softened up. After a spell, we got to be friends."

"Why'd it take you so long to tell me about Aunt Esther?"

I looked down. "I was scared you'd light out for Seattle to find her and maybe never come back. You're the only piece of Era I've got left. If I lost you, son, she'd be gone for good."

"Don't you have pictures of her or anything?"

"Mattie cleared out everything of Era's." I paused. "She said she couldn't compete with a ghost. And maybe she was right—she's the one standing beside me now, raising the kids and holding things together while I'm laid up with my back busted again."

"So you just forgot about Era?"

"No, son, not at all." I shifted, trying to make him see. "A man can't ride two trails at once, not when it comes to love. I gave my heart to Era, and when the good Lord called her home, she took a piece of it with her. Damn near broke me in two. But then I found Mattie, and I learned a man's heart can love again. I loved Era. I love Mattie now. Back on the prairie, Mr. Rhodes would say you can't build a future sittin' in yesterday's saddle. At some point you've got to ride on. That doesn't mean I've forgotten Era—I never will. It means I can't live in the past."

I shook my head, the words twisted up inside me. I tried to make him see, but A.J. just stared, like he figured the pain or the medicine—or maybe just too long in this hospital bed—had gone and made me crazy.

That night, alone in bed, I thought about how the good Lord had blessed me with both Era and Mattie. These two women were as different as sunrise on the prairie and sunset on the mountains—each shining in its own way, each stealing your breath. No man could rightly say which was better, and I'd had the joyful privilege of experiencing the love of both.

Era was gentle as spring grass with a sweetness I never deserved. She dreamed of a home full of children's laughter, Sunday dinners, and quiet peace. But she never got to see that dream come true. Losing her was like losing the morning sun—left me cold and lonesome, with shadows stretching long.

Mattie was cut from tougher cloth. She'd weathered storms most women couldn't stand upright in. She didn't just dream of a home— she shouldered the weight of one. With her it was grit as much as tenderness, the kind that keeps a man upright when the world's set to knock him to his knees.

Era was a cool drink after a long ride. Mattie was the fencepost you tie your reins to when the wind's howling. And I'd needed both, just at different times on my restless journey.

The next day A.J. was beside my hospital bed earlier than usual. He was twisting his hands and chewing his lip like something heavy was weighing on him.

"Son, just spit it out."

"There's something else Aunt Esther said. I've been turning it over all night."

I nodded for him to continue.

"She asked me about the twins, and I had no idea what she meant. Then she told me I had a brother and sister—Arle and Arleen. Why am I just now hearing this?"

"I'm sorry," I said. "I should've told you long ago. Sometimes life moves so hard and fast a man don't get the chance to speak his mind."

"Dad, that's a mighty big thing to keep from me. First you didn't tell Mattie about Eddie or who Fern really was, and now this. Makes me wonder what else you haven't told me."

"There are no other secrets."

"Then where are Arle and Arleen?" He looked me square in the eye like a man.

"They were born just before your mother died. It was a hard stretch—working full time, laying the woman I loved in the ground, tending to you and two babes. Felt like I'd stepped into quicksand— the harder I fought, the deeper it pulled me under. Truth is, I didn't know what to do."

"So what happened to them?"

"They needed a mother and a home, and I couldn't give that to them. So I adopted them out to families that promised to love them. Places that could give them everything I couldn't."

"You ever heard anything about them?"

"I think about them all the time. They should be about thirteen now. Arle's in Coos Bay, Arleen's in Portland."

"How could you just give away your own kids to strangers?"

I lowered my head. "I did the only thing I could think of at the time. The children's welfare folks swore these families would care for them. Said the kids needed to pull close to their new homes and any contact from me would only confuse them. So I let them go."

"Why didn't you adopt me out too?"

"You and I were already close—the way you looked at me, clung to me, wanted me to tuck you in each night. I couldn't let you go. And when I started seeing Mattie, she thought you were the sweetest boy she'd ever met."

"But couldn't she have taken care of the twins too?"

"We were just courting then, and that seemed too much to ask. The twins needed a home quick, and Mattie and I didn't marry for another six months. All I can say is I did what I thought was best. Maybe it was right, maybe it was wrong. But it's what I did, and I have to live with it."

A.J. nodded slow. I couldn't tell if he understood or agreed, but he let it rest. Still, I saw something in his eyes that told me the matter wasn't fully settled.

I spent a month and a half flat on that hard hospital bed—it near drove me crazy. If it hadn't been for A.J., I don't reckon I'd have made it. But a week before Christmas, I escaped. I told A.J. I was feeling good enough to go home.

"But the doctors say you need to stay in traction for another two months." A.J. tried to look stern, as stern as a fifteen-year-old can manage.

"I don't give a damn what the doctors say. I'm leaving this place today—with or without your help."

"You've got my help." He shrugged.

"We need to be home for Christmas. I need to be there for Mattie and the kids."

"Let me call Aunt Esther, see if she'll drive us to the train station."

"That's a powerful idea. But when we get back to the ranch, best not mention your Aunt Esther to Mattie."

He nodded like he understood.

Twenty-four hours later, I was sitting in front of our fireplace with Mattie and the kids gathered round. My back hurt like the dickens, but I didn't let on. A thick brace of metal and leather kept me straight as a fencepost pounded into bedrock. So long as I kept it cinched tight, the pain stayed bearable. The ache was there, sure enough, but Christmas with my family made it all worth it.

The next day A.J. went out to cut us a tree. I wanted to go with him, but Mattie wouldn't let me leave the house. "The last thing we need is you messing up your back any more than it already is."

Erroll jumped up. "Can I go with A.J.?"

"If you bundle up and don't get in your brother's way," she said.

"So you won't let me go," I said, louder than I intended, "but you let a five-year-old boy go."

"I don't want to offend you," Mattie said gently, "but our five-year-old can walk straighter and pull more weight than his pa. That's just the way it is right now."

My pride was ready to argue with her, but my good sense knew she was right. So I just shrugged and moved closer to the fire.

An hour later they came back, and we all went to work trimming the tree. To my eyes, it was the finest Christmas tree I'd ever seen. Mattie set a candle in every window, hung five stockings by the fireplace, and laid out gingerbread men that filled the room with the sweetest smell. I slipped penny candy and oranges I'd bought at the Seattle train station into the stockings, while Mattie handed out scarves and mittens she'd made for each of the youngsters. She'd wrapped them neat in old newspapers, and the kids tore into them with squeals and laughter. It was a simple Christmas—nothing fancy, nothing store-bought—but nobody complained. Truth be told, we were just thankful to be together.

By the end of January my back had mended some. I could shuffle about—stiff and slow—but I managed to feed the chickens, milk the cow, and push the goats into the barn come sundown. Still, most days found me sunk in a chair by the fire, the hours slipping past as I stared into the flames and dreamed of better days.

Then one evening, after the kids had gone to bed, Mattie sat down beside me. I could tell she had something on her mind, but I waited, letting her find her words. "Allen." She took my hand the way only she could, her eyes meeting mine and reminding me how good it felt to be home. "Could you bring the cradle in from the barn?"

I smiled. "When will we be needing it?"

"Not until summer, most likely." She leaned close, and I caught the sweet smell of sugar and cinnamon clinging to her apron.

I kissed her and said, "Ma always told me children are the Lord's best blessing. She used to say a house full of 'em makes a man richer than any bank ever could—and I reckon she was right."

Late in July of '38, on a day so hot all A.J. and Erroll wanted to do was sit in the river and eat watermelon, a healthy boy was born. I was excited as a cowboy who'd roped a runaway steer.

"What should we name him?" I asked the next morning.

"I'd like to name him after my grandfather. He died before I was born, but I've heard he was a good man."

"Then so be it!" I said. "What was his name?"

"Robert." Her face lit with joy.

I froze. Surely I hadn't heard right. Not Robert. Not the name of my boy who'd died in Montana—the loss that had torn Eddie and me apart. Any name but that. I turned away and buried my face in my hands.

"Are you all right?" she asked, her voice full of concern.

I forced myself to look at her and cleared my throat. "Robert is a fine name. It was the name of my son who died."

"Oh, I'm so sorry. We can choose another."

"No," I said softly. "It just caught me by surprise."

She reached across and took my hand. "Then maybe that's all the more reason we should use it. To honor both my grandfather and your boy."

I sat there quiet, my chest aching. It had been a long, long time since I'd lost him, but moments like this made it feel like yesterday. His little face still came to me in dreams—the sound of him crying, the silence that followed. A man buries a lot in his lifetime, but some losses never stay buried. Finally I nodded, slow and heavy. "Robert it is. That way the name will hold real meaning."

Tears welled in her eyes, and she pressed my hand tighter. "Then he'll carry a name tying the past to the future."

I managed a smile, though it trembled. Speaking the name still stung, but this time it was different—like a scar that marks its territory, reminding a man where he's been.

The baby quickly became the heart of our family. A.J. made sure he never went short on milk. Erroll talked to him steady—about the weather, the animals, whatever book he'd pulled from the library. And Mary, just four years old, wouldn't take her eyes off him. The minute he fussed, she was there—holding, comforting, playing with his toes until he laughed.

The world felt steady again. I was back to ranch work near as strong as before my accidents. A.J. and Erroll were at my side each day—splitting wood, tending the orchard, working the garden, hunting deer in the hills or ducks down by the river. Life was good, and I was thankful for every bit of it.

Then at the end of September, after the boys were back in school, I received a strange letter with no return address. Standing at the mailbox at the end of our drive, I tore it open. The page was plain white, typed with no signature.

On September 22, 1938, Arle Chester Bradburn, age fourteen, of Coos Bay, Oregon, was accidentally shot by a close friend while they were cleaning a twelve-gauge shotgun. He was rushed to Wesley Methodist Hospital in Coos Bay, where he died the next day.

That was all it said. Nothing more.

I sat down hard on a stump and read it again. And again. My hands trembled, the words blurring, but I couldn't stop staring at them. Questions crashed into me like a freight train. How could this have happened? Was it my fault for giving him up? Why would the good Lord allow such a thing? I knew there were no answers, but the questions wouldn't quit.

And then a memory rose up clear as day—Arle as a baby, no bigger than a loaf of bread, bundled in a blanket. I remembered the way his little fist wrapped around my finger, how his chest rose and fell as he slept against me. I could still smell the faint sweetness of his hair, hear the soft noises he made in his sleep. Back then I'd promised him the world, but I gave him away instead. Now he was gone, and all I had left was the weight of that broken promise.

Then another picture came to me—his sister, Arleen. She had the same dark eyes, only hers watched the world wide and wondering, like she was trying to take it all in at once. I remembered her tiny cry, thin but determined, and how she settled quiet when I hummed to her. I had given her up the same as her brother, and though she was still out there somewhere in Portland, it felt like I'd lost her too.

At last I folded the letter, slipped it back into the envelope, and slid it into my pocket. Then I rose slow from the stump and walked up the lane toward the house, each step heavy as if I carried the weight of both children I'd given away. What near broke me wasn't only losing Arle—it was knowing I'd have to set this sorrow in Mattie's hands and look A.J. in the eye to tell him the brother he never knew was gone.

Winter turned to spring, but the ache of that letter never left me. Some losses follow a man like his own shadow. Mid-April A.J. quit school. He'd almost graduated, but that wasn't important to him. Mattie wasn't happy. She tried every argument she could think of, but the boy's mind was set. I told him plain—it was either work or school. Two days later he was down the road at the Round Prairie Saw Mill, loading lumber into boxcars. Hard work, long hours, but the kind of labor that puts muscle on a boy and makes a man out of him.

His reason was simple: he wanted a car, his own set of wheels to claim his freedom. He had his eye on a 1936 royal-maroon Hudson Terraplane. Grant swore it was the fastest car on the planet for the price. I just hoped A.J. would prove a better driver than his old man.

By the fall of '39 he'd saved enough to buy it. A week later he shook my hand, hugged Mattie, and then bent down to Erroll and Mary. He mussed Erroll's hair, told him to mind his chores, and lifted Mary into his arms one last time. She clung to his neck until he set her down gently and kissed her cheek. Little Robert just cried, and A.J. took his hand. "Life's an adventure. If you don't explore it, you'll never know what you've missed." Robert looked at him curiously, and stopped crying.

Then he climbed behind the wheel. His aunt up in Seattle had promised him a bed and a job with the Boeing Airplane Company, and he was set on going.

I sat on the front porch and watched that Terraplane sail down the lane, a red streak in the sun. The dust rose up behind him, hanging in the air long after he was gone. And as I sat there alone, it hit me square—this must've been what Pa felt the day I rode off so many years ago. I suppose it takes leaving home and riding your own trail for a boy to become a man.

But that didn't mean I wasn't hurt.

BRAZIL

It was hard to not have A.J. at home. I didn't realize how much I'd miss him. Over the next few days my heart turned into anger. I knew it was foolish and selfish—but it was still there. I held onto this anger for him leaving for more than a month. It was a stubborn, tight-fisted anger, like a hungry barn cat clamping down on a mouse and refusing to let go. That is, until Mattie faced me in the kitchen one frosty morning and told me plain and simple to quit it. She said he was just a boy being a boy and it was foolish to let such a natural thing ruin a perfectly good bond. So I swallowed my pride, wrote to him, and told him how much I loved him. After that he sent a letter near every month.

But the more I thought about Arle's death and the miles between me and A.J., the heavier the loss of my three older boys from Eddie pressed on me. Where were they? What kind of men had they become? Did they still carry bitterness toward me for not being there when they needed me most? The questions circled in my head until they near drove me crazy.

Just before Christmas I wrote Eddie's sister, Mary, asking for their addresses. She answered within the week—George and William were in Los Angeles, John in Kansas. I set my hand to paper, one letter for each of my boys, pouring out my heart. I laid my failures bare, told them I loved them, and asked them to write. Then I waited. Every time the postman came my chest jumped, hoping for an envelope with one of their names. Days turned to weeks, and still nothing.

So I tried again, another letter to each, holding tight to hope. But the months dragged on quiet, and no answer ever came. In the end, I was left with nothing but silence—and silence like that follows a man the way the echo of a night train rolls across a lonesome prairie.

When A.J. heard how it nearly broke me in two, he said he'd write to them himself. Two weeks later he had letters from all three half brothers, and through his words I came to know the shape of their lives.

George Allen, forty now, was not doing well. Unemployed and living in a run-down flophouse on Bunker Hill Avenue in downtown Los Angeles, he'd spent ten years in the Coast Guard and picked up a taste for alcohol that had near ruined him. I hated to hear it. I'd hoped the memory of his mother's drinking would've kept him straight, but it seems it didn't. George had once written me steady—back when distance kept us apart, he was the one who kept us connected.

John Lewis, thirty-nine, was a carpenter in Wichita, Kansas. He was happily married to Mary Alice, and they had a little girl he called the light of his life. John had always been the quiet one, more sensitive, even-tempered. I reckon he felt caught in the middle, so he just withdrew into his own world. I was proud of how he found a good trade and was doing his best to be a fine father.

William Henry, thirty-seven, owned a small house ten miles south of downtown Los Angeles. He was an electrician for the Standard Oil Company, and a devoted family man, with his wife Dorothy and their four little daughters. He was the toughest for me—proud, stubborn, carrying a chip on his shoulder. Truth is, I had been hard on him too—said and done things I still regret.

A.J. asked each brother if they'd please write to me. He told them I was truly sorry for all the ways I'd let them down. George said he was too ashamed of himself and the mess he made of his life to face me. John said it was too tangled up inside him—feelings he'd buried deep and didn't want to dig back up. And William said he'd never have anything to do with me, and wouldn't forgive me for leaving his mother, not until hell freezes over.

I sat with those words for a long while. I could respect George's shame, and I could understand John's retreat. But William's answer cut clean through me. A man can weather silence, even carry shame—but to be told outright you'll never be forgiven, not till the end of time—that's a weight that settles deep in the bones.

Meanwhile, the world was falling apart. Each evening after supper I'd listen to Edward R. Murrow on the radio, reporting on the war in Europe. I didn't much like what I heard, but I'd known men like Hitler out on the prairie—men with dark hearts who'd steal a neighbor's land and claim his cattle as their own. Power-hungry thieves who lied like it was second nature and believed it was their God-given right to rule the earth. In April of 1940 Hitler took Denmark. By May, Luxembourg, the Netherlands, and Belgium had all fallen. In June his forces stole Norway and France. By late summer the bombing of England was building night after night. Each month things grew worse. The president promised America would stay out of the war in Europe, but I wasn't convinced that was possible. A man can sidestep trouble for a spell, but sooner or later he's got to take a stand. To me it felt like America was drawing closer to that place—sure as day turns to dusk. But still something deep inside me was hoping we'd stay out of the war. I'd seen too much death, and I didn't know how much more I could stomach.

It had been nearly a year since I'd last seen A.J., and I'd learned the hard way what it costs when a man drifts too far from his kids. So toward the end of August I boarded the train for Seattle. A.J. was turning eighteen, and I wasn't about to miss it. We spent two full days, talking nonstop about everything—his mother, his three half-brothers, life on the ranch, dreams he had of owning a house looking over the water. But we mostly talked about the war in Europe. The Boeing Airplane Company, where he worked, was building B-17 bombers.

"The company says that sooner or later America has to join the war," said A.J. "And we are building the best machine ever. It's fast, high flying, and can take anything the Germans throw at us."

"Roosevelt said he'll keep us out of the war," I said, "and I hope he's right."

"So you just want to sit back and watch Europe fall?"

"No, but we can't get involved every time some crazy gunslinger reaches for his revolver."

"They have most of Europe. They are edging their way into England. I hear that their next victim will be Russia, then Northern Africa. After that what will they set their sights on? South America? The United States? The whole world?"

"He's not that crazy!"

"Dad, I respectfully disagree," said A.J. with a fire in his eyes that said you'd be better off wrestling a grizzly than continuing this fight. "If we don't stop him, who will?"

"It's a problem, but not our problem. A man has to determine when to stand up and when to walk away. Hitler is an ocean away. And that is our protection."

"But in time they will develop long-distance bombers and more powerful U-boats. We are just delaying the inevitable."

"Maybe so, but too many of our young men will die."

"They'll die to protect the rest of this country." He faced me like a man.

"That is honorable, but..."

"And when we finally enter this war, I'll be ready to fight."

"I'll be proud of you, son, if it comes to that—I'm hoping it won't. But let's not cross that river until we get there."

A.J. leaned back, jaw set like he'd already made up his mind. "If the call comes, Dad, I don't want to be the last man to stand. I want to be the first to step forward."

I stared at him across that kitchen table, the lamplight catching the hard lines in his young face. For a second I almost argued more, but then I saw something else flicker there—still just a boy, shoulders not quite filled out, eyes a shade too wide for all that talk of war. I reached over and put my hand on his arm.

"You got plenty of time to prove yourself, son. And no matter where life takes you, don't forget—your old man's proud already."

He gave me that half-grin, the same one I'd seen when he was chasing calves across the pasture back home. For all his fire, he was still my boy.

Two days later I was riding the rails south, the steady clack of the wheels carrying me away from Seattle and that lanky eighteen-year-old with war in his eyes. His words kept echoing—"If we don't stop him, who will?" Pride sat heavy in my chest. He'd grown into a man quicker than I'd ever expected, ready to fight for something bigger than himself.

But right alongside the pride came dread, sharp as a knife. I'd buried too many already and the thought of burying another of my own kids was a weight I wasn't sure I could shoulder. I tipped my hat low, let the rhythm of the rails roll under me, and prayed Roosevelt was right—that the ocean stayed wide enough to keep the war off our shores.

Sixteen months later everything came crashing down. It was December 7, 1941, a grey, damp Sunday afternoon, with a thin low-hanging mist masking the river. Outside the cabin, the world slept in a strange hush, waiting for the deafening cry that would change everything. Inside, Mattie and I sat near the fire—she was knitting a sweater for A.J. with three-year-old Robert asleep in her lap, me reading *A Long Winter* to little Mary. Suddenly Erroll threw open the door, "Something is happening!" The panic in his voice forced me to my feet.

The long loud blast of a car horn pushed away the quiet. "What in the world!"

"We've been attacked!" shouted Grant from his car.

"Attacked? What do you mean?" I asked, not believing what I'd just heard.

"Turn on the radio," he said. "I'm telling the neighbors." Then his car disappeared into the low-lying fog.

I ran into the house and heard President Roosevelt's familiar voice boom from the radio: "The United States of America was suddenly and deliberately attacked by naval and air forces of the Empire of Japan."

It hit me hard, like a punch to the gut. My hands were shaking, and for a moment, I thought I might even cry. All I could do was sit near the fire and listen—stories of ships burning, young men going down in that far away harbor in the middle of the ocean, planes overhead raining fire on everything below.

Two weeks later A.J. came to the ranch with his arms filled with Christmas gifts for us all.

That evening we all crowded around our small table for a feast— fried chicken, baked bread, mashed potatoes, corn and cucumbers from the garden, homemade applesauce. "You shouldn't have brought so many gifts," I said.

"I didn't know how long it might be until I saw you again," he said. "Or if I ever will."

"Son, what are you talking about?" said Mattie as she filled his plate.

"I'm joining the Navy sometime in the next few months. I'd sign up sooner, but Boeing needs me to get as many bombers built before they can train a new crew."

"I figure every man's got to do their duty." I shot him a smile of respect.

"Yes. Most men my age in Seattle are signing up."

The next week was as bittersweet as a campfire burning low— warm for a spell, but knowing a cold night was closing in. When I stood beside him at the train station, saying my goodbyes, I couldn't let go. I held on tighter than I ever had, fear twisting deep in my gut that if I loosened my grip, I might never hold him again. But then the whistle blew, and I let go, and he was gone.

In September of '42 A.J. went to naval training at Farragut Station up at Sand Point, Idaho. That's where they told him he was bound for Brazil—he wasn't even sure where that was or what it had to do with the war. But he said a good Navy man obeys his orders, and he promised me he'd write every chance he got. He kept that promise through those three years in uniform, though Brazil felt like a million miles away. For a plain cowboy like me—never set foot on a ship, never flown in an airplane, never been beyond these borders— that's about what it was. I studied every letter like a man studies the horizon for a storm. He couldn't believe they sent him clear down to Brazil, and it rankled him some. He'd signed on to be in the thick of it—in Europe or the Pacific—not parked on some coast a thousand miles from the fighting. But I was glad for it. The thought of him dying in battle would've split me clean in two. I took off my hat to the boys who gave their lives, but I couldn't bear to set another cross on that hill above the orchard.

On a cold, snowy day in January of '43, A.J. boarded a train east to New York, then climbed aboard a transport bound for Brazil. They sent him clear to the far eastern tip—a base called Natal. German subs were prowlin' the southern Atlantic, sinking ships, so the Navy put our boys there to guard the lane. That was the closest jump to Africa, and every day ships steamed out of Natal—freighters and troopships loaded with trucks, ammo, rubber, coffee, even canned beef. His job was to keep the U-boats off 'em. Every safe crossing was one more step toward Berlin, one more step toward ending the war.

Convoy duty, he called it. Long lines of tankers and transports sliding east while his patrol boat kept watch. Most days it was nothing but endless hours—eyes on the water, ears on the sonar, the monotony near driving a man cross-eyed. But now and again a

U-boat surfaced, and the war showed its ugly face.

I almost lost A.J. twice in those three years. He never wrote me about either incident, but later he told me about both in intimate detail. The first involved battle, the second carelessness. And the good Lord reached out each time—holding back the sea and keeping my dear son from the jaws of death.

The first incident happened shortly after he arrived. It was late in the afternoon about five miles off the coast of Brazil, sun setting red over the swells. A.J. was watching the water when he caught it — just a glint, nothing more. But as he focused in, he knew exactly what it was—a periscope cutting the water like a thin silver knife.

"We've got a target!" he shouted. Suddenly the whole ship came alive. Boots moving fast across the deck, guns swinging, depth charges rolled into place. But before the first canister could drop, the periscope was gone. The captain swung her around, sonar men pinging the deep, every man aboard holding his breath for the echo.

Then they had it. A hollow return—steel down below. Orders flew. "Stand by depth charges!" The first one splashed in, seconds later the muffled boom shuddered through the hull. More followed, each blast rolling the sea over like thunder in the deep.

But the ocean struck back. A.J. said there was a sickening crack, then a roar from below. Every man grabbed hold. A torpedo slammed the patrol boat broadside, close enough to lift the deck under his boots. The ship rolled hard to the starboard, steel screaming as the sea came crashing in. Men scattered like dry leaves in a storm. A.J. never saw the ship's side rush up—only felt it smash into him. The next moment, cold black water closed over his head.

He said it was like a steer slamming you into the dirt—breath gone, lights out, nothing left but darkness. He didn't remember the ship burning behind him, didn't remember the scramble of his mates in the sea. He only knew he woke three days later, flat on his back in a hospital cot, skull bandaged, body aching like it had been beat six ways from Sunday. A Navy doctor told him he had a concussion, some bruised ribs, but nothing that wouldn't heal.

He told me that when he finally opened his eyes, he didn't know if he was dead or alive. Took a nurse telling him he was going to make it before he believed it. Said he was fortunate. Some of his mates never came back. Just oil on the water. Empty bunks. Silence where men ought to be. He told me he never forgot the stink of diesel and smoke that rode the wind before the blast, or the way the sea itself heaved under those charges. And he never forgot the silence after—the kind that falls when you've lost shipmates.

When A.J. finished telling me that story, I just sat quiet, hat in my hands. My boy had stared death in the eye on the open Atlantic, and only by the grace of God did he come back. Three days out cold in a Navy hospital, head wrapped, ribs aching—while other boys never opened their eyes again.

I thought of their parents, how they must've got the telegram that splits a heart wide open. And when A.J. told me how close he'd come, my chest ached like a fresh wound. Only chance and Mattie's prayers kept him standing while his mates went under. I'd never seen Mattie pray so much as when A.J. was in Brazil. It reminded me of Ma—Bible open on her bed, hands folded, her head bowed. Every night, every morning, without fail. I prayed for A.J. too, but not the way she did. I just wasn't as faithful about it as Mattie.

That night, after hearing about his close call, I walked out back alone and stood by the orchard, looking up at the stars. The wind moved soft through the branches, whispering like voices of those who'd gone before. I bowed my head and gave thanks that I didn't have to plant another cross. But I knew it could still come to that. The war was far from over, and my boy was still out there, scanning black water, waiting on the next periscope to break the sea.

The second incident could have also ended badly. The way A.J. explained it, Ponta Negra was nothing but a long stretch of golden sand with a fishing village made of a few shacks. One Sunday afternoon a couple of sailors rode out there from Natal. They were wrung out from convoy patrols—eyes stinging from salt spray, nerves jumpy from chasing phantom subs. That beach was like another world. They tore into the water like kids. Warm, rolling waves, sun bright as new brass. A.J. floated on the water, staring at the clouds overhead, and for a spell he dreamt the war was over. It felt like freedom—simple, carefree, without the world on his back.

But as he drifted, the current carried him further and further from shore. It caught him and dragged him sideways, out toward the open Atlantic. When he looked around, he knew he was in trouble. At first he fought it, thought he could break free. But the more he strained, the more it pulled. The shore shrank to a thin line, and fear set in deep. His arms went heavy as lead, lungs burned, and for one dark moment he thought it was his time to meet his Maker.

Then he remembered something Grant had once said about rivers—don't fight the water head-on. So he breathed deep and swam parallel the coastline, letting the current carry him slowly toward shore. Every stroke felt like his last, but little by little that sand drew closer. Finally his knees struck bottom, he crawled up on the beach coughing salt water, and collapsed face-down in the sand. He lay there, still as a stone, until he had the strength to stand and join his friends.

But he never told them what had happened—never told anyone until he told me. He just tucked it away, a lesson burned deep, a reminder that a man's got to stay on guard, no matter what. He was thankful to be alive. Truth is, so was I.

Those years in Brazil were hard on me. I thought of him every day, prayed for him more than I'd ever prayed anything before. By the time he shipped home in '45, with the war over and the enemy defeated, he was dead-tired and ready to be home. Three long years of sun, sweat, salt spray, and patrols had worn him down. But he returned in one piece, thank the good Lord. Too many good men never did.

TWO WEDDINGS

"This is the best Christmas ever!" Erroll, now thirteen, announced with the excitement of a cowboy who'd just broken his first horse.

Mary, eleven, and Robert, seven, cheered in agreement.

A Christmas tree glittered with silver tinsel in the corner of the room, and Mary placed a porcelain angel with a lace gown on its top. I stretched a strand of colored bulbs—red, green, blue, yellow, orange—across the ceiling. It was the fanciest Christmas we'd ever had. Mattie baked enough cookies and pies to feed the whole county, and she filled that cabin with more warmth and color than four walls had any right to hold—cinnamon in the air, quilts on the chairs, and a quiet happiness bright enough to make you think spring had come early.

The war was over, Germany and Japan had surrendered. Rationing had ended, except sugar. Many of our soldiers were back home, including A.J. He arrived at the ranch the Saturday before Christmas, and we all went upriver to the little white church the next day. I'd never seen it so full—people packed in, thanking the good Lord that the world had returned to normal. The spirit was as hopeful as fresh tracks leading home through drifting snow—except for Nancy Mayborn, whose husband never came back. Too many husbands and sons never came back.

A.J. was as cheerful and talkative as I've ever seen him. The navy had done him good—deep tan, strong arms, respectful confidence.

This was a man who knew what he wanted and was determined to get it.

Before training he'd sold his Hudson. Now he was back driving a brand-new Ford super deluxe coupe sedan—dynamic maroon with a V-8. He'd driven it straight through from Seattle to Ruckles in eight hours.

"That's faster than the train," I said when he arrived late on a freezing afternoon.

"I should hope so." He smiled. "They say it can hit a top speed of 100, though I've only taken it to eighty."

"Well I must admit it's the sharpest looking machine I've ever laid eyes on."

After supper that night A.J. leaned forward at the kitchen table, the little ones hanging on his every word. To them he wasn't just a brother—he was a war hero.

"I'm so glad to be back in Seattle," he said. "Brazil is in the past. I've got steady work at Boeing for now—day shifts, checking parts and tightening bolts. Pays the bills, but it's not where I aim to stay."

Mattie looked at him, curious. "Then where?"

He smiled, proud but a little shy. "The fire department Station Thirty-Two. They've got me volunteering nights—drills, hauling hose, riding out when the bell rings. It's not full-time yet, but if I stick with it, I'll get there."

I studied him for a moment. "That's a hard road, son. Smoke, heat, and plenty of danger. You sure?"

"I'm sure," he said without blinking. "After the war, I can't just punch a clock. Fighting fires feels like something that matters."

The kids sat wide-eyed, and I felt the truth of it—my boy was still chasing dreams, only this time in his own backyard.

"Also I've met someone."

"You mean a girlfriend?" Mattie said.

And A.J.'s smile broadened and he nodded. "Met her at a dance."

"Tell us about it. Did you dance with her?" Mattie asked, folding her hands, a smile tugging at her lips.

A.J. chuckled. "Didn't have much choice. First number I'm just standing there, trying not to look lost, when this girl comes right up—blue eyes, blonde hair, little blue ribbon in it. Said her name was Elsie Buxton. Before I could answer, she had me out on the floor."

The kids laughed, and even Mattie's eyes lit with curiosity. I asked, "And could you keep up?"

He shrugged, grinning wide now. "I managed. We danced near half the night. I told her about Brazil, the convoys, the patrols. Then she told me that she also worked at Boeing, and about every dream she had. We didn't run out of words until the music stopped."

"Tell us more," said Mattie.

"She's a year younger than me with two older sisters. She's got a close family, her father is a baker, her mother is strong and sensible. Her grandparents came from Switzerland, and she's mighty proud of that. Elsie was born in Seattle and has lived there her whole life. She's sweet and smart and not afraid of the world. I think she might be the one."

"And how long have you known her?" I asked.

"Six weeks. Maybe the best six weeks of my life."

"That's not long."

"I know." A.J. paused. "Things look good so far, very good. I hope she's the one, but it's still too early to know for sure."

I sat back, watching the light in his eyes. He'd fought a war, bought himself a fine car, and now he was talking about a girl with ribbons in her hair. I hoped he was right. Lord knows after all he'd seen, my boy deserved someone dependable by his side who'd make him better.

Three months later A.J. and Elsie got engaged, and early in August we drove to Seattle for their wedding. Somewhere near Portland a red roadster shot out of nowhere and cut across the road in front of me. I slammed the brakes and swerved right. My front bumper caught his back wheel and we jolted to a stop. Robert screamed from the back seat, and Mattie's head struck the windshield hard enough to crack the glass. For a moment the car was filled with silence except for the tick of the cooling engine. Then everyone started talking at once. Mary calmed Robert, I checked Mattie's head—just a lump, no bleeding—and Erroll went over to the roadster to see about the other driver. He was a young fellow about Erroll's age, shaken but unharmed. Ten minutes later we were back on the road to Seattle with a bent bumper. We were still rattled, but grateful it hadn't been worse.

That wasn't my first scrape behind the wheel, and it wouldn't be the last. Driving a car never came natural—it put me on edge. Ever since I ran my Model T off the road back in '37, I'd hit my share of ditches, trees, even other cars. More dents and busted glass than any neighbor I knew. I was good with a horse, in the saddle or behind a wagon, reins fitting my hands like they belonged there. But a steering wheel never did. Sometimes I wished I could go back to the prairie, where a man and his horse didn't follow roads—just chased the horizon with the wind in his face and a dream in his eyes. But a car was a necessity, and that day it was the cheapest way to get my family to Seattle.

That evening we arrived at A.J.'s flat and he introduced us to Elsie—tall, slender, and as serious as a cowboy crossing deep waters. But the two were in love. You could see it plain in their eyes, in the shy smiles they shared, and the way her hand found his like it had always belonged there. I'd never seen my boy so happy.

Two days later they were married at University Lutheran Church, the little chapel on the green. The place was small but full to the rafters with friends and family. Sunlight streamed through the stained glass, laying sparkling colors across the wooden pews. Elsie walked the aisle in a simple white dress, no frills to it, but she carried herself with such grace that every head turned. A.J. stood tall at the altar, shoulders back like a man ready to carry any burden life gave him. When she reached him, I swear his face lit brighter than the candles.

The vows were spoken soft but sure. Their voices didn't carry like a preacher's, but they carried enough—everybody in that chapel heard the love in them. When they kissed, the bells rang out over the green, and for an instant the world felt right, like all the hard years had led to this one moment of pure joy.

We shook their hands, hugged them, and wished them well. I told my boy I hoped he and Elsie would be as happy as Mattie and me. His eyes shone when he said he aimed to try. That was when I knew his dreams would come true. Mattie and I were proud of him—prouder than words could say—Era would've been too. A.J. was everything a man could hope for a son, and maybe even more.

The next morning we packed up and drove home—it was harvest time in the orchard. Mattie made me keep the speed down, and she gripped my arm every time we crossed an intersection. I figured that crack in the windshield reminded her I wasn't exactly the best driver in the world. Back home, life slipped back into its rhythm. I worked the orchard, Mattie canned peaches and corn, and the kids started school. The years turned over quick after that.

A.J. settled in Seattle with Elsie, and we bent our backs on the ranch, one harvest after another. Time runs faster than a wild horse the further a man gets from his prime. The world turns to a blur, and he wonders how much longer he can sit high in the saddle. Still, he clenches the reins and rides on.

By then, the eyes didn't see as true, the legs didn't carry as strong, the voice didn't call as clear. A man slows so much he can't pull a gun fast enough to protect his family if trouble came calling. Yet when I see the wrinkles deepen and feel the ache in my bones, I take comfort in this: my mind rides steadier, my memory keener, and my heart bigger than it ever did in younger days.

November of '48 marked seventy years I'd been walking this wide stretching earth—wrangling its problems and savoring its fruits. Mattie, the kids, and even the neighbors figured it was cause for a celebration before age caught up with me and threw me from the saddle. I was grateful for their kindness, but truth be told, all that fuss just made me feel old. But for this one Saturday, time stood still as frost before dawn and I could catch my breath.

It was a simple party, the kind I could stand. Grant came over with some neighbors, and A.J. and Elsie made the trip down from Seattle. I wasn't big on parties, but everybody meant well. Mattie baked the biggest cake I ever laid eyes on, and we carried it down by the river. We sat in the shade, eating cake and watermelon, kids splashing each other and skipping rocks across the current, folks telling old stories and laughing till it hurt. For a while it made me feel like a boy again, back in Nebraska when summers stretched forever and Big Beaver Creek took the edge off the heat. It wasn't fancy, but it was honest, and for a spell it felt like the world had slowed enough for me to enjoy it.

But a month later Erroll headed off to college, and I found myself standing in the yard watching him go, same as I once did with A.J. It never got easier, seeing a boy of mine strike out on his own. He was full of hope, shoulders squared like he had the world ahead of him, and I was proud—but it left the orchard rows feeling a little emptier.

The years carried him quick—college classes, Navy service, even a spell on some far-off island in the South Pacific. Then came a letter about a girl he'd met, and the next time I saw him, his talk was full of her. Soon enough they were engaged, and I knew he'd found his path same as his brothers had.

And just like that, five years—five springs, five harvests, five Christmases—were gone, shaved clean from my life. Suddenly it was July of '53 and Erroll was getting married to Becky Freeman, sharp as a whip and full of promise. She carried Eddie's fire, Era's kindness, and Mattie's grit. They'd met at college, but when he shipped off to the Navy and she took a nursing job in Portland, their love lived in letters. Hundreds of them. In one, he asked her to marry him. In the next, she said yes, and promised she'd follow him wherever the trail led. So seven years after A.J.'s wedding, we were getting ready for another.

Mattie and Mary didn't trust me behind the wheel after a few more mishaps, so Mary, now nineteen, drove us. At least that way they knew we'd make it to the wedding safe. I sat in the passenger seat beside Mary, while Mattie and Robert sat in the back. It took her two hours to reach Cave Junction, a hundred miles south, though I could've made it in half that—maybe that's why they didn't let me drive. That day was one of the hottest I'd ever known—so hot the thin white taper candles melted before they were even lit. The little church was packed full, which made it worse. I sweated more than a cowboy riding through a wildfire with an empty canteen. I wiped my forehead and wished I could dunk my head in a horse trough.

But there was no escape. Somehow the Shasta daisies and lady ferns tied to each pew didn't wilt. Sunlight filtered through stained glass and washed the room in a pink glow. The setting was beautiful. The music swelled and the room hushed. Erroll stood at the front with the pastor on one side and his best man, A.J., on the other. Seeing two of my boys up there filled me with a pride so strong I almost cried. Then Becky stepped into view, that long flowing white dress making her as pretty as any bride I'd ever seen. When Erroll caught sight of her, their eyes met and his smile was like nothing I'd ever seen before. She smiled back, and in that instant there was something powerful and pure between them. The music fell away, and in the stillness he took her hands and spoke his vows with a confidence that showed he meant every word—without question.

Mary leaned close to her mother and whispered, "That's what I want—to be a bride with a man who'd sacrifice everything for me."

"Just be patient," Mattie said, giving her hand a gentle pat. "There's a lucky man out there who'll love you like a dream come true."

"I hope so."

A moment later the pastor's voice rang out: "I now pronounce you husband and wife. You may kiss the bride."

The room erupted in applause as Erroll and Becky sealed it with a kiss, then walked back up the aisle together, smiling like they had the whole world ahead of them.

After the reception wound down and folks were drifting toward the doors, I found a quiet corner with my two boys. A.J. had his tie hanging loose around his neck, and Erroll was grinning like he couldn't quit if he tried. "You did good today, son," I said to Erroll, clapping his shoulder. "Better than good. Made me proud."

Erroll ducked his head a little, that same boyish habit he'd had since he was small. "Thanks, Dad. Feels right. Becky's... she's everything."

"I can see that plain as day." I turned to A.J. "And you stood tall up there beside him. Makes me glad just to see the men you're both becoming."

A.J. gave me that half-smile of his. "We learned from you, Dad."

I shook my head and chuckled. "Maybe you learned in spite of me. Either way, you turned out fine." Then I pulled them both into a rough hug, and for a moment I didn't care who was watching. "Just promise me one thing—stick together. No matter where this world sends you, both of you stick together and have each other's back. After all, that's what brothers do."

They nodded, serious now, and I saw it in their eyes—they meant it. I held on to that moment for the rest of my days as one of the sweetest memories a father could ever have.

Outside the church the heat of the day finally broke, a cool breeze moving through the trees as the last of the guests drifted away. I thought back seven years to A.J.'s vows in Seattle, and now Erroll's here in Cave Junction. Two beautiful weddings, two unforgettable days. Both my boys standing tall with brides at their side. A father couldn't ask for more.

NOT WHAT I THOUGHT

I had three little girls. Three beautiful little girls—each from one of my three wives. Fern, with her soft brown hair and tender heart, was caught between her mother and me, and she was gone at twenty-eight. Arlene was born in the tuberculosis sanitarium. Her mother died when she was just eight months old, and not long after I kissed her goodbye and handed her over to strangers in Portland— never to see her again. And then there was Mary, with her red hair and loving smile. She'd do anything for her mother or me without us even asking. But now she was headed for trouble, and none of it was her doing. These were just sweet, innocent girls, pure as spring rain, and I let all three of them down when they needed me most. That guilt rode with me every day, like a shadow that never left my side.

A month after Erroll's wedding, Mary landed her first job as secretary at Myrtle Creek High School, nine miles south of the ranch. I'd never seen her so excited. She bought a simple print dress with a full skirt—pretty and professional—the one she'd been eyeing at Rice Brothers Mercantile all summer. She looked like a million dollars, and I let her drive the Chevrolet to work. Principal Childress was impressed—he said she was one of the best students he'd ever seen. She could type sixty-five words a minute, take shorthand at a hundred, and handle every office machine without trouble. The job started at a dollar an hour, and by the end of the first week she felt like the richest girl in town. To celebrate, she drove the Chevrolet down Main Street to the Dairy Queen, ordered a chocolate sundae, and handed over a nickel and a dime, proud to be paying her own way.

Suddenly a tall man, just a few years older than Mary, stepped to the counter and laid a crinkled dollar bill on top of her coins. "Excuse me, miss, but I'd be honored to pay for your sundae."

"Thank you, but I've got this."

"I'm sorry, but I insist." He picked up the coins and dropped them back into her hand. He winked at the girl at the counter. "And I'll take a sundae for myself too."

Mary looked him over, unsure whether to feel offended or grateful. He wore a plaid wool shirt with the sleeves rolled to his elbows, suspenders holding up blue denim pants, and heavy leather work boots.

"I don't take gifts from strangers," she said.

"Then I'd better introduce myself." He untied the bandanna from around his neck and wiped the sweat from his tan face. Sawdust drifted from his dark hair. "I'm Ed—"

"Ed Freese," she said quickly. "You have quite a reputation in town."

"Is that good or bad?"

"You tell me," she said. "Star athlete, skirt chaser, real boozer."

"I haven't had a drink in three months."

"That's a good start."

"Please don't judge me from my past," he said. "I've grown up a lot since those days."

"I hope so."

He stepped back and studied her face. "You look familiar."

"From high school," she said. "You were a few years ahead of me, so we never had any classes together. Besides, I was shy—kept to myself. You...well, you were popular."

Anyway, that's the story Mary told me when she came home that afternoon. She said they sat at a table outside, ate their sundaes, and talked near two hours. Mary was as giddy as a horse turned loose in an orchard full of ripe apples, her cheeks still pink with the memory.

"He asked me to the movies at the Rio tomorrow night. They're showing *El Paso Stampede.*"

"That's a hard movie to turn down," I said.

"I figured it would be something you'd like to see."

I chuckled. "Seen enough real stampedes to last me a lifetime, but I reckon it might be good fun to watch."

"But what should I do? I've never been on a real date."

"Ed comes from a good family," I said. "I know his father—member of the Eagles Lodge, damn good poker player. Works construction, been building houses on the west side. Straight shooter, proud of his boy."

"He should be." Mary sat down beside me. "He was captain of the football team, most popular kid at school. Half the girls dreamed he'd ask them out."

"And here you are trying to decide what to do? What'd you tell him?"

"I wanted to say yes on the spot, but that sounded desperate. So I told him I'd think on it and call him tomorrow at ten."

"Is he a gentleman?"

"As far as I know."

"Does he have a job?"

"He's been logging with a crew west of Canyonville. Said it's hard work but pays well."

I nodded. "It surely is."

"He told me he's got bigger plans—maybe doctor, businessman, even politician."

"Well, I hope it ain't politics. I'd trust a dog with a chicken in his mouth more than a government man."

Mary laughed but twisted her hands in her lap. "Do you think I should go?"

"If he picks you up at our front door, looks me in the eye, and promises to treat you like a lady, then he's got my blessing. But if he lays a hand on you wrong, he'll find himself staring down the barrel of my shotgun."

"I'll be sure to tell him that," she said with a nervous smile, then leaned over and kissed me on the forehead. For a moment I just sat quiet, realizing my little girl wasn't so little anymore. I'd ridden stampedes, confronted rustlers, and buried too many loved ones, but nothing cut deeper than watching time steal away my children. All a man can do is tip his hat to the years, pray they're kind, and hope his daughter rides a gentler trail than the one he rode.

Fall in southern Oregon on Clarks Branch Road comes on quiet, like a lantern lit at dusk. The hills put on coats of gold and crimson, maples flaring bright against the steady green of fir and pine. The air sharpens with woodsmoke and the sweetness of fallen leaves. Mornings start with a frosty mist marking every word you speak, and by afternoon the sun breaks through, warm as a fresh cup of coffee. The orchards hang heavy with prunes and apples, their fragrance riding the wind clear across the valley. And when the day fades, the ridges burn with color until the last light slips west, leaving only the hush of crickets and the promise of rain.

By the end of November the last leaves had blown clear, the bushy-tailed squirrels had their acorns buried deep, and the cold wind forced your hands deep into your pockets. This Thanksgiving was different than any other. Mary was rushing about cleaning every nick and cranny of the house. Robert was out sweeping the porch. Mattie fixed enough food for an army. They even dressed me up in my Sunday best and made me promise to be well behaved. The whole thing made me as uncomfortable as a chicken staring at the chopping block. I even started regretting letting Mary invite Ed over for dinner. She'd been seeing him for two months—high school football games, movies, long walks through town. But this was the first time we'd ever shared a meal in the same room with him.

We all gathered at the table, dishes set perfectly in place, steam rising off the potatoes and green beans, Mattie still fussing in the kitchen. Ed sat beside Mary, straight-backed and polite, trying his best to make conversation.

"I hear you used to be a logger," he said, glancing my way.

"That was a long time ago." I nodded.

"I worked in the woods for a season myself, but now I've found something better—a lot better."

"I heard you work in the auto parts store in town," said Robert.

"He not only works there," said Mary, "but he's the general manager."

"So the young man has drive," I said, placing a napkin in my lap like Mattie had taught me.

"Without drive you can't get anywhere these days." He smiled. "And when I'm not at the store, I spend my time outdoors." He looked up, a little spark in his eye. "I also hear you're a fisherman?"

I raised an eyebrow. "I've been known to cast a line now and then."

Just then Mattie brought in the turkey, golden brown and filling the room with the smell of sage and onions. Robert sat tall at the end of the table, hair combed slick, and Mary glowed with pride as she looked at Ed. She looked as pretty as I've ever seen her.

Plates were passed, knives and spoons clattered, and for a few minutes there wasn't much talk—just the shuffle of serving dishes and the quiet satisfaction of plates being filled. Then Ed set his fork down before taking a bite, leaning back like a fellow about to spin a yarn.

"Stopped in at the tackle shop in Roseburg last week," he began. "Old timer there talked me into trying a new fly. Didn't look like much, just a little scrap of deer hair and tinsel, but I figured I'd give it a go. Got up before daylight, drove east till the South Umpqua was steaming in the cold. Third cast, the water just erupted. Steelhead hit so hard I near lost the rod. Twelve pounds easy. Fought him twenty minutes before I brought him to the bank."

Mary's eyes shone like lanterns, Robert's fork hung forgotten in midair. I set my coffee cup down slow. "Steelhead on a fly rod in November," I said. "That's no small thing."

Ed puffed his chest a little, pleased with himself. Mary reached for his hand under the table, and I felt my jaw tighten. I'd seen men brag on catches, broncs, even bar fights, all with the same grin he wore now. Talk was easy. But life wasn't measured by stories told over turkey and biscuits. It was measured by how a man stood steady when things got rough—whether he could hold fast to his word, same as he held fast to that fish.

I buttered another biscuit and passed the basket along. No sense in saying more. Time would tell if the boy was worth the trust my daughter was already giving him.

Ed wiped his mouth with his napkin and leaned a little closer. "You know, Mr. Stephens," he said, "I was thinking—next Saturday I'm heading back up the South Umpqua. Water ought to be just right after this cold snap. Maybe you'd like to come along. I'd be proud to share a stretch of river with you."

Mary's eyes went wide, hopeful. Robert perked up, waiting for my answer. Even Mattie paused, one hand still on her knife.

I sipped the last of my coffee, let the silence stretch a moment. "Been a spell since I swung a line on that river," I said finally. "But I reckon I could stand a morning on the water."

Ed grinned, quick with relief. "I'll bring an extra rod."

I gave him the faintest smile. "Don't worry about the tackle, son. I can still tie a fly or two of my own."

Mary beamed, Robert went back to shoveling potatoes, and Mattie slid a slice of apple pie onto each plate.

"This is the best tasting pie I've ever had," said Ed.

Thank you." Mattie blushed. "The secret is in the crust."

"As for the rest of the meal—you're a mighty good cook."

After dessert we cleared the table and played cards and checkers. I beat him three times in checkers before the evening wound down.

He stayed until eight, and then he and Mary slipped out to the front porch to say goodbye.

All in all, he seemed like a fine young man. It was only later I found out how wrong I was.

A month later, on Christmas Eve, Ed joined us at the little white church up the river. That really got the people talking. They'd never seen Mary with a fellow beside her singing hymns—and especially not one who looked at her like she was an angel plucked right off the top of our Christmas tree. The preacher told the story of baby Jesus and the bright star over Bethlehem, same as he did each December, with shepherds and wise men standing watch.

Ed was listening close, like he'd never heard about the manger before. Maybe he hadn't. As far as I could recall, his parents weren't the church-going type. Anyway, he didn't nod off or anything like that, though it was a bit distracting, the way he kept holding Mary's hand, easy but sure, like he wasn't letting go. It didn't seem proper in church, and besides, it was bound to fuel the rumors even more.

After the service, Ed drove Mary back to our house for a special Christmas applesauce cake—with raisins and walnuts, topped with caramel glaze—which Mattie had baked for the occasion. Then, to my surprise, he pulled out a neat stack of wrapped packages—one for each of us, except Mary. He said hers would come later.

Robert tore into his and found a steel-tempered hunting knife, sharp enough to skin a deer. Mattie unwrapped a Kenmore three-speed electric blender, shiny as a new dime. When it came to me, I shifted in my chair. I wasn't used to strangers handing out family gifts. I was the provider, and I'd already figured Ed had spent more money than he ought to.

And then I saw what he'd set in front of me. The biggest gift yet. A Winchester hunting rifle.

I set it down carefully. "I can't accept this."

"But you have to," Ed said.

"I don't have to do anything I don't aim to," I told him.

"Yes sir," he said, straightening in his chair. "But next fall—I got this foolish dream of us hunting black-tailed deer up on Buckhorn Mountain."

"What about me?" Robert piped up. "I've got this brand-new knife. The two of you shoot the deer and I'll skin 'em."

"That's up to your dad," Ed said with a grin.

I looked at Robert, then at the rifle. "She's a pretty little thing."

"A walnut stock and a thirty-inch barrel," Ed said proudly.

I picked it up and ran my hand along the smooth wood. Truth was, I still didn't trust a gift that big. It didn't sit right, a young man spending that kind of money on me. But Robert's eyes were shining, and I couldn't bring myself to snuff out that kind of joy. So I simply said, "Thank you".

Still, all these special gifts got me wondering. They were kind gestures, sure enough, but deep down I knew we were being bought off. And I didn't like it—not one single bit.

Later that night, after we'd all gone to bed, I heard voices out on the front porch. Ed and Mary. I knew I shouldn't listen, but I couldn't help myself.

"Would you like to open your gift?" he asked.

"Of course."

A moment passed.

"Oh my," Mary whispered. "It's a ring."

"And would you grant me the honor of marrying you?"

"Oh—no. I mean...oh yes." She sounded as flustered as I'd ever heard her. "But I've only known you three months."

"The best three months of my life."

"But this is much too fast. I'm pretty sure I love you, but I need more time."

"If you love me, why would you need more time?"

"You're the first boy I've ever dated and..."

"Do you know half the girls in town would jump at the chance to marry me?"

"That's probably true, but I'm not the sort of girl who makes quick decisions. I'm mighty flattered, but I need to think about it. Besides, have you asked my dad?"

"No." A pause, then his voice was sharper. "Why would I ask your dad? You're the one I want to marry, not him."

"But I trust him. I want to know if he believes this is right and good."

"So you're turning me down?"

"I'm asking you to be patient."

"I can't believe this." His voice rose, loud and sharp. I started to swing my legs out of bed, ready to teach him that no man talks to my little girl that way. But I stopped myself, listening.

"I'm so sorry."

"I thought this would be the most romantic night of my life," Ed snapped. "Me proposing to you on Christmas Eve."

"It was the most romantic thing that's ever happened to me," Mary said, her voice trembling.

"Then give me back my ring," he barked. "If you don't want it, I know plenty of girls who would."

"But Ed—"

"Maybe I was a fool to think you were the one."

"I'm not saying no, Ed. I'm saying not yet."

"You don't understand—I thought we had something real."

"Ed, please, let's just talk—"

But a moment later his car roared to life and sped down the lane. The door opened, and Mary came in, sobbing. I started to get up, but Mattie laid a hand on my arm. "I think this is something a mother needs to deal with," she whispered.

I lay back, staring at the ceiling, every muscle tight. That was the night I first knew Ed's charm was only skin deep, and sooner or later my daughter would pay the price.

Mary sobbed for over an hour while Mattie comforted her in steady tones. A little past midnight Mattie slipped back into bed. "Everything is going to be alright."

"What is Mary going to do?" I asked.

"She'll talk to Ed tomorrow. She needs to see where things stand once he's calmed down."

"I know where things stand. If he gets anywhere near my daughter, I'll kill him."

"Hold your horses," said Mattie. "Your daughter loves him."

"How can that be after the way he just treated her?"

"Love doesn't always walk beside still waters."

I let out a long breath. "That's for sure."

When the house finally went quiet, I just lay there listening to the stillness, broken only by the wind brushing through the firs outside the window. Sleep never did come. There was grit in my gut and a bad taste in my mouth. Ed wasn't who I—or any of us—thought he was. I eased my shotgun from the corner, to the foot of my bed. Mattie called it foolish, maybe she was right. Back when I rode the prairie, we had a way of dealing with no-good, yellow-bellied snakes like this. But what if Mary truly loved him? What if she needed me to let her handle it? What if Ed came crawling back on his knees asking forgiveness?

I wasn't sure what to do. And besides, there wasn't anything more I could do that night—but tomorrow, I told myself, I'd figure it out.

ONE MORE CHANCE

I admire a man who owns his mistakes.

But that don't mean I trust him. I kept my eye on Ed the way I watch the sky for rain come harvest. Clouds can fool you, and so can men. That thought rode with me into a bitter January night at the Eagles Lodge in Myrtle Creek, where the smoke hung thick, the stories were loud, and the poker tables were full. That's where Ed came up to me, hat in hand, ready to settle things. He looked tired and red-faced. I pointed to the chair next to me, and he sat down.

"I heard you and Mary patched things up," I said.

"Yes. I was a real jerk a few weeks back at your place. I had my mind set on something, it didn't go the way I thought, and I lost it."

"I heard you two out on the porch. Your voice carries."

"I've apologized to Mary. Now I need to apologize to you."

"I don't much like how you talked to her."

"I don't like how I talked to her either. I was angry and mean. There's no excuse for what I said or how I acted."

"Promise me it won't ever happen again." I looked him square in the face.

And he looked at me—hands shaking, feet shuffling. "I promise." He said it strong and steady like he really meant it.

"I'm giving you one more chance, and that's it."

"I know I've lost your trust, and I'll do everything I can to earn it back."

"I hope you do. But let me tell you—it won't be easy."

"The things in life that matter most never are," he said. "But I'm willing to fight for them."

Something in me wanted to like that boy, but down deep I just wasn't sure I could.

That winter came colder and wetter than most. Three storms rolled through and left the ranch buried in snow—the kind that seeps into your boots and stays in your bones. Through it all, Ed kept trying to prove himself. Every Friday night he took Mary into town, and most Tuesdays after work he bought her a chocolate sundae at the Dairy Queen. She told me he was quiet, respectful, and that things between them were starting to warm. I kept my mouth shut.

One dry Saturday he drove out to the ranch and asked if I'd like to go fishing with him. He stood there humble as could be, hat in hand, polite in a way that made it hard to turn him down. For a moment I almost said yes. But the river was running high, and I wasn't ready to sit side by side and pretend the past had been washed clean.

He tipped his hat. "Maybe next time."

I nodded, though I wasn't sure when—or if—that time would ever come.

But then spring came, and I found myself on the river with Ed. It wasn't my idea—Mary asked in that sweet, insistent way of hers, saying it would mean a lot if I gave him an honest chance. I pushed back, but she wore me down, and I couldn't bring myself to disappoint her. So at first light on a cloudy April morning, we set out on the South Umpqua and hauled in three chinook salmon. He was gracious enough to let me keep the catch. Two weeks later we tried our luck on Calapooya Creek and came home with a string of trout. Mattie fried them up golden, and Ed ate at our table that night, careful with his words, like a man testing thin ice.

Mary was happy—maybe happier than I'd ever seen her. She walked lighter, smiled more, and giggled with a freedom I hadn't seen for nearly a year. She told me love meant forgiving and forgetting. I said Ed was walking a better road, but I was an old cowboy who'd watched too many trails turn bad. So I kept one eye on the campfire and the other on the storm clouds.

She just smiled. "You can keep watching the clouds if you want, but I know where his trail leads."

Maybe she was right, but I'd learned the hard way that hope could buck a man quicker than any horse. Still, watching her smile, I reckoned it might be worth holding the reins a little looser this time.

The two of them walked the riverbank gathering wildflowers, same as I once had with her mother. They rode horses through the hills north of the ranch with rain pouring down, soaking them clear through. And at night they sat on the porch, staring into the endless sky, counting stars and trading dreams, laughing like colts let loose in spring grass. They even took a few trips—drove the rim of Crater Lake, sat through a Shakespeare play in Ashland, and cheered at a Fourth of July rodeo in Eugene, with Mattie and me tagging along. After all that, I had to admit I might've been wrong. Maybe the two of them were good for each other. Maybe they'd make a fine couple. But I still wasn't ready to lay down my guard. Not yet.

Mary's twentieth birthday fell on a hot Thursday, July 29, 1954. Mattie set a fancy spread down by the river—cold fried chicken, corn on the cob, sliced watermelon, lemonade, and a three-layer devil's food cake with fudge frosting from Lawrence's bakery. This was no ordinary birthday.

When the picnic was done and Mary blew out all twenty candles, Mattie and I stretched out for a nap while Robert waded the shallows after crawdads. Mary and Ed wandered upriver hand in hand, the late July sun throwing long ribbons of light across the water. She bent low to gather wildflowers and tucked them into her hair until she wore a crown of meadow blooms. I heard her laugh float back on the breeze, light and easy as water slipping over stones. They stopped near a bend where the willows leaned in, their branches swaying slow in the evening air.

For a long moment Ed just looked at her, holding her hands like he never meant to let go. His throat worked as if the words were stuck there. Finally he drew a deep breath, reached into his pocket, and dropped to one knee.

"Mary," he said, voice trembling but steady enough, "from the first day we sat together at the Dairy Queen, I knew you were the one I wanted beside me. I've pushed too much at times, and I'm sorry for that. But you've made every day brighter than the last, and I can't imagine a life without you. I hope I'm not moving too fast." He paused, swallowing hard. "Would you do me the honor of being my wife?"

For a heartbeat she stood frozen, flowers trembling in her hair, eyes wide and glistening. Then she let out a small laugh that broke into a sob, covering her mouth with both hands. "Yes," she whispered, then louder, "Yes! Yes, Ed—I'd love to be your wife!" She threw her arms around his neck, laughing and crying all at once.

Ed rose and pulled her close. "You've just made me the happiest guy in this whole wide world," he said, voice rough with joy.

"And I'm the happiest gal," Mary answered, her cheeks glowing as bright as the sunset spilling across the river.

I'd been watching from a ways off, giving them their space, though my heart was pounding hard in my chest. My little girl didn't look so little anymore, standing there with wildflowers in her hair and love shining in her eyes. The sight hit me hard and sweet all at once—like watching the colt you raised from birth run off strong and free across an open pasture. Proud as I was, it stung too, knowing she was slipping out of my hands into her own life.

Ed turned toward me, still holding Mary's hand. His voice was steady, but I caught the nerves flickering in his eyes. "Mr. Stephens," he said, "I'd be honored if you'd give me your blessing to marry your daughter."

I looked at Mary, then back at him, taking my time, letting the weight of it settle. Finally I said, "If Mary's ready, then so are Mattie and me. You've got our blessing."

Ed smiled wider than I'd ever seen, and when he shook my hand it was the grip of a man set on keeping his word. Mary leaned into him, radiant, and I just stood there quiet, thankful and aching all at once.

Summer faded and on a crisp fall morning with mist pooled low in the valleys, Robert and I headed up Buckhorn Mountain with Ed. The air smelled of pine and damp earth. We pitched camp in a green meadow where the grass was still wet with dew, three days' worth of gear stacked neat beside the fire ring.

I carried the Winchester rifle Ed had given me last Christmas. For months it had sat in the back of a closet gathering dust, a reminder of the worst side of him. But time has a way of sanding down hard edges, and after nine months of steady respect, I reckoned a man deserved a second chance—especially with Ed's ring on Mary's finger.

That night by the fire we traded tall tales, the sparks rising into the black sky like prayers. We laughed and sang old cowboy songs like the past had never happened.

At first light the next morning, the meadow was silvered with frost. A raven cut across the ridge, its cry sharp against the silence. That's when I saw him—a five-point buck standing proud against the skyline, steam curling from his nostrils in the cold. I raised the Winchester, settled my elbows against my knees, and slowed my breathing. The world seemed to hold still, waiting. I steadied the sights, squeezed the trigger, and the shot cracked through the pines. The buck dropped where he stood.

We hurried up the slope, boots crunching frozen ground. Robert's eyes shone, wide with boyish pride. Ed gave a low whistle.

"Clean through the heart," he said, kneeling by the buck. "That was some shot."

I helped with the first cut, then stepped back and let Robert and Ed do the rest—skinning and quartering, their hands working fast and sure. I watched, proud that the next generation was carrying the weight, and proud too that this old cowboy, seventy-six years behind him, still had it in him to stand his ground and provide for his family. It felt mighty good to show these two that I had a good eye and a straight shot.

Ed slapped me on the back, grinning wide. "I only hope I can still shoot like that when I'm your age."

I just smiled. Robert glanced at me like he was memorizing the moment, a story he'd be telling long after I was gone.

We hauled the meat down to camp, but I kept those antlers. Cleaned them up myself and hung them in the cabin over the fireplace as a reminder of the good old days. I was mighty proud of those damn antlers.

I was hoping for a fine Christmas Eve. Nearly everything that year had gone better than I thought possible. We gathered at the little white church up the river, same as every year. Robert, Mary, Mattie and I sat near the back.

"I'm sure Ed will be here any minute," Mary whispered as the music began.

But he wasn't. Not when the service ended, not when the crowd spilled out into the cold night.

"He's just running late," Mary said. "He'll be at the house soon."

We went home and waited. Supper grew cold on the table. Mary barely touched a bite before she turned to me. "Dad, let's call his folks."

We did. They said he'd left for our place three hours earlier.

Mary's eyes filled with worry. "We've got to find him. What if something's happened?"

The two of us climbed in the car, Mary driving. Several miles out she cried, "There's his Chevy!"

We pulled up beside his '53 Bel Air, Surf Green with an ivory top shining under the neon of the Roaring Ranch Roadhouse. My gut sank.

"Damn fool," I muttered. "It's his car."

Inside, the room was dark and smoky, the jukebox blaring Hank Williams' "Your Cheatin' Heart." Ed sat hunched at the bar, a beer in hand. Mary marched straight to him, and I stayed at the door. This was hers to handle. Truth is, if I stepped in, I might not stop at words. I shoved my fists deep in my pockets and listened.

"Ed, what are you doing here?" Mary asked, her voice tight.

He turned, eyes glassy. "Stopped for a drink."

"It's almost nine."

"Lost track of time, I guess," he slurred.

"I've been worried sick."

"Nothin' to worry about, Honey." He pulled her close and tried to kiss her. "C'mon, have a drink with me. It's Christmas Eve."

She shoved him away. "You're drunk. And what happened to your eye?"

He rubbed at the bruise, smirking. "Oh, this? Might've gotten in a little fight."

"A fight?"

"A couple fellas at the pool table got mouthy," he muttered. "Nothin' serious."

Mary's eyes flashed. "Ed, you promised me. You promised things would be different."

"I slipped, that's all. One beer too many. Won't happen again."

She stood there for a long moment, then said, "Get your coat. I'm driving you to your parents' house."

He blinked, startled. "But my car?"

"You can pick it up in the morning, when you've sobered up," she cut in. "You're not driving anywhere tonight."

Something in her tone must've cut through the drunken haze, because he tossed a dollar on the counter and followed her toward the door, shoulders slumped like a boy caught in the wrong. I stepped aside to let them pass. For a second his eyes met mine, and I swear he shrank two inches under the weight of my stare.

The three of us drove in silence, the only sound was the tires humming over the frosty road. When we pulled up in front of his folks' place, Mary parked and said, steady but soft, "Good night, Ed. Please don't make me ever do this again."

He mumbled something that might've been an apology and slunk up the walk. Mary sat there a long moment before turning the car back toward the ranch. Neither of us spoke. The tires crunched over the gravel, and the silence settled like a weight between us. Then she hit the steering wheel hard. "I'm so disappointed."

I nodded.

"How could he ruin two Christmas Eves in a row?" Tears streamed down her face.

I gave her my white handkerchief.

"I thought he loved me."

"I think he does," I said softly.

She laid her head on my shoulder and cried like I hadn't seen since last Christmas. "It doesn't feel like it."

I wanted to say that I understood—that I've seen this pattern before in Eddie—but the words felt hollow. So I kept quiet, letting her tears fall, knowing some pain just needs to be waited out.

Twenty minutes later, when we got home, she went straight to the window, still in her church dress, shoulders shaking as she looked out at the yard. I laid a hand on her shoulder, and she whispered, "He said he'd change."

I didn't have the heart to tell her that sometimes a man's promises are like storm clouds—you never know if they'll bring rain or blow clear. All I could do was hold her and hope, though down deep I feared she was hitching her life to a man who wouldn't weather as well as she thought.

The next year was like a cyclone tearing through a general store. Everything was a blur of disaster and disorder. Lightning struck the barn, animals scattered. Thunder shook so loud I couldn't think. Mary cried. Mattie cried. Ed drank. I drank. Ed and Mary fought and got married and fought even more. Mary moved out and she moved in and moved out again. Doc Smith gave me nitro for my heart and morphine for my back, but the medicine was only a distraction. Nothing made any sense. The days spun faster and I felt like I'd fallen off my horse and he was trampling me with his hoofs. It was a nightmare that wouldn't stop. All I could do was close my eyes, praying the storm would pass and the sun would rise so I could find my life again.

Mattie and I sat in the little white church along the river for Christmas Eve service. Same as last year—except this time it was just the two of us, since Robert was off with a girl from the city he'd taken a strong fancy to. The sanctuary was full, but I paid no mind to the crowd. I needed some peace, a chance to breathe. Quiet hymns floated around us. I reached over and held Mattie's hand, loving her more in that moment than I ever had. Ma would've told me to pray for calm and for an end to all the chaos.

So I bowed my head. "Dear God, be with my kids. Protect Mary. Bless the ranch. Mend my heart and strengthen my back. And thank you for Mattie. Amen."

It wasn't fancy, but it felt good to let the words out. Ma always said God listens, even when the prayer isn't polished up like a preacher's. And God knows I'm no saint.

I opened my eyes and looked up. Soft light poured through the stained glass, scattering color across my face. The Good Shepherd stood there in a blue robe with a white lamb cradled close. Behind Him, the golden sky and green hills glowed as if alive. For a long minute I sat still, certain he was looking straight into me with eyes so gentle it felt like a whisper meant only for my ears: Everything is going to be alright.

I wanted to believe Him. But no words came. I just sat there, still as stone, while tears rolled down my weathered face and darkened the floorboards beneath my polished boots.

CUT THE DAMN THING OFF

Near the end of a long trail, a man sleeps heavy—hard and heavy—and the past comes riding back to meet him. Memories I thought were buried, or prayed forgotten, rose up fresh as if they'd happened just yesterday. What's left to a man at the end is nothing but the faces he loved and lost? Some sweet, a few bitter, all stitched into the hide of who he's been and what he's lived. And in those still hours, the women of my life came back to me, clear as day.

It started with Eddie—the prettiest girl I ever saw, red dress and high heels shimmering in lantern glow. Her laughter spun through the night until the cry came when the bullet struck, riding the stage with me through Yellow Jacket Pass. Whiskey clung to her breath, her hair wild against my cheek. And I can still see her eyes drifting toward that cowboy she was flirting with outside the Broken Spur in Duff, chasing a freedom I could never hold. And that's when I knew she was gone.

Then came Era—so innocent in that pale blue dress, lace collar, lavender trailing after her. I held her close through the blizzard of '13, huddled together in our flat above the tailor shop. Each morning I carried the calm glow of her blue eyes as I headed out to work. And I still see her in that open-air pavilion at the sanitarium, the two of us clinging to every moment in wicker chairs, steady as prayer, though we both knew her days were numbered. And there was nothing either of us could do about it.

And at last there was Mattie—she came to me walking down the aisle in a satin dress, ivory glowing like lamplight. Later I saw her again, eyes blurred with tears, standing before three tiny crosses. I smelled the cinnamon bread she kneaded, flour smudged across her red cheeks, her heart breaking even as her hands stayed steady. And I sat beside her on the porch, listening to the river's rush while her needles clicked soft and sure in her lap, peace woven into the sorrow.

These were the trails my mind wandered as the months slipped by. Near the end of the trail, the future feels unsure. All a man has left is his past, and that's where his mind goes when he's got nowhere else to ride.

But memories can't hold a man forever. The living world has a way of barging in when you least expect it. Still, here I am with my boots in two worlds—yesterday, and today—and I'm keenly aware that just around the bend there's another world waiting, quiet and patient.

I was riding steady on a humid day in July of '58 when Ed pulled me off my comfortable chair on the front porch where I was half asleep and threw me into the backseat of his Chevy Bel Air hardtop.

"What the hell are you doing?"

"Taking you to the hospital."

"Why?" I tried to open the door, but he'd locked me in.

"Because your daughter told me to."

"Why would she do such a thing?"

"Because Mattie's worried about you."

"There's nothing to worry about." I set my hat on my lap. "I'm doing just fine. Don't need anyone fussing over me."

"Mattie says ever since you fell off that horse and bruised your thigh you haven't been the same."

"That's 'cause it hurts." I rubbed my leg. "A horse will throw you now and then—just the way of a cowboy. I've taken more hard falls than you've seen winters. So just let me be."

"She says all you do is sleep."

"So what if I'm sleeping more? It's none of your damn business."

"It's been three days," Ed said in a way to calm me. " And each day you're worse, not better."

"When you're old, you don't heal near as fast as you once did. Getting dragged around to some stupid hospital doesn't make your bruises fade any quicker."

"She says your leg started out swollen—bright red and purple. Now it's dark blue and cold."

"Injuries happen," I said. "Give it time."

"Mattie thinks you should have a doctor look at it."

"I don't trust doctors."

"She says your leg smells like rotting flesh," he said, eyes narrowing on me. "That's infection—and that's bad."

"I soaked it in whiskey and took morphine for the pain."

"Is it helping?"

"Too early to tell, but it don't hurt as much."

"Allen, infections and rotting flesh aren't nothing. Mattie's right."

"Doctors make big deals out of nothing," I said.

"Maybe, but this isn't nothing."

"Doctors treat you like you're dying."

"That's how they keep you from dying."

"Well, if I am dying, can folks just let me be? I sure as hell don't need anyone hanging over me with tears or pity. None of that ever fixed a bad leg or set a man back in the saddle. So they can keep their fretting—I aim to face this my own way."

"Mattie loves you too much to just let you be. If you don't know that by now, you're a fool."

"Sounds like you're dragging me to the hospital whether I want it or not. So let's get it over with."

Half an hour later, we arrived at Mercy Hospital in Roseburg. Ed swung the Bel Air up to the curb and killed the engine. Before I could protest, he was around to my side, hauling me out by the arm. My right leg buckled and I nearly hit the pavement.

"Dammit, I can walk," I growled, but Ed dragged me toward the entrance all the same.

The moment we stepped inside, three nurses closed in around me, one rolling a chair, another peeling back the blanket, the third calling for a doctor. I shoved away their hands. "I can walk on my own."

"Not for long you won't," one of them shot back, steering me toward a gurney.

A doctor came striding down the hall, face grim, eyes sharp. "What happened here?"

"He fell off a horse three days ago," Ed said. "His right leg's swollen, dark blue, and it smells rotten."

The doctor bent low, lifted the blanket, and gave one look. His face hardened. "Gangrene. We need to operate now."

My stomach knotted. "What kind of operation?"

"Amputation," he said, plain as day. Then he looked me square in the eye. "If I can save enough to take it below the knee, that'll be better. But if not, I'll have to take it higher."

The words hit harder than any fall. A man needed his legs. I'd ridden broncs, driven cattle, felled timber. Without my legs, what was I worth? Half a man? Just another burden? My hands gripped the side of the gurney, knuckles white.

"There's no other way?" I gritted my teeth, not feeling so good.

"Not if you want to live," the doctor said. His voice was steady, no give in it. "It's your leg or your life."

I thought of Mattie. She'd tell me straight that life mattered more than pride. She'd rather have me alive with one leg than buried whole. And she'd be right—but that didn't make it easier to swallow.

Anger flared hotter than the pain. I slammed my fist against the rail. "If there's no other option, then just cut the damn thing off!"

I woke to the smell of disinfectant and the low hum of voices in the hall. The first thing I felt was absence—my right leg gone, heavy blankets falling flat where it should've been. For a moment I thought it was some kind of nightmare. Then the pain hit, sharp and throbbing, and I knew it was real. The stump was heavy with bandages, tight and pulsing, as if the rest of me still hadn't figured out it was gone.

Mattie was there, sitting close, her eyes red from crying but her hand steady on mine, like it had always been. Mary stood on the other side of the bed, arms crossed tight against her chest like she was holding herself together. Even Robert was in the room, standing back with worry on his face, never having seen his pa in such sad straits.

"You're awake," Mattie said softly, trying to smile. "The doctor says the worst is behind you. You made it through."

I swallowed hard, throat dry. "Made it through to what? How the hell is anything gonna be all right without a leg? How am I supposed to feed the chickens or care for the goats now?"

Mary leaned in, her voice gentle. "You'll get used to it, Dad. Folks do. People learn new ways."

I shook my head, bitterness rising in my chest. "Get used to it? How the hell do you ever get used to something like this?"

Mattie squeezed my hand tighter, her voice low but firm. "One day at a time. That's how. And you won't be alone."

I closed my eyes, not ready to believe them, but holding on to her hand like it was the only thing keeping me from falling clean away. It wasn't very manly, but it was all I had.

I slept the rest of the day, and the next morning I asked the nurse, "When can I get out of this place?"

"The doctor says it'll take about two weeks for the wound to heal."

"There's no way I'm staying here for that long."

"You'll need to talk to the doctor about that," she said, patting my hand like I was a sick dog.

"Young lady, nobody tells this old cowboy what to do. I let the doctor take my leg, but he can't take my freedom."

I sat up and threw the blankets off. The sudden shift knocked me off balance, twisting my body until spasms of pain shot up my right side. I yelled out and dropped back onto the bed, swearing like an outlaw caught by the sheriff.

The nurse reached for me. "Easy now."

I shoved her hand away. "Don't touch me. I'm a lot stronger than I look."

The doctor came in, arms folded. "Stronger maybe, but not smarter. If you rip those stitches open, you'll be laid up twice as long."

"I'm not staying here two weeks," I snapped.

He stood his ground. "You nearly died, Mr. Stephens. You've got one leg left and you're alive, if you want to keep it that way, you'll rest until that stump heals. Otherwise, you won't walk out of here at all."

I glared at him, jaw tight. "We'll see about that."

Four days later, I talked Ed into breaking me free. He wheeled me out when no one was looking and loaded me into his Chevy. We raced back to the ranch, gravel spitting under the tires.

Mattie and Mary were waiting on the porch when we pulled in, both of them looked furious. The doctors had warned they wouldn't take the blame if things went wrong, but I'd always been restless as a gambler betting on a bad hand. I wasn't about to die in a hospital bed. If I was gonna heal, I'd do it at home. And if I was gonna die, I'd do that at home too.

"What have you just done?" Mary asked Ed, her voice gentle but tight.

"He wanted to come home," Ed answered.

"But the doctors said he wasn't ready."

"Your father asked me man to man," Ed said, "and I gave him my help."

"Mary, don't blame him," I cut in. "You might not agree with me leaving the hospital, but I just couldn't stay. I felt like a steer penned in too tight."

Mattie stepped down from the porch, her hands tightening in her apron as she looked at me. "And what happens when that wound tears open? What happens when infection sets in again? You think you're stubborn enough to fight death twice?"

I couldn't look her in the eye. "I just want to be home."

Her shoulders eased, though her voice stayed sharp. "Then you'll rest, Allen John Herbert Stephens. You'll do what the doctor said here under my roof, or I swear I'll drag you back to Roseburg myself."

I nodded. I might have been too worn out to argue, but that didn't mean I still didn't have a heap of fight left in me.

The next two months were hell. It's hard to admit, but I was half the man I used to be. There were more things I couldn't do than I could. This ranch was bound to break me. I couldn't ride horseback or herd cattle. I couldn't milk cows or muck stalls. I couldn't mend fences or chop wood. And that was just the beginning of the list. More than once, I caught myself wishing I'd died on that operating table in that damn hospital up in Roseburg.

I sat at the kitchen table staring at my single boot, unable to pull the damn thing on without help. The words choked their way out of me, rough and raw. "Mattie, I've got to give up the ranch. It nearly kills me to say it, but a seventy-nine-year-old man with just one leg has got to face the god-awful truth that his ranching days are over."

She froze, the dish towel still in her hands. "What are you saying?"

"Ed found us a house in town—two blocks from him and Mary. Fair price. He says we can move in as soon as we're ready."

Her eyes filled, but her voice stayed steady. "Do you think you can let go of the ranch?"

I swallowed hard, my throat dry as dust. "Sometimes you've got to face it—the day's done, the chores unfinished, and all you can do is lay it down."

Three weeks later we sold almost everything we had on Clarks Branch Road and moved to 320 Northeast Rice Street in Myrtle Creek. I'd lived at the ranch for thirty-eight years, Mattie for thirty-two years. Here was where we'd raised our kids, buried our losses, held each other close, weathered storms, and grown old together. Mattie wept as she said goodbye to our home. And I just stood there, leaning on a wooden crutch, trying to keep my balance, and put my hand on my chest. My heart hurt, and tears or words or even prayers, couldn't lessen the way I felt at that moment. But now we had a new home, and somehow, together, we'd make it ours. It wasn't the life we'd dreamed, but it was the one left to us. And if life had taught us nothing else, it had taught us how to survive whatever challenges came our way.

And then came November 13, 1958, my eightieth birthday. A.J. and Elsie came down from Seattle. Erroll and Becky, with their three little kids, drove from Portland. Mary and Ed, along with Robert and his girlfriend, dropped by.

Our new house was a small gray single-level bungalow pressed close to the street, with a white picket fence out front. A tidy place—fit for a banker or a shopkeeper—but not near enough land to plant a decent garden or keep a couple of goats. Still, that's what life had come to. It sat in a residential neighborhood about ten blocks from downtown with a park, a church, and a school all within walking distance. Not that walking was something I could do anymore.

We packed into a living room about twelve feet wide by eighteen long, with a large picture window facing north to the street. A dark blue couch sat against the west wall, and across from the window stood two leather recliners—one for Mattie, one for me. This was where I spent most of my days, reading or staring out at the world:

old men walking their dogs, children racing toward the schoolyard, young couples strolling hand in hand, giggling at some secret only the two of them shared.

On the south wall, behind our recliners, hung four framed photographs: one of Ma and Pa standing in front of the soddie in Nebraska, one of my brother Erroll in his Marine uniform, another of Mattie and me walking across a field not long after we were married, and one of our four kids when they were still young. Along the east wall leaned several messy stacks of books—some read, some waiting to be opened—westerns by Zane Grey, mysteries by Agatha Christie, volumes by Steinbeck and Hemingway, and a collection of short stories by Flannery O'Connor that Mary had given to Mattie, since both of them had come from Georgia.

It was a wet Thursday, gray with the promise of winter, when we all squeezed into that little room and the first request came: "Tell us stories."

"Tell of the boy who ran away from home," said A.J.

"The one who stole Pa's horse early one morning, before anyone was awake, and rode off into the wide-open prairie," said Erroll.

Then the questions flowed so fast I could barely keep up. What was he thinking? How old was he? Why did he do it? Where did he go?

After I retold the story, they all said, "Tell us more." And then more, and more, until I thought the well was dry—but still the stories poured forth.

At some point, a man is left with nothing but stories—of a different world, when he was a different man. So as I told them, we drank beer and ate cake, laughing and crying and holding on to each other. The night grew late, eyes grew heavy. I hoped the party would never end, though I knew it would. Sooner or later, everything ends. The room grows quiet and the lights get turned down.

As the couples left for their own homes, Mattie and I were left alone with our stories and our memories. Each one as precious as a speck of gold sifted from black sand in some long forgotten stream bed, somewhere out on a far away prairie.

Time has a way of washing away the extra edges and frantic fantasies of who you thought you were, making you smaller and purer, until there's nothing left but memories. And those memories live on in the stories you tell—and the stories others remember about you.

In the end, the stories are all you have. Once they're gone, you slip into the shadows. But you smile, knowing every trail you rode and every storm you weathered—it was worth it. Every damn minute of it.

A CLOSING THOUGHT

Here I am an old cowboy with one leg, a bad heart, and a broken-up back waiting for my final sunset. I hope it's full of more brilliant oranges and blood reds and golden yellows than I could ever imagine. Wouldn't that be a hell of a sight? But in the meantime, while I'm waiting to hang up my hat, I wonder what wisdom my folks would send my way. Ma would tell me to look up and thank the good Lord for every breath you got left. Pa would probably say to look down and keep your shoulder to the plow. In my own stubborn way, I'm doing a little of both.

After all, I never thought I'd ever make it to my eightieth birthday. Figured I'd be buried in some shallow grave on the prairie or lost in a frozen snowstorm in the Rockies or simply laid to rest with the white crosses on the ridge above the ranch. But I suppose I was just too ornery to kick the bucket at a respectable age. So here I am, looking back on my life as if it were something worth remembering—maybe it was, maybe it wasn't.

But A.J. gave me a notebook and told me to write. I asked him, "Where should I start?"

"At the beginning," he said, "and then just let the story go wherever it wants to go."

And that's what I did. I wrote what I remembered—filling a lot of pages and using more words than I ever thought were in me. Some came easy, some came hard, but it all came spilling out like water flowing from a stream after a hard rain. In the process I discovered that I wasn't half as smart or courageous as I thought I was, but I was honest. That's the one thing I was. I was also lucky—damn lucky.

So here at the tail end of my story, I've finally figured something out—something others likely learned long before me. As I sit in the fading light of this cockeyed rodeo, I see it plain. It wasn't the cattle or the miles that made me. It wasn't the train, nor even the land. It was the women who came into my lonely life—Eddie, Era, Mattie— each stealing my heart, shaping my future, and leaving their mark like tracks on a long trail west, tracks that grow deeper with every step and never fade.

And that's enough trail for one man.

ACKNOWLEDGEMENTS

First of all, to the many conversations with Grandpa Stephens.

Then to conversations with Mattie, A.J., Erroll, Mary, and Robert.

These conversations were the foundation for all these stories. Special thanks to Tami Stephens, Becky Gendren, Sarah Miller, Rick Arnold, and Jerry Spires for reading and providing feedback. Also to Amy Livingstone's excellent design and technical help.

This is a true novel. But when stories are about family, how true can they be? Grandpa Stephens had no trouble adjusting a detail here or there to make a story more engaging. How often he did that, I have no way of knowing. And stories told over decades have a way of twisting, softening, or sharpening themselves without permission.

That said, this is the closest to the truth I can find.

ABOUT THE AUTHOR

Steve Stephens has served as a counseling and clinical psychologist, life coach, seminar speaker, radio talk show host, university professor, and author. He lives in the Pacific Northwest with his wife, surrounded by beautiful gardens. Their children and grandchildren visit often. He likes to tell them stories.